Nokota® Voices

Forever Fields

By Julie Christen

Print Isbns
B&N Print 9780228624585
Amazon Print 9780228624592

BWL Publishing Inc.

Books we love to write ...
Authors around the world.

http://bwlpublishing.ca

D0068151

Dedication

To Jake, Sherri and Jodi who shared this ride in
so many ways.
To my own little Prairie dog, Paisley, forever in my
heart.
In loving memory of Holiday who was the
inspiration for Paisley's Journey.

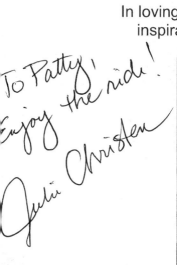

*People always need dreams. Their whole lives,
they must dream.* Lois Lowry

Acknowledgement

Nokota® is a trademark breed name developed
by Frank and Leo Kuntz and the Nokota Conservancy
in Linton, ND.

Thank you, Nancy, of BWL Publishing, Inc. You
are wonderful. And thank you to my cheerleader,
Dean Hovey, for the endless messages that kept this
author in motion.

Table of Contents

Spring

Wetu

Chapter 1

Hike up your big girl panties and quit the waterworks, said my dead grandma as I fiddled with a tattered photo of her daughter. My mother's black hair swirled in the wind; she sat bareback on a wild-eyed buckskin colt in front of a house I didn't recognize. A carved sign next to her showed a diamond shape with a large letter F in the center and two smaller Fs on either side. I wondered if she heard the voices too, wherever she was. Did they tug at her until she finally followed?

It's time, Gram nudged.

Though Gram had been dead for five years, her voice prodded me from the edge of my bed. I reached for my suitcase and stuffed the picture of Mother into my pocket. I took a deep breath and stepped toward the door. My heart thumped in my throat as the wheels ricketed across the warped wood floor. I

7

stopped to look one last time at the snapshots taped on my wall. Friends. Smiles. Boys. Group hugs. Cheeky kisses.

Lies. All of it.

I wasn't like them. I never had been.

Bitterness boiled up inside me, but I kept my temper in check. I had a tendency to ruin everything with my temper. Tonight, I wouldn't let that happen.

I swallowed and glanced at the framed photograph above my dresser. There sat Gram. She stared at me, unsmiling, black-and-white, hands folded neatly in her lap, wavy hair tied back. She was young in that picture. In her prime, I supposed. I slipped her off the wall and held her close.

Move it, she said.

A twinge in my jaw shot straight to my spine and latched onto my skull. Doubt. I hesitated at the top of the stairs.

Then came the pat-a-tat rhythm of Prairie's little border collie paws. My shoulders eased, and my jaw relaxed. It *was* time.

My stocking feet shuffled as I hoisted my suitcase with one arm and held Gram close in the other. Prairie stepped close behind, ready to cushion my fall. I could see myself sailing down all fourteen narrow steps, waking *them*.

Dad and Cindy, *gag,* knew I'd be leaving soon. And after today's drama, I figured they'd be disappointed if I was still around in the morning. But I wasn't about to risk listening to one of their common-sense talks about what a normal seventeen-year-old girl ought to be doing.

That rotten third step creaked as usual. Prairie and I froze. Listening for stirring. Only a fan's hum. The grandfather clock's tinny tick-tock. The kitchen faucet drip.

Prairie made the first move. I trusted her. We sneaked like burglars through the living room. But the only things I'd be taking were mine.

I grabbed a Floral Daze notepad off Cindy's home office area, formally known as the dining room. The stationery she designed and sold sprawled like floral leprosy over our oak table. I shook my head and sat at the kitchen counter, my gut churning. I scrawled the words "OVER MY DEAD BODY" on a butterfly note then stuck it to the fridge with a smiley face magnet.

A *Horse and Family* local magazine lay buried in the mess of old mail. I ripped out the dog-eared page and read the circled ad one more time. Just a few weeks ago, during a late-night cookie sneak, I found it haphazardly lying open on the counter. Someone had spilled coffee on one of the pages and left a big blotch right next to a "Help Wanted" ad for a ranch hand and grounds keeper. Normally, I wouldn't have given a flying flip about something like that, but when I looked closer, it seemed to bounce off the page at me.

*F*orever *F*ields *F*arm: Equine Retirement Center

FFF was scrunched inside a diamond graphic next to the heading. A flash of the photo with the sign next to my mother and that wild-eyed buckskin blinked in my mind.

I found directions on my phone to Sheldon, North Dakota.

Prairie looked up at me with perfect amber eyes.

"Food."

Her triangle ears snapped to, so we whisked into the breezeway. I pulled off the Tuffy's lid and took out a plastic bag with a small roll of hundreds in it, perfectly preserved. The product of countless hours working at the Farmer's Market and squirreled away allowances that probably should have been spent on a wardrobe. Prairie sniffed and started licking it.

"Don't worry," I whispered. "I packed your things already." I waved the money bag in front of her. "This is for me." She let out a grunt sneeze.

"Are you ready?"

She opened her mouth to pant smile and wagged her tail hard.

I egged her on. "Are you ready to go?"

She panted louder as her butt wrenched from side to side. Her tail banged against the screen door.

"Okay, okay, okay. Shhhh." I smiled.

I slipped into my worn cowboy boots, gripped the suitcase handle, and shouldered a canvas bag. Out the breezeway window, I looked over our farm. I knew this place like every crease in my mother's photo. Every knoll and tree and pond and valley played a part in making me. The view forced memories to wash over me. Some fond and loving. Others cold and hateful.

Mist rolled down the slopes of the meadow shimmering in the moonlight. The shadowy branches of the willow tree in the pasture draped in peaceful sleep. The barn, its sagging roof, crooked sliding door, and flaking paint showed how tired it was.

Doubt lurched inside my stomach.

Snap out of it, Gram echoed.

In one breath I could have turned around and slunk back to the safety of my bed. Then something soft brushed against me. Prairie's patient, golden gaze said, "You are not alone."

I eased open the screen door. Its rusty spring ached open, and we escaped into the night.

* * *

Oscar's door burped and I flung in my bags. Oscar, a 1975 Chevy Scottsdale, my first vehicle, paid for with my own cash. I silenced my phone and tossed it in the glove box where I planned to leave it. After I checked the connections to the trailer and tested the lights, I hopped up into the truck bed and climbed over a few hay bales to check on Prairie's provisions in the chest behind the cab. She traveled light.

As I slid over the side like a super hero, my jeans caught on a rusted hole near the gas cap, and ripped, just before my feet hit the gravel. I sucked in my breath to squelch a screech and grabbed my thigh. An inch-long slit marred my paisley jeans. My *favorite* jeans. The only jeans in my closet that truly understood my rear. Blood peeked out from under a halo of powdery rust blending into the other swirling colors on the denim.

I kicked Oscar's tire, blew a strand of bangs out of my face and hissed at my truck, "Wouldn't you like that? If I marched my wounded tail straight back into the house and left you here to rot in peace?" I grumbled as I searched for my first aid kit in the back seat. "Or better yet, land in the ER with tetanus! Well, not so lucky today, *mister*. Just got a shot in the butt last fall for track." I waved a bottle of antiseptic and a Band-aid at the dashboard.

After doctoring my cut, I washed off my jeans with some trough water and stuck a piece of super-duty duct tape on the tear. Those pants were a museum of memories. Every stain and frayed edge reflected snippets of me. Flawed, but sturdy.

I faced the barn, but doubt turned my head toward the warm glow of the porch light.

Did the light just flick off in my bedroom? It must have been moonlight playing tricks.

Get your head straight, Gram ordered.

"Right. Head straight. Shake it off, Paisley." I focused on the barn.

"Phsst," Prairie sneezed and bumped me from behind.

I touched the massive sliding door and heaved it open. "This is it, ancient one."

Whispers in the rafters greeted me. The resident mourning doves stirred, and a waft of hay and dust fluttered down. Prairie sniffed out scurrying mice and attempted to terrorize Ernie, our last barn cat. But quickly enough she flopped down in a loose pile of hay. She knew she was no match for that tough-as-nails, three-legged, one-eyed, crimp-eared orange tabby tomcat.

11

For a moment in the moonlight, I allowed myself to bask in memories. The countless horse books I'd read in the hay mow. The dizzying heights the tire swing had taken me. The endless batches of kittens. The sleepless nights spent in the stalls keeping a sick horse company.

"Hhrrr hhrrr hhrrr." Journey reached his head over his stall door.

Melt. "Hey there, Handsome." I rubbed the stark-white shield under his tangled forelock. My chestnut knight in shining armor. He listened to my whispers and tuned in to my movements as I groomed. I know my way around a horse.

In no time, his mane and tail flowed like a silken waterfall and his sides shimmered coppery in the dim light. I patted him on the shoulder. "You look good." He snuffled my pocket for a treat.

Unfortunately, when it came to my own grooming, you could say the buck stopped in the barn. The fashion police at school reminded me of that daily, *especially* when it came to my paisley jeans. It's funny how that made me wear them even more.

If I'd had it my way, I'd have worn my thrift store jeans every day with an un-tucked super hero t-shirt and my mousy hair whipped up in a ponytail.

Wait ... I *did* have it my way most days.

I caught a glance of my cracked reflection in an old mirror we hung between the stalls to entertain the horses. The moonlight silhouetted my skinny neck stretching up toward my high cheekbones. My dish-water blonde ponytail dangled behind my head. Shadowy hazel eyes glinted back at me.

Who did I think I was? Did I actually think I could do this? It hurt to breathe and my jaw ached from clenching my teeth.

A warm, earthy breath puffed at the back of my neck. I turned to Journey who looked at me straight on. His eyes told me, "I believe in you."

* * *

Ernie meowed from the tops of the stalls and walked along. A carefree, three-legged daredevil. I followed beneath him next door to Boss Girl. She stood dozing in a corner, one hind leg bent, head hung low.

"Hey, BG," I whispered. The last thing she needed was getting jolted out of a perfectly good dream of the old days when she and Mom ran barrels or raced the wind in the clover field.

As my eyes adjusted, I began to make out the vague contours of her bony hips and swayed back. Age left its mark.

My defiant voice from earlier that day echoed in my head. *Over my dead body!*

Then Cindy's sticky voice, *It's the humane thing to do.* This coming from someone who'd never touched, much less owned, a horse in her life.

I reminded myself again, *I'm not like her.*

Then Dad, "I don't see any other options. Unless you want to start paying the vet bills."

And me, "She's only twenty-five! What kind of idiot puts down a horse that's paid for herself ten times over in winnings just because she's retired?"

"Paisley Alberta Noon, that's enough." Dad had pulled out the middle name weapon.

"*Mom* would never allow it." I had no problem pulling out the Mom weapon.

Silence.

I blinked out of the memory. None of that mattered anymore. In fact, I was glad it happened. It was just the catalyst I needed to finally listen to the voices tugging at me to leave for the last year. Their whispers became clearer, yet I still couldn't understand their words. And Gram's had become unbearable. My choice was made.

The noise of the stall door was just the persuasion Boss Girl needed to lift her head and nicker a soft greeting.

"All right, mi'lady. Aren't we looking lovely this evening?"

She arched her slender neck and stretched her refined Arabian head to me.

"Aw, Boss Girl. You know I always have a little something for you."

I reached into my pocket for a mint, and she slurped it out of my hand before I could even pick the lint off of it. The sound of her slow crunch, crunch in the darkness made me smile.

I tussled her sparse forelock. "That's right. Simple pleasures, BG. Simple pleasures."

A wave rushed over me as I stood with my mom's horse. I would protect her. I listened to her steady breathing while I groomed her dappled coat until it shone even in the darkness. Gliding my hand over her side, my fingers felt her ribs just slightly, her eyes closed in contentment. I patted her rump.

Determined to keep moving before doubt invited itself in again, I grabbed her travel bandages. Once I had her wrapped, careful and swift, I said, "Let's move."

Prairie's ears shot up. In a flash she sat at the stall entrance.

"Are you going to make yourself useful?"

She picked up a ratty lead rope from the dirt. Its snap had long since broken off and both ends were frayed like noodles. It might have been blue and white at one time.

"Not with that old thing, you're not."

She sneezed at me and trotted off toward the trailer. It dragged on the ground hanging out both sides of her mouth.

Boss Girl and I looked at each other and sighed simultaneously.

I haltered BG and led her to my slant-load trailer, which I bought at an auction with my own money. Gram taught me the art of perennial propagation, and we had furnished a hefty portion of the county's front lawns and backyards with flowers and shrubs, earning a respectable sum each year. My trailer was rusty and needed a paint job, but the floor was solid. Parked in the shadows of an oak tree, I swung open the door, thankful for having greased the hinges.

"Ladies first." I unlatched the lead from her halter and bowed low as BG loaded herself. We could just as well have been off to a barrel race or western pleasure show for all she knew. I waited until I saw her munching on the hay hanging by her window before I set the divider in place. Then I went for Journey.

"Come on, Mister. Quiet now."

Journey sank his head low to the ground and picked up each foot a little more carefully than normal. I kid you not. He tip-toed like a Scooby-doo cartoon right in next to Boss Girl. They touched noses through the divider.

Prairie appeared as I closed the door and secured the latch. That dirty old rope still hung out of her mouth.

"Thanks so much for your help, girl." I wondered if dogs get sarcasm. "So much for border collies being *working* dogs. Now drop it and hop in."

I opened the door, and she jumped up shotgun. She sat straight as a kid at boarding school, rope in mouth and a resolute look in her eye. I knew better than to fight her on this one.

She just blinked and looked out the window. It was all I could do not to roll my eyes.

* * *

Experience has convinced me Oscar's got a split personality. I never knew what kind of mood that Scottsdale would be in. Sometimes he'd turn over and purr like a kitten. Other times, he'd screech like a yeti. I cringed at the thought of the latter in the still night. In fact, I slid my clammy hand from the key in the ignition and leaned back for a nervous breath, to settle the whirligigs in my stomach.

Then I saw Gram. On top of my duffle bag. The portrait, that is. Her eyes still as stone just watched me, waiting. She had been like that — always watching and waiting for me to make a decision for my obstinate little self. Prodding me on with some quip remark. In the picture the little curve at one corner of her mouth told me she was with me as I sat behind Oscar's steering wheel all sweaty-palmed.

That woman was my hero. I wanted so much to be like her.

Prairie sat in the truck with a determined look she could only have gotten from being around me way too much. Glancing past her to the porch light, I wondered what kind of decision I was making this time.

Then it came to me. Gram, though she'd been dead five years, would be with me. She would swish away any mess I got myself into. From behind the glass, the crinkle in her left eye winked. She *got* me. No matter how big of a brat I was. She knew I had to learn things my own way.

I leaned forward and turned the key. Vvvrrrum hummmm.

"Helloooo Kitten."

Prairie pant-smiled and let out a "whuff." The ratty rope dangled over her canines.

"I guess that means we are on our way." Ghostly butterflies fluttered in my rib cage.

As we inched down the driveway, gravel crunched beneath Oscar's tires, and I said my silent goodbyes to the only home I'd ever known. I slowed to a stop at the mailbox that read "The Noon Family: 445 Aurora Way." A sadness tensed my shoulders because I honestly could not remember the last time it had felt like a *family* lived at this address.

It was time.

Enough with the mush. Get on with it! Gram said.

"See ya 'round, suckers," I sneered to my past.

Oscar's grimy headlights lit the way as I began my cruise north and west toward the plains of North Dakota.

Chapter 2

Oscar's engine hummed as we bounced along through Minnesota. I thought about my mother, especially when I blew past a billboard for AhhSpa.com. It said they could "heal your mind, body and soul." *Gag.*

Fernie Greene, my mom, was a zen master. Or at least she thought she was. That's how I got my name. To her, a paisley was half of the yin and yang symbol. It makes most people think of gaudy sofas and heavy curtains, but that was my mom. She had her own way of seeing things.

"You brought balance into my world," she would say as we rode double on Boss Girl's round back across our four-hundred-acre farmland. "I'm the yin and you're the yang."

"What's that mean, Mommy?" my five-year-old self would ask.

"It means you are the part of me that makes me whole."

"Was something inside you missing, Mommy?"

"Yes, Miss Paisley Alberta Noon. It certainly was."

"What was missing?"

I was five. I didn't get it.

"Balance, my little filly. Balance. Before you came along, I could never do this…"

She would reach her dark Lakota arms around me to take my pale hands in hers, fling our arms out far, and give BG a squeeze in the ribs. Together we would fly across the meadow, nothing but legs and wits keeping us upright. My screeches of joy were drowned out by the wind and my mother's war whoops. Her hair whipped behind us, streaming black and wild. I wondered often if I was like her.

Unfortunately, my *dad* ... was zenless. Still is. He's a sensible Scandinavian trying his darnedest to make an honest living. Peter Noon is his name, and soy beans were his game. He called it "the rich crop." We were not rich.

His and my mom's relationship, I was told, was a classic case of opposites attract. He indulged her sporadic phases — I guess you could say he found her interesting. She, in turn, happily provided a little thrill and that feeling of newness ... constantly. That was until she got bored and realized it was all a big mistake. Again, so I was told. Mom packed up her yoga mat by the time I was seven, and we've never spoken of her since. Though I've wanted to.

So *I* became the one with something missing. That's when the voices started, in my dreams first.

At that point, Gram stepped in. Thank God.

When my Lakota Grampa Joe Greene died of a heart attack just after Mom left, Gram packed her bags from their dried up hog farm on the neighboring acreage and tromped onto our front porch.

Nothing like her free-spirited daughter, Gram was focused, tough as barbed wire, and hot tempered as a bull. Though certainly not my yin or yang, she loved me. And somewhere inside that love, she tried to fill an eternally empty space.

Dad was scared to death of her. Not surprising. It doesn't take a genius to figure out who the alpha dog is when you watch your scrawny father cringe deeper into the couch cushions at the sound of your grandma's boots clomping through the kitchen to ask what the hell he'd accomplished that day.

"Good Lord," she'd say to him, "you act like you're the only one in this family who's lost someone. Hell, you act like you're the only one on the *planet* who's lost someone." She would usually then take her

19

frustration out on the mountain of dishes teetering in the sink. "Fern was my only daughter. And Paisley's momma, for cripesake."

I suppose I shouldn't have been so shocked when she died. Let's face it, not many kids lose their grammas to the wickedness of a howling Minnesota blizzard.

Truth be told, though, it should have been my dad. He's the one who should have set out into that twenty below howling blizzard. The horses had panicked when the wind blew a hay feeder right straight through the fence gate that led into white nothingness.

Gram went out instead. Gram had gotten them back. And then, Gram was gone.

I hated my dad for letting her go. I hated *her* for going. I hated my horses for being frightened. But most of all, I hated myself for letting her see me that night, with my tear streaked, pleading face.

So I learned to suck it up. Brave face. It's safer — for everyone — that way. And the voices continued in my dreams. But I didn't listen, just swatted them away like flies.

When Dad met and married Kewpie doll Cindy a couple years later, the house no longer felt like my home. I was alone.

I knew whatever I needed did not lie in the little town of Grover, Minnesota.

I sat on Oscar's springy vinyl seat, my dog at my side, and two horses safely in tow. I was on my way to discovery. Like a quest. Like a super hero just discovering her powers, or a hobbit trekking across Middle Earth. Maybe like my mother.

* * *

As sunshine reached into Oscar's cab, I listened to his steady growling while we banged along a poorly maintained, two-lane highway. Spring thaw potholes and swells riddled the asphalt as we drove between marshy wetlands of messy cattails and winter flattened swamp grass. Sadly, it reminded me of my hair. Hence, the ponytail.

Prairie was curled up, her head on that ratty old rope. She watched me. She did that a lot. I know she counted on me to keep them all safe. I grabbed Gram's photograph and wedged it between the dashboard and windshield. Prairie's head popped up and tipped.

"Our trip's talisman."

I ruffled her silky head, and she plopped it back down, satisfied.

I dug around blindly in my bag to find the want ad and directions. I tried to read my chicken scratch notes written with Purple Mountain Majesty Flower Daze photo-safe marker. I shook off the vision of Dad and Cindy waking up and slowly going about their Saturday. I figured it would probably take them half the day to notice the empty barn and missing dog.

After a few hours on the road, we neared the first horse-friendly rest area on my list. Prairie sprang up in her seat and perked her ears at me as I eased my rig onto the exit. I started to break at the top of the off ramp when suddenly a loud bang rocketed my heart into overdrive. Then *thump, thump, thump.* I wrestled with the steering wheel and stomped on the brake as we rounded the corner. The trailer moaned and banged and swung this way and that, rocking with terrifying momentum. Journey and BG's hooves clanged sharply against steel walls.

Prairie got thrown to the floor where she splayed out her legs. She bravely snatched Rope off the seat.

One of the hay bales I had stacked too high tipped and tumbled right off Oscar's truck bed and rolled away down the road in my side view mirror. A yowling wail came from the back. I shot a look out the sliding window only to see Ernie, the three legged, one-eyed, crimp-eared suppose-to-be-in-the-BARN cat suction cupped to the glass!

"What the…? Holy …!"

"Woof!" Prairie finished my thought.

But I couldn't worry about the cat. I had to get my rig under control. Panic devoured my nerve. I *did not* know what to *do*.

Then I heard it.

Breathe, Paisley. Breathe. Gram's voice was hauntingly calm. Then I saw it. Gram's eyes flickered, I swear it, wedged up on the dash.

Breathe, she said.

So I did. Eyes glued to her photo.

Time seemed suspended. I relaxed my grip, and followed, rather than fought, ever so slowly and carefully guiding it back to the right path. The lurching behind me began to subside as I continued my dance with the wheel. This way and that. Until the music finally stopped and I pulled over.

The dust of the gravel roadside billowed past me. Finger by finger I plucked my hands from the wheel. Prairie crept onto her seat wide-eyed.

"You okay, girl?"

She nuzzled her head under my shaking hand, and I felt the blood flow in my veins. We both panted and looked at Gram, flat and lifeless.

"Yeeowow yeow wow wow!" We whipped around to see an orange tabby belly and three orange tabby legs clinging to the back window like a bumper sticker.

"Ernie, what in the…"

"Woof!"

"… are you *doing* here?"

I opened the rear sliding window. Like a drunken sailor, he scrambled into the cab looking pathetic as ever. Emergency Nurse Prairie snuffled him furiously. Then, once satisfied he was indeed in one piece, she plunked half her rope on top of the duffle bag where he collapsed.

"I guess we've got a roadie." I scratched Ernie behind his crimped ear. His eyes rolled back, and he purred like a Harley. Prairie pant-grinned. "Either of you know how to change a flat?"

Chapter 3

Hunched over, head hanging between my knees, I digested my situation. Oscar's rear tire was flat as my hair, the rim bearing all the weight. My first thought was to call 911, but my cell was dead.

Here was one of life's most common do-it-yourself moments, and I had no clue.

I looked as far as I could see in all directions. Desolate. A brook gurgled nearby, and crows cawed in the distance. Apparently, no one else existed anymore.

Doubt's fingers crept into my chest as tears streaked my cheeks. I pulled out my mother's crinkled picture and cupped her in my hands. Her eyes were gentle as Grandpa Joe's, yet alive with fire like Gram. I focused on the sign with the three Fs next to her and something washed over me, reviving me.

Gram's voice reached out. *Get it done, Paisley.*

Shoving the photo back in my pocket, I wiped my face with the back of my sleeve, shook off my pity party, and marched straight for Oscar's glove box. The yellowed truck manual was warped, and half the pages were stuck together, but I managed to find the "How to Change a Flat Tire" section. Prairie propped herself over the opened window and looked down to give a gargly "wow woowoo…" cheer. Boss Girl and Journey hung their heads out their windows to "hrr hrr nicker" encouragement. I set to work.

Oscar can make me mad as a wet cat, but for some deranged reason, I thought he was perfect. I have since the first time I laid eyes on him two years earlier. Back when the time I spent with my dad could actually be fun, and back when I still felt like I meant something to him.

I was fifteen with just a farmer's permit. Dad was driving me home from school when I saw "RUNS GREAT! $700!" in the window of an old yellow and white truck in a church parking lot.

We approached an old guy with a scraggly gray ponytail and a John Deere cap.

"Ahhlo!" He reached out his hand while trying to get out of his lawn chair next to the truck. "You interested in this old boy, girly?" He slapped the hood and a rusty powder rained onto the asphalt.

Dad had a strange expression as he looked at the man. Like he maybe recognized him. Then Dad started his hustler thing. "I'm willing to bet this baby needs a little repair work. Am I right?"

"T'ain't a thing wrong with this ol' boy that a blind eye can't cure. This truck has stories to tell..." He waggled a bony finger at me. "... and *make*."

When I saw his near toothless grin, my heart melted – for him *and* the truck.

"Right, right." An awkward pause. Dad sounded like he couldn't peg what was so familiar about this guy. "Where've you been with it?"

"Used to work wit my brother out in Nort Dakota."

Dad spoke pensively. "I've got some ... uh ... *distant* family out there. What did you say your name was?"

I leaned out the window to see them both. Dad gave me a hesitant glance.

"Lenny. Lenny ..."

HONK, honk! A semi blared going by.

There *was* something going on, but I was too excited to try to figure it out.

After a test drive, Dad wrote a check, we got the title and exchanged handshakes.

"You've got some stuff in here still. I'll get it for you."

Lenny waved his hands. "Nope. Nope. Don't bother, girly. The deal's done. It's all yours."

"Even … this?" I whipped out a Baby Ruth and waved it at him. This old codger and I could have been buddies in a heartbeat. "Split it with ya?" He gave me a semi-toothless grin, so we shared a candy bar in the church parking lot sitting on the tailgate of my new truck.

I remember thinking I would probably never see him again. Half the people we meet are temporary, tiny marks on our lives. But I couldn't help feeling his part in my story was not done.

Dad handed me the title like he was presenting an award. "Congratulations, Paisley. You are now the proud owner of possibly the oldest truck on the planet."

I ostentatiously took it. "Thank you very much, Mr. Lenny…" I focused on the last name since I hadn't heard it earlier, "…Tuson."

* * *

I nearly killed myself changing Oscar's tire. Seven scraped knuckles, two gravel-bloodied knees, and one heck of a goose egg later, change it I DID! I flung my arms out and gave a war cry.

BG and Journey whinnied. I'd tied them to the side of the trailer.

I danced around the whole rig. "Oh yah. That's right." I caught my reflection in the window and kissed my biceps. "Who's the big tough girl now? Huh!"

Prairie and Ernie looked at me like I had scrambled my noodle, but I just made a crazy face at them, which made my goose egg throb. I loaded the horses and got back in the truck. Oscar's springy seat folded around me as Emergency Nurse Prairie snuffled furiously. Ernie rolled up on my lap, purring. I laid my head back, exhausted, and closed my eyes.

That's when the first dream came.

It started with the voices, the ones I don't understand. I stand alone in the center of all things. Ethereal shapes circle me. They move the grass and the clouds and the wind. Plumes sway overhead, back and forth. Manes and tails sail. Grey ones. Running. A sinuous, metallic river. Heavy hoof beats drum the earth.

My hair glows. My skin electric. I am strong. I am like them.

I am like them.

Then, faces peer through the smoke. Dark, human faces. They look at me. Waiting.

Whinnies and knickers flutter on the wind. Screams pierce the air. Through the din … all those voices. They are calling.

Chapter 4

Scenery crawled by. Painted clouds swept across the endless sky. Rolling landscape stretched endlessly. Round bales hunched like resting buffalo in perfect lines far out in the fields. Black specks of cattle dotted the hillsides. The sun soaked into my skin through the window. And I drove and drove into the heart of North Dakota prairie.

"Arms up!" I squealed as we coasted down a pretty decent grade on a gravel road into a river valley. Rocks spat out from Oscar's tires. He ground in like a champion keeping us straight as a corn row.

"Woof!" Prairie reached her front paws up onto the dashboard, disgusting rope dangling like a bulldog's drool. Ernie, on the other hand, scrambled under the seat. It's not like I was pulling g-forces or anything — I wouldn't put my precious cargo in danger — but after driving through flat grasslands for the last hour, this felt like a roller coaster.

Trees grew thick at the bottom of the hill, a rare sight other than shelter belts lining fields. But when we got about half way to the bottom, something else drew my attention. Or should I say the *lack* of something. I couldn't find the road, just gushing water. A flooded riverbed barreled across where there was *supposed* to be a bridge.

Prairie looked at me wide-eyed. Even Gram's photo looked a little panicked, but then I heard her say, *What now, Paisley Noon?*

"Prairie, get down," I ordered, and she immediately obeyed curling herself and her rope around Ernie. "Alright, Oscar, easy does it."

I tried my darnedest not to shut my eyes as I eased the brakes so Oscar wouldn't seize up and twist. I released the brake then eased on it again.

I took a deep breath and angled for a tractor turn-off into a freshly disced field just twenty feet or so from the water. We had slowed enough to make the turn, but it still felt too fast.

Gram's eyes, steady and true, watched from the dash. I heard her voice ring through clear as a cardinal call. *I got you.*

Then, smooth as silk we veered toward the tractor turn-off and thumped to a jarring halt. The sound of water rushing water coursed over the rattling of Oscar's engine.

I sat frozen. Prairie lifted her head, twitched her eyes and ears around in every direction then, satisfied the coast was clear, hopped up onto the seat next to me and panted with Rope dangling over her teeth.

A gust of air escaped me, "Holy ..."

"Woof!"

My voice shook. "Well, that was fun."

Prairie sneezed and pounced against the passenger door to get out, and then Ernie climbed up and limped over purring. Clearly, I was the only one in need of a little recovery time. Eventually, for the second time that day, I shakily undid my seatbelt and checked my rig.

Journey reached his nose out of his window and tussled my ragged ponytail with his big lip. I swear he said, "Do it again!"

I let them stand outside tied to the trailer, each with a bag of hay, while I sat next to Ernie on Oscar's warm hood and tried to collect my nerves. Prairie and Rope investigated the area. (Yes, I've succumbed to the fact that it's *not* going away. It has a name now.)

"Helloooo down there! Is everything alright?"

29

Prairie galloped to my side, and we hiked up the incline to greet the farmer.

"I say, is everything alright there, girly?"

The vaguely familiar term "girly" stopped me in my tracks as the man continued toward me. "Lenny?" I whispered. Visions of the man I'd bought my truck from floated in front of me.

I must have looked pretty strange parked there in his field, but I tried to smile into the sun. I may not have the greatest people skills, but Gram made sure I knew my manners.

"What do you think you're doin' out here? Can't ya see the bridge is out?"

Jeez, I felt dumb. "I seem to have missed my turn, sir."

"Is that so?" I could've lived without the sarcasm. "Where is it yer lookin' for?"

I pulled the magazine page out of my pocket and showed him the ad. "A place called Forever Fields Farm, sir. Do you happen to know where I went wrong?"

"Course I do." He grabbed the page and looked at it closer. Then he surveyed my rig. "You handled yourself pretty well there." His eyes twinkled at me.

I didn't know how to respond to that, so I just asked, "Do you think you could show me the way?"

He tipped his Carhart cap up. "Well, if you think yer able to turn that rig around, you can follow me. It's a good mile back."

"I can, sir. Two shakes of a banty tail."

"Off with ya, then."

I loaded up the horses while Prairie herded Ernie back into the truck. As soon as I had Oscar back on the gravel road, the big John Deere tractor drove up next to me in the field. The farmer waved me to follow. He even looked like Lenny Tuson, right down to his grey pony tail.

Sure enough, about a mile back down the road, the tractor turned left. No wonder I missed it. A sorry excuse for a mailbox peeked out of a thorny thicket of Russian olive trees and wild chokecherry bushes blocking the weather-beaten sign that barely read: For ver Fiel s arm.

Prairie and I looked at each other.

"This is a driveway?"

I couldn't see the end. It must have been more than a mile long. Then Lenny-not-Lenny flagged us to continue down that way without him, so I rolled down my window and gave him a thumbs up. "Thank you!" I hollered, but he didn't seem to hear, or care, and headed north back toward the river. "Okay, girl," I said to Prairie, "I think we can handle it from here."

"Whuff." Pant smile.

We limped along due east over potholes and divots with the sun at our backs spotlighting the scenery. All along the south side out Prairie's window was a continuous wild row of chokecherry bushes with crabapple trees and Russian olive trees springing up randomly. The grass in the ditches grew cab high as it waved us on in the breeze. On the north side of the driveway, the freshly disced field ended with a run-down fence line, and cottonwoods stood tall, limbs reaching for the sky.

Then I heard it, or rather … felt it, like a pack of Harleys on my tail. The rumbling grew louder, so I stopped and got out to look around. Journey and Boss Girl figured it out first. As soon as I heard them whistle and stomp, I knew too.

Multiple ear-splitting screams coursed through the cottonwoods, and drumming legs ran toward us. The ground shook as a herd of the wildest looking horses I've ever laid eyes on came thundering into the shadows of the trees. Dirt flung far and wide. Manes and tails whipped the wind. My heart raced, pounding in rhythm with the hoof beats. Sleek, charcoal gray bodies streamed past catching glints of sunlight from the breaks in the budding canopy.

As I peered closer, I could see their necks were thick and burly. Their legs were sturdy and strong, yet wild feathery hair adorned their fetlocks giving their hooves wings. Their dark eyes and broad foreheads bore the mark of intelligence. A few held their heads high with their upper lip curled to catch my scent in the wind. They moved as one mass like a flock of birds.

But one, a smallish, black-speckled blue roan, looked straight at me. Even at their pace, I could tell. He was looking right at me. And I looked back. And we ... *saw* each other. Like time was slowing down around us so we could meet. It was then that I heard these ghostly whispers of words I did not know whoosh at me, swirl around me, and then curl right back into the herd's wake as they passed on by.

Some kind of crazy possessed me, and I found myself racing along behind them with my arms stretched wide and whooping and hollering until tears streaked my face. I yanked the band out of my ratty ponytail and whisked life into my matted hair. Prairie raced alongside me, smiling with filthy Rope sailing along.

Eventually, my legs couldn't keep up with my heart. I sagged to a stop. Bent over gasping for air, I lifted my head and watched the herd round the bend and head north into distant grasslands.

Prairie and I plopped on the dirt and stared in their direction. I wiped the tears from my cheeks. I couldn't be sure if they were from the wind or from me.

Prairie herded me into the truck, but she didn't have to work very hard because I was ready ... so ready.

We drove around the corner, and chills rushed over me when I saw the ranch. I pulled the picture from my pocket and held it up. Aside from a coat of paint, the two were the same. Oscar grumbled along slowly, and something fluttered in my chest.

Out-buildings lined the drive on both sides. Prairie wagged her tail and propped up on her window. Even Ernie balanced with his one hind leg on my lap to look out. A couple of men went about their business while we rolled straight ahead. I drove past rusty corrals and dilapidated shelters and sagging barns. But the visible wear on the place did not read ruined. Rather … seasoned, like Gram's favorite cast-iron pan.

In a rough pasture behind a row of little cabins, several swayback horses nickered at us then went back to munching the new spring grass. A few of them laid in the afternoon sun, eyes and heads drooping. These were not the same sleek, charcoaled bodies that had thundered their way through the trees. These were the elderly.

I whispered, "This is the place, BG."

Journey and BG whinnied tender calls to each little cluster. Sweet neighs and gentle murmurs echoed back and forth. I relaxed.

We drove onto a turn-about encircling a massive, dried-up, cement fountain. I shut Oscar down and exhaled with him as he hissed, clicked, and tinged a sigh of relief. We made it.

And there it stood. On the corner of the porch. The sign from the picture. The carved diamond around the letters fFf.

"Forever Fields Farm."

I sank back in my seat visualizing my mom on that wild-eyed buckskin standing next to it in real life. I held the photo up again, and there she was, as real as my imagination would allow. The breezes tossed her hair and played with his mane. Her smile came to life, and she looked at me longingly. I dared not move for fear of chasing the vision away.

"Yip whuf!" Prairie brought me back.

I blinked a couple times and the picture laid flat and lifeless again.

I scuffled Prairie's ears. "Okay, miss task master." I looked around. "What do you think? Will this place do?"

"Owf."

Everything was overgrown with moss and weeds. I thought about the ad in the magazine. "Grounds Keeper" it had said. Oh, my good Lord.

I stepped out of the truck and as soon as my boots hit the dirt, that place had a feeling to it. It fit me. Like the way my worn-out paisley jeans slid effortlessly over my rear. Or the way my feet folded into my garage sale boots. Most importantly, I could tell there was a story here, a *real* story riding on the wind over endless open acres.

I dared consider it — maybe *mine*.

Chapter 5

The screen door on the front porch squeaked open and slammed shut behind a tall, scrawny, red-haired kid. He wore a Spiderman t-shirt and purple velour pants two inches too short and no shoes. I admired his daring. Thick, crazy curls twisted wildly out of his head. This kid needed a serious haircut.

He scrunched up his face and adjusted his plastic-frame glasses, his deep brown eyes magnified as he focused on me. "Uh...excuse me? Can I help you?" he asked all nasally.

I straightened my own Avengers t-shirt and pulled out the want ad. "I'm here about the ad. You need a hired hand?"

"Uh...I don't know." He sounded kind of perturbed, then slapped his bare feet to the far end of the wrap-around porch and hollered, "Mother!" He glanced at me and bellowed, "Berta Greene!"

Greene?

I didn't have time to think about the lady's last name because he said to me, "Why's yer hair so crazy?"

Without thinking my hackles shot up, and I loaded one heck of a nasty come-back, but he just stood there on the porch picking his nose like a champion. What was this kid's *deal*? He looked like he could be at least a junior in high school, but everything else screamed eight-year-old. Since I had a sense that something was just a little off here, (and *I* had actually fired the first hair shot, just not out loud) I decided to stand down.

Just then, a holler came from the main barn, "I'm coming! Hold your horses, Knut!"

The massive barn door slid open a crack underneath a sprawling gabled roof and, expecting a body to match the size of both the barn and the booming voice, I was shocked to see a tiny, tow-headed woman emerge. Her feet splayed out when she walked toward us, and for some strange reason I got the impression that she was a well-educated woman, like she had been places ... places I could only imagine or read about in books or see in the movies. She walked as though she knew who she was, from the inside out. Each stride and flap-swing of her arms and toss of her head appeared completely on purpose. No pieces missing.

As she came closer, I saw dense, white-blonde hair that cupped her head. Creases drew themselves across her face but settled in most comfortably by her eyes. Tiny badges of honor after every belly laugh or each sun-drenched day in some exotic locale where she'd just finished learning how to hog-tie a giraffe or trim the perfect bonsai.

She raised one hand to shield her eyes from the afternoon sun and waved the other at me like I was some long-lost friend. Then she flashed the brightest, toothy smile I ever did see.

"Welcome to Forever Fields Farm, Paisley Alberta Noon. I've been expecting you!"

* * *

So here's what happened inside my head:
YOU'VE BEEN *WHAT*?
And here's what happened out loud:
"Huh?"

"I've been *expecting* you," she said matter-of-factly. "Peter said you should be arriving about now."

When I just stood there, mouth agape, her warm smile faded into a cute little smirk, and she thumped her hands on her hips.

More scholarly words escaped me. "Peter? As in Noon? As in my dad?"

With another sure-as-the-sun look, she answered with an absolute, "Mmhm."

"I … I … don't understand."

"Well, honey, not to worry, because I do." Her eyes glinted. "I'm your Auntie Alberta. Your daddy is my baby brother." And as if that wasn't enough to knock me into next week, she added, "and … I might as well tell you now because I gather little ol' Peteypoo hasn't yet …" she squinted harder at me, more serious, "Your mother's older brother was my husband for 25 years."

That did it. I was going to barf.

"Holy Saint Francis, honey!" She rushed to catch me before I fainted right there head first into the gravel. "C'mon. Sit down on the step here now."

She thrust my head between my knees and held my hair back. My head spun with questions and … I don't know … *betrayal*.

The want ad in my hands stared at me, the coffee stain so conveniently splotched in exactly the right spot. It mocked me for a sucker. Dad must have planted it for me to find. He knew I'd go for it too. I thought with dim realization that I hadn't given him enough credit all these years. He knew me *too* well.

Breathe, Paisley. Breathe. I heard Gram from the far corners of my mind.

My eyes started clouding and sending that oh so attractive twinge through my face prepping for a waterworks extravaganza, but I shoved it down, deep inside before any real tears materialized.

When my vision cleared, I asked, "Wh…what did you say your name was?" I didn't look up, just stared between my knees at the flakey white paint on the step.

She took a deep breath. "Alberta … Greene."

I whispered, "My middle name is Alberta."

"I know, sweetie." She rubbed my back firmly. "I know."

We sat there for some time in silence. The wind had died down to nearly nothing. An early evening chill rippled ghostlike over the grounds. BG and Journey stood calm without a murmur from the trailer. Oscar pinged and ticked. And when I raised my head, I saw Prairie and Ernie staring out the window.

That's when I snapped out of it — when I looked at my rig and all its precious cargo. They were counting on me to take care of them. I had brought them here. So it was time to shake off whatever freak-out session I was having, deal with information overload later, and be a grown-up.

Gram's voice echoed in my head. *Atta girl. Get on with ya.*

I turned to face this woman who said she was my aunt and said, "My horses need water."

Ms. Greene sat up straighter then slapped her knees as she pushed herself up. Her smile returned. "Well of course they do. Let's get you settled in." Then she hollered so suddenly it nearly jolted me out of my boots. "KaahNooT!! Get on out here and help us unload!"

"Aww MOTHER! I'm BUSY!" came nosepicker's nasal whine from inside the house. He had retreated shortly after our hair critiques.

She looked at me and grumbled, "Busy my behind."

I raised an eyebrow.

Yelling again. "Put down whichever comic book you're thumbing through for the thousandth time and come on out here to meet your cousin properly!"

She was tough. I liked that.

"They're called *graphic novels*, Mother." Crazy Hair emerged with a pathetic not-fair-to-me look and messed with his wild, red curls. He looked as though he'd jumped off the page of one of his *graphic novels*, but I wasn't sure if he was hero or villain. We eyed each other with tangible wariness.

Ms. Greene introduced me. "Knut, meet Paisley Noon. Your cousin from Minnesota."

He scooped up his syllables at the end. "Uh...mm...well..." It was more a groan. Then he surrendered, "Nice to meet you ... Pasty."

I was not amused. But neither was Ms. Greene.

"Knut, you of all people should know how it feels to have your name mispronounced," she said with a no-nonsense ring I recognized from times when Gram would ask me if I really did think it was a good idea to stick my tongue out at my father.

"Yah." He directed his words at me. "It's Kah-noot."

I raised my hands trying not to let this kid get to me. "Hey, I'm all over that. So ... I'm Pays-lllee." I slapped my jeans. "You know, like the pattern."

He just scrunched up his nose and poked his glasses up, while we all stood there.

"Green Lantern or Thor?" he asked.

I glanced at Ms. Greene who looked at me with a little smirk, and then they both crossed their arms and narrowed their eyes awaiting my reply.

"Duh, Thor," I said pointing to my Avengers t-shirt.

They eyed each other approvingly and then stared at me like I was supposed say something now.

"Uhhh... Aquaman or ..." I swear they leaned in a little. "Iceman?"

Knut let his mother take this one. "Aquaman, especially in the summer. Iceman's too high maintenance."

It was her turn. "Batman or Tarzan?"

Knut sucked in his breath.

I barely had to think for this one. "Tarzan. I'm a naturalist." They didn't even see that one coming. "Wolverine or Beast?" This one was all Knut's.

His face sobered and he raised his eyebrows till they were clear over the rim of his glasses. We stared each other down like gunslingers.

Cool as cauliflower, he said, "Beast."

I pressed an imaginary loser button. "Ehhhh. Wrong! Wolverine all the way. Nothing can beat adamantium."

He stuck his pointer finger in the air and addressed me like Professor Hank McCoy from the X-men would have. "Ah. But intelligence, my dear, is the sharper weapon against evil!"

I did a double take. He was good.

Sky blue laughter erupted from Ms. Greene as she flung her arms out and squeezed our shoulders. "My, my goodness. You two are going to get along quite well, I see. Quite well."

I wasn't so sure, but it all did make me smile.

"Come." She scooted us both off the porch. "Let's get our guests comfortable."

"Okay!" he whooped as he hurled himself, limbs flailing, off the porch over to the truck. I thought Prairie was going to waggle herself right out of her skin. "Can I let them out?" he cried.

I looked at Ms. Greene who said, "Knut is our animal whisperer around here. They'll be perfectly fine."

Waving, I hollered, "Go ahead. Just keep an eye on them." I totally knew Prairie didn't need anyone to *keep an eye* on her. I couldn't lose that dog if I tried. And Ernie had his own agenda, as always, so he would take care of himself, but I wanted to make sure everyone here knew I was in charge.

As Knut and Prairie flomped around the yard playing and chasing with Rope, I could see out of the corner of my eye Ms. Green was looking at me.

When she spoke, she turned to watch them play. "It'll be nice having a dog on the farm again. Just this winter we had to say goodbye to our old sheepdogs." She seemed to be looking far off into the distance now. "They were good dogs. Cancer took the one, and loneliness took the other." Silence for a moment. "Loneliness is the true silent killer." Another pause. "We got them when they were pups. My gosh, that was nearly fifteen years ago now." She chuckled and focused on Knut and Prairie bouncing like jack rabbits in the tall grass. "Yes, it'll be good to have a dog on the farm again."

My heart went out to her. I couldn't imagine the day when I would have to say goodbye to my best friend. Dad had brought her home one day a few months after Mom blew us off. I was seven. The neighboring farmer's purebred Border collie just had an "unexpected" litter, which basically means one of several intact, gallivanting males had, shall we say, made the most of one romantic, moonlit evening.

Dad thought a puppy would be a good distraction for me. From the moment I took her furry little body in my hands and we looked into each other's eyes, I knew (and I think she did too) that I had found much more than a "distraction."

I looked at my dog with pride. "Prairie is a really great dog, Ms. Greene. She'll carry her own weight around here."

"I don't doubt it a second." Her tone changed slightly. "You know, Paisley, everyone here brings a special talent to the farm. Knut's is working with the smaller animals, every one of them. Sometimes I think we should have named him after Saint Francis of Assisi." She laughed and pointed to the statue of the patron saint of animals peaking around the corner of the fenced-in front garden. Gram had had one similar to it in our perennial beds, but this one was so tangled in vines I thought he might choke.

Knut had Prairie leaping clear up to his shoulders, and then he made her sit, turn a circle, and lie down.

"Hmm." I wondered about my *talent*.

Changing the subject, Ms. Greene clapped her hands. "Let's get your horses to the barn."

Soon as I snapped the lead rope to Journey's halter and started leading him out of the trailer, he knew I was edgy. It made him snort and arch his neck.

I closed my eyes and took a deep breath. Journey pressed his head against me steadying my heart. "No worries, right Handsome?"

I turned around to find Ms. Greene staring into my trailer. A little gasp escaped her, and she touched her mouth. She was looking at BG, and I think I saw tears well up in her eyes.

"Hello Boss Girl. It's been a long time."

"Hrrr hrrr hrrr."

Ms. Greene stepped into the trailer talking gently to BG all the time. "Aren't you a beautiful sight for these old eyes."

She led BG out of the trailer. She rubbed between her eyes then over the poll and down her sleek Arabian neck. Boss Girl really did still look as beautiful as her ancestors.

"How did you know her name?"

Ms. Greene led BG to a freshly prepared stall. "Oh honey, this horse and I go way back to days before you were a twinkle in your daddy's eye."

Journey hrr hrred softly as we followed them.

After we took off travel wraps and scooped grain into buckets, Ms. Greene said, "We'll keep them in here for a day, like we do with all our new equine guests. These stalls open up to a nice prairie view paddock, so we'll be able to see them from the house. You can move them to the corral over by your bunkhouse tomorrow.

"Bunkhouse?"

"Yep. Bunkhouse," she said again. "Peter said you wouldn't want to impose by taking up in the big house with me, not that it's all that fancy by a long shot. I figured you might like your own space, at least until winter hits."

Winter? I had been living so in-the-moment that I hadn't really considered how long I would be staying. I *had* come here looking for a job. An epiphany hit me. The world would not stop in the fall when school started. I'd dropped out a month before graduation. I would just move on with … life.

I swallowed. "The bunkhouse will be fine."

We took a walk down The Drive, that's what she call the driveway, which ran straight south from the house. Then it turned a sharp right to go straight west down The Lane, the mile and a half long road that led to the mailbox. Knut skipped along and swung a stick getting Prairie to leap like a fool, higher and higher each time. I was surprised to see Rope dangling from his back pocket.

Ernie, griping little half meows, hobbled after me on his three legs, so I stopped to carry him. Cradled on his back in my arms, he purred and took in the view.

Ms. Greene laughed. "I have to say, that cat looks like he's been through the gauntlet. Can he still mouse? Our barn cats have dwindled in the last few years."

"Oh, he can mouse, believe it or not."

"I believe it." She chuckled as she scratched Ernie's crimped ear while he lounged there gazing up at us with his eye.

I got the nickel tour as we strolled. I liked how I didn't have to do much of the talking with her around. She was really good at keeping awkward silence at bay. And she didn't drill me, or sneakily try to get me to talk. I was thankful for it.

"You can see here," she pointed to our left, "we've got the hay shed right close to the big horse barn. You can help yourself to as much as you like for BG and … Journey, is it?"

This woman knew *everything*.

"Yah. Journey."

"Missouri Fox Trotter, right?"

In my mind, I truculently threw my hands in the air.

"Mm hm," I said.

Obviously being a woman of fine intuition, Ms. Greene seemed to pick up on the fact that I didn't feel like chatting. "Ahh. I thought as much. A fine-looking head and excellent lines on that one, mm hm."

He *is* impressive, but so few people I know actually appreciate such things about horses. The compliment caught me off guard.

"Thanks," I said and felt the corners of my mouth curl upward.

We held eye contact for just a few steps. Then she smiled softly. I think she wanted to put her arm around me, but something told her not to. I give off this anti-hugger vibe, probably because I didn't believe most hugs.

The only *real* hugs I'd ever gotten (the kind where your body presses in, and your arms hold tight, and the squeeze is so true that you could just lie your head on their shoulder and close your eyes) had been from two people: Mother and Gram. And that was it. I convinced myself that I wanted to keep it that way too, one thing that belonged to the three of us alone. *Real* hugs would be just ours, forever.

"That right there, you can see is our chicken coop," she graciously dissipated any awkwardness clinging in the air. "And then Knut's barn over there."

"My barn! That's my barn!" Knut squealed. "Let's show her, Mom!"

"You can show her some other time, after she's settled, Mister."

He tore off toward it. Prairie went half way with him then turned around to see if I was coming. When she saw I wasn't, she glanced once toward Knut, raced toward him to yank Rope out of his back pocket, and then trotted back to my side. Looking up at me, I swear, she was laughing from all the fun. I balanced Ernie in one arm so I could ruffle her ears.

"That big pole barn away down there is the machine shed with a mechanics shop in back. Always something noisy going on, but I tell you, they work pure magic inside."

I was dying to know who "they" were, but I didn't ask.

Ms. Greene stopped and pointed to our right at a row of four buildings. With the exception of a Quonset at the end, each had an old-fashioned hitching post in the front, stacked wood on south sides, a corral and three-sided shelter in the back. The corrals all opened up to a long, narrow pasture that spanned the length of all three bunkhouses on up to the fenced in yard of the big house. It stretched westward toward the cottonwood stand where I had seen the band of wild horses. I peered through the distant trees to search for any sign of them, but they weren't there.

The first bunkhouse, square and squat, needed a paint job. All the shades were crookedly pulled down and a pair of crumpled boots sat on the tiny porch. A menacing assortment of knives glinted on the railing. In the corral out back, a sturdy little strawberry roan snoozed in the lean-to. Its back showed the sweaty outline of a saddle. It had the same thick neck, sturdy legs, and feathered feet as the ones from the running herd.

The next bunkhouse was wide with a sprawling front porch.

"You can probably see we have mostly men helping out here." She whisked a finger toward a pair of socks and boxers hanging over a railing. She must have caught me cringing because she laughed out loud. "Don't worry. They clean up okay."

"Of course." I half smiled.

"This one, my dear Miss Paisley, will be *your* little palace," she said with a sweeping gesture. I stopped in my tracks to catch my breath. Her movement reminded me so much of my mother while we rode

BG through the clover fields. I could almost hear her war cry whoops and hollers in the distance.

"This one is *yours*, Paisley," she reiterated with a head nod.

Prairie gave me a get-with-the-program head-bump on my calves. I swelled with emotion as I took in the quaint, light blue cottage, complete with white porch and shutters. A wooden swing hung off to the side of the door that had a welcome sign painted with blue and yellow and white flowers.

As I stood on the simple rug in the entrance, I could see the entire cabin. In fact, I could take three or four steps in any direction from the center of the room to be in the kitchen, bathroom, bedroom, or living area. But what it lacked in size, it made up in charm. It was clean as a whistle. A simple, mission table, white eyelet curtains, black kettle on the woodstove, and ivory pitcher and basin on the dresser in the bedroom. I felt like I had been time-warped back to the days of Little House on the Prairie, and at any second Laura Ingalls would come bounding in. I had a sudden urge to wear braids.

"It's simple, but you should have everything you need. You have hot water in the bathroom over there, as well as at the little sink here in your kitchen."

"It's perfect," I said.

Prairie trotted in and carefully coiled Rope in the corner by the door before she set straight to work sticking her nose into everything. Ernie slunk around checking for ... ew, I didn't want to think it.

Ms. Greene commented, "Well, I see they're making themselves at home. You've got a new mattress and blankets in the bed nook, and I thought you might like that old sofa in the corner by the woodstove. There's nothing like cozying up to the warmth of cottonwood kindling in cast iron on a drizzly evening. You'll have all your meals up at the house with the rest of us."

"It's perfect," I said again as I stared around the room. I must have had a silly grin on my face, but I couldn't help it.

The "nook" (which would qualify to most people as a closet) had a west window overlooking the corral and shelter, and I could hear the ticking of a fancy, little clock on the nightstand by the tiniest bed on the planet. Prairie jumped up and flopped down like it had her name on it. Ernie followed suit.

"I hope you don't mind, but I took the liberty of putting together a little desk area over here by the south window. I know *I* need a space to organize my thoughts now and then."

Three steps to the left stood a sturdy wooden desk. The chair had brass casters, wooden arms, and a leather back and seat. A pillar candle flickered in the center of an abstract piece of diamond willow. I went to the desk.

I trailed my finger along the back of the chair then pulled open the skinny drawer until I saw a ream of stationery with wispy paisley designs. An array of pencils and pens lay next to it. (Oddly, I thought of how much Cindy would have liked the set.) Then, I saw the corner of a picture frame in a drawer. Like molasses, I took it out. It was the same picture I had in my pocket, only this one was in pristine condition, protected behind glass and a burnished gold frame. My mom sat on that wild-eyed buckskin. In this shot, however, she held her windswept hair off to one side, and the horse's head tipped up more. But it was the same moment.

"Where did you get this?" My voice rang too sharp, and my words came too fast.

Ms. Greene looked a hundred percent prepared for that very question. "I took it."

Process, process.

"Fern and I were once very dear friends. No … sisters."

My head started to spin a little. And though I desperately wanted to talk about it, I fell into query overload. Thankfully, Ms. Greene could tell that now was not the time.

"You unpack and get settled. There's kindling in the stove. Start it before long. The nights still get chilly around here this time of year."

She moved around the room as she talked, and I stood there like a lump.

"I've stocked your mini-fridge and cupboards in case you get hungry. Breakfast is at six AM, and I promise you, you won't want to miss it. Baker Bob works wizardry. And he's famous for his chokecherry jelly made from our very own trees." She stopped at the door. "Is there anything you need, Paisley?"

Uuum… that was a loaded question, but I just said, "I could use an aspirin."

She grinned, but not in a mocking way. Half-way out the door she said, "Medicine cabinet, top shelf. See you in the morning."

* * *

That night I sat on the sofa sipping a juice box, trying to fully take in my surroundings. Ernie was curled up on my lap purring but remained ever watchful of the corners and floorboards. Prairie sprawled on the floor soaking in the warmth from the woodstove.

Above the crackling and popping of cottonwood sticks drifted the sound of muffled voices. Men's voices. Deep and … yes … I do believe they sounded … burly. And boots. Lots of clomping boots. I heard some hearty laughing, but mostly low conversations. Part of me wanted to watch them through the kitchen window, but I did *not* want a bunch of *guys* catching me spy on them. So I just sat there, bouncing my foot across my leg, until my juice was sucked dry, and … I could stand it no longer.

I scooted Ernie off my lap and found myself on hands and knees giving Prairie the *shhh* sign. She pricked both her ears at me and then crawled on her belly right along beside me. We skulked to the sink and pressed ourselves ever so slowly upward.

Several boots were propped up on the railing and strands of smoke curled away. One man stood with his back to me. I could only see long, black hair draping well to the middle of his back. In the glow of the lamp posts lining The Drive, the hair swayed back and forth like a sheet of black silk. It was mesmerizing.

I stood up tall. Prairie looked at me wide-eyed. I could not help myself. I *had* to see who belonged to that hair. I think I had my whole face pressed against the window by the time *the hair* decided to move. I heard indistinct goodbyes among the men then he walked down the porch steps with a dog, which bore a silhouette more like a wolf, jogging at his side. They walked toward the hitching post where a dark shadow of a horse waited for him. His full-length coat swung side to side, and … *the hair* swished at me like it knew I was watching.

When he climbed effortlessly into the saddle, he sat still as stone, tall and collected. Then all three (dog, horse, and man) moved as one shadowy figure under the lamplight. His dog trotted on ahead in the darkness, but I swear it turned its head and saw us. Prairie, now standing on hind legs next to me on a step stool, gave the tiniest whine. It made my scalp tingle. I followed the man on the horse as far as the window would allow.

Just before he stepped out of sight, the lamp light in front of my cabin filtered down on him, and he turned to look at me full on, eye-to-eye, the distance between us irrelevant. I froze, horror-struck.

He was … beautiful. And I was … busted.

So, like a mature modern woman, I screamed and ducked. I smacked my elbow on the floor but squelched my cries. Emergency Nurse Prairie snuffled me to make sure I'd live.

Humiliated, I held my breath. Ernie crawled back on my lap as the easy clip-clopping of hooves rode away.

Chapter 6

That night, I dreamt the wild horses wisped around me like ghosts. I stood in the wide-open prairie. Grass swished high as my head. Hoof beats pounded an earthy rhythm as I turned and turned with them, breathing them in. I raised my arms to the clouds and turned. I closed my eyes and turned. I turned and turned with them until nothing but swirls of smoldering manes and tails filled the canvas of my mind, ethereal vapors embracing me.

Harmony washed over me. I stood, lean and beautiful ... balanced ... inside their circle. My hair flowed softly in their airy stream, every strand free, blonde and amber. My limber body swayed with the coneflowers. I sensed all things around me. Long, silken sheets of black hair and a wolf's eyes mingled among the ragged horse hair. Trees ladened with berries streaked the mist like blood. Rushing waters flowed at my feet.

The horses whispered secrets to me as they wrapped me in their warm blanket. Voices. Familiar and urgent. They summoned me. And I know who I am. My purpose clear. I know what I have been called to do...

But I would not remember in the morning.

* * *

At 5:00 AM I slipped out of bed. And by *slipped*, I mean shinnied my legs out from under the covers. Heaven forbid I disturb the two fur balls monopolizing the surface area. Prairie laid flat on her back with legs splayed out for all to see her under-things, and Ernie sprawled full length doing a nice road kill impression.

I'm not normally a morning person, but I was so jacked about being someplace new that I couldn't have stayed in bed any longer if you paid me.

I began my typical morning ritual. Shower. Check profile in the mirror. Try sucking in gut to achieve proper boob-to-belly ratio. Give up on said ratio and pull on paisley jeans, Iron Man t-shirt, and garage sale cowboy boots. By that time, my sidekicks were both yawning and stretching next to me ready for breakfast. I found a ceramic bowl in a cupboard and filled it to the brim with the dog food I had packed. Unfortunately for Ernie, I hadn't planned for him, but Aunt Bert had brought him a can of tuna, so he was in heaven.

While they ate, I brushed my blonde mop into a wet ponytail. I rubbed my eyes and slapped my cheeks until I looked like I was ready to be somebody.

Before we could leave, though, I had some important *decorating* to do. The bunkhouse needed two guardians, I decided. Gram and Mom. I propped both their pictures on either corner of the desk then stood back to assess. Prairie canted her head.

"What?" I asked her quizzical look. "Switch them?"

Prairie looked straight up at me and pant-smiled.

"Alright." I made the switch. "Better?"

She studied the ensemble for a moment, her head moved ever so slightly back and forth, then she gave a single, concurring "*phst*" and trotted straight to the door to collect Rope.

As we walked down The Drive in the crisp morning air, I tried to suppress the giddy schoolgirl in me. What if *he* came to breakfast? Ms. Greene had said "… the *rest of us.*" I can hear the stimulating conversation now.

Ms. Greene: Paisley Alberta Noon, meet Shadow Boy. SB, Paisley. Eggs anyone?

SB: Yes, please ma'am, I'll take some of those eggs you have there. Hi Ms. Paisley Alberta Noon. I'm fabulous and flawless. Jelly?

Me: Oh, hey yah, I'd love some. By the way, I'm the one who was stalking you through my kitchen window last night. Pass the toast.

Ugh! My stomach about lurched into my throat, so I tried focusing on the quiet landscape. Not a breath of wind stirred. A heavy fog shrouded the grounds, and I wished I had my jacket. Some horses blew out their noses in the corral behind the neighboring bunkhouse, but I only saw milky figures if I squinted. I was anxious to get Journey and BG moved in behind my place. I would feel much better knowing they were close.

Once I reached the big barn, I shoved open the door to the tune of a couple hrrr hrrrs and a whinny-nicker-snort.

"Well hello to you too," I said softly, glad to see those familiar faces reaching for me over their stalls. "There's my handsome chestnut man and my fine silver lady. How *are* we this morning?" Journey snuffled all the strange new smells in my clothes and hair like a giant Labrador. BG wiggled her nose into my pockets for treats. I scratched one's mane and rubbed the other's cheek. Their hay racks were already full, and their buckets had been cleaned and filled with fresh water.

Good Lord. How early do people get up around here?

Once I had checked for signs of travel swelling or stiffness and found none, I realized I couldn't put off the inevitable. I had to go to breakfast ... with everyone else ... and be social ... like I *enjoyed* eating with strangers.

I felt Journey's big head give me a shove out the stall door as Gram's voice cheered.

Go get 'em.

"Deep breath. Right."

I worked my knuckles as I walked to the big house, up the three front porch steps, and knocked on the screen door. I could see inside just fine, the main door was swung wide into the entrance, and I could hear some clanging dishes and chatting. I waited only a moment before I saw Ms. Greene peak around the corner and say, "Why Paisley, dear! Good morning, good morning! Come in, come in!"

Prairie bumped my legs shoving me through the door. She and Ernie stayed on the porch.

Ms. Greene hollered, "Help me carry these place settings to the sup deck. Baker Bob's just taking the rolls out of the oven." She gave such a charged expression you would think cinnamon rolls equaled Christmas.

A staircase with a diamond willow railing reached up in front of me, and I could have gone around either side of it to a spacious living area and down a long hall or to the kitchen. A framed aerial photograph of what I assumed was the farm hung on the wall. From what I could tell, the property was configured like a fat U with the long drive running down the center out to the road that went to the bridge.

The "sup deck" was a four-season porch connected to the kitchen. It had a sweeping view of prairie lands and hay fields. A side door led out to a long cedar deck.

Three squares a day were served here. Never fail. Hungry or not. In fact, I was told I didn't have to eat at all if I didn't want to, but if anyone wanted to remain employed at Forever Fields Farm, they had to attend mealtime. Turns out we were expected to share our plans for the day, the events that ensued, and whatever else the spirit so moved us to divulge (so sayeth Ms. Greene). Regardless of the cozy smells wafting around me, my intestines tied knots that would make a boy scout proud.

"How do you take your coffee?" a sweet voice echoed from inside the oven. Baker Bob emerged. He was aged but fit as a fiddle, tanned to a crisp, with a trimmed silver beard, and a buzz cut. I tried not to stare, but it was pretty hard not to notice his neck tattoo of a dove with its beak pointing right at an ugly scar that ran jaggedly down the side of his cheek all the way under his chin.

Ms. Greene introduced us. "Bobby, this is my niece, Paisley Noon. Paisley, meet Baker Bob, our magician in the kitchen. Thanks to this man," she swung an arm around him and, since she was so short, reached way up to pat his chest, "no one at Forever Fields Farm shall ever have a grumbly tummy. And that's saying a lot considering some of the bellies we have to fill."

"Oh, Bert, how you go on." He flung his arms around her into a hug, and I think he blushed. Then he wiped his hands on a pristinely white, fitted apron before extending a greeting toward me. "My, my, it is a pleasure to me you, Miss Noon. Goodness, you do have the Noon nose!" He took a photographer's step back then said while sweeping flat palms in a circle, "But the rest of you, I swear, screams Greene."

"Um. Thanks?" I said.

I felt a fraction of awkward pause after I shook his hand. I think he wanted to hug me, but my anti-hugger vibe came through loud and clear. As I glanced around the room, averting eye contact, I was drawn to a metal baker's rack in front of the east window. On it sat rows and rows of jelly jars that gleamed like jewels as the morning sun began to pierce through the fog.

He offered me kind words instead. "Well then, your coffee. How do you like it?"

I said, "Oh yah, um, if you have some creamer, I'll fix it myself."

He waved a spatula. "Suit yourself. It's in the fridge. Compartment A, Sector 3, Station 1." He winked at Ms. Greene.

I didn't want anyone to think I might be, you know, *stupid*, so I opened the fridge and stood there studying its jam-packed yet orderly layout. Compartment A? *Uhh... crud,* I thought.

Then I heard a nasally voice say, "Creamer's right there, dingbat."

I bristled.

Knut reached around me, pulled it out, and set it on the counter. He made a quick attempt with his finger for the frosting bowl, but Baker Bob swatted him. "Wash up, Little Man."

Ms. Greene was on Knut like slime on snot, which was good because I was a fraction away from cold-cocking him. "Knut! What have I said time and time again about name calling?" she reprimanded. "*What* do you say?"

Sheepish, but doubtfully sincere, he sing-songed, "Sorry Paisley."

Hm. He got my name right at least.

I said, "We're good, Knut." I wasn't here to make enemies.

"Wonder Woman or ..." He scrunched his face. "... Storm?"

Everyone froze. This seemed to be his way of making nicey nice.

"Easy," I said, "Wonder Woman. Helloooo. Can you say wicked accessories?"

Everyone breathed a sigh and waited for my volley. At least that's what I think they were doing. I honestly didn't get this game.

"Okay. The ladies today, huh? Well, how about ..." (Insert dramatic pause while Paisley pulls this one out of her...) "Invisible Woman or ..." *Think, P, think!* "... uhh ... Aunt May?"

Knut tilted his head like a puppy that just heard you sneeze for the first time. He ran his hands through his nappy, red hair. I looked to Ms. Greene and then Baker Bob, but they let Knut work through this on his own.

Finally, with complete conviction, he answered, "Aunt May."

"Seriously?"

"Yep. Mmhm. She's wise and ... and ... *loves* Peter Parker. Every superhero needs an Aunt May. A superhero for a superhero."

This kid, though something about him made me want to feed him a knuckle sandwich, was growing on me.

Ms. Greene said, "That's a lovely thing to say, Knut. Don't you think so, Paisley?" She set some dishes down and walked over to him.

I sensed a hug coming on.

When I saw her swing her arms around him, I noticed his reaction wasn't exactly receptive. He dipped his head over her shoulder and pushed up his glasses. She kept hugging him. Baker Bob grinned and frosted cinnamon rolls.

I replied awkwardly, "Yah. That was really nice."

She started smoothing his hair with her spit dampened fingers and straightened his Green Lantern t-shirt. As I watched them interact, I remembered Gram's hugs and thought about how she meant each one, regardless of how I received it. Sometimes I hugged back, sometimes I acted like it was such a bother. I wished I could race back in time and hug her — *really* hug her — every single time. She had been, after all, *my* Aunt May.

A gruff voice interrupted the moment. "It's 6:15 and there's not a speck of food on the table yet. What the hell is going on here?"

The man from the tractor stood in the hallway. Dirty and sweaty, he looked like he'd rolled in the dust and run through a sprinkler. He didn't acknowledge me standing there fixing my coffee.

Baker Bob wasn't shaken one bit. "Take off that hat, mister, and go get yourself washed up. You hear, Griff?"

Grunting then stomping were the only reply.

57

Good morning, Griffin dear." Ms. Greene motioned for Knut and me to scoot our butts into the sup deck then whispered, "Give your Great Uncle Griff a little time to warm up. Food usually does the trick."

Seriously? Great uncle? I thought. I needed a spreadsheet to keep track of my questions. But I followed Knut's lead without hesitation around to the back of the table. Eight place settings, but the rough oak table could sit ten easily. I looked out the windows to try to spot that herd of horses still tucked inside my head, but I only saw grass rippling under a veil of rising mist.

Ms. Greene continued, "I see you've already gotten a start on that downed fence." She gave Griff a motherly look, "You *really* should wait for the boys to get out there to help you. Their backs can take it."

More grunting. He tossed a straw cowboy hat onto a wall hook. A ringer. "Can't wait around all day."

I remembered how much he had reminded me of Lenny when he showed me the way to the driveway, but right now, the resemblance escaped me.

"What do you mean *all day*?" Two new voices piped in from the hallway. They sounded like trouble. "Crimeny, Griff. The sun's barely got her panties on!"

Baker Bob stifled a chortle. "Wash up you two. We're almost ready."

They sauntered over to the sink, and I watched them shove each other for the soap then flick water everywhere.

"Meet your second cousins, Paisley." She eh-hemmed for their attention, and they whipped off their caps. "Heath. Henry. This is Paisley Alberta Noon, my brother Peter's daughter."

Definitely not used to her calling my dad "brother."

Dim realization dawned across their faces then they looked at me like I was some long lost relic. Or was it fresh meat? They appeared to be in their early-twenties and acted like teenagers, but not in the same way Knut looked seventeen but acted eight. These guys were just real hyper goofballs.

"Nice to meet you, Miss Paisley," said the lanky blonde as he swept into a bow. "Name's Heath, like the candy bar. Ain't that right, Knut?" Heath made a single-handed quick-draw motion at him.

A pop of laughter burst out of Knut sitting next to me at the table. He snorted even. I guess I missed the joke.

"I am Henry, like the O'Henry your-so-friggin-awesome candy bar." The stocky, buzz-cut one did a double-handed quick-draw at Knut, which earned an even louder snort.

Me being an only child, I imagined these two characters as big brothers. Annoying, I supposed, but somehow protective and fun too. Like most of the brothers I read about in books or heard about from kids at school. So I tried to be cool and not get too girly-grinny excited to meet them. I went with a nonchalant, two-finger wave-type salute instead.

"Yo. Good to meet ya."

Yo? I cringed at myself.

They both looked at each other with smothered grins at my marvelous first impression but sucked it up when Ms. Greene gave a knock-it-off-and-sit-down glare.

She brought out plates piled high with English muffins then went to the baker's rack and grabbed two of the sparkling red jars.

"Go ahead and get started," she said. "Paisley, you're in for a real treat." She tapped the top of one of the jars with a butter knife.

Knut dove in, elbows on the table.

I was starved and dying for a distraction, so I swiped some jelly on a muffin. The second it hit my tongue my taste buds went berserk. At first it made me pucker, but then immediately shifted into cool sweetness.

"Wow," I said and stared at it, amazed.

Henry bit into one and said with a full mouth, "I know, right? Friggin' awesome, huh?" Then he snapped the other half down the hatch and grinned, red jelly smeared across his chin.

Bert smiled knowingly and went back to the kitchen saying, "I'm telling you, Robert, you could make a fortune if you put that jelly on the market." She looked at me and bragged, "This jelly wins blue ribbons at the county fair every year." Then she wagged a finger at Baker Bob and said, "Norse Drive Market in Valley City would love to sell it for you, I'm just sure of it. They're such nice folks."

From where I sat, I could see Baker Bob's ears redden. "Oh come on now, Bert. It's just a little hobby. Going commercial would ruin it."

She waved her hand. "I'm just saying."

"Hey Berty," asked Heath flinging his wavy blonde hair out of his eyes, "where's River? It's not like him to be late ..." he stuffed his mouth with a big wedge of cantaloupe from the fruit bowl, "... like us." This, apparently, was a hilarious joke warranting elbow nudging and, yes, more snorting on all three boys' part.

After pulling himself together, Henry, not too notably concerned, added, "He left the bunkhouse way before we were up. Jesse was gone too."

"Sorry I'm late, everyone," said a rich, low voice from behind the French doors. And for a heartbeat's second I thought the voice might produce Shadow Boy. But then I glimpsed the dark-haired, clean-cut cowboy around the corner before he continued, "I hope you all didn't wait to start on my account."

"Not at all, River." Ms. Greene hustled over to take his coat and hat. "You go wash up. We've had a lazy start today."

More grunting came from Griff buried behind a newspaper at the end of the table.

The man they called River nodded graciously as she took his things. "Ma'am." Then he glanced again at me. "Who's the new recruit?" His tone rippled gently, and his sun-wrinkled eyes were kind.

Straining to reach the coat hooks, Ms. Greene said, "That fine, young lady you see there is none other than Peter and Fernie's daughter, Paisley Alberta Noon. Isn't she just the spittin' image of them both?"

His eyes smiled first then the rest of his complexion followed. "You don't say. Well, I'll be. She finally made it."

"She sure did. Right on time." She winked at me and clapped her hands, "Paisley hun, this is River Lightfoot. He's what I guess you would call your uncle-in-law, but more importantly a dear, *dear* family friend. He's been at Forever Fields Farm since its inception."

He swished his fingers through impeccably trimmed, slightly graying hair then rubbed his hand on his jeans before he reached between Heath and Henry to shake my hand across the table.

"Pleased to meet you, Ms. Paisley. I take it that was your fine-looking little Border collie and three-legged cat acting as greeting committee out on the porch?" His pearly smile and calloused, firm grip melted my insides for a second. He was *that* nice.

"Yes, Prairie and Ernie. Pleasure to meet you, sir." I ran the words back through my head and gave the slightest hint of a smile when I decided I had nailed that intro.

Knut bounced in his seat like he had to pee. "Five, Riv! High five!"

"K-man!" They smacked hands. River poked at Knut's shirt. "Green Lantern today."

Knut beamed.

"Nice choice, my man."

Heath chimed in, "Aw, I don't know. I think Mighty Mouse would've been better."

Then Henry, "No way. Knut, you need to stock up on Wonder Woman t-shirts." His eyebrows danced as he cupped his hands way out in front of his chest.

I covered my mouth to trap my own snort this time.

River scuffed both their heads as he backed up from the table. "That's enough, you two. I swear we need to reverse the numbers of your age."

"Twelve! They'd be twelve!" Knut pointed and mocked.

They elbowed each other and mouthed their superhero preferences at Knut. He nearly busted out of his skin trying to keep his snorts under control.

"Oh, for cripesake, people! Can we get a move on, or should I go scrounge up some berries and grubs for myself? Am I the only one who actually needs to get work done around here at some point today?" Griff definitely needed food.

"Okay, here we go!" Baker Bob announced. Two huge trays of gooey, melty cinnamon rolls balanced on both hands.

Ms. Greene followed with a cooker steaming with sausage, peppers, and eggs. "Make room for more, boys ..." She caught herself then grinned so wide it's a wonder she could form any words, "I mean boys *and girl*."

I twisted my mouth and looked out the window into the fog while everyone gave their full approval. My leg began its nervous bouncing, but then I heard the ice water in everyone's glass start to jingle, so I forced my knee down with my hands. I felt like a weed sticking out in a well-established flowerbed, and I had to make a choice. Was I going to be an ugly, noxious weed that gives you hives and sticks you with pricklers? Or would I be the kind you just weren't expecting to pop up in that particular place, but you're glad it did, so you give it some space and sunshine ... and let it grow?

All I wanted was a little space.

"Thank you," I said.

They were all staring at me waiting for more. My heart raced and my palms got all sweaty, so I rubbed them on my jeans. *Where are my words?* I thought.

I looked around the table. Seven faces looked back at me. Baker Bob stood in the doorway untying his apron. Ms. Greene reached for her napkin. Knut scrunched his nose like a fly had landed between his eyes. Griff peered over his newspaper. Heath and Henry licked frosting off their fingers. River sat with perfect posture and an expression like ... well I'm not sure what he was *really* thinking, but I couldn't help feeling like he was ... rooting for me to say something spectacular.

I had come here in search of safe haven for my mother's horse and employment among strangers. Instead, I found myself in the middle of an unfamiliar framework. Family. They all seemed to accept me so quickly. (Well, maybe not Griff.) I felt like I was *supposed* to be here

Trying to swallow the sandpaper that had somehow grown inside my mouth, I searched for ... something spectacular.

Then I heard it. Gram's voice. She'd come to rescue me.

Get a grip, P. It's not the Spanish Inquisition. Just tell them how you feel.

She never did sugar coat advice. I wouldn't have listened if she did.

"Thank you, everyone, for having me. I'm glad I'm here, and ... I hope I can show you what a hard worker I am, and ... since I'm going to be taking care of the grounds, I think you'll all agree that I'll have plenty opportunity to prove myself." Everyone gave me a charity laugh for that. "And..."

Tell them how you feel, P.

"I really appreciate being a part of …" I looked around the table at the food and the faces, "all of this." My face burned hot, and I dove for my orange juice. Not as graceful as one might hope, but I think I managed a decent *pretty weed* impression.

"Paisley, my dear," Ms. Greene said, "We are lucky to have you. Let's eat."

"AMEN!" growled Griff.

Chapter 7

Everyone dug in, talking and razzing, and asking questions. Even crankster Griff softened once he had some meat in his belly — a little.

Where I *used* to live, especially after Gram died, meals were like scavenger hunts — cereal and toast or peanut butter and jelly. At best, Dad would take me out to eat at the nearby bar for chicken strips on the weekends. I guess sometimes we would order take out and bring back boxes of Chinese and spread it all over the big dining room table. That was actually kind of fun. But when Princess Cindy moved in, we had to say buh-bye to the dining room table so she could sprawl her Floral Daze business crap all over it. I really learned my place in my family when I discovered Cotton Candy Dream coordinating marker and stationery bundles took precedence over me.

My stomach purred as I waved sayonara to fend-for-yourself days. I sat there in the sup deck and ate and savored and chewed and relished, giddy with the idea that I'd get to do it all over again at 1:00 and then again at 6:30! Digest and repeat.

"Now Heath and Henry," Ms. Greene pointed her fork at them, "I want you fixing that south fence line first thing today. I'd like to move The Old Ones over there soon."

Henry answered for them both. "Yes ma'am. We'll get right on it."

"Then round half of them into the south paddock." She looked to Griff across the table. "Griffin. River. I presume you'll be starting your spring trimming today when you come in from the field?"

"That's the plan," Griff said between slurps of coffee. "As long as that fence gets taken care of." He gave a one-eyed glare over his mug at the twins.

"It'll get done," said Henry with a mouthful.

Griff twitched a bushy eyebrow.

"Anything you need us to do after that? Or can we keep working on our ..." Heath sent a shifty, blue-eyed glance my way then finished, "... top secret assignment?"

Seeing them high-brow each other, I imagined some crazy, hair-brained projectile mechanism. A horse apple catapult or maybe a super-powered water gun to fill troughs from the comfort of the front porch.

"Just get your chores done before you keep working on that contraption."

They both grinned and said in stereo, "Yes ma'am!" as they high-fived.

Knut wanted a piece of that action. "High-five!"

"Yah dude! Want to come to the junk yard with us again, buddy?" Heath asked.

"Of *course* I do!" his voice cracked.

Ms. Greene rolled her eyes and continued, "River, what got you up so early this morning? The boys say you and Jesse were gone before they rose."

River explained in buttery tones, "I told Tate I'd come over first thing to check on that mare of his. He stopped over last night. Says she's about to drop her foal any time now." He took a slurp of coffee. "He's pretty excited about this little one. Sire's Smoke-N-Ash."

Last night? Tate? Shadow Boy. Hopefully no one noticed my chattering heartbeat.

Everyone ooed or ahhed at the mention of Smoke-N-Ash. Ms. Greene even eyed me and winked like to tell me this was a big deal and all.

"Mmm-mm. That Tate Maycomb's got big plans. Big plans," she said, and all heads around the table

66

nodded in silence. "Griffin, I presume you'll be discing up the northeast section. How did the west field go yesterday?"

"Clockwork. If this weather keeps cooperating, we should be ahead of schedule." His gruff voice had mellowed. "Might even have time to plant some silage corn down in that south pasture I never got to last year."

"Say, could you do me one little, bitty favor, though?"

He wiped his mouth with his napkin. "Name it."

"Can you plant a little flax this year? It makes *such* a view. I do love a nice view."

Griff's sun-baked eyes became tender, and I saw a corner of his mouth twitch like to hold back a smile. "Done." He cleared his throat and pushed his chair away. "If you all don't mind, daylight's burnin'."

Ms. Greene leaned back in her chair like she was pretty darned proud of herself for coaxing a smile out of Griff, if just for a moment. "See you for lunch, Griffin."

He grabbed his hat and clomped out, surly as ever again.

River patted his belly. His blue western shirt fit flat and taut. "Robert Baker, I do believe that was one of your finest, sir."

"Thank you much. Got a secret ingredient in the eggs this time."

"Well, keep it coming, is all I'm saying."

"Will do, Riv."

"I'll be over at Tate's. Gonna make sure that baby gets here safe and sound." He gathered his coat and hat. "Miss Paisley, it was a pleasure to meet you. Welcome to the crew." He winked and tipped his hat.

I managed a "Thank you, sir" and he was off.

Henry grabbed his ball cap and rubbed his stubbly blonde hair. "What's for lunch, BB?"

"Yah." Heath smashed his cap on forcing blonde locks to flip out the sides. "You aren't gonna snub us with sandwiches, are you?"

"Oh, good Lord, you two." Baker Bob was stymied. "You've still got breakfast on your chins, and you're worried about lunch!" A vein popped out of the dove on his neck, and the crease of his scar deepened as he scowled. It made him look awful tough.

"Never mind them, Bobby." Ms. Greene calmed him with a couple pats. "You boys git. Git now." She grabbed a tea towel and snapped it at their rears. "Out, out!"

The boys jauntily accepted their comeuppance and hustled out the door. I'm telling you, it was quite a scene, tiny Ms. Greene shooing those two strapping young men out of the house. She was the boss. No bones about it.

"Well, Pasty Spoon, you better help clean up," Knut said.

I gave him *a look* as I picked up my plate.

His mom didn't miss a beat. "I heard that, young man."

"Sorry." He hung his head like someone just took his birthday away.

Something told me he was just, in some sardonic way, trying to make friends with me.

"We're good," I said. Then, to prove I held no grudge, I pointed to my t-shirt, "Ironman or Hulk?"

His eyes lit up. "Ironman ..."

We both said in stereo, "Wicked accessories."

Ms. Greene watched us with one of those "Awww ... isn't that sweet" looks.

"What's my job today, Mom?" he asked.

"I think it would be good for you to set up an area for new kitties. Make sure they have a safe place in your barn before you let them roam free.."

"Yesss!" he cheered. "I'm gonna raid the Quonset for some stuff to make a playground."

68

Ms. Greene appeared to enjoy watching him get excited. "Fine, but chores first."

"Paisley." Her voice rang my name. I was the only one left without an assignment.

"You and I are going to have a talk."

* * *

Prairie greeted us at the porch. Ernie was nowhere to be seen. The west side of the porch had a swing overlooking the disaster zone front yard, but Ms. Greene and I sat in some over-sized, sea green Adirondack chairs on the east side overlooking the horse barn. BG and Journey stood with their heads over their paddock fence. They simultaneously turned to look at us then returned their gaze to the rolling prairie.

I searched the cottonwoods for the wild horses. There was still no sign of them.

Ms. Greene sat back with a satisfied sigh, kicked her feet up on a stool, and laced her fingers behind her head. "I love the mornings. So peaceful. Full of possibilities." Her blue eyes twinkled in the sunrise.

I slouched and bobbed my head.

Shielding her eyes, she squinted into the sun burning off the fog. She took a deep, meditative breath. "Paisley, we try to live a simple life here. Sustain ourselves as best we can. In the meantime, we attempt to do good things." She looked at me square on. "What are you good for?"

Prairie's ears pricked. This woman reminded me so much of Gram. And Mom. And a tiny bit of Dad. I loved that, and I hated that.

"What am I good for? I…"

Suddenly, there came a hollow yowling from under the porch. Both Miss Greene and I startled to the edge of our seats.

Ernie, haggard as ever, hobbled out from under the porch and up the steps, his one eye staring at us,

69

and a limp, pink-tailed body dangling in his mouth. With a satisfied grunt, he plopped the mouse down and looked back and forth at us for approval. Then he licked himself.

Miss Greene gave me a bolstering look. "It seems *someone* is proving his worth, bright and early. Not bad, for a one-eyed, crimp-eared, three-legged tabby tomcat."

I held back my eye roll and substituted a sheepish grin. The little guy *had* earned an ear scratching.

Prairie, always the task-master, left Rope coiled and picked the mouse up by the tail, clearly needing to dispose of the filthy thing properly.

Miss Greene sprang up from her chair. "Let's get that to the garbage." Prairie followed straight on her heels, all business. She plopped it into the trash and got a good ear ruffling.

While we walked to the giant fountain in the turn-about, Miss Greene's feet splaying to the sides and arms flapping out and in, she pulled out a paper and flattened it on her quilted flannel shirt. A list of things to do with teeny, tiny words from top to bottom.

She held it out at arm's length. "Well, well. *Grounds keeper*. It's been an awful long time since a green thumb worked magic around here." She stuck up her thumb and gave a look of disdain. "You'd think with a name like Greene, I'd be a miracle worker." Her gaze retracted slightly. "Well, I did marry into the name, I guess. Lane was the miracle worker." I could feel her look at me as we continued walking around the yards. "Everyone in his family could make things grow. Everyone." She was still looking at me.

The heaviness of a question weighed me down. Gram's familiar, tough voice rang in my head. *Spit it out.*

"Lane. He was … your husband? And my uncle?" I asked.

70

I could hear a hint of smile in her voice, but I did not look up. "Yes. My true love since the day we met at the Sheldon Summer Shindig barn dance."

Finally, I looked at her. We stopped walking.

"That was the day, I met Lane … and your mother. Fern. His sister."

Air suspended in my lungs.

"Your dad and I met your mother and her brother Lane." We started walking again. "I met my *best friends* that day."

"Best friends? But I never even knew you existed until yesterday," I said. Pressure pinged behind my eyes, and I clenched my jaw.

Easy Paisley girl, Gram tried to back me off.

I hadn't meant to sound accusive, but that's how it was coming out. "How is that possible?"

Rein it in.

Now I could learn about my mom. And me. I thought maybe she could tell me who I am like.

Prairie hopped inside the empty fountain to sniff around. Cracks and weeds webbed intricate lines. I let my eyes follow each one like I was looking for something important. *Anything* to not look at my … aunt.

My aunt.

"Paisley," she leaned toward me, "Believe me, I *wanted* to be a part of your life. But sometimes …" she turned to look down the long drive, her posture straight as that carved fFf post just feet from us, "sometimes life throws you a few sidesteps, and things don't turn out the way you think they're going to."

I did an inward eyeroll at that.

Lose the attitude, P.

But Gram…

I mean it. Hear her out.

"Fine."

"No. It's not fine. But it is the truth. And that, my dear, you can always count on here at Forever

71

Fields." She looked me in the eye and slapped her hand on top of mine, holding it firmly. Her blue eyes coaxed reflections of my dad to the surface. "I am your Aunt Alberta. Like or lump it. Can't pick your relatives." She clapped my back but not hard.

This lady was unflappable.

"You know what, Miss Paisley? I think we ought to save the rest of this conversation for another time."

I'm sure my face screamed *Agreed*.

She winked. "Tell me what you think should be first?" Her mood fluttered light and airy like her smile as she reviewed the to-do list.

"There." I pointed into the vine and bramble-infested area where Saint Francis peeked out crying for help.

Atta girl. Just what I woulda picked.

Gram would have worked magic here. I pictured her rear end in the air, weeds flinging and flying every which way, until it was sculpted into a topiary garden with dolphin-shaped shrubs spewing wisteria vines out their blow holes.

Aunt Bert replied with a high brow, "Are you sure?"

I think I heard a challenge. We stepped through the swirly iron gate. It screeched and a flock of finches flushed.

"Yep. Game on," I said as I eyed the scene.

"My, my. Aren't we ambitious?"

I sounded cocky, but I think she loved it. "I need tools."

* * *

Armed and dangerous with clippers, shovel, hand saw, and wheelbarrow, that yard didn't stand a chance. At least, that's what I tried telling myself. I had never actually tackled such a huge project alone before. Deep down, I was a little overwhelmed. Aunt Alberta was watching me too.

72

Remember, P. Go slow. Take your time. Get to know it. Piece by piece.

"Piece," I whispered to the voice inside my head. I think Aunt Alberta heard me.

"I'll let you and your project here get to know each other a little."

The familiar sentiment of her words startled me.

She patted Ernie on the head as she walked up the steps and disappeared into the house. Prairie and I remained, staring at the yard.

"Well girl. Where do I start?"

My dog never needed prodding when it came to an honest job. She and Rope trotted about, head low, searching. First, through the thicket. Then around a crazy-limbed flowering tree groped by wild vines and thistles. She looked in each corner, meticulous as ever. Finally, she stopped at a mass of tangled creepers and popped up onto what I could only assume was a bench buried in wisteria vines next to Saint Francis' tiny peering face. She plopped Rope on it and gave me a lop-eared pant-smile.

Bark.

"That's the spot?" I wheeled my tools over. "Then I guess that does it."

Once I discovered it was a huge arbor with a swing, my mission presented itself. Prairie must have seen the glint in my eye because she went into play mode: front legs down, butt in the air, tail waving like the starting flag at a drag race.

Eying my most powerful artillery — the graphite Craftsman loppers with brass bypass blades — I threaded my tiny hands into leather work gloves then wielded it over my head and hollered like a barbarian, "Release the swing!"

Prairie leaped, Rope trailing in the wind like a banner, wild abandon in her eyes. Then she raced in wide circles, yipping like a warrior.

Of course, I didn't attack recklessly. After all, Gram's orders were, "Take your time. Go slow." So after all the fanfare, I picked my way through, one snip at a time, carefully pulling and trimming like picking cockleburs out of Journey's tail. I let my mind drift as I worked.

I wondered again how Aunt Alberta knew Boss Girl so well. I get that she and Mom were friends, but it had been so long. Nearly eighteen years.

An hour later, I stole a glance at the horse barn. Then at the swing. It was still buried. I thought maybe I should take a few minutes to check on my horses ...

Bark!

"Oh... you try untangling this mess then," I barked back at my task master. But when I looked at her, Prairie stood rigid facing out the swirly gate.

Bark, bark!

Her hackles stood up. She whipped toward me, and then back toward The Drive. She was confused. Or worried. Or excited about something. It bugged me that I couldn't read her quite right, so I went to her.

On the far end of The Drive, a dark figure moved slowly on horseback toward the house. And though I could make out no details, somehow, I knew.

My heart started fluttering. In just moments, the figure of a dog appeared jogging alongside the rider.

Shadow Boy.

I shoved my hands in my paisley jeans pocket, and suddenly, for some stupid reason, I wished I owned another pair of pants.

Get a grip, P.

"No kidding, Gram."

I couldn't get myself to look away. The rising sun made his jet-black hair gleam. It mesmerized me again. Prairie and I stood like topiaries peeking around the gate at first, but as he drew steadily nearer, we both trickled out into the open drive, drawn like magnets. Standing there, watching them. Approaching. Horse, man, dog.

Prairie's head sank even with her top line and her ears pressed forward; eyes fixed.

And then, I could see his face. Clear, smooth, dark. Beautiful. His hair parted hard down the middle then fell in silken sheets behind broad, straight shoulders cloaked in a full-length oil skin coat that draped over his horse's rump. He swayed only slightly with the rhythm of his smoky mount, each hoof step sure and steadfast.

He fascinated me.

Shadow Boy stopped just twenty feet or so away. He dismounted, agile as a cat despite the heavy drover. His dog stood at his side, just like Prairie at mine, and together they began walking toward us like one being — Shadow Boy's eyes unwavering on me.

A lump formed in my throat all sticky and hot. The flutter in my chest got thicker and thicker until I heard it pounding in my head, vibrating my bones.

The pounding and vibration became bigger than me. It was of the earth. I only glanced at the popping gravel for half a second, but when I looked up, Shadow Boy had re-mounted and loped past me with a cocked eyebrow and an easy smile. The pounding became rumbling, and the rumbling became thunder. My heartbeat matched it.

Prairie started after them then turned to bark her unmistakable command, *Come! Come now!* She snapped me to my senses, and I realized what was happening.

Boss Girl and Journey whirled in their paddock. Heads high. Tails high. Eyes wide. Nostrils flared.

The herd was coming! The wild band of blue and gray smoke of my dreams raced north of the house. Mindless, I flew to them. Again, Prairie and I chased my dream. I had to be near them. Once I reached the fence, I leaped onto the middle rail and propped myself up. The mob moved as one shifting this way and that. In the lead was a charcoal stallion with a roany brown face, jet black mane and tail, and rippling muscles.

My mouth hung open and I found myself speaking out loud words I thought were only in my head. "What *are* you?"

A silken voice said. "They are Nokota."

Startled, I looked toward the voice. Shadow Boy, still astride his horse but right next to me now, stared out at the scene.

"And I am after ..." he searched the mob, "*that* one." I followed his outstretched hand to the charcoal stallion with the roany brown face.

Shadow Boy's countenance drew me in. He looked like he'd been plucked out of another time. The smell of leather and hard work emanated from him like incense burning slow. His deep brown eyes roiled with mystery. The refined lines of his cheekbones and jaw sat smooth under dark skin, flawless yet seasoned with seriousness, which made it hard to guess his age. He was so ... different ... from anyone I'd ever known. But one thing was certain: the longer I looked at him, the steadier my heart beat.

Like a drug, I took a deep breath, and I became weightless as a leaf on the water. The horses from my dreams raced through the prairie grasses before me. I wished time would stop for me, as it seemed to have for Shadow Boy.

I whispered into the wind, "Nokota," and the word caught on a flurry of cottonwood tufts swirling in the herd's wake. I did not know what the word meant, but somehow ... I knew these horses already, like a part of me I've always known was there but didn't know how to see it.

When they drifted to the top of a swell and stopped to graze, I turned to look again at the man next to me on his smoky mare.

He said, "They carry the quiet songs and stories of our ancestors upon their backs. If you listen, you might hear them." Shadow Boy spoke to me as though he'd known me his whole life. Our eyes connected full on. Frozen for a moment. Unwavering. Soft and honest.

I wanted to tell him I *did* hear them. That their voices came to me. Though I did not know what they said. But I only stood there watching the dust settle.

Just to the side, our dogs stood with their heads pitched downward, their noses barely touching.

"Our dogs," I said, "They seem to like each other, huh." I kept my eyes on them.

After a slightly awkward pause, he replied, "It seems."

His voice was simple, just like his answer. I liked that. I could deal with that.

"I'm Tate Maycomb, your neighbor."

A hand extended toward me, and I reached hesitantly to shake it.

"You must be Paisley Noon."

I looked at him — deadpan — had everyone on the planet known I was coming here?

I said with a hint of smile, "I am. Are these your horses?"

"They are," he said.

Normally, this would have registered as awkward, but for some reason I didn't feel like filling the air with words. Instead, we listened to the quiet sounds of the morning and watched the horses. Their tails swished lazily as they nibbled at the grass. Meadowlarks sang in the distance, and the day continued to awaken right there before our eyes.

"Come on, Prairie," I said at last. As lovely as standing there with a handsome guy watching horses all day long sounded, I knew I had to earn my keep. "Time to get back to work."

Whine.

Tate smiled. "I … believe Kola has made a favorable impression upon her. He has a way about him for such things."

"I guess so," I said. "I've never known Prairie to shirk an opportunity to get back to work. Usually, I just say the word and she snaps to." I shook my head but had to laugh a little. The two dogs had some sort of kismet going on, all sniffing close and leaning on each other. I guessed a few more stolen moments wouldn't hurt. I turned back to the herd and rested my head on the fence. "I would like to learn more about your horses someday, Tate," I said, unable to peel my dreamy gaze from them.

Again, Tate's voice was soft and honest. I could somehow tell he was looking at me when he said, "I would like to teach you about them. Very much, Paisley."

I looked up at him and, again, we held eyes for a small moment. I was expecting it to feel weird, but somehow, it still was not. Not in the least. I squatted down to fluff up Prairie's silky ears and scratch Kola's dense chest. "Come on, Prairie, let's get back to work." This time, Prairie leapt to my side, tail wagging, ears flopping happily. Her pant-smile had sort of a glow to it. "Good girl," I said. "Should we go find Rope?"

Her ears and mouth snapped shut like she was trying to think where she'd left It.

Tate said, "It was a pleasure meeting you, Paisley Noon."

I gave him a little wave as we walked away and said, "You too, Tate Maycomb. Good luck catching your stallion."

His smile curled up on one side. "I will not need it, but thank you all the same." Then he nodded and trotted off.

As I walked back toward the house, I saw two figures standing in the windows of the sup deck. Aunt Alberta and Baker Bob leaned against each other with silly little smirks on their faces.

Chapter 8

My senses tingled clear as the blue North Dakota sky above me. Vivid images of what I imagined the arbor and swing looked like in its day filled my mind. Before I existed.

Swift and sure, without hardly even thinking, my hands flew through the bramble. Soon I made a loveseat swing reveal its peeling white paint and cradling curves. Flagstones emerged in a courtyard beneath my feet, rough and dull, puzzle-pieced together inside mossy frames. Before I knew it, white lattice work arched up over my head, and I wove a wisteria vine in and out like an Easter basket. At last, I cleaned Saint Francis and placed him in front of a struggling rose bush with a handful of birdseed in his outstretched basket.

I stepped back with Prairie. Together, we stood in awe. I swiped a sweaty strand of hair from my eyes. Ernie rubbed against my leg.

"You aren't the only one who can show off a bit of handy-work."

Merroww.

"Of course, it's no *mouse*. But all in all, not bad, if I do say so myself."

"But does it work?"

My heart jolted against my ribcage at the sound of the smooth voice, and I whipped around to find Tate standing there. His horse stood untied next to the fountain. Kola lay in the grass next to the gate.

Prairie's tail swished on the flagstone.

"You're back already?" I said surprised.

"Already?" He looked at the sun high in the sky. "It's nearly noon."

I shook my head a little shocked. "Well, my my, how the time does fly," I said looking over my project.

"Does it work?" he restated.

"Only one way to find out," I said and invited him into the garden.

He smiled soft as a feather and brushed past me to sit on the swing. It rocked with a little click and a squeak, singing a steady rhythm.

"It's not finished," I said. "It still needs some work."

His silky voice replied, "Paisley Noon, yuwípi (yoo WEE pee)."

The words sank right into me, and my throat got tight at the back. My name sounded like it had floated in on a wind from ages past. A warm wind that untangled the knot in my shoulder. A soothing wind that lifted my head to face him.

His eyes were, as before, honest. "It is magic," he said and smiled with a nod.

I tried the word, "Yuwípi." It rolled off my tongue as natural as when he said it. It made me grin with pride.

Prairie, tongue lolling, sprang onto the swing next to Tate and licked him as if he'd had a peanut butter facial.

"Prairie!" I scolded. Her eyes flicked at me then straight back to him. "I'm sorry. I don't know what's gotten into her."

"It's alright." He scruffed her black and white fur. "She is studying me."

Then Ernie clawed his three pathetic legs up Tate's drover all the way to his shoulders. He rubbed his one-eyed, crimp-eared face all over the poor guy's head.

"Oh my." I laughed.

Tate sat there like a circus act, grinning wide. Prairie put her paw up to his chin as though she needed to check his profile. Ernie curled around his neck to make a cat-tail mustache and licked inside his ear. *That* did it. This guy was never going to come within a hundred feet of me and my personal-space-invaders again.

Tate just let out a yelp of honey laughter and scrunched up his face to endure the torture while he hugged them and ruffled their shameless furry heads.

We both laughed until all I could do was hold my stomach and try to catch my breath. It felt good to smile so hard. Good that it was real.

So when Tate said, "Care to join me?" and patted the swing seat, I did.

We talked about simple things. Like the yard and the plants that were actually trying to grow in it. He surprised me with his knowledge of perennials and shrubs and general landscaping.

"That crabapple over there in the far corner will bear fruit like none other. See how it blossoms? It is in love with the soil here. Like so many things at Forever Fields."

I digested that. And I hoped for a moment that this place would be as good for me as it is for "so many things."

"And do you see over there, creeping from the shadows?"

I strained to see some baby-green jutting through a mat of dead leaves hidden in the shadows of some lilac suckers under the front porch.

"I see them. Lily of the Valley, it looks like. No?"

"Indeed. Though, it has been many years since they have bloomed. They must be released from the shadows."

This guy did not talk like anyone I had ever known before. And I got the feeling he wasn't just talking about the flowers right then.

Eventually, we got talking about our horses. There's one topic I have no problem rambling on about to anyone willing to listen.

He listened.

So he got to hear about the love of my life. My handsome knight in shining armor. Journey.

"Journey and I," I told him, "have had our own language since I was seven years old. A touch, a look, or even just a *feeling* is all it takes sometimes. We understand each other on a level different from that of any *person* I've ever known. Next to Prairie, he's the best friend I've ever had."

Tate just sat and swung.

"I can't imagine life without him," I said.

"And Boss Girl," he asked eventually, "as you call her. What of her?"

How could I skirt around the topic of my mother abandoning me?

"She's nearly 30 now. Pure Arabian. You should have seen her in her day. Quite the show circuit she ran." I crossed my fingers for no questions. "She's a sweet, sweet horse with more stories to tell than even I know about. I figure she's due for a good rest."

"I would say so." He looked through the garden gate toward BG standing at the edge of her paddock staring out onto the prairie. "This place is good for resting souls."

Hmm. That sounded … cryptic, like he'd aimed the remark at me, not Boss Girl. This guy barely knew me, yet I got the feeling he had a better handle on *Paisley Alberta Noon* than I did.

Suddenly, I felt the conversation had turned too personal, so I shifted focus.

"Did you get that stallion you were after?"

"Oh yes. Mazaska is waiting for me in the pen behind River Lightfoot's cabin."

"Mazaska?" He'd pronounced it mah-ZAH-skah. "Do they all have names?" I couldn't imagine anyone being able to single out and actually name so many wild horses.

He simply replied, "Yes," in a way that made me feel kind of dumb.

"You see Kala, there?" He pointed through the swirly iron gate to his horse snoozing by the dried up fountain. "Wiyaka Cikala is young. Three years only."

I studied her for a moment. "Wiyaka Chikala?" He had pronounced it wee-YAH-kah chee-KAH-lah, and it flowed off his tongue like the breeze stirring her mane. The little smoky mare opened her eyes and looked to us.

"What do they mean? The names? Kola. Mazaska. Kala."

He turned to me, "They are Lakota words of the Sioux Nation." Here, his eyes turned sad, almost worried. "I try to keep it fluid on my lips for fear it will die in me like so many others. Our elder translators are aging, and so few of the new generation want to learn. It is a difficult language." His eyes softened and a long strand of that black hair slipped down over his eyes as he paused and looked me straight on. "But beautiful."

For a fleeting, stupid moment, I let myself believe he was referring to me again. I held his gaze, dying to tuck the dangling strand across his silk chocolate cheek gently behind his ear.

But I knew better. So instead I asked, "Teach me?"

He blinked, swiped the strand back, and then pointed to his horse. "She was born in a pasture beneath a great oak. An eagle's nest sat high in the tree, and when I found her, already taking her first steps, the prairie winds blew tufts of downy feathers upon her like snow." A smile lit his face. "Wiyaka Chikala. Little Feather. Kala for short."

"Wiyaka Chikala," I tried again, but it didn't sound *nearly* as cool. "Little Feather."

He grinned. "Yes."

Next, I learned that Kola means *friend*, and I have to admit, I melted a little when I found that out. I'd never met anyone before who, like me, considered their dog an actual friend, not just a pet. Then I learned that Mazaska, the stallion's name, means silver because of his rare metallic coloring.

"You know," Tate tried to explain, "they should produce many fine foals for me ... if I pair them wisely."

A-a-a-and that's when I got up. No talk about *breeding*. Oh, don't get me wrong. He was perfectly proper and pretty adorable, but we were stepping dangerously close to snapshot land, and I wouldn't allow it. Time for Paisley to grab the reins and steer this stagecoach.

"Don't you have an important foal coming this morning?" I talked too fast and fidgeted for my gardening tools. "Aunt Alberta and River mentioned something about it at breakfast."

A moment passed before he rose easily from the swing and picked up a trowel for me. "Indeed, I do. River is watching Zica Hota. Gray Squirrel. He said he would sound the bell if the time comes, and I've not returned."

"The bell?" I asked.

"I live just beyond that grove of cottonwoods below Berta's south field. The old dinner bell on the porch of my trailer can be heard for miles across these rolling prairie lands."

Dinner bell. Wow. Like settler days. God forbid he just call him on his cell. But the ad for this job *had* said "No electronics," so I guessed they dealt with serious coverage issues. Funny how I hadn't given my phone a second thought since I arrived.

"I need to get back to work before I go and get myself fired on my first day for lollygagging." Still talking too fast.

He grinned but moved toward the gate as he said, "Family cannot be fired at Forever Fields. Only loved."

I froze. A warm something-or-other fanned through my chest. Again, my brow released its clutch. How did this guy *do* that? I so desperately wanted him to stay, but I knew he couldn't (for more reasons than

84

that foal). And though I'd just spent the better part of an hour talking with him, my tongue twisted into a knot.

"I ... well ... I ... uhn ..." Genius.

A ripple of kind laughter floated on a breeze. I looked to him, helpless.

"Perhaps we could take a trail ride, you and I. I would like to see this Journey of yours."

Just as I was about to release the world's most un-cool *Oh my gosh you've got to be kidding,* there came a screeching and hollering like none other from the far end of The Drive. We both bolted through the gate to see a cloud of gravel dust kick up. Both dogs stood on alert. As a utility vehicle came closer, I recognized the green souped up Gator that had been parked outside the machine shed earlier. Its driver honked and swerved.

Tate was the first to see. And understand. He swung around, drover and hair whirling in unison like black flags, "Get Alberta!"

His urgency stunned me. Paralyzed. I could make out my cousin Heath behind the wheel, his blonde locks flapping in the wind.

"Go! Paisley Noon! Get help!" Tate commanded then wheeled into a dead run toward the ATV coming in at top speed.

Just before I ran for the house, I saw.

Henry, my other cousin, sprawled out in the cargo bed, his strong arms clinging to a limp body flung over him.

Chapter 9

"He's not moving!" Heath screamed over the engine.

The dogs barked incessantly as they swarmed the ATV. Aunt Alberta and Baker Bob flew off the front porch. Everyone stopped short when Henry and Tate dragged Griff to the fountain bench.

His face was as ashen as the clouds moving in from the west, and his body looked so small and fragile underneath his heavy work pants and canvas vest. I barely believed it was the same curmudgeon I had breakfast with just hours ago.

Knut came running out of his little barn, legs and arms flinging everywhere. "What's going on?" His red curls flicked in the late morning sun, and his purple high-water corduroys clashed with his Green Lantern t-shirt.

Aunt Bert took charge like a drill sergeant. "Knut, get your superman cape, you hear?"

"What's the matter with Uncle Griff? Someone wake him up."

Though I couldn't put a label on it (and it honestly bugged me as bad as uneven stirrups), this kid … my cousin … I could tell would not be able to handle the real situation going down in front of us.

"Just do as I say, Knut. We're gonna take a ride into town, and we need a superhero. Now go on."

He hesitated a fraction of a second, but sure enough marched straight into the house with such a look of single-mindedness that even *I* thought he could have been Clark Kent steeling into a phone booth.

Berta waited to make sure he'd gone inside then gave a quick nod to Baker Bob before she barked orders. "Tate, get River. We're going to the ER."

In a whisk of motion, Tate blazed down The Drive on Little Feather with Kola racing behind. And just like that, they vanished into the prairie grass.

"Get his feet up here, Heath, and take those heavy steel-toed boots off him. Mind his head, Henry! Robert, toss that old wheelchair from the Quonset into Clifford and pull around. Paisley, get a blanket from the house."

I just stared at her with a stupid look of shock on my face.

She clapped at me. "Quick like a bunny, Paisley Noon. Would someone mind telling me what the hell happened?"

As I rushed into the house I heard Henry start to blubber about how they'd found Griff on the south fence line, the one Henry and Heath were supposed to take care of before anything else. A tattered patchwork quilt hung over the entryway bench, so I grabbed it and ran back.

Henry continued explaining, in tears now. "I know we were supposed to do that first, Berta, but we just …"

Heath picked up, "We just needed to set up a couple things in the machine shed, and, well, one thing led to another, and …" His voice cracked. The two guys looked miserable. I tell you. Miserable and guilty. "He's just so damn stubborn …"

Henry finished, "We found him in the dirt next to a corner post. Damn if he didn't pull it out on his own, Bert."

"Oh sweet lord almighty, Griffin Cy Tuson," Aunt Alberta said to the sky, "You went and gave yourself a heart attack, for Chri-sake."

Tuson? Did she really just say *Tuson*?

87

Before my brain could manage much more than *Wasn't that Lenny's last name?* Baker Bob came flying up The Drive from the Quonset in a one ton, king-cab, fire engine red pickup truck with shining dual exhaust. By the time they had Griff carefully sprawled out in the back of the cab, an old Bronco with wood grain sides pulled up.

River rolled down the window. "Let's go, kids."

Heath, Henry, and I piled in the back. Knut with red cape sailing "flew" from the house and hopped in shotgun. He *so* did not pick up on the tension and bounced up and down wide-eyed, ready to save the world.

"Buckle up, big man. We're gonna make time."

* * *

I barely remember the ride into the whopping town of Valley City. And by whopping, I mean population 6,826 according to the blur of a sign on the edge of town just below a looming billboard advertising Stone Bank, Insurance, and Real Estate. A polished man in a cheep suit and a pearly smile that flashed a little *ting* star said, "Remmy Stone. He's got you covered."

I wondered why Aunt Alberta didn't just call an ambulance, but I learned later that the even *more* whopping town of Sheldon (population 396) didn't have one. By the time an ambulance wiggled through the maze of gravel roads to the ranch, we would be pulling in the parking lot.

River tuned the radio to a country station to keep Knut distracted. So aside from the staticky Grand Ole Opry songs, we sat in silence. Heath and Henry on either side of me stared out their windows. Heath bit his fingernails until they bled. Henry wrung his cap .

I tried to figure out how Griff and Lenny could coincidentally have the same last name. Or maybe they spelled it differently. No. Deep down, somehow I knew they were brothers. I'd seen it the moment I laid eyes on Griff in his tractor yesterday. But who knew if I would ever be able to talk to him about it now?

I put that thought out of my mind. Though I didn't know him, I wanted to see what kind of person he had tucked under that growly outer shell. I had seen a fragment of it at breakfast whenever Aunt Bert spoke with him. If Lenny Tuson's blood ran in his veins, I knew so much more lingered inside Griffin. I do, after all, know a thing or two about shells and how to hide *all sorts* of things underneath — funny things, smart things ... worthwhile things. Shells keep you safe and hidden from the world. Hard and unyielding. The thought of losing another person like me was unsettling. I didn't want to be the last of my kind. Alone.

I remembered like it was yesterday, that first time I met Lenny Tuson and my truck. And I remembered how I'd had a feeling that his part in my story would reprise. Now I was sure of it.

* * *

Within twenty-five minutes, white-coated doctors escorted Griffin Tuson on a stretcher, still unconscious, through the Emergency Room double doors.

We sat in the waiting room on olive green vinyl chairs. Mine had a crack in the seat that pinched my butt every time I moved. This was definitely not how I expected to spend my first day on the job. And though I felt awkward being there, I have to admit that I also felt a hundred percent part of this family already. More so than I had ever felt on Aurora Farm with Dad and Cindy. These people ... my family (still sinking in) ... took zero time to get used to me. Amazing.

Fortunately, as soon as we had arrived, Knut got swept away by the nurses. They treated him like a celebrity. It seemed he came here often enough to

89

have a following. One nurse (I heard him call her Penny), as soon as she saw us all come barreling into the ER, gave Berta a knowing glance then started in on a superhero contest with him. She took him under her arm, which he shrugged away from at first until she said, "Knut. I have some very special patients who could use your super powers STAT. What do you say we pay them a visit?"

He was all over that. I saw Aunt Bert sigh as they walked down the hall to the pediatrics wing.

Aunt Berta put on a tough show, but I noticed how she nervously patted Baker Bob's knee occasionally with one hand and worked her rosary beads with the other. Once, Bob placed his tattooed hand over hers and held it for a moment.

I saw River look at her from the line of chairs across from us. I tell you it was a look like nothing I'd seen in a very long time, so long I'm not sure if I ever actually saw it for real but maybe just dreamt it. The softness. The kindness. Like worn old boots slipping effortlessly over aching feet.

This was love. Not the romantic kind, just pure and simple love. Wanting *good things* for those who are important to you.

Finally, Dr. Bjorn, a white-haired elderly man who had to stoop when he spoke with tiny Aunt Alberta, told us Griff had stabilized, but it would be a couple more hours before he finished running tests.

Baker Bob, attempting a buoyant attitude, slapped his knees. "I think we could all use some grub. Griff wouldn't want us all starving on account of him."

No one seemed too interested, but I'm pretty sure I heard some muffled gargling coming from Heath and Henry's stomachs.

"Good idea, Robert," said Aunt Bert. "Why don't you take everyone to the café, and bring back a sandwich for me and Knut, will you?"

River didn't budge. "I'm staying here with you." And by the sound of his voice, there was to be no discussion on the matter. "The elders and Tate should be here soon to start the healing ceremony."

She gave him a misty look then started digging in her purse for some cash.

Baker Bob waved her off. "Don't worry, Bertie. I got this."

I looked back at River and Aunt Bert sitting there, heads down. They could have been praying, I guess. I wondered what River had meant by "healing ceremony." Part of me wanted to stay too, but Heath grabbed my arm and pulled me out the doors, like this was not our place right then. So I wondered all the more.

* * *

Billy's Café was the greasiest diner I'd ever seen. My boots stuck to chipped black and white tiles as we walked the length of the pitted lunch counter lined with red vinyl swivel stools. Baker Bob led us past the few bib-overalled patrons straight to the sounds of clanging plates and silverware, banging pots and pans, and sizzling burgers.

"Billy!" he hollered over the racket.

A hulking man (far too large for the close quarters of that kitchen if you ask me) turned from the deep fat fryer and grinned with his whole bushy-mustached face. He mashed his hands on his apron and extended a burly greeting to Baker Bob.

"If it isn't Robert Baker! My god, it's about time you showed your ugly mug in this joint. Where've you been hiding? That little Greene giant working you into your grave out at that washed up ranch in the middle of nowhere?"

Bob reciprocated with a sturdy, two-armed handshake and laughed. "Oh hell no. I never worked a day in my life. Don't plan on it either."

Both their forearms bore identical tattoos of a shield with two swords and lightning bolts crisscrossing.

Billy's eyes flicked to the rest of us. Heath and Henry sat at the end of the counter, but Bob swung his arm around me for a side hug. My first instinct was to duck away. Every fiber squirmed for freedom, but when I felt his warmth and soft fingers pressing gently into my arm, I gulped deep and made myself stay.

"Billy Lindstrom," Bob said, "Meet the newest recruit to Forever Fields. Miss Paisley Alberta Noon. Fern and Peter's daughter. Isn't she the spittin' image of her mother?" He squeezed me closer and rocked a little. I smiled.

"Well, I'll be dipped in sheep dung if this isn't a pale-skinned little Fernie Greene standing right before me."

Um. Awkward.

"You're just as lovely as your mother ever was," he added then reached out to shake my hand. And though I usually reserved my dishrag handshake for strangers, I decided I'd better give this guy a strong, sturdy one or he might come at me with more than I bargained for, like a full belly-hug.

Bob said, "This beast and I served in the Marines together."

They flashed their tattoos and rubbed their stubbly hairdos. I nodded, a little surprised, but not shocked. They both looked the part on the outside, but Baker Bob hadn't come off like that ... on the inside ... I guess you'd say.

Billy came back, "Served up *slop* most of the time, that is."

"We were mess sergeants," Bob explained. "Taught me everything I know. He did."

Billy leaned toward me and whispered loud, "Not my *best* recipes. Saved those for myself." He winked.

Baker Bob slapped his back, "You remember the twins, don't you Billy?"

"Are these the Greene boys?" Billy's voice rattled like the blown speaker in Oscar's passenger side door. "You two were just skinny, snot-nosed trouble-makers about yay high last I saw you." He held his hand at his belly.

"Just taller now," Bob said. "Heath. Henry. You remember Big Billy Lindstrom don't you? He taught you how to shoot your bb gun."

Heath stood, wiped his hands on his coveralls, and removed his cap before extending a well-mannered greeting. "Course I remember. Good to see you, Mr. Lindstrom." Then he ran his fingers through his golden waves and stuffed his cap in his back pocket. Nerves still flashed across his face as he looked at his brother. We were all still thinking about Griff, of course, but the twins seemed to be worse off.

Henry, muscles taut, tapped up the brim of his cap. "Mr. Lindstrom."

A palpable moment of silence hung amidst kitchen clatter.

Bob explained, "Griff's in the hospital. We're waiting on some tests. Think he might have had a heart attack."

Billy nodded soberly. "Ah. I see," he said. "Did they start the ceremony yet?"

"They were about to shortly after we left."

"Mmhm. Good," Billy said and gave a sharp nod before clapping at us. "Only one cure for the worries, you know." He looked at me as though the answer should be obvious. When no one replied, he bellowed, "Four Big Billy's Buffalo Burgers comin' up!" He swung into action.

At some point between my first bite (of the most massive hunk of ground meat I ever did see slopped between two buns) and my last, a vaguely familiar, shiny man strode into the café yammering away on his cell phone.

"No, no, NO. You misunderstand, you see. It's called dee – pree – shee – ay – shuh – nnnuh. Look it

93

up in your old Webster, will you," he sneered then hollered as he stuffed his phone inside his suit coat. "Billy! Get me a Reuben, ASAP!"

Baker Bob tensed next to me but kept still. Then Billy, wiping a glass, stood grimacing in the doorway to the kitchen. "Be right with ya, Remmy."

The shiny guy drummed at the counter and twitched all jittery, like he had pop rocks in his skin. He didn't acknowledge Billy or anyone else. Just pulled out his cell phone seventeen times and fidgeted. "Make it to go, and don't you dare go using any of that day old rye crap from Nose-Dive Market, you hear. I want *your* homemade stuff or I will walk straight out that door."

I can't be sure, but I thought Billy muttered something like, "If only."

The gold watch on this guy's wrist slipped up and down as he worked his satiny striped tie. He wore a navy blue suit, a starched white shirt, and patent leather black shoes. Late twenties maybe. His jet black hair was slicked back with a little tuft sticking out in front. I think you might have called him handsome if his eau-de-jerk stench hadn't permeated the room.

To my surprise, Henry spoke first. "Norse Drive Market runs an honest business, Mr. Stone." Henry did not look away from his buffalo burger. "Everyone knows it."

Remmy contorted his face like he bit lemon. "Who asked you?"

My stomach knotted as I watched Henry slowly stand up, and though Remmy had a few more inches of height, Henry's t-shirt stretched over his biceps.

Heath swiped a paper napkin across his mouth then stood tall and lanky behind his brother. By the looks of his cheeky grin, nothing would have eased his nerves better than pummeling something (Perhaps, say … a shiny jackass?) right then. Clearly this was not the first time, and I dared guess it

94

wouldn't be the last time, the twins had taken on a guy like this.

Baker Bob, still chewing, diffused the tension. "Hey guys, we'd better get back. Bert will wonder where we are." He had sidestepped any mention of Griff or the hospital. "Billy, can we get those other sandwiches, please?"

Eying Bob carefully, Billy feigned levity. "Right here. Heads up!" He tossed a paper sack with Bert's, River's and Knut's lunch in it. "Don't be a stranger, Bobby."

Bob gave his Marine buddy a reserved smile. "Let's get a move on, guys."

The twins didn't argue but gathered their jackets, eyes never leaving this Remmy Stone.

He, however, puffed up to an insulting stance, buttoned his suit coat, and fussed with his cuff links as we exited. Bleeding sarcasm, he said, "You all have a nice day, now." A twinkle star shot from his impudent smile … *ting*. I suddenly realized where I'd seen him before. The man from the billboard. Remmy Stone.

* * *

Myocardial infarction. Yep. You guessed it. Massive heart attack. It turned out Griffin Cy Tuson would indeed NOT be dying that day. When Dr. Bjorn gave the news, you could feel the whoosh of relief sweep the room.

"It's important to remember a full recovery from this particular kind of episode could take months. He won't be allowed to do much around the farm for some time." The doctor added with friendly sarcasm, "Which I'm sure will come *quite naturally* for him." His eyes twinkled. "I'll give you a full write-up before he goes home at week's end."

95

Baker Bob chuckled and spoke for us all, "Don't worry about old ornery britches. We'll make sure he follows your orders to a T."

Dr. Bjorn went on calmly, like he had no doubt, "The healing ceremony is well under way." Then he squeezed Aunt Bert's hand and smiled.

"Thank you, Karl," she said, and though her countenance remained rock solid, I think I heard a crack in her voice.

He replied, "He'll be ready for visitors after they're done. I'll send River out to get you. You take care, Alberta." He gave a polite wave and shuttled through the ICU double doors.

Heath sprang to life first. "I'll go see how Knut's doing." He grabbed Henry's slumped shoulder and power rubbed his brother's stubbly blonde hair. Then he bounded off to the pediatrics wing.

Henry just stood there head hanging. Bert and Bob went to him when they heard him suck in a sob. They made a circle hug with him and rubbed his back.

Faintly, I heard a drumbeat. The "healing ceremony" I later learned was Lakota tradition. The steady rhythm rolled soothingly through the quiet waiting room.

I heard Aunt Bert say real soft and in time with the drums, "It's alright now. It's gonna be alright." She took out her rosary and whispered some prayers as she rubbed each bead.

Part of me really wanted to be inside that circle. Another part wanted to know what was going on in Great Uncle Griff's room.

Rattling joined the drumbeats now.

Many minutes passed like that, listening to the ceremony through the walls, watching Bob and Bert comfort Henry. Drifting through the walls, voices sang vaguely familiar words I did not understand.

More drums. More rattling.

Then I realized the words were like those in my dreams, and I knew this was the language of my

96

ancestors (half my ancestors, I guess). Where did I belong in all this?

I closed my eyes and swept myself onto Journey's back. Running. Running like the wild Nokota through the head-high prairie grass out to the horizon until Journey said to me, "Hold on! I will show you."

The drumming and rattling and singing grew louder, a heartbeat.

And then there was silence.

Gram's voice came to me. *I will show you.*

I clamped my eyes shut. *Thank God, you're still here,* I said. *I'm alone.*

Never, Paisley Alberta Noon. You know better.

Can't help it, Gram.

Now you listen to me. Wish on them all the good things your sorry little self can muster. This is more about who you are *than you know.*

Yes ma'am. But which part belongs to me?

All of it.

Understanding washed over me. It didn't matter which world I belonged to because both were a part of me. In fact, maybe that's the way it's supposed to be — a perfectly blended combination of everything spinning the world around and around like in my dreams.

I closed my eyes and conjured up good things to wish on them, just like Gram ordered. I thought of blooming gardens and green grass. "Blue skies and puffy clouds. Fresh hay and the murmur of horses in an old barn. Rolling prairie and a faithful dog," I whispered.

"Kittens rolling in the dust and sunshine," said someone else's voice which made my eyes dart open to find … my family … standing with me. Knut held Aunt Bert's hand and leaned against Heath. His red cape dangling behind him. He just looked at me with the most innocent expression, like waiting for my comeback. I hadn't meant to speak my thoughts out loud. It just happened.

Magic hung in the air. Kind faces looked at me.

"Porch swings and crickets," I said.

After a moment Aunt Alberta said, "Grandfather clocks ticking."

Both Knut and I smiled at her.

"Warm kitchens on rainy days," said Baker Bob. Aunt Bert mmhmmed.

Heath said, "Frogs and tadpoles in the crick." He elbowed his brother.

Henry didn't lift his head, but I noticed a hint of smile as he thought about what to say. "Girls in cut-off jeans."

The group murmured a laugh but went quiet again. So there I stood, wouldn't you know. Part of the circle.

Suddenly everyone's eyes shifted to look behind me. Standing tall in the double doorway was Tate Maycomb. Long hair fallen to the side; drover draped heavily over his arm. I don't know how long he'd been there, but it must have been long enough to have understood what we were doing because he said with a simple smile and weary eyes, "An ornery old man defying the spirit world once again."

* * *

Three long-haired, sun-baked men in traditional Native American clothes passed us in the hallway on our way to Griff's room. One carried a drum and the other two carried boxes full of colored kerchiefs and other things I couldn't see. Their drawn, wrinkly faces eyed me carefully, but they greeted everyone with warm sincerity.

In the darkened hospital room, Griff lay limp and still. River stood tall at his bedside, but the lines in his face made him look spent.

"Hey ..." Aunt Bert said just above a whisper, "How we doin'?"

Pale and withered, Griff barely raised a finger to greet us. Aunt Bert scooted to his side and held his hand, which he appeared to appreciate but said nothing. Tubes stuck to his wrinkled arms and poked out of his gown leading to all sorts of lit up, beeping equipment.

Baker Bob moved in, "Leave it to you, old man, to cheat death again. Eh?" He gently wiggled Griff's foot through the bed sheets. "What does this make now? You must be working on life number twelve at least." Bob's hearty laugh eased the seriousness in the room.

Griff grunted and rubbed a scar on his head. His gravelly voice sounded oddly small. "I guess it might be something like that." Then the room fell to silent again.

Henry, with nothing short of a pleading look on his face, slowly went to Griff. His eyes were already red as he searched for words. "Griff ... I ..."

Griff closed his eyes and shook his head. "No, kid. There's nothing to be said." Then he roughly patted him on the cheek. There would be no blame placed on anyone here today, nor would there be *any* day. Henry forced a smile but broke down anyway as Griff rubbed the boy's stubble blonde head.

Our somber mood weighed heavy in the room. No one seemed to know what to do until Tate walked over to Griff's bedside and looked at him like he had something important to say, but he seemed to hold back. He looked up at us as though he wasn't sure if this was the right time to tell us whatever was on his mind.

"Before I came here ... I stopped at my place to check on the horses and close things up. I didn't know how long I would be gone, you see."

Griff asked, "Is everything okay, Tate?"

"Oh ... I think you could say that," he said with a suppressed grin. "I just didn't want to say anything until I knew ... you'd be alright."

Knut voiced what we all were thinking. "What is it?"

Tate's eyes brightened with an intoxicating, sly smile. "A newborn filly foal nickering a song for her mama."

Surprise burst out around us.

Griff smiled and reached for Tate's hand, "Congratulations, son." I swear the color flushed right back into his cheeks.

"I knew you could do it!" River shook Tate's hand too and pulled him in for a hug. Then he looked him straight in the eye, serious, "Zica Hota have any trouble?"

"None at all," Tate replied. "Gray Squirrel is a good broodmare."

Aunt Alberta clapped her hands, "I knew it! I knew that pair would make a winning combination! It's all going to work out, Tate." She flung her arms around him and held on. "You just wait and see."

River stood close and said real low and proud, almost a whisper, "The first of many."

Tate closed his eyes tight as he hugged Aunt Bert back, and I couldn't help but notice how his expression radiated elation and concern all wrapped up in one.

Knut flapped his arms as he did a prancy dance in place hollering, "What color is she, Tate? What color?"

"Well this is the amazing thing, you see," Tate began, and I could tell we were *all* relieved to be hearing a happy story. "This little one came out like neither her sire nor her dam." His expression became animated. "You know how Smoke-N-Ash has a coat like a velvet thundercloud?" Knut emphatically nodded his curls up and down, up and down. "And you know how Gray Squirrel has the body of a silver fox, but her

100

head is the color of fine chocolate?" Tate walked around to each person as yeses and mmhms and uhuhs filled the room. "Well this little girl came out white as a ghost ..." He swiped both his hands past his widened eyes. "... except for ..." Here he paused and stood still as stone. "... the medicine hat." Shocked gasps rifled through the thick hospital air. Tate flashed the most brilliant smile.

Now the nurses and orderlies began to gather to hear him tell his story. He moved to include every person. Something fluttered in my chest as he came my way. "And do you know what she did all the while she struggled onto her spindly legs and wobbled to her mama?"

Knut, beside himself with excitement, screamed, "What Tate? What did she do?"

Tate laced his fingers behind his back and waltzed over to him. Every single person smiled in anticipation as he rocked back and forth on his heels, clearly having just as much fun telling this story as we were having listening to it.

"She sang," he said simply. I could see his amusement at our puzzled faces. "She came out singing a whinnying song. This singing, it woke up the whole herd. They came running in from all directions to lean upon the fences and echo her song to her." He swept around the room again stopping right in front of Knut. "She sang her little song in between slurps of her very first meal." He stepped quickly over to a group of smiling nurses. "She sang while I helped Sica Hota wash her." He stopped in front of the twins. "She sang while I raked the stall and filled it with clean straw." He stopped in front of River, Berta, and Bob. "Then, in the warmth of the morning sun ..." Here he looked around the whole room. "...she sang herself and her mama to sleep."

Everybody aawwwed and tipped their heads. Myself included. It was quite a story.

"What's her name?" I said in such a small voice, I barely heard it.

But he did. Tate's coffee brown eyes melted me to the core as he strode over until he was so close I had to look up to maintain eye contact. I drank in the musky smell of his un-tucked muslin shirt. He looked at me as though he'd known me all his life and said, "I thought you'd never ask."

I just tweaked an eyebrow and crossed my arms. The hospital staff had drifted back to their duties. My family waited silently, except for a few laughs when I started tapping my foot impatiently. I wasn't the only one wanting to hear his answer.

"Isn't it obvious?" He continued to look straight at me, and though I wanted to glance around the room for a little help, I never flinched.

"Oka Wana Gi."

I did not look away but searched his eyes for the translation. I could tell from the murmurs of approval and resumed conversations that pretty much everyone else knew what it meant. This Lakota language was definitely on my To-Do-List. And judging by the playful little smirk on his face, Tate seemed to be enjoying my torment a trifle too much.

Trying to think of what I knew about the filly from Tate's story, I forced my mind to come up with a guess. All white. *White as a ghost*, he'd said. Singing. Singing, singing, singing her little filly song. "I don't know. If she was mine, I'd call her Ghost Song or something cool like that." I flicked my ponytail.

I could feel everyone's stare. Aunt Alberta had such a look of amazement on her face I thought a fly might buzz right into her mouth. The twins nodded in unison as though mildly impressed for a second. Baker Bob nudged River and the two gave each other a high brow.

"What?" I demanded, a little perturbed.

Then Tate said, "That's it," and took my hand. A wave of warmth radiated from his gentle, calloused fingers. I just let my hand lay limp in his. "That is what Oka Wana Gi means." He squeezed ever so softly. "Ghost Song. At least, something close enough to that."

Then he smiled at me so earnestly it filled me right up from my pinky toe to my crimson ears. My breath skipped and I found myself grasping his hand. I'm not sure if anyone else in the room was paying any attention to us since they'd all started chatting amongst themselves, but it would not have mattered. All I saw was Tate Maycomb holding both my pale hands now, one raven tendril enticing me to sweep it back and pull him in. We breathed together, in and out.

In this moment, somehow, I knew that this man smiling back at me, holding my hands close, held a special place inside my circle.

Our heads nearly touched when he asked breathlessly, "How is it you know my thoughts?"

"I didn't." *Did I?* "I mean, I don't. I just took a guess." *Didn't I?*

His eyes twinkled as he grinned at me then slowly, ever so tenderly, kissed the tips of my fingers, which sent a flame to the depths of my belly. All because I guessed a newborn filly's name. How the heck did I pull that one out of my …

"Afternoon all!" boomed a voice that nearly jolted me out of my skin.

The room went frigid. My family stood locked, staring at the individual greeting us so loudly. Remmy Stone, popping a breath mint, leaned against the doorway like he owned the place.

Baker Bob growled. "Aw no you don't." He used his Marine Corps frame to back Stone out of the room and down the hallway without even touching him. River, Bert, Heath, and Henry backed Bob like a posse.

What was *with* this slick creep? Did he follow us here from the café? I looked to Tate to see his reaction. He'd whisked away to the back corner of the room where I could only partially see him hidden behind a curtain. My hands ice cold. Empty. Before I could even steady my heart knocking around like a caged bird, Remmy's vortex sucked my attention.

Griff ordered, "Keep an eye on them and tell me what's goin' down."

I threw a confused glance at Tate hidden in the shadows before I crept down the hall close enough to hear.

"My, my, my," Remmy's tone came slow and bored, "If it isn't my dear old friends Berty Greene and River Lightfoot. I do hope everything is okay. Unless, that is, you've just finally decided to appreciate the wonders of modern medicine and bring the whole fam damily in for a check-up. Ay?" He turned toward the twins and Bob with an over-exaggerated crude gesture. "Turn 'n cough, boys!"

The cheesy wide grin cutting his face made me want to gag. No one replied.

"What? You mean to tell me old Riv here hasn't been stirring up your stick-n-daisy tea to cure all that ails you?" He looked up steadily from examining his fingernails. "Ssshhocking."

My aunt took only a fraction of a second to shift into a Greene Giant. All four foot eight of her swung into action. Arms flapping jauntily side to side, smile like the sun, feet splaying out, she strode over to this Stone dude and stuck out her hand. "Remington, my goodness, how *are* you? It's been such a while. You look so..." She paused to look him up and down with the confidence of a full-bellied mountain lion. "... fancy!" I'm not sure how or why she maintained such civility. "How is the homestead holding up? That old twelve-bedroom shanty filled up with handsome little babies yet?"

He wasn't going for the niceties. "Save it Berty." He nearly slapped her as he flicked his hand in the air. River and Bob jerked, but she didn't flinch, just stood there with a concrete, pleasant smile.

"You know," he went on, "you're fourteen and a half months late on your insurance payments. Sure hope whatever's brought you in search of the excellent services of the good people here at VC Mercy Hospital," he winked at the nurse in the hall who watched him with disdain, "isn't going to cost more than you can write a check for." He turned to the nurse again, this time landing an eye on her cleavage, then back to Alberta with a bland look. "A *good* check, that is."

I thought Heath and Henry might lunge right out of their skin to go after him, but both River and Bob shook their head.

Aunt Bert, unshaken, smiled a little harder and crinkled her nose while she reached up to straighten his red and yellow striped tie and pat him exactly twice on the chest. "Oh don't you worry your little head over us, dear. We'll make do as always. I do appreciate how you've accommodated us during these tough times, you know. I'm sure it can't be easy on you either. You take care now." She turned away, head high, before he had a chance to say a word.

I poked my head back in Griff's room. Tate was gone. "Aunt Bert set him straight."

Uncle Griff grimaced and crossed his arms.

So I'd heard it twice now. Billy's ruff voice resounded among diner racket, *"... that washed up ranch out in the middle of nowhere."* Now this, if there was any truth to it, about not paying the insurance. I started to put a few things together. No cell phones, no TV that I could tell, piles and piles of wood stacked outside the houses — all under the guise of "living simply." Worst of all, and it seeped into my gut like bad Chinese, all the "hired" help consisted of family. The topic of wages never came up.

Though I wasn't sure about a lot of things in life right then — like how exactly I'd fallen into this circle, or where Tate had disappeared to, or what the voices in my head said, or why I'd dreamt of Nokotas before I knew they existed — of one thing I was fairly confident, and it froze me to the bone like a Minnesota blizzard daring to steal everything important from me.

Forever Fields was going under.

Chapter 10

By the time we got back to the ranch late that afternoon, we were so emotionally exhausted Aunt Bert told us to just take the rest of the day off.

"Come on, Knut. Let's go inside. I want you to sift through that new box of comics that arrived last week. Penny says those kids want to hear you read to them." She disappeared into the house without so much as a nod to the rest of us. Knut waved, but we were left kicking dirt and standing around the dead fountain.

Prairie came running from the barn and nearly barreled me over. I sat on the fountain's edge while she snuffled all the hospital smells out of me. I gave the spot next to me a slap and she popped up, ears draped. I leaned into her and ran my fingers through her silky black fur. Those amber mother hen eyes peered into me. She put a little white paw on my knee.

Heath leaned against the iron fence of my project yard. "If I didn't know better, I'd think Remmy kind of got to her this time."

Henry couldn't help himself. "I knew I should've cold-cocked him when I had the chance at the diner." He ground his fist into his palm, flexed and paced.

Baker Bob sat down next to me and started working Prairie's ears. "Oh I wouldn't go getting too worried about Alberta. It's been a fairly tough day for her. For all of us." Something in his eyes hesitated before he blinked it away.

"And what's Tate's problem?" Henry said.

My heart skipped a beat at the mention of his name. I tried eyeing everyone to see if they were looking at me. Heat radiated from my face. River and Bob looked at each other then to me like I was an adorable kitten. Heath plucked at the stray vines poking through the fence then rolled his eyes.

Henry kept pacing. He reminded me of a Jack-in-the-Box getting cranked and cranked up until … snap … BAM! I felt sorry for him. He obviously had no clue how to bottle himself up tight as a drum until he forgot his emotions even existed. Second nature for me, like breathing.

But then, I didn't want that for him or *anyone* here. That was no *skill*, more like a curse. I should be taking lessons from *him*. The more I thought about it, the more I felt sorry for *myself* (because *that's* so attractive).

"He can't be near him for two seconds, Henry," Heath replied to Henry's accusation about Tate. And I wasn't sure if he meant Tate couldn't be near Remmy or the other way around.

"Well, if anyone should be standing up to that scumsucker, it should be his …"

"That's enough!" demanded River, the strong lines of his jaw flexing. His crinkled mahogany eyes flicked at me so fast that if I hadn't been looking, I wouldn't have known. But I *was* looking, and I *did* see.

I wanted to know how Henry had intended to finish his sentence. That meant I had to pipe up and be a part of this conversation.

"What did you mean, Henry?" My words sounded small. I barely recognized my voice. I tried again. Stronger this time. "Why *did* Tate leave?"

Baker Bob attempted to appease my curiosity. "It's a long story, from a long time ago."

"No, it isn't." Henry sounded like one more crank oughta do it.

"Henry." River stood taut.

108

Heath flung his hands in the air. "Seriously you guys, if she's going to be a part of this family ..." He stopped to look at me as though appraising my value. "She deserves to know about ..." Again, he paused, "... how things *are* around here."

The pleading look that followed managed to move River. He sat next to me on the curved cement bench but didn't speak.

Bob said, "I think the young man may have a point, Riv. No secrets from family."

River took his cowboy hat off and rubbed his evenly grayed head. He looked tired, yet quiet concession smoothed the lines of his face. "You're right. You're both right."

Henry stopped pacing. I sat motionless waiting for someone to *pah-lease talk to me!* No one seemed to want to start. It made me nervous, but Prairie patted my leg. I wiggled my fingers into her fur and looked at the four men.

"I want to know. Whatever it is. Trust me. I can take it." Astonished at myself for actually speaking up, I rolled with it. "Big, tough girl?" Even I heard the question mark, but I'd had a fair share of shocking news in my life, and somehow, I managed to survive it all.

The final crank set Henry off. "Tate is Remmy's brother!"

Prairie and I jumped.

"And they hate each other! They've hated each other since anyone can remember! And what's worse, Aunt Bert is in debt up to her eyeballs to him! Tate has big dreams and no cash, fresh out of college. Forever Fields is supposed to be his partner, but any idiot can see this place has about had it. So where does *everyone* around here go when they need money, to the only person who ever seems to *have* any money."

"That'll do Henry!" River boomed.

"No, it will *not* do," Henry snapped. But when River seared him with a steady look, he became eerily calm. Someone needed to get Henry a punching bag or a yoga class at the *very* least. Even when Heath tried to settle him down with a single hand on his shoulder, he shrugged it off, leaving Heath hanging. I got the feeling he knew better than to interfere when Henry got like this. My gut told me Heath had lost a few brawls to his beefier, hot-tempered brother.

Heath tried again, "Look man, we know you're upset about Griff, but let's try and keep our head here. Okay?"

"Well if we didn't have to work under that sleaze-ball's shadow every waking minute ..." He gripped both hands behind his head, stared a hole into the ground, and took a settling breath.

Heath blew out relief, "I know, Brother." They slapped hands and held firm.

I picked up genuine remorse when Henry spoke. "Sorry, Paisley. I didn't mean to go off like that. You don't need to hear it." He shook his head. "But they're brothers, for cripe sake. You hear me?" He squinted. "*Brothers.*"

When he pulled Heath in for a long, full-on hug (you know, the kind that usually makes my skin go all wiggly), I tried to remember the last time I'd felt that passionate about anything, much less my family. Nothing but a blinding white snow-covered farm came to mind.

The afternoon sun shone down in the turn-about as shadows of the western shelterbelt crept toward us. Soft nickers echoed from Journey and Boss Girl's paddock. Ernie hobbled out of the bushes and proceeded to curl around each of our legs, purring and stopping for an ear scratch.

At first, I thought it odd how no one spoke, but as duress lifted, I realized how beautiful it was to sit there surrounded by people who know each other so well that they didn't have to yammer on just to fill the empty space. It felt as comfortable as a sun-soaked hay mow with swallows swooping in and out.

Just one thing was missing. I looked down The Drive hoping to see his silhouette coming like this morning. I didn't care who his brother was. I didn't care about the financial situation.

Prairie flipped her head under my hand to make me keep petting her. I hadn't realized I'd stopped. River and Bob sat with their hats in their hands, inspecting the tops of their boots. Heath took off his cap, closed his eyes, and shook out his wavy blonde locks as he leaned back. Henry sat scratching Ernie curled up like a baby in his arm. A dab of drool spilled out of my cat's mouth.

I turned to look at the fountain's centerpiece and wondered how long it had been since it had worked. Three tiers of fluted bowls with a seahorse sculpted at the top where I assumed the water came shooting out. How nice it would have been to hear a little trickle, just to settle our nerves. I plucked a weed out of a crack.

Calm and easy just like his name, River began, "Your Grandma Ruth, Paisley, was the second child of four."

Gram's voice groaned, *Aw here we go.*

I sat up real straight and careful. "Big Tough Girl" had not prepared herself for a story about Gram.

River looked me in the eyes like I was a filly, and he was sorry to break the news, but I'd be going for my first ride today, and it might be bumpy as a washboard, but you've got to start somewhere.

"Her two younger brothers are none other than our very own Griffin Cy Tuson and a man named Lenard Angus Tuson, whom I believe sold you that truck parked by your bunkhouse. I'd recognize it anywhere."

I let out a little gasp but clamped my mouth shut with a hand. I didn't want to interrupt him, but DANG … I just knew it!

111

He continued, "They also had an older sister, Tilda Layne Tuson. All four children were born and raised on the outskirts of your hometown in Grover, Minnesota. Their folks — your great-grandparents — Olive Baker and Brush Tuson were lucky enough to have claimed one thousand acres of the most beautiful land in the entire tri-state area. Your father Peter still farms some of this very land of which I speak."

Aurora Way. I knew it like the back of my hand. I picked at a corner of duct tape still patching the rusty hole Oscar had made in the thigh of my paisley jeans.

I think River could tell something bugged me because he continued telling the story with a lighter tone. "It was quite the scandal back then, you see, because it was not ... how should I put this ... *socially acceptable* for a white woman to marry a Lakota. They were quite the case of opposites attract too. Sweet little Olive, with her Scandinavian translucent skin and flaxen curls. Then Brush, with his cocoa skin, jet black hair, and the distinct ability to defy anyone who claimed authority over him. But young love being what it is, the rules of social propriety held no meaning to these two."

Baker Bob piped in, "Lord, ain't that the truth. And did you know Olive Baker was my father's sister? My aunt."

It took me a second, but finally I made the connection. "Ohhh. Baker. That's right! Billy called you Robert Baker at the café today."

"We've all got a connection here. Be it close or distant, blood or marriage, we truly are *family.*"

"I got the sense," I said with a grin. Finally, FINALLY, some answers started crawling out of the cracks.

River nodded, leaned his elbows on his knees, and went on, "The four kids of this forbidden couple were the talk of the town. Tilda Layne, the oldest, had white-blonde, straight as an arrow hair, toasted skin,

112

and an attitude fit for her Scandinavian name — mighty battle maiden. Your grandmother Ruth Aurelia — though she went gray early in her tough years of hog farming with Joe — had the finest, silken, ebony hair you ever did see, but her skin shone like pearls. She was known, as you might imagine, for her passionate strength."

I closed my eyes and stroked Prairie's head. I imagined Gram in her younger days. She stood on a hill in my mind, a west wind blowing her hair back like a wild Nokota mare. A tenacious look in her eye. The image made me smile.

"The two boys, Lenny and Griff, could just as easily have been twins. They had hair that flowed like copper waves past bronze shoulders. Both had a knack for trouble, but they worked hard and were known for their dedication to a job.

"Eventually, Olive and Brush grew too old to work and wished to spend their golden years retired in the cabin the family had built by a lake on the farthest western reach of their land. They had always expected their four children would continue to farm, but when Tilda, Ruth, Lenny, and Griff inherited all that land, well, let's just say things didn't go as they expected."

"Noooo sir," Bob chimed.

River took a deep breath. "By that time, the sisters had grown up and married, and the brothers went off to find their own fortunes. Your Grandma Ruth married Lakota hog farmer Joe Greene. When they had Fern and your uncle Lane, they settled on the farthest eastern hills in that homestead you grew up in, Paisley. Did Peter or Ruth ever tell you that?"

"Never." I wasn't able to bite back the bitterness in the word. Why hadn't I ever heard any of this? I mean, I kind of understand why Dad didn't tell me. He and I never had conversations, especially after Mom ditched. But *Gram*? I thought of all people on this planet that she would have told me things about our

113

past, our history. Now I wondered how many other secrets she'd kept from me. She would be getting a ghostly earful from me soon.

Apparently sensing my inklings of betrayal in the awkward silence, River changed the subject. "And Tilda Layne, your great-aunt, married a Lakota named Pacing Horse. They believed deeply in preserving the land, and they wanted their only child Jill to grow up in a place where nature came first, man second. They let the tilled acres return to their natural state and made an honest living mostly from Tilda's garden goods at farmers markets and Pacing Horse's gift for farrier work and saddlery. This is where I came in. Their daughter Jill and I were married just out of high school, and since my parents had recently passed, Tilda and Pacing Horse took me in as their own."

This surprised me. I felt sad that he'd lost his parents, but I didn't know what words to say. I sidestepped it. "So did you go to Grover High too?"

"No, my little sister Moon and I learned from my parents and our tribe members. We went to the Prairie Island Indian Community schools for enrichment, but mostly we learned from the land. My mother showed me the healing powers of plants. My father taught me everything I know about the way of the horse. I have not failed one yet. Then my father-in-law showed me the art of a farrier."

"River here is one of the few *true* horse masters of the prairie plains. You can't learn the things he knows by sitting in a classroom," Bob said. Then he nudged my shoulder. "Not that I condone dropping out of school or skipping college. I just know it's not for everyone."

Amen to that! I thought. I wanted to learn from the land like River.

"Not for everyone, true," River said, "but most definitely for some. Like my sister Moon and Tate for example."

The mention of his name made his absence gape in front of me. I looked again down The Drive for him. I looked through the western trees for his herd. Searching for any sign that he might be close. Nothing.

Trying to sound casual, I stretched a little then focused on a tiny mat of fur on Prairie's neck. "So uh, how does Tate fit into the picture?" I kept fiddling with the clump of fur even after I'd untangled it.

I heard a smile in River's voice when he went on. "He's my nephew. Moon's son. She took both him and his brother in when their parents died in a car wreck. My sister Moon rescued them from foster care.

"You see, after I married Tilda and Pacing Horse's daughter Jill, Moon went on to further her education at the University of Minnesota to complete her doctorate in equine veterinary medicine. By the time she finished her schooling and settled in with a thriving practice, she felt ready for a family."

"Tate and Remington," I breathed.

"Yes. But Remington's birth name is Chante. It is the Lakota word for heart."

Both Henry and Heath snorted at this but said nothing. I gauged by the way they listened to the story unfold that they perhaps had never heard it told this way.

"Tate — pronounced tahk-tay in Lakota — swept into her life like the wind he was named after, filling her emptiness like a well-spring. But Chante did not take the transition so well, as you might guess. And though he still had his brother, and though Moon did her best to care for him and raise him, the anger inside his heart grew too strong. Sadly, I have learned through my years that there is so little one can do to ease the aching of another's heart. Especially that of a strong-minded young man just beginning to search for purpose in the world. Powers of reason deflect off such an individual once he sets his mind on his own course."

Here River paused, I think for my benefit. After all, there I sat, little miss runaway. I'd gotten it in my mind that I belonged somewhere other than with my dad and Cindy. Sure, I ended up gullible enough to land precisely where they had wanted me all along, but the fact remains, no one could have talked me out of leaving. I had my grandmother's stubborn streak.

Lord, yes, she sang. I hung my head and smiled.

"Chante wanted nothing of this new family or the ways of the land which Moon tried to teach them. Jill and I did what we could before we moved out here, but Moon was essentially on her own. Tate, however, took in every word she offered, every thought she shared, every lesson she taught. Eventually, she put him through college to learn the ways of business and it allowed him to grow into the man we know now. Gentle and wise beyond his years. For these reasons, Tate Maycomb is Forever Fields' best hope."

Heath leaned in and asked, "What about Remington? I mean, Chante? How did he end up such a degenerate fool?"

River's eyes turned sad. "On the morning after a deathly blizzard — the very same that claimed your grandmother, Paisley — Chante resolved to erase his life." He swept his palms smooth from one side to the other. "Clean slate himself just as the snows had done to the land in a single night. Start over ... alone. He told his confused little brother nestled under a patchwork quilt, "We are no longer family. I want nothing of this life with the land, nothing of that woman or her money ..." River's words halted in his throat and our silence was palpable. " ... nothing of *you.*"

My heart weighed heavy inside my chest. I felt a crevice etch across my brow.

"Chante changed his name to Remington Stone and took off for the western plains of North Dakota after whispers of oil fields and great wealth. And great wealth he did indeed find. But not the kind that counts for anything. Just money.

"It broke my sister's heart and nearly destroyed Tate all over again. Moon claimed responsibility for Chante leaving the way he did. Could she have done more? If she had just said this or that? Tate cried many days and nights, and no matter how many times Moon whispered in his ear, 'Cante chante sica yaun sai ye,' do not have a sad heart. But as with most things that threaten to cleave our hearts in two, the pain dimmed in time. Though no such injury can ever truly heal. We only press on and try to find threads of good in people to stitch the wound together again and again. Tate cannot be near his brother. For it rips the wound open. In time, that will change."

I sensed River had scars of his own that were probably still healing, and I wondered desperately what happened to his parents and his wife Jill, but I didn't press. I was grateful for what he had been willing to share.

Henry asked calmly, "So ... how is it Remington ended up living around here? I mean, it couldn't have just been a coincidence."

River took a deep breath, kind of like he was trying to figure the best way to explain this part of the story. "No. It was not. According to a few of our friends in Valley City, Remmy moved into the area as soon as he heard some Tusons from Grover, MN had moved out here. You see, he knew the four children of Olive and Brush had inherited all that land and figured they were wealthy. So he moved here to try to worm his way into their lives. But when Griff and Lenny Tuson turned him down flat, knowing how he'd abandoned his family, Remmy went and bought up as many properties as he could get his greedy fingers on. When he realized how unstable the weather around here can be, he began the insurance business then he added the real estate end to it too. The man has much money and intends to keep it that way. I

117

think Remmy holds a grudge. The way he treats families in need here proves I'm right."

Heath looked like he was calculating an algebraic equation. "Yah, but how did Lenny and Griff make this place famous? I think I know some of it but just bits and pieces."

River and Baker Bob gave each other an exhausted look, and just as River drew in another breath to begin again, Bob stood up and noisily stretched his back before announcing, "I think *that* part of the story, my dears, will have to wait for another time. Look at the length of these shadows. My spaghetti sauce has been simmering by its lonesome all day and the rest of our meal won't cook itself."

River shared a grateful smile. "He's right. The ponies won't grain themselves either."

Heath stood, stretched, and pulled his crumpled ball cap out of his back pocket. He smacked it a couple times on his jeans before smashing it on his head. Blonde wings stuck out all over, and he gave his brother one of his cheeky grins. "Hey man, you two want a little *time alone*? I'm sure P here can help me get the Old Ones in for chow."

Henry was still cradling a mighty comfy looking Ernie. Henry put Ernie down carefully then tried to brush all the hair off his shirt and jeans and face. "Whatever, you twig." He swung and missed Heath's hat then challenged, "Last one saddled up showers last! Brrhrrrhrr!"

They both took off like bucking colts toward their bunkhouse where their matching bays waited. I envied them. How they could move with their emotions as easily as a chickadee flits from branch to branch. I wondered how that must feel.

I glanced once more down The Drive. Prairie herded me toward the barn.

The crease between my eyes melted as I heaved open the wooden doors to the sounds of hrrr hrrr and feet swishing in the hay. Warm and dusty smells rushed through me. I closed my eyes to revel in it. When I opened them again, I saw my handsome knight, the star on his forehead calling me in. My fair maiden hung her silver head over the stall's top rail, doe eyes soft. I grabbed a brush. They nuzzled for treats, and we wound ourselves into our human/horse knot scratching each others' backs and ears until it was hard to tell where one of us started and the others ended. Bliss.

I thought about the web River had spun trying to explain some of the families and connections that made up the history of the ranch. It was hard to remember which one led to another and which ones branched where, but one thing remained as clear as my love for the two warm bodies surrounding me — we were all connected. And *that*, I began to understand, was what mattered.

I don't know how much time had passed when I decided to take a last deep breath and give my horses a final pat. Though the day had definitely not been what I'd expected, contentment filled my bones as I stepped out of the stall.

I strolled through the barn checking out its stalls lining the north side — all opened up to the prairie view Alberta mentioned. Each had a white board with a name and feeding instructions. Methuselah: four cups senior feed, six cups soaked hay cubes. Harper: two cups weight builder grain, one scoop glucosamine. Preacher: one quarter strip eye ointment, three cups warm beet pulp mash. The Old Ones, as they called them, were well cared for here.

The barn had cement floors, a draft of fresh air, and not a stick of straw out of place. It had a washing station, a long neatly stocked tack room, grain bins and cupboards full of buckets, supplements, and tools. Most impressive was what looked like a vetting station with every kind of bandage, spray, herbal tincture, and salve concoction you could imagine. It even had a tall refrigerator with a glass front displaying herbs like a florist, as well as racks of prescription meds. No rinky-dink operation.

Right across from Journey and BG's stall, was a little room with its door slightly ajar. Inside … chaos. I'm talking train wreck. Dirty, broken crap piled high. It didn't fit. I just shrugged and closed it up.

On my way out, a silhouette stood in the barn doorway. Prairie barked once and shuffled off wagging her tail toward the shadow. Journey grunted and reached instantly over the rail to touch me. He wasn't too sure about whoever stood at the entrance.

When the figure took a few steps out of the sun, my heart skipped right into my throat.

"I'm … glad I found you," Tate said.

Chapter 11

"You…" I choked. *Where is saliva when you need it?* "Were looking for me?"

He took off his long oilskin, flung it over a rail, and sauntered toward me. He wore an un-tucked muslin pull-over shirt. A thin string hung loosely tied at his chest, draping over flawless umber skin. His worn jeans hugged him then flared slightly at the bottom to bunch around the base of his scuffed work boots.

"I wanted to explain," he said, "why I left like I did. At the hospital."

To my surprise, his breath came quicker. His rounded shoulders sloped ever so subtly underneath the shirt.

"You don't have to explain anything to me," I offered, knowing full well he'd tell me anyway.

He hesitated. "I know I don't *have* to." He focused on the tie strings at his wrists and twiddled them in his fingers. Then he looked at me, full on. My knees wobbled. "I *want* to."

Gulp. "Okay."

Prairie flomped in the dust by a stack of hay bales then crossed her front paws and looked at him all serious, like this *better* be *good*.

He took more slow steps toward me and started talking in low buttery tones as he moved his hands with his words until he stood an arm's length away from me. Journey flung his head at Tate's shoulder shoving him to a more respectable distance.

I patted Journey softly. "Sorry. He can be a little … protective." I rubbed his star.

Tate's eyes lit up. "Ah. This must be Journey. Knight in shining armor."

"Yep."

Journey blew snot and shook his head.

"The one and only," I said. "I … think he might need some time to warm up to you."

"Not to worry," Tate said completely unabashed. "I came prepared." He shrugged his hair over his shoulder and dug a fistful of chopped carrots out of his pocket.

Impressive.

I heard Journey say, "Now we're talking," as he dove for the treats.

We both snickered at how easy he was to win over. I buried my face in his mane then kissed him smack on the nose. "Hey mister, save some for Boss Girl."

BG slung her head over the rail and looked at us expectantly. All the carrot pieces were gone, but Tate held up a finger. "Wait one moment, Madame." He reached into his back pocket, this time producing a peppermint. BG slurped it up and closed her eyes as she crunched.

Doubly impressive.

"Well, that does it," I said. "You are officially on their good side. Congratulations."

He smiled, and it made my heart flutter into the rafters with the mourning doves. But I kept my distance.

Tate gave a similar version of the story River told out at the fountain earlier. Less about Olive and Brush Tuson, however, and more about life in the Prairie Island Indian Community with Remington.

I heard the heartbreaking honesty in his voice. He held no detail back. Dead center in my chest, a less familiar reflex pinged. Once again, I found myself in uncharted emotional territory, and I didn't know if I was supposed to make a break for it or nestle in and enjoy. I'll tell you what. The latter sure seemed like a fine idea, but being conditioned the way I had been for the last several years of my jaw-locked, brow-creased life, my shoulder pinched instead.

Just listen, Gram whispered.

Instinct, however, made me casually back away. A whiff of warm breath puffed against my cheek and Journey dipped his head over my shoulder.

So there I stood. Gram on standby. My knight guarding me. Prairie watching like a hawk. I was safe.

Then I listened. Really listened. I had a feeling Tate needed to tell this story. Like to say it out loud would ease the pain he felt from it living inside him. He didn't weep or choke up or even seem to get nervous once he started. He just told his story. And I listened.

By the time he'd gotten to the part where Remington left, we found ourselves lounging on a couple hay bales. Ernie had wormed his way onto Tate's lap and sprawled out till his head hung over while Tate scratched his belly.

After a few moments of silence, I dared a question that had been nagging me for a while. "So ... what led you here? To North Dakota, I mean. To Forever Fields?"

"River and Jill Lightfoot."

"Oh?" I said surprised. I was still trying to wrap my head around the family web. Seriously, I needed a spreadsheet to keep it straight. I looked at him hard. "What about before them? How did Lenny and Griff put this place together?"

Tate dove into the story. "Those two brothers came here together years ago before a single fence post marked this land. They bought a tractor and a handful of quality broodmares and stallions with their portion of inherited land back in Grover, Minnesota. They made it great in its early years, back when I was just a kid. River and Jill used to bring me on weekends when Moon was on call. She trusted them to teach me to work hard. They made me earn my keep. I baled hay, trimmed feet, tended to the sick and old, and shoveled more manure than I thought humanly possible." He looked into the rafters, smiling, and shaking his head.

"What was this place like? Back then. Before ..." I looked around the weathered barn, "... it aged? What did they do here?"

"Bred, trained, and sold horses. Those guys were the best in the tri-state area, maybe the country. When Griff is not around, River and Alberta tell about how the two brothers worked so well together that rarely would you even hear them speaking. Just moving as one. Like they knew the other's thoughts. People would bring their prized studs and mares from all over just so they could say the Tuson Boys trained their horse. They took a special interest in gaited breeds, like your Missouri Foxtrotter, Tennessee Walkers, and Rocky Mountains."

Journey hrr hrred and blew out over our heads. We both reached up to scratch his cheeks. I had a strong suspicion that Journey had come from the workings of the Tuson Boys.

"On rare occasions, they took in a wild horse off the plains," Tate continued. "One such wild horse, they tell me, a buckskin stud named Wild Eye, they received on trade from another set of brothers out west in Linton, North Dakota. The Kuntz brothers. The founders of the Nokota breed. He was the first Nokota horse on this ranch."

Wild Eye. I tried not to show it, but my mind whirled to the photo in my back pocket. My mother on a *wild-eyed* buckskin. I'd always assumed it was a mustang, but it *had* to be the one Tate was talking about. I *sensed* it. Like my left butt cheek was tingling even.

"Really?" I tried to contain myself. "Was this Wild Eye the one to start your herd?"

124

"He was. I started working on bloodlines while I finished college."

Tate went on to tell more of Alberta's and River's stories. "Crowds would gather to watch the Tuson brothers work their magic. The finest came to Forever Fields. This place was ablaze with business for many years.

"It wasn't until the brothers had a falling out that the place began to suffer. Griff worried about becoming too commercialized and wanted to back off to keep the smalltown, personalized feel to what they did with each horse. Lenny wanted to expand, hire more hands, build more barns, put on more clinics, and charge more money. The brothers could not agree.

"Griff tried to keep the ranch going after Lenny moved back to Minnesota, but the business didn't have the same draw. The brothers were the magic. Griffin has forever resented Lenny for abandoning him and the ranch.

"River and Jill rousted Alberta and Lane to take it on. They tried to save it, though they were never able to restore it to its former glory. After time they found a new direction."

"What 'new direction'?"

"The Old Ones and Throw-Aways. Although mostly Old Ones these days."

I wanted to know more about these Old Ones and Throw-Aways, but I had a front-runner question nagging at me. It pained me like you would not believe, but I had to know, "What about Mom and Dad? Where were they? If they were all such *good friends*, (gagging) why didn't they partner too?"

Eyeing me hesitantly, he said, "I'm told they went back to Minnesota to … start a family. Fern was not one, I guess, to settle down in any one place for too long, but Peter, not being much into horses, wanted to try to make a go at farming the old homestead, so they went back."

Tate was able to give me the facts in a way that made it all just kind of make sense.

I said, "So Lenny lives in Minnesota. He sold me my truck, you know. I didn't know who he was at the time, but I could tell he and my dad were acting weird once they realized who the other was." I studied the ground. "How could they not recognize each other right away? And why keep me in the dark?"

"I would only be guessing," he said shaking his head and scratching Ernie's half ear. "But it might have something to do with your mother. I have heard them speak, River and Alberta and Griff, of how she had once stolen and broken the hearts of many." He laid a still hand on Ernie's cheek. "They tell of how she could ride the wildest horse, even Wild Eye, until it was tame. How her Lakota beauty and manner made everyone love her and envy her. She flew in and out of lives like the prairie wind sweeping over the grass and whistling through the trees. All anyone could do was smile when she was with them, cry when she was not." He paused.

Neither of us looked up for a long while. Prairie scooted over to me until she was leaning hard against my leg, Rope lay like a wet noodle across my boots.

I knew exactly what he was talking about. Riding bareback with her through Olive and Brush Tuson's meadows, she filled my life. Then she left me. And Dad. And Gram. Like it seems she did everyone she pretended to love.

"That figures," I said as though it didn't bug me one bit that she abandoned us. Like it was no big deal that she left during the most fragile years of my life, when a girl needs her mom to teach her things that a dad or Gram just can't.

Tate looked at me.

"You don't have to feel sorry for me," I said more bitterly than planned and sort of unladylike scrambled to my feet. "Actually, it makes total sense that Dad didn't want to have anything to do with things that

126

reminded him of her." I stroked Prairie's head and looked into her amber eyes for strength.

At that moment, a tremendous clanging dinner bell pierced the air.

"Time to go," I said.

He repeated, "Time to go."

Neither of us moved.

"I'd better get home." He blinked.

"Yah. Of course. You better go."

As he walked away, I reached for Journey's star. *Okay?* he asked me. I held his cheeks in my hands. We both closed our eyes for a moment then I kissed his eyelid to thank him for watching over me.

I whispered, "As long as I've got you."

He exhaled deeply with a nostril flutter. *Always,* he said.

From the corner of my eye I saw Tate had stopped at the barn door. He'd been watching me.

"There you are!" Aunt Bert came tromping up. She crossed her arms and studied us. I heard an unmistakable brightness in her voice. "I thought that was Kala ..." I swear she was stifling a giggle. "...hanging out by Boss Girl. Will you be joining us for supper, Tate?"

Though I still focused on rubbing Journey's forehead, I felt Tate's eyes peel away from me. "No. No I don't want to impose. I was ..." His voice returned toward me. "... just leaving."

"Really?" She sounded truly disappointed. "Where's Kola?"

"Home, watching over our new little one. He wants to protect little Oka Wana Gi."

"Oh!" Aunt Bert clapped her hands. "How is our little medicine hat Ghost Song doing?"

Tate smiled as he reached for his oilskin drover coat, "She is the most beautiful foal I have ever seen, Alberta." The pride in his eyes warmed my heart which fluttered toward him. "She is the one we have been waiting for. I feel it in my bones."

"The luck of the medicine hat," Aunt Bert said. A mourning dove's coo filled the rafters. "Please stay for supper, Tate. I know you do love Baker Bob's spaghetti. Kola has things under control. I'd trust that wolf dog more than most humans!" She laughed, but I knew she meant it. I was glad to see her in such good spirits.

Tate must have been thinking similar thoughts. "How are you doing, Alberta?" He paused and looked down. "I know how horrible my brother can be." He kept his head down and his voice attempted to mute the shame. "I ... apologize for leaving. I should have done someth-"

"Nonsense, Tate Maycomb. Nonsense! The day Alberta Greene can't take on a wormy little weasel like Remington Stone is the day you'll be shoving her six feet into the dirt."

Tate and I looked at each other surprised then grinned. He said relieved, "Alright, Alberta. I hear you."

"Besides," she continued, "I just had to sort through a few things for a minute. Trust me, I believe I did indeed devise one ingenious plan up there in my stuffy little office. I did. Now I'm just itching to let you all in on it too." She waved us in.

Tate didn't follow her, however. I hated seeing each arm slide into his coat sleeves.

Bert thumped both her hands onto her tiny hips. "Now take off that damn coat and both of you get your rears into the house for a decent meal. Lord in Heaven knows we could all use some family time after such a day. Just think how cheesed Griffin would be if he knew how late we are getting to supper!"

Tate looked at me. I shuffled my toe in the dirt and bit the side of my lip trying not to grovel and beg him to stay. Then those almond eyes of his smiled gently. "Alright. For Griff's sake."

"That's more like it! Just wait till you hear my brilliant idea."

128

In the sup deck, with mountains of steaming whole wheat spaghetti and turkey meatballs on our plates, Aunt Bert offered a hand to Baker Bob on her right and Knut on her left. "Let's all just take a moment before we dig in."

Knut took my hand like no big deal then dunked his head down and closed his eyes. I'm not sure why, but I got a little nervous and glanced around the table. Butterflies pinged around in my stomach while I looked across to Baker Bob and River joining hands, and then River and Heath, and then Heath and Henry, and then Henry reached across the table for Tate's hand. All heads bowed in silence. All but mine.

Tate's hand, soft and warm, brushed against my forearm. A flurry of delicate wings twirled inside me. I felt his fingers glide smoothly, yet with a hint of hesitation, to work their way into my hand, which I had already instinctually clenched into a fist atop the duct tape on my bouncing thigh. I closed my eyes and let him to take my hand.

I expected someone to start saying grace like Gram had made us do on Sundays and holidays, but no one said a thing. Silence permeated the room. I just sat thinking about everything that had happened since I'd arrived.

I'd discovered a family I never knew existed. I had a job that made me feel like I could earn my keep. Still, I felt I had more to offer, I just didn't know what. Something that really mattered. It whispered indiscernibly in the far reaches of my mind.

Tiwahe. (Thee WAH hay.)
Gram?
Tanké (Thahn KAY).
Definitely not Gram.

Hunka (HOON kah). Cuwé (Choo WAY). Tiblo (TEE bə lo). Ciyé (Chee YAY). Misuŋka (Miss OON kah).

The ice in our water glasses started jingling. Then the floorboards beneath our feet started vibrating. The wall of windows looking onto the north prairie pasture started rattling. Even the antique chandelier clacked above us. I felt Tate squeeze my hand. It made me look up.

What's going on? I only thought the words, but my expression must have said it loud and clear because he lit a breath-taking smile and turned to the windows.

Everyone half-stood at their seats to look outside. Knut let out a squeal and leaped from his chair to press his nose right up to the glass. The rumbling grew louder like a constant thunder. That's when I knew. My skin tingled from scalp to toes. The Nokota were coming!

I thought briefly that they would be old hat for those living here. These guys probably got to see the herd all the time. But you would have guessed it was the first time for everyone the way they peered out the windows like kids waiting for Santa.

Heath shouted out, "They're on the move!" His blue eyes sparkled.

River put a sturdy hand on his shoulder.

Bob said, "Why, Tate. You never told us we'd be getting a dinner show!"

Tate laughed, "I guess they missed me when I didn't come home."

Knut cheered, "They're coming to find you, Tate! They're looking for you!"

The rumbling grew.

"Who do you suppose'll be leading that pack of homely plugs today, Aunt Bert?" Henry asked rubbing his meaty hands together.

"I don't know, Henry," she answered slyly. "How much you willing to put up?"

Tate playfully spoiled their fun. "Sorry you two. I penned Mazaska this morning."

Bert and Henry moaned.

Silverware tinked against the plates. Vibrations worked up through my insides.

To my surprise, Tate grasped both my arms like he had the most exciting news EVER. He paused only but a moment while we locked eyes, and then he said, as though royalty was about to enter the room, "Miss Paisley Alberta Noon, I would like to formally introduce you to ..." He paused a second longer and turned me slowly until I faced directly out the sup deck's wall of windows — a front row seat. "... *the* mightiest of all stallions that ever did grace the prairie plains."

The thundering hooves pounded a drum roll. I thought they might trample the farmhouse.

Knut's voice cracked, "Here they come!"

Tate flung his arms wide, "Direct descendant of Sitting Bull's war ponies ... Grandson to the great Wild-Eye ... Smoke. N. Ash!"

Call it crazy or whatever you want, but everyone in the room, myself included, applauded as the herd bounded out of the western tree line and into open prairie. Smoke-N-Ash flung his gray head, his mane and tail whipping in the wind like the flags of a pirate ship. His war cry resounded over the deafening thunder. The last bits of sunset glistened over his metallic body making him look made of steel rather than flesh and blood. His band pounded behind him obeying his every command. Their thick necks and muscled frames drifted gracefully in rhythm as they came into view.

My own two horses pranced in their pen to the east making such a fuss I thought they might bust out to join the wild herd. Journey fox-trotted and showed-off, his head and tail high, whinnying for all he was worth. I laughed out loud imagining my legs wrapped around him, a fistful of bronze mane, flying out to meet them, clumps of dirt sailing behind us as we floated with their every move. Even Boss Girl reprised her ancient desert bloodline, arching her neck, flicking her feet and tail, auditioning to be the newest member of Smoke-N-Ash's harem. They were *all* beautiful. *All* perfect in their own unique ways. But the haunting voices hissing in my mind told me the Nokota were different.

My mind attempted to slow the scene down, and I honed in on a few at a time, taking note of every detail. The generous-sized heads with tiny hooks on the tips of their ears. Their low-set tails. Sturdy, thick-boned legs, square quarters, and feathered feet. Perfectly designed to charge up the steepest valleys and endure the roughest terrains. It whispered, *Nokota.*

Smoke-N-Ash turned his herd away from us in a wide, sweeping circle, only to come barreling back down the slope heading directly toward the house. My mind swept to my dreams. Circling. Circling. Circling me. I closed my eyes and found myself in the field with them, standing in the center of their circle, breathing deeply. The prairie winds lifted me off my feet. It released my dishwater hair from its ponytail and blew sunrays into each thickened strand until it glowed like spun silk. They whispered to me again, calling. *Nokota.* They needed me. *Nokota.*

All fell silent. I opened my eyes and realized I'd said their name aloud. The herd stood less than a hundred yards away, heads down and grazing peacefully. Everyone at the table had already returned to their seats and stared at me with knowing eyes. My breath came quickly, and I felt my face flood red. A ponytail band hung from my fingers.

I crawled back to my spot at the table and put my hair back up. Aunt Alberta's voice washed over me helping me force back the embarrassed tears. "It's okay, honey."

Oh if they would all just quit looking at me.

"They speak to us *all* at times, Paisley."

I quickly looked at her. How did she know?

But did they hear the voices *every* night? And get swept into a wispy circle of faces and horses? Or were these dreams specially reserved for teenaged girls *losing it*?

"We are lucky to still have conversations with them. We're their hope, Paisley," River tried to explain. "The Nokota is a lost breed. They depend on us to bring them back. To help them thrive again like they once did in the days of great Chief Sitting Bull of the Lakota Sioux and his favorite war pony Fear His Shadow. So few remain." He nodded out the windows. "This herd of Tate's holds some of the strongest blood from the original horses of the late 1800s. They are as pure as the laws of nature will allow. History runs deep within their veins."

Tate concluded, "It's up to us to make sure they have a future."

I looked at Aunt Bert. "Forever Fields isn't just a retirement home, is it?"

She smiled tenderly at Tate and twirled spaghetti onto her fork. "Not anymore."

Everyone chortled and kept eating, but Tate went on, "But the Old Ones are just as special in our eyes."

Everyone nodded.

"They have lived a life of hard work and dedication to a master who believes they have earned a rest."

River summed it all up. "We provide peace at Forever Fields."

Aunt Alberta added, "On a rarer occasion, we take in a problem horse or a sick one from the auctions — a Throw-Away. We rehabilitate those and show them how to partner with humans again. Then we help them find the right person to take them home."

Like what Great Uncle Griff and Lenny did, I thought.

Heath slurped up a noodle and smiled with spaghetti sauce on his chin. "We won't give up on them."

"In fact," Henry went on, "we got a client coming soon to drop off a retired racehorse, and a gal's coming tomorrow to take a look at the pony Knut's been working with. Right, my man?"

"Yep," Knut said and stuffed his mouth. "She bites."

I had a hard time finding my words. The people around this table had hearts so huge they clearly sacrificed much for paychecks in order to make it all possible. I was a part of it now.

We all had a gift. We *belonged* here. For the Nokota. For the Old Ones who deserved a peaceful resting place, or for those who had not yet found their place in the world. And something deeper told me ... *Hunka. Cuwé. Tiblo* ... my part was bigger than I knew.

Suddenly, Aunt Alberta put her fork down and announced, "Well, lady and gentlemen," she sent me a wink, "I've made a decision."

Chewing stopped.

Baker Bob asked, "Oh really now? What is it?"

"Well," she started, "in light of recent events," she paused and shook her head, "and seeing how this farm just *cannot* handle losing such a valuable worker as Griffin," she swallowed, "I decided to ask Lenard to move up here and help out a bit."

Forks and knives clinked onto plates. No one moved. I shot Tate a curious look. He cocked an eyebrow.

Perturbed, she poked her fork at River and Bob, "Oh *come on*. Like you two didn't think about it at all? Who else do you suppose could work with a horse as well as Griffin can?"

I saw a vein in Henry's neck as he started, "But he ..."

"But. He. *Nothing*. That was a long time ago."

134

Heath just looked down at his plate.

Silence.

"She's right," said River. "It's a good idea." He raised his glass to toast.

Bob followed suit. "Agreed. Let bygones be bygones."

Tate said, "I would truly enjoy having Lenny around again. I've missed the old Cayuse."

Knut threw up his glass spilling a little and said, "Me too! Great Uncle Lenny belongs here just as much as any of us. I like his stories."

They all murmured consent, especially having heard it from Knut, I think. He had a way of saying such difficult things so simply. I took a good guess that the drama they alluded to was what Tate had told me in the barn about Lenny abandoning the ranch ... and his brother.

Being a somewhat impartial party, I raised my glass too. "I agree. I knew the first time I met him a couple years ago, when we sat on Oscar's tailgate and split a Baby Ruth candy bar ..." When I saw smiles and nods, I finished, "... I had this strange feeling I'd see him again. Like his part in my story wasn't done yet." I swallowed then added, "He *needs* to be here."

That was quite a speech for me, but it just burst out like I'd been talking to these people all my life. No sweat. I think I turned a corner that night. Of course I knew I might end up hair-pinning around as soon as the road got rocky, but right then, I let some confidence settle in and make itself at home.

I lifted my glass higher and eye-balled Heath and Henry. I didn't care about the drama. "To Lenny. And Forever Fields," I toasted, and it seemed to spark a fire.

"To Griff," toasted Henry. "May he make a speedy recovery and get back to griping at us. And ... may he not kill his brother when he gets here."

Knut wanted in on the fun. "To my new cousin!" He nudged me with his shoulder and looked down at me goofily through his thick glasses and curlicue bangs. I chuckled.

"To possibilities and grand ideas," said Heath nodding to Aunt Bert, but I wondered if he was also referring to his and Henry's secret contraption hiding in the back of the machine shed.

"To Smoke-N-Ash and his prodigy," toasted Aunt Bert as she nodded to Tate.

He replied, "To the Nokota."

River's voice rolled like water as he toasted simply, "To family."

Summer

Lakota: Bloketu

It is observed that in any great endeavor, it is not

enough for a person to depend solely on himself.

~ Lakota Proverb

Chapter 12

Great Uncle Lenny said yes in a heartbeat to Bert's request. Clearly, he harbored no hard feelings about the falling out so many years ago. But he had several clients in Minnesota he needed to finish up with before he could just leave for who knew how long. Turns out Lenny never quit working with horses, which I had a hard time picturing since the old man who'd sold me Oscar had seemed kind of worn out. But I *also* remember, like it was yesterday, his spry attitude — sharp as a tack.

Griff had no say in the matter as far as Alberta was concerned. So when he came home from the hospital and found out that his no-count-low-down-good-for-nothing-abandoning brother would be coming to the ranch in a few weeks, all he could do was frump around and stew on the rickety front porch of his bunkhouse amidst his hanging socks and wood carvings. It kind of made me nervous to watch — even from the safety of the fenced in yard — him leaning back in a beat up rocking chair, scraping at stick after stick with one of the knives from the glinting collection stuck into the railing. Curled up wood shavings spat out over his propped up bare feet.

"He'll come around," everyone assured me at one point or another. "He always does."

Hmph. I'll believe it when I see it.

Spring took off down the road like a hornet bit it in the butt, and summer came charging in like a herd of red buffalo. When I lived in Grover, I remember *easing* into the heat of summer. By the time my birthday rolled around on July fourth, the lakes were finally warm. But at this ranch in Sheldon? Heat swept in with a haze over the prairie slopes by mid-June. And though the instant warmth made the perennials in my garden pop, weeds came with them.

I'd gotten the Lily of the Valley underneath the porch cleaned out right away so they could stretch and get some air. For a couple of short weeks, their perfumes transformed my workspace into one of those hoity-toity health spas you see in the movies. It only needed some robed rich people lying around with cucumbers on their eyelids and some hot, shirtless guys offering to rub oil all over you at the snap of your fingers. Toss in some lofty harp music plus a babbling brook and ... voila ... you got yourself a million-dollar money maker right in the middle of Nowhere, North Dakota. Okay, I didn't plan to propose the idea to Aunt Bert, but I did resolve to get the driveway's fountain working somehow. In the meantime, a symphony of chickadees, whinnies, and an occasional crow or hawk flying overhead accompanied me.

Along the far west line of the iron fence, I discovered daylily spikes poking out of the matted mess. Daylily fronds would make a nice border over there with happy orange faces reaching toward the sun.

Once I got that line cleared, I discovered wild chokecherry bushes on the other side of the fence just before the cottonwood shelter belt. I had a perfect view of where the Nokota run, which made me think about Tate. Often. But trust me. I was not about to go all batty eyelashes. Nope. Not me. Paisley Alberta Noon has much more self-respect than that. Never mind the flutters in my chest every time he looked at me or I heard his name.

Eventually, I turned to the north fence. Blocking the view to the north pasture, stood the mangled crabapple tree said to produce like no other, according to Tate. He had pointed out how much work it needed. Wild vines threatened to choke the few blossoms trying to peek out of the branches, so I carefully snipped and unwound the gnarled mess, taking every precaution not to mar the bark. Before I knew it, a perfect little tree emerged, clean and unscathed. I'd given it a chance to thrive again.

The garden had a ways to go before I would consider it finished, but Saint Francis of Assisi smiled in the sun which now reached his stony face as he fed chickadees from his basket.

One morning while I worked on the flagstone paths, I heard a phone ring inside the house. It came from the opened window of the upstairs room, which I assumed was Aunt Bert's little office. I didn't *try* to eavesdrop, but I couldn't help it, especially when I heard Dad's name.

Aunt Bert's voice started out bright. "Peter! How are you, baby brother?"

I dropped my tools. Frozen as though if I moved, she'd know I could hear her. I knew Dad had somehow planned for me to end up here, but I didn't understand it all.

"Yes, she made it right on schedule … yep … Hardly a scratch on her … just messing with you, Peter … no … She's fine."

Dad was checking on me. Suddenly, I felt a pinprick of guilt for leaving him the way I did. And I kind of wanted to run up there and ask to talk to him, to tell him all about Forever Fields and the people and the horses. But then a dark cloud crossed over the sun and darkened my thoughts as well ... he *wanted* me here. He and his precious Cindy planted that fake help wanted ad and obviously told Aunt Bert they were sending me to live with her. Plus, he knew about all these people — *my family* — and never said so much as a word about any of them. The thought was enough to erase my guilt, so I stayed put and listened in.

"... of course ... very useful."

Seriously Dad? You thought I'd get here and be a slouch? I thought he knew me better.

"No, no, no, don't worry about that. I figured it out soon enough."

Ah ha! Confession.

"Maybe you should tell her yourself ... You sure?"

I did not want to talk to him. Not now. Maybe not ever.

Her tone deflated slightly. "Okay ... yes you're probably right ... yep ... time will do the trick, I'm sure. You know, Peter, you are still welcome to ... Oh. I see ... But I thought maybe for her birthday ... Alright then ... yes, perhaps that'd be best."

Almost imperceptibly, I felt my heart sink. This would be the first time I'd celebrate my birthday without him. It's not like we ever did anything too special. No kiddy pizza parties or sleepovers. That's never been my thing. Besides, landing on a holiday usually meant everyone else in the world was busy with their own deal. Dad just made balloon-shaped pancakes for breakfast, took me to the Grover Fourth of July parade, and watched fireworks on the beach afterward. Even after Mom left and Gram died. But I frowned at myself for caring if he ever came to visit. I'd found the yin to my yang. My emptiness filled up more and more each day. This was my home now. This was my family.

I would be eighteen — an adult — this July fourth. I told myself Peter Noon had no place in my story anymore. He and his wife were a blurred chapter of my past now. With a little more time, they would be completely erased chapters. My stomach lurched.

Right, Gram's sarcasm echoed in my ears, *good luck keepin' that lie up for long.*

I swallowed a lump in my throat, ignored her, and went back to work.

* * *

Every morning, Tate rode down The Drive on Little Feather with Kola padding at their side. Prairie and Rope ran out to greet them then she and the wolf dog went romping off into the woods while I took a break with Tate on what we now called "Our Swing" next to Saint Francis.

"This garden," he said to me one morning, "already has new life. The transformation you have made is impressive." He swept a stray lock of hair behind my ear. I couldn't help but wonder if the transformation he referred to was that of the garden … or of me.

In the few short weeks I'd been here, I not only felt a change in myself, but I saw it too. In the mirror my hazel eyes gleamed greener than I'd ever noticed before. My hair grew thicker, making it so I only had to twist a band two times instead of three or four. My skin took on a sort of biscuit tone offsetting my hair which now had sunny, flaxen streaks running through it. I felt myself stretch and tone daily as I worked in the garden and kept up Journey's and BG's paddock behind my bunkhouse. I pitched in wherever anyone needed me, especially since we were short a hand, what with Griff laid up most of the day and Lenny still on his way.

Right after lunch, I would help Aunt Bert in the vegetable garden just beyond the sup deck. She had a nice open space where the Nokota swung by now and then. I helped her put in rows and rows of every produce Baker Bob requested. Potatoes, peppers, tomatoes, peas, corn, squash, onions, lettuce. You name it. Even though the sky hadn't so much as spat on us since early June, and we maintained a diligent watering routine using the artisan well, I had a feeling our fall harvest would rival any big city farmers' market.

In the late afternoon after the most intense heat from the sun started to drop off, River would call me and the guys over behind the horse barn. I used Oscar to haul hay bales and water tanks back and forth from the pastures to the barns. That old truck never skipped a beat. The dirtier he got, the better he ran.

All in all, Forever Fields cared for somewhere around thirty head. I counted the Old Ones, our own using horses, plus the *Not Yets*. That's my new name for the Throw Aways. I cringed *every time* I heard that term. They just hadn't found their place yet.

I quickly learned names as I discovered which horses were friendly and which ones needed time to warm up to me. Take Jimmy Not Yet for example. He was a sixteen hand, blood bay American Saddlebred who had once spent his days dancing around a dressage arena with a spoiled brat, daddy's little princess propped up on his back until he tore a ligament in his hind leg. She sent him off to auction quicker than you can say Snot Nose. Jimmy had a bad attitude. But he healed quick enough with River's herbal poultice concoctions and slow-and-steady rehab routine. Now Jimmy could out-maneuver all of us like nobody's business with those fancy steps of his. River said he'd be back to winning ribbons in no time. The hardest part would be finding Jimmy the right home. He seemed pretty jaded. We would grill anyone interested in him, make sure they'd be a good fit.

River told me one day, "I promise each Not Yet a forever family. If I can't find the right someone for Jimmy, then he will dance the days away in our meadows until I do."

This is how it was for *every single* horse on the ranch.

Methuselah, the chocolate Rocky Mountain horse with the flaxen mane and tail, was Aunt Bert's first horse at Forever Fields. The day she hauled him home from auction, he became her go-to horse. River says a horse will live longer, and with a better quality of life, if they feel they are of use to someone they love. I'd say it worked for old Thusie. He was thirty-five years old. Aunt Bert fed, groomed, and blanketed him herself every evening. Like a ritual.

Once in a while, we'd get a call asking if we could take a horse for one reason or another. Rumor has it Bert never turns anyone away. Even the little Shetland pony with the bushiest, rattiest mane and tail you ever did see. And as Knut said, she bites. Everyone. Her owners had bought her for their kids to ride around on in the yard a few summers back, but no one could get near enough to tack her up, so they called Forever Fields. Knut is on a mission to clean that little pony up, teach her some manners, and find her a little human buddy.

I worked hard to learn their stories. Heath and Henry showed me which ones needed special feed and which ones needed certain supplements or medicines or leg treatments. From shots to shoeing, those twins had a way of making anything fun, so it was easy to learn.

Journey took to rounding up horses like a born-and-bred cow horse, which he *so* was not. But oh did he love the action. Anyone could see the glint in his eye as I saddled him up and put him to work. He'd kick up a dust storm prancing out to the pastures

143

glistening like a copper penny, all full of himself, and then he'd dig in like a pro, snorting and spinning while we rustled up whichever cluster River needed. I clung to him like a starfish and zigged and zagged with his every move, sweat trickling down my neck and back. Above the wind in my ears, I heard him whinny, "YeeeHaww!" I laughed out loud as we whipped around scrambling to get our job done.

Sometimes Tate would come over with Little Feather to help out. My heart sang racing around the fields with him. He laughed at our not-so-textbook maneuvers. I refused to think what I must have looked like out there, all sweaty and caked with dust. But we didn't care, Journey and me. We lit on fire doing our thing.

Prairie bolted around the pens making the horses stay right where they were supposed to. Tongue lolling, she took to ranch life just as I'd expected. Perfectly. In fact, between the attention she got and having an actual job that honed in on every DNA molecule in her scruffy little border collie body, I'd say Prairie came darned close to being the happiest dog on the planet. Horse apples and trough water were just bonuses.

Ernie, on the other hand, could often be found "supervising" (with his *one* eye, mind you) the goings-on from atop the one corner post that stood in the shade of a box elder tree. I'm pretty sure one time I heard him say, "Carry on, worker bees. Fine job. Carry on." Then he jumped down and licked himself.

Knut introduced me to his ornery goat he named Flash Goaton (oy), and a little flock of ducklings. Plus, Aunt Bert had made good on her promise to get him a box full of kittens. They kept him pretty busy, so I pitched in when I could. We made a kind of jungle gym that allowed them to get pretty much anywhere in the barn. For the ducks, we created an entire water park consisting of garage sale plastic swimming pools, Clementine boxes, and Slip N Slides. Heath

144

and Henry even helped us rig up a misting system to keep them cool and dust-free.

One day while Knut and I sat on straw bales playing superhero, while the kittens crawled all over us, I marveled at the fact that I had once, not so many days ago, considered him a strange and annoying twerp. Outside his barn, Knut looked like he didn't know if his arms and legs were coming or going, but inside, he knew exactly how to handle those animals, like they were the part of him that gave him control over the rest of his body ... and his mind. He fascinated me. So much, in fact, that I found myself making excuses to "help" him. He didn't need help.

The only place I most definitely was *not* welcome was the machine shed. If I ever so much as stepped one pinky toe too close to that place, Heath and Henry chased me off. Which was fine by me. They had that place locked up tighter than a nuclear weapons plant, probably booby-trapped to the hilt.

I asked Baker Bob one morning while I helped peel hard boiled eggs in the kitchen, "What do you suppose those twins have cooking up out there?"

"Ohhh," he let out a deep breath, "I imagine they're working on a contraption that'll one day save the world." He gave a hearty laugh at the idea.

Suppertime was my favorite meal. River seemed to make a habit of *needing* Tate to stick around late enough most days so that Aunt Bert would insist he stay to eat. *Those two.* And Baker Bob! I tell you. But I didn't find myself interfering with their little shenanigans since it always resulted in more time with Tate. I didn't see him putting up a fight either.

Each night, I sat in my little bunkhouse at my desk and pulled out the stationery Aunt Bert had given me. I tried to make sense of my feelings. Sometimes it cleared my head, and other times it left me more confused. More often the latter. Not only did Tate defy the things I knew about guys, he broke all my rules on friendship too. No amount of flowery paper or sea foam green ink could work it out for me (though I'm sure Miss Floral Daze Home Wrecker Cindy would beg to differ).

While Prairie slipped into her nightly coma and Ernie curled up on my lap, I wrote. I had to lay Mom's picture face down for the most nights. I'd learned maybe too much about her and the past lately. I just didn't feel like facing her and dealing with that mess. So with Gram to my right, reading every word from her portrait by the dim light of the desk lamp, I wrote about everything I could remember. I made notes about the flowers I discovered in the garden, brainstormed ideas to get the fountain going again, and logged the names and descriptions of each horse I'd met. I recorded quotes someone said that day. I drew pictures of the place and portraits of my family.

I worked my butt off to carry my weight, but I still got the feeling I had something more. It worried me.

While I wrote, I listened to the comforting sounds of low, muffled voices from the bunkhouse next door, but some nights (the nights when Griff went to bed early two cabins down) — he made me nervous) I followed the faint trail of pipe smoke and joined River, Tate, and the twins on their porch next door. A cacophony of crickets and frogs pierced the misty darkness while they told me stories of days-gone-by, often stories of Griff and Lenny, how magical they were with horses. How they anticipated each other's moves without words. How they could gentle a colt in minutes.

"Mind you," River said, "they had their struggles too, but I'll be hard pressed to think of a time they didn't come through in the end."

We sat in quiet, and then I asked the question I knew everyone was thinking. "How's it going to work? You know, when Lenny gets here? I mean Great Uncle Griff won't even sit on the porch with us because we might start talking about the old days."

NOKOTA® RANCH

the largest and oldest

herd of Nokotas®

in the World

Nokota® Horse

The Nokota horse is the native horse of North America with immense history and regal presence.
They are a distinct breed, with superior health and emotional intelligence.
Frank Kuntz and his late brother Leo Kuntz have been managing this feral herd of native horses, which they carefully acquired from Theodore Roosevelt National Park during the removal in the mid-70's , before they introduced domestic breeds and have bred and created a pedigree for over 40 years.

Henry added, "I wonder where Lenny's going to sleep. Crammed in here with us?"

Heath offered, "We could clean out the old tack room and shove all that junk in the Quonset. Or he could have the room across from Bob downstairs in the big house."

River thought a while. "I don't know the details, but it'll work out once he get's here."

"I can't wait to see him," I said. "I want him to tell me all about the old days."

Tate looked concerned and drew his feet in from off the railing. "You know, your Great Uncle Griff is a really good storyteller. He just takes extra care deciding who gets to listen. I'll bet, Paisley Noon, he would like to tell you a few things if you gave him a chance."

I looked at him like he'd sprouted antlers. "Are you kidding? Griff can't *stand* me. Seriously, I swear the man growls when I walk by."

Heath said, "He's a surly one alright, but he has his moments. Ay, Henry?"

"That's a good man, P," Henry said leaning forward to look me in the eye. "You could learn a lot from him."

Okay. Was it just me, or did it seem like they were ganging up on me? Because *oh* that is *so not* cool. Cornering Paisley Alberta Noon never ended well for anyone involved. I mean, *come on*. Were we talking about the same person? You know … Griffin Tuson? Mr. Crabby Appleton himself? Skepticism ground a scowl into my brow while the rest of me prepared to pounce on the next poor soul to speak.

Just as I was about to snap some retort, River's voice floated on the night air. He spoke to no one in particular and stared out into the misty darkness. With it came smooth strains of comfort that calmed me like a gentle hand on my shoulder telling me … listen.

"Grandmother, Grandfather," he said, "Your words taught me, inspired me, but your actions showed me the way." Slowly he spoke. "Grandmother, Grandfather, you lived your lives, winning, losing, laughing, and crying. You earned your wisdom. Help me be like you."

All five of us sat in silence listening to the frogs chirruping. I didn't know what to do, what to say. So I thought about the words.

Finally, Tate explained. "We Lakota have a strong culture because our grandparents, great-grandparents, and great-great grandparents persisted in their quiet ways. They preserved the essence of what we are. If we choose, we can see them walking with us, riding with us."

River added, "Having Griffin still with us in the flesh is an honor."

The words made me feel very small. Chopped me down to size like I knew I deserved. Still, I didn't envision a heart-to-heart story-time with Uncle Griff any time soon.

* * *

The morning of July fourth, I celebrated my own Independence Day at five AM with my horses, cat, and dog. My eighteenth birthday. Official adult now. But as I sat on the edge of the water trough watching the dew glisten in the paddock ... I didn't feel different. Journey and BG munched on the oats-and-molasses treats I made with Baker Bob, Ernie hunched over a full can of tuna, and Prairie lay in the grass with a meaty bone I swiped from yesterday's roast. In the neighboring paddocks, I saw River's paint Jesse, Heath and Henry's matching bay quarter horses Edison and Einstein, plus Griff's little red roan Nokota named Bullet. They all stuck their heads over the fence and whinnied. They wanted in on our little party.

I smiled and looked up at the sky. Popcorn clouds drifted in slowly from the west meeting the early sunrise with hues of pink and orange. Warm, quiet mornings like this always set my head to daydreaming.

Part of me missed my dad, and I dared to wonder if he was thinking of me. This day had been the only day I could count on to be the same *every* year. No matter what. Up till now. The thought formed a lump in my throat.

You're finally grown up, just like you always wanted.

"Yah. I guess. Doesn't feel that different. Actually, it feels kind of weird, not being with Dad and all," I whispered.

But you wanted this, remember?

"Sure. Of course." I shook off any lingering childhood sentiments.

Get a move on, Gram commanded.

I couldn't help noticing the extra insensitivity in her tone, but I shrugged it off as *just Gram* and made my way to the sup deck.

As soon as I walked down the hall to the kitchen, I could see the lights were off and something glowed. Then I heard it. And it stopped me in my tracks.

A chorus singing. Bad singing. But really, *really* beautiful singing.

"Happy birthday to you…" they all chimed.

Baker Bob stood in the middle holding a plateful of balloon-shaped pancakes with a candle stuck in them. Everyone else, Bert, River, Knut, Heath, Henry, even Griff stood around the flickering light and sang to me. Goosebumps tingled up my arms, and I was thankful for the dim lighting since I could feel my face blushing crimson.

Happy Birthday, Paisley, Gram said tenderly. She knew all along.

Aunt Bert hugged me close, and I whispered, "How did you know?"

She squeezed me. "I have my ways."

* * *

Aunt Bert asked me kind of out of the blue, "What say, Paisley, you and I go into Valley City today and do us a little shopping?"

With a mouthful I managed, "Wha- fo-?" I assumed she needed help picking out some annuals or barn supplies from the tack store.

"Well..."

She shoved her hash browns around on her plate.

"... I just thought it might be nice to spend a little girl time together. A birthday treat."

Everyone at the table stopped with raised eyebrows. Naturally, I heard snorts escape Heath and Henry as they choked on some genius remark. My face radiated heat.

Baker Bob cut them off though. "I think that sounds like a lovely idea, Berta. It'll do you two some good to get away from all this testosterone for an afternoon."

"That's precisely what I was thinking, Robert," she said with sass. "Besides, the way I figure it, once Lenard gets here ..."

Griff clanked his fork and knife on his plate and growled just like he did *every* time anyone mentioned Lenny.

Bert continued with aplomb. "Once *Lenard* gets here, we probably won't have much time to ourselves, you know?" She paused and took a bite, craftily avoiding eye contact for just a second. Then, like she couldn't contain herself anymore, she zeroed in and poked her fork at me. "And blast it, honey. I can't sit by one more day watching you go about your business with those duct taped jeans and ratty t-shirts. You're just too beautiful a girl for that."

My hand swept straight for the duct tape on my paisley jeans, and I about wanted to go crawl in a hole.

150

"But I ..." was all that came out. And though I really wanted to get all up in arms over the thought of someone taking my favorite pants away, *or* the fact that I'm pretty sure she just indirectly insulted my sense of style, deep down I knew it was true.

Knut asked innocently, "What's wrong with her pants?"

Thank. You. Kah-nut. Though he was probably the last person who should be dishing fashion advice. Today's ensemble? Green jeans showing off his ankles and an orange Flash Gordon t-shirt.

River tried, "Maybe you ladies could go and pamper yourselves at that new fancy salon or something." He kept on eating like this was a perfectly normal conversation for him. "Get your hair done up or your fingernails clipped."

Bless him for trying. I decided to put him out of his misery. "No thanks. I'm fine. I'd be happy to help you finish weeding that row of raspberries, though."

Clanking silverware amplified the awkward silence.

Then my aunt turned briskly to Baker Bob and asked, "Say Robert, didn't you say you happened to come across a flyer at the grocery store just the other day for the Twenty-Fifth Annual Sheldon Summer Shindig?" I swear she sounded like she'd rehearsed this very line.

Then Baker Bob leapt out of his chair and bounded to the fridge to grab a flyer. "Why yes, Alberta. Yes, I did. Look at right here." It was like watching a bad high school play. "And wouldn't you know it? It's tonight. Complete with a horse show, dance, and fireworks!"

My heart slid right up my windpipe. My *God* did that sound fun. *Must not let on.*

"Sweeeeet!" Heath and Henry high-fived, pumped, clearly not in on the act.

"Oh no," Knut grumbled. "Dances are dumb." I wasn't convinced he meant it.

"Shindig?" I swallowed. "Tonight?" I reiterated the obvious just to mute my excitement.

"Yep. Tonight. See?" Bob held up the flyer and pointed to the date and time. "Right there. Starts at seven o' clock, on the dot."

I drew in a deep breath, closed my eyes, and slumped against the back of my chair. Even though it sounded like fun, I wouldn't know anyone. My mix-and-mingle skills stink. I felt my head shaking side to side.

But when I barely opened my mouth to say, "No way," Aunt Bert asked like a happy goldfinch, "River, didn't you say Tate would be attending too?"

"Yes ma'am. You know it's his favorite event of the summer."

Damn. They were good.

Chapter 13

"Welcome to the Ahhhh Spa. May I spritz you?" breathed a black-haired waif at the door.

Here we go.

"Yes, you certainly may, dear," said Aunt Bert as she yanked up my sleeve for a misting of offensive perfume. She got herself a shot and we were escorted through a long, dimly lit entrance past flickering candles, watery vista murals, and stone sculptures — all to the tune of some lilting Zen music. Our hostess drifted vapor-like a few feet ahead.

"Are you sure we really need this, Berta?" I asked. I *so* did not sign up for this.

"Oh, it'll be good for us," she replied in her typical no-nonsense way. "It's easy to forget to take care of yourself when you live on the farm. No excuses today."

She grabbed my hand and smiled like the sun. I couldn't possibly have argued. And though I dreaded every second of the poking and prodding and staring and glaring once anyone caught sight of all my flaws (not to mention the disaster I knew clothes shopping would be), I could tell Aunt Bert really did want this for me. I could tell this day wasn't just about shopping and massages or manicures. She and I had the whole day to ourselves, just the two of us, and I have to admit, that gave me reason to smile back.

Waif lady stopped us at a mini-bar next to a burbling fountain. "May I interest you in our mint and rosemary infused ice water with cucumber and lemon?"

153

Aunt Bert, clearly up for anything, answered for us both, "That sounds lovely."

We continued down the hall to a shadowy sitting room with big, squishy chairs. The room sported a bamboo garden in a sandbox complete with boulders and a couple of straight rakes. Ten bonsai trees with little scissors next to them lined a ledge the length of the room. Faded memories of my mother flickered in and out of my mind. She would have dug this. I think the whole Buddha-slash-mind-slash-body connection thing must skip a generation.

"Please, make yourselves comfortable and cleanse for a moment," our lady whispered then disappeared through a door camouflaged as part of the cherry wood panel wall. Very Scooby-Doo.

Aunt Bert looked around for two seconds then picked up a rake. Mimicking our hostess, she said all breathy, "Come on, Paisley, let's ... *cleanse our minds.*"

I thanked God up in heaven she wasn't taking this too seriously. I grabbed the other rake. With reed flute music piped through the hidden speakers in a couple of fake boulders, we acted like a couple kids while we drew our designs in the sand. She stomped her tiny size-five footprints through my lines, and I dragged my rake through hers. Then we trimmed a few leaves off every single one of the bonsai trees before we sank into the swallow-you-whole chairs.

When the secret door opened again, a tall, fragile man dressed in all black emerged. His dark hair stuck up in front with a white streak right up the center like a unicorn. He took precise steps toward us then laced his long fingers.

"Welcome," he whispered, "I am Andre, and I shall be your guide throughout your stay at the Ahhhh Spa." He looked down at us through black-rimmed glasses.

We looked at each other, stuck in our chairs, and tried not to snort.

Andre took a deep breath, and I think I detected the slightest hint of an eye roll. "Please," he said, "follow me."

We scrambled out of our chairs. He ushered us down a mushroom beige hallway lined with ocean blue doors. For some horrible reason, the colors made me think of Dad's new wife Cindy and her stupid Floral Daze markers and stationery, which brought back memories of that train wreck shopping day I'd had with her a couple years ago when she tried to cure my fashion disability. Trust me. I'd bolt out the door faster than you could say *Bonsai* if things started going like that day. So far so good.

"We begin with massage. Right this way, please." He entered a room with two padded tables. "Disrobe to a level of your comfort. Brittany and Bethany will be with you momentarily."

Aunt Bert gave me an "Oh goody" look and pulled me in. Andre bowed as he left. Before I could even get my bearings in the candlelight, she had already pulled off her jeans and t-shirt then reached for a fluffy terry robe.

Gulp.

It felt like middle school gym all over again. This would be a major stretch for me.

"Come on, Paisley. You can leave your skivvies on," she cheered holding out my robe.

"Have you ..." I hesitated before reaching for it. "... done this often?"

"'Course I have," she said. "I guess your daddy never mentioned how I spent some time in Thailand, huh."

"No, he never did." I didn't have the heart to tell her he never told me she even existed. "What did you do over there?" I snuck behind a tri-fold screen to change.

"Oh, Lane and I spent a couple years in the Peace Corp."

"Really?" I asked, surprised.

155

"Yep. Sure did learn how to live on a shoe-string. But it also showed us how a little effort put forth by an able body or two can turn things around, no matter how dire the situation."

I paused. "Is that why you took over Forever Fields?" Robed, I came around the screen.

"The way I see it, Paisley," she said leaning against one of the tables, "good things *want* to happen everywhere. It just takes good *people* to bring them to life."

That made me smile. I knew she thought I was one of these good people, or she never would have let me become a part of the ranch's story. I wanted to say something, but naturally I couldn't find the words.

The door opened. "Greetings," said two nasal voices in unison.

The platinum blonde on the right shook Aunt Bert's hand. "I'm Brittany." Her wedge-cut hair reflected the candlelight.

"And I'm Bethany," said the other as she offered me a firm handshake. Her bright red ponytail ran straight as a pipe down her back.

Both girls had the same sloping nose and high cheekbones like an elf out of a Tolkien novel. They wore white smocks, and as my eyes readjusted to the dark after the door closed, I saw dainty tattoos scrolling the corners of their eyes.

Were these chicks for real?

Aunt Bert nudged me out of my stare. "Nice to meet you both," she said.

They both tipped their heads at precisely the same time and at the exact same angle before saying in stereo, "Shall we begin?"

I won't go into the gory details, but just know that Bethany found muscles I did not know existed. Mostly ones balled up in knots. Aunt Bert lay face down next to me ooing and ahhing like she was in nirvana. I laid my face in the doughnut trying not to writhe in pain. Heavy lavender fumes filled my sinuses like water balloons as Bethany's merciless knuckles gnawed at my shoulders, apparently attempting to beat my muscles into submission.

By the time our half hour was up, and she asked if I'd like to reschedule for later in the week so she could "finish the job," I decided I liked my tension knots right where they were.

Bert, on the other hand, looked loose as a goose when Brittany and Bethany escorted us in our terry robes to the hall again where Andre awaited us with two new cucumber drinks.

Brittany bowed and said, "It's been a pleasure serving you."

Then Bethany said, "We hope you enjoy the rest of your day at the…"

In unison like a couple feathery droids, they chimed, "Ahhhh Spa," and faded away.

Seriously, I thought I'd stepped onto the Starship Enterprise.

Andre whispered, "This way please," and he led us to a more open room with lots of windows overlooking a garden area. He situated us in two ergonomically correct barbershop swivel chairs looking out at a crimson Japanese maple. Goldfinches flitted here and there.

"Candice and Evelyn will arrive shortly." He shuffled into the hallway again.

"Well," sighed Aunt Bert, "that was nice. Wasn't it?" She rested her head.

"Yah, um, it was quite an experience," I attempted. "What's next?"

"Mani-pedi." She inspected her fingernails and wiggled her bare toes.

I had left my socks *on*. Dread seeped into my throbbing muscles.

A boisterous voice came from behind. "There's our beauties, Ev!"

Bert looked at me with a tireless "Oh what fun" smile and to my surprise, it relaxed me, her confidence. Kind of like Gram. Oddly, that made me a tiny bit sad, and a smidge guilty.

A gravelly voice said, "I see 'em, Candice."

Both ladies scuttled around our chairs to greet us. Candice was a fleshy woman in a floral Mumu. It looked like she'd spray-painted rouge on her broad cheeks. Evelyn, wearing jewel encrusted cat-eye glasses, skin-tight fuchsia leggings, and a dangly black tank top, was fence post skinny and wrinkly as a raisin. Their hair was a modernized version of a bee-hive.

And could they *talk*!

The moment Candice wheeled up to me on a rolly cart to start hacking and scraping away at the scaly, quarter-sized calluses on my heels, the two ladies started in on the latest town gossip. Every now and then Bert and I would catch each other's "Did I really just hear that?" glance, but essentially, we just let the ladies have at it. By the time they finished soaking our feet, I was thankful I didn't know any of the scandalous people in their stories.

"And did you *hear*," Evelyn half-whispered to Candice as she reached for a pumice rock, "about what that horrible man Stone did?"

Aunt Bert froze right next to me at the mention of his name.

Candice propped my foot up on a cushion and shook her head. "What did that louse do now?"

"Well," Ev said like someone just belched in church, "he's gone and called in the loan Norse Drive Market's had with him for five years now."

"You don't say?"

"Mmhmm. I hear Lars Anderson asked for an extension on his June payment on account of that new baby he and Shirley just had and their three oldest at Valley City State still. I guess they're having a bit of a time making ends meet, you know. Well, that Stone creature told 'em it wasn't *his* fault they got pregnant so unexpected like, and that ... get this ...

maybe they'd think twice next time and learn how to manage their finances better."

"He. Did. Not!"

"Yes, he did. And then ... if you can believe the balls on this cur ... he handed them a business card and said he'd be happy to be their financial advisor if they needed to learn a thing or two about handling money."

"Well isn't that just a kick in the pants. Those sweet Andersons don't deserve it."

"Mmhmm."

They both shook their heads as they clipped our toenails down to nubs. My knuckles had turned white from gripping the chair. Out the corner of my eye, I could tell Bert's head was turned down and away. I imagine she felt both fear and shame. Shame for the boy once named Chante Maycomb (*Heart* for crying out loud!) who had abandoned those who loved him and went off to learn how to hate, so hard and cold. And fear perhaps (and I was just guessing at this one) for herself because she owed Remmy Stone a boat load of money.

Before I could wrap my head around it, Candice asked me, "Color, dear?" She displayed a tray of every color polish on the spectrum.

"Oh, no. I don't need polish."

Now *that* silenced them. Evelyn looked at Candice. Candice looked at Evelyn. They both sat stunned holding their trays.

Aunt Bert to the rescue. "I'll take some of this ..." She strained to read the name on the bottle. "... Purple Mountain Majesty."

Why did that sound familiar?

Evelyn, who'd clearly had a cigarette (or a thousand) in her lifetime, said, "Ooo. That's a nice one." She unscrewed the top. "You know, the nicest gal from Minnesota makes this stuff."

Candice's bell-toned voice curled at me. "Just a little touch of color, hun?"

159

I looked over the tray for something I could stomach at least until I got home. (We'd be stopping at the drug store for some remover, mind you.)

"Well, how about this one?" I pointed to a beigish one.

"Oohhh. Look at here, Evelyn. We've got ourselves a trend-setter." She high-browed Evelyn as she fan-fared the bottle. "You know that Harper's Bazaar says this is one of the season's hottest styles."

What's Harper's Bazaar?

"Hmph. No wow factor if you ask me, but something's better than nothing," she rasped.

"It'll look lovely on you, hun," Candice assured me.

Not that I cared, but I was curious. "Can I see the bottle?"

"Of course, dear." She started stuffing cotton wads between my toes.

The bottom of the bottle read "Amber Fields of Gold." It was … tolerable, I decided.

I asked, "What brand did you say this is? A Minnesota woman makes it?"

"Yes, yes," Candice answered. "It's called Floral Daze by Cindy Petals."

The bottle slipped right out of my fingers and crashed to the ground.

* * *

I stared at my painted nails while waiting for the hairdresser. Candice had yelped when I dropped the bottle, but she just cleaned it up and grabbed the same color from Evelyn's tray. I couldn't get over the fact that my stepmom had somehow crept into my girl's day out with Aunt Bert. At least I was ninety-nine percent sure it was her. She made nail polish? Much less, marketed it hundreds of miles away.

160

I sat in my robe and stared at my reflection in the mirror. Even though I thought I had run away from Grover and left all of its memories behind in search of all things new, elements from Aurora Way Farm kept working back into my life. Lenny Tuson, coming soon to live with us at the ranch. Dad knowing full well I would end up here and calling to check up on me. Tate and his tyrant brother born and raised in the Indian community practically next door to my childhood home. Now Cindy's Floral Daze stamp on the very same polish that glossed my fingers and toes.

Did I escape at all? A not-so-tiny part of me (and I can't quite believe I'm saying this) didn't really seem … to care. So I did what I knew Gram would tell me to do. *Roll with it.*

"Something gnawing at you, Paisley?" Aunt Bert asked snapping me out of my thoughts.

I looked at her in the mirror. My gut wanted to say something about it, but I didn't want to wreck our pretty decent day.

"Not a thing, Bert," I said. And meant it. "I'm just kind of surprised at what a good time I'm having."

She smiled back at me and winked. She clearly had no intentions of allowing dark news about Remmy Stone get to her.

Andre's whispery voice interrupted us. "Ladies, your hair designers have arrived." He bowed and backed away as two impeccably well-groomed individuals sauntered toward us.

"I'm Tink," said the perky bleach blonde as she extended her hand to me.

"And I'm Kit," said the equally perky curly red head as she reached to shake Bert's hand.

While Kit and Bert discussed options, Tink took out my ponytail and laced her fingers through my hair. "Where do you get your highlights done?"

"Highlights?" I asked. "I've never had highlights."

She looked at me then back to my hair then back to me again. I felt like some freak show specimen. Any minute men in white coats would whisk me away to a lab and study me for science.

"Really?" she asked.

(Enter snot.) "Yah. *Really.*" I saw myself roll my eyes in the mirror and was glad Aunt Bert had already gone to the sinks. I have never, never shelled out hard earned cash for hair coloring.

Tink just kept sifting my hair through her fingers, staring at it. She tipped her head this way and that, and I was reminded of several dumb blonde jokes, which I won't repeat here.

My leg started bouncing. I'm not one to think much about my looks. I always figured Mom must have stood too close to paint fumes or something while that part of my genetic code tried to develop.

I opened my mouth to tell off Miss Beach Party, but she cut me off instead. "I'm sorry," she started, and I braced, "I'm just so dazzled by these natural highlights. So pretty. I've never seen anything like it."

My mouth gaped open like a barn door. *That* I did not expect.

"Uhh..." I replied.

"So what did you have in mind?" When I only sat there dumbstruck, she looked at me in the mirror and reiterated, slower this time, "What are we going to do with your hair today? You know, cut? Style?"

I replied with a genius, "I dunno."

"Well let's get you shampooed and give you time to think about it, n-kay?" She tilted her head and bobbed like a cheerleader.

Once I leaned back into the porcelain sink and the warm water spray began massaging my head, I closed my eyes and tried to just relax. I felt all of Tink's attention seep through her fingers into my scalp as she rubbed and lathered and rinsed. Tingling sensations spider-webbed down to my neck and into my shoulders. The crevasse in my brow released slightly, like when I'm with Tate.

He'd be there. At the dance. Part of me worried. Worried about things I usually couldn't give a rip about. Like if he'd notice my freshly done nails. Who was this ... *girl*, and where did the aliens take the real Paisley Alberta Noon?

I hadn't a clue what I should tell this lady to do with my scraggly mop — "natural highlights" and all. And then there would be shopping. Even *I* knew duct taped paisley jeans and a Captain America t-shirt wouldn't cut it. That whole endeavor would require serious, professional help. Lord help Aunt Bert.

"There we go. All done," Tink chimed as she eased me up and wrapped my head in a towel. "Did you decide?"

I said as honestly as I could without sounding too pathetic, "I ... was hoping you might have some ideas."

"Oh I'm full of them!" she proclaimed.

"Good," I said not quite able to believe what was about to come out of my mouth. "Just ..." (Deep breath.) "... do what you think would look best." (And release.) There. My eye twitched like a woodpecker on steroids had perched inside my skull.

Tink's eyes lit up like I'd just given her the Perkiest Employee of the Month award. "Are you sure?"

(Inhale. Exhale.) "Yep. I'm sure."

"Well, we've got to accentuate these highlights all over here, and then we need to give you some lift right here and a little more animation in this area ..."

I tuned her out, closed my eyes, and forced myself to think of something else.

Chapter 14

On the kitchen countertop in my bunkhouse, a fan stirred the dry air. My paisley jeans slumped over the back of the desk chair. Though my heart ached for them (or my *butt*), their faded knees and worn hem looked exhausted and, quite frankly, due for a rest. Captain America lay crumpled on the floor. Prairie and Ernie sat like spectators as the afternoon sun streamed in. Through the bedroom window, I saw Journey and Boss Girl staring in at me from the pen. Journey perked his ears like a bunny and flung his head up and down. I heard him holler, "Lemme see!" If I let him, he'd come in and sit on the rug.

Gram's serious black and white face watched from her vantage point on the writing table. Even Mom on her wild-eyed buckskin watched. I didn't have her out all the time yet, but something told me she'd like this.

Trying to get a full-length view of myself in the rippled windows, it looked like someone else's reflection.

I looked down at the floor and, just to make sure they still belonged to me, wiggled my gold painted toes peeking out the end of new sandals. Then I allowed my eyes to continue upward across flare-legged jeans that hugged my thighs then eased up over my pooch belly.

I bit the side of my lip as I touched the gauzy fabric of my tunic top draping past my hips. I trailed my fingers across the turquoise stones and simple brown stitching around parts I'd almost forgotten were there. I felt my cheeks get warm. I guess there's nothing like an androgynous baggie t-shirt to make a girl forget she is indeed a girl.

I swallowed a lump and forced myself toward the entry mirror. Though I'd seen it from way too many angles at Norby's Department Store in Valley City, I still hadn't quite adjusted to my new look. The reflection showed me someone I didn't know. And even though my knee-jerk response was a Grand Canyon split brow, secretly … I *really* wanted to know her.

She had this honeyed glow to her skin that brought out the green in her hazel eyes like an emerald at the bottom of a riverbed. Her ginger-blond, wavy layers curled here and there framed her sun-kissed cheekbones, and bangs dangled playfully across her forehead. When she flicked her head, her hair floated with life then gently settled back down, light and airy.

She made me smile.

A chorus of happy nickers came through the screen window in the bedroom, and I heard Prairie's tail thump. Ernie even hopped down to rub against my legs. My fan club.

"So I take it you all approve?" I gave a twirl.

Whinny. Pant. Purr.

Best critics ever. If only they could prepare me for the rest of my evening.

* * *

I didn't have the nerve to go inside the house for supper, so I stopped at my garden to swing with Saint Francis for a minute. White clouds thickened and tumbled in slow-motion. We needed rain to settle the dust and cool things off. A warm breeze pulsed through my hair. I rocked back and forth. I closed my eyes at the butterflies in my gut.

The spotlight never suited me much. I knew I'd be standing under a big one as soon as I stepped through the sup deck's French doors. I dreaded the gracious "Aw, don't you look so pretty" comments River and Bob would be obligated to say. And Griff? I supposed he'd ask me who I was trying to impress (to which I would have zero come-back). The only one I figured I didn't have to worry about was Knut; he'd probably wonder what everyone was making such a big deal about. But what kind of smart remarks would I have to deflect from Heath and Henry? Let's be real here. This could get ugly.

I closed my eyes. Deep breath in. Swing. Deep breath out. Swing. Hear the birds and the wind in the treetops. Focus on the murmurs and munching of horses over the fence. Vision the Nokota on the prairie. Listen to the clip clop of hooves coming up The Lane. Swing. Breathe. Swing. Hear Prairie's little paws scuttle off to chase something. Swing.

"Good evening, Miss Paisley Noon."

Startled out of my gizzard, I clutched the swing chain. Tate leaned against the swirly iron gate, grinning wide as the prairie and holding three daisies in his hand. I yelped and wished to high heaven I could hide behind a bush. I had no idea he'd be coming for supper, although I had no reason to think he wouldn't, I guess.

Somehow, I managed, "Tate. Hi." I could not get myself to look at him. I had this sinking feeling he'd think I looked silly or that I was trying too hard.

I heard a smile in his voice as he walked toward me. "May I?"

"Of course." Still no eye contact, but I slid over and crossed my arms.

Awkward silence.

"These are for you." He handed me the daisies and leaned in, but I masterfully averted his eyes by quickly taking the flowers and focusing on them.

"Thanks," I said. "They're pretty."

I felt him lean back and rock.

More quiet.

"You know, Paisley. I was thinking," he said matter-of-fact, "we still haven't gone for a trail ride."

I rearranged the three flowers over and over. "That's true. I guess we ride together enough around here."

"That's work. I mean for fun. Right now. What do you say?" He asked as though nothing in the world would make more sense.

"Oh," I replied, caught off guard, "I don't know, Tate. I'm ... I'm not ... uh..." Right then, it would have been just as easy to speak Chinese than say *out loud* that I wasn't "dressed right for it." (God, strike me dead, please.)

"Come," he said slapping my knee as he got up. "Get your boots and Journey."

Finally I looked at him. Truth be told, (though I honestly can't quite believe it myself) I was a little miffed that he hadn't even mentioned anything about my new look.

Enter Obstinate Brat. "I can't. They're expecting me for supper any minute now." I stood up and stuffed my hands in my pockets.

Gram's voice came at me swift and hard. *Nice, Paisley. Blame everyone else.*

Completely unabashed, he said, "Nonsense. I have taken care of supper." He flashed a smile and swept an arm toward the front porch. "What would you say to a birthday picnic?"

As if on cue, Baker Bob came flouncing out the front door carrying something. "Here you go, Tate. Just like you ordered." Bob grinned like a fox as he handed over Tate's saddle bags and nudged him with his elbow.

"Perfect, Bob." Tate gave me a whatcha-gonna-say-now look. "Well. Shall we?"

Baker Bob had such anticipation on his bristly face, I thought he might bust if I didn't say something soon. Then Prairie snuck up behind me, grumble-wuffed and bumped my legs.

Tate said kind of smug, "I'd say the popular majority thinks you should say yes."

I knew I was defeated. "Oh really?" I began an equally smug saunter toward him. "And what if I don't *want* to get my *clothes* and *hair* all *dirty* before I go to the *dance* tonight?" We hadn't said a thing about the Sheldon Shindig.

He started walking toward Little Feather and said over his shoulder, "Then I'd say there's nothing like riding across the open prairie to break in a new outfit and test drive a new hair-do."

He *had* noticed.

He extended a hand. "Picnic with me, Miss Paisley, and allow me to escort you to the dance this evening."

Flutter. "I suppose."

Baker Bob practically skipped back to the house. I saw all the faces in the windows quick turn away. But they were busted.

* * *

"Hah!" I yelled then dug my fingers into Journey's silky mane as we swept through head-high grasses into the east prairie. Tate and Little Feather matched our strides. He sat up straight as an officer, his muslin shirt flapping in the wind and his hair waving. Together we galloped toward the reaching horizon, away from the crisp outlines of thunderheads creeping up in the west like snow capped mountains. The welcome smell of rain sharpened my senses to a razor's edge.

168

"Follow me!" he hollered as he flashed a smile that about made my stomach flip then he banked northward on a grassy tractor road.

"Where are we going?"

"The Swale!" Wiyaka Cikala surged ahead like lightning.

A drum beat sounded in my ears, steady and powerful. I looked around but saw nothing. I held Journey back to search the landscape's flowing slope. *Takúyapi. Takúyapi. Takúyapi.* (Tah KOO yah pey) Ancient voices thrummed to the beat of ghostly drums.

I looked to Tate. He and Kala race ahead.

At the top, silhouetted against the sky, stood the Nokota.

The beat shifted. *Tiwáhe. Tiwáhe. Tiwáhe.* (Tee WAH hey)

Heads shot up. Tate and Wiyaka Cikala galloped straight for them.

Journey was inconsolable. No way would he let that little mare beat him. Snorting and flinging his head, we lurched toward the silhouettes on the hill. I let his mane slash at my cheeks, gripped his girth with my legs, and let loose his head with a wicked, "Hah-ssss!"

The ground beneath me disappeared as tears streamed from my squinted eyes. Strong and sure, he rocked forward and back. I tucked my head in close to his sweaty neck. Journey swallowed up the ground until we raced just a length behind Tate and Little Feather. We swung wide around the back of the herd stirring them up. Tate let out a whoop and a cry so very like the ones that echoed to me from the distant memories of my mother. He motioned for me to take the herd's left flank and, just for fun, we pushed them north across the top of The Swale.

Charcoal bodies ran so close alongside us, I could have reached out to touch them. Black manes and tails whipped the air. Snorts and pounding hooves beat the rhythm now. *Takúyapi. Tiwáhe. Takúyapi. Tiwáhe.* Intoxicated with sweat and prairie dust, I urged Journey along with them. Together, we flew.

I heard Tate's whistle and saw him flag us eastward.

In order to swing the herd, I had to push Journey up toward Smoke-N-Ash running at the front. I shrieked a sound I did not recognize as my own, and Journey screeched with me. I gripped with every muscle in my body as we coursed past each one. *This*, I tell you, was a drug. A manifesting, spirit altering *drug*.

When we reached the top of The Swale, we started down the other side into what I can only describe as a cozy valley-like intersection of two slopes. Lush grass blanketed the bottom. Tate and Kala rounded the herd to slow them then came toward us at an easy lope.

Journey's muscles loosened as he settled into his smooth four-beat pace. He played now, kicking out in front and flicking his tail, but I could have balanced a dictionary on my head as both our butts wiggled side to side fox-trotting along. By the time we reached Tate and Little Feather, we had neatly deposited the herd at the base of The Swale. Smoke-N-Ash ran the ranks, checking on each mare and Little One.

I wanted, for all I was worth, to grab Tate's hand and spread my euphoria through him, but the look on his face showed he already shared it.

"Quite a ride, yes?" he said as he jogged Kala next to us.

I slowed Journey to a walk. "I'd say so."

Tate grinned cheekily. "I'd say we broke in your hairdo."

I rolled my eyes and ran my fingers through the rat's nest. Nothing he could say would kill the major buzz I had going. The thought of what I must look like made me laugh out loud. Then I laughed at the fact

170

that *clearly* he cared less about my hair than I did most days. And I laughed even *harder* at the thought of how I'd worried for even a second about it.

Breathless, I asked, "Where to?"

"The Spring." He peered south. "Down there."

Down into The Swale toward the thick grove, our horses worked their way carefully through bramble on not much more than a deer path through chest high daisies and daylilies. Then we came to a woodland trail which led to a small clearing right next to the prettiest little crick you ever did see, like something out of a Tolkein meets *Little House on the Prairie* book.

Tate hopped off and flung his arms out. "Our picnic spot. Will it do?"

I looked at the tiny yellow and white flowers popping in the shadows along the trickling creek bed. The sun beamed through the canopy showcasing wild chokecherries.

"It's perfect," I said.

"I had a feeling you would like it." He slid Kala's bridle off her head. "Come down. They won't wander far from this sweet spring grass."

As soon as I slipped off Journey's bridle and loosened his cinch, he moaned in pure bliss eating so voraciously I swear he breathed through his ears. He wasn't going anywhere.

I laughed. "You'd think I never fed him a day in his life!"

"No horse can resist this grass." He pulled off the saddlebags and started walking. We picked the last of the June berries lining the creek until we came to an enormous tree that had fallen across creating the perfect sitting bridge. We laid everything out and swung our feet like Tom and Huck. All we needed was a cane pole and straw hat.

"Watch," Tate said as he held a berry up.

"Watch what?"

"You'll see."

171

He tossed the berry into an eddy behind a boulder. As soon as that berry touched the water, four or five little fish leaped at it, tore it apart, and absconded.

"Let me try!" I squealed not intending to sound like a little girl.

I tossed a berry in. Seven, maybe eight fish jumped this time. I couldn't keep my eyes from lighting up like a kid watching fireworks.

"I might have ridden more lightly had I known Baker Bob packed this." Tate laughed and lifted high out of his saddlebag a gallon-sized bag full of smooshed berries.

We both cracked up and kept tossing. We ate and talked with our mouths full, making each other laugh and pretending to push each other in.

When I looked downstream and saw two sets of eyes looking back at us through the brush, I grabbed Tate's thigh. "Look!" I whispered. "Over there. Do you see them? I think something's watching us."

He squinted a little in the direction of the eerie eyes, then chuckled. I whipped my hand away and started to get up. "Fine. Stay here and get eaten by a pack of wolves, why don't you." I was teasing ... sort of.

He tugged my hand. "Paisley," he said. "Look again." He pointed to the trees then whistled.

Out from the brush sprang Kola and Prairie with Rope dangling between her teeth. Those two trouble-makers splashed through the water, smiling and (I mean it) *laughing* at what a good joke they just pulled on old, gullible Paisley Noon. We had told them to stay home since we planned to ride into town for the Shindig, but *clearly* they did not listen. Tate kept chuckling. I'd been had, but I giggled in spite of myself.

The dogs romped off into the woods, and we both fell silent listening to birds and the stream.

"Teach me a new word," I asked, "in Lakota."

172

"Which one?" he asked.

"Anything."

He looked around, pulled a cup from his saddlebag, and stepped nimbly off the tree trunk.

"Do you see this? This is the stream's point of origin. The Spring." He pointed to a burble of water coming out of the rocks at the edge, filled the cup and returned to my side. "Wiwila mni."

I took the cup and waited for his translation.

"Springwater. Try it."

I let the icy liquid, clean and pure, ripple down my throat. "Wiwila mni."

Tate smiled and nodded as he moved a strand of hair out of my eyes.

"Teach me about the Nokota," I said. I'd wanted to ask about the voices, but I didn't know how to bring it up.

He tweaked an eyebrow at me, "That's not such a simple request. There's not enough time in the circling of the sun to do such question justice. But I will tell you this much: The Nokota horse is capable of something most horses are not, with the exception of your Journey."

We watched Journey make a glutton of himself. Dainty Little Feather, however, stood dozing in a spot of sunshine.

"What do you mean?" What did my horse have uncommonly in common with Nokota horses?

"The Nokota, Miss Paisley, have an extraordinary capacity for affection. Not unlike that which I have been so honored to witness between you and Journey over the past weeks. Once love and trust are established, they develop an indestructible bond with their human companions. More so than any other breed. I believe this is because they know their history of near annihilation when they were driven from their people. The Lakota. Before the breed name *Nokota* was uttered, our ancestors believed deeply that these horses were their takuyapi — relatives. Ciyé (chee

YAY). Tanké (thahn KAY). Kola. Brothers. Sisters. Friends."

The familiar words caught my breath.

"When great Chief Sitting Bull surrendered at Fort Buford in 1881 and was forced to adapt to life on a reservation, white armies tore his carefully bred horses away. Some, it is said, they secretly kept for themselves, for even *they* could not deny the greatness in these war ponies — the compact design, stamina, and heartiness. But the white officers *claimed* the horses were diseased and unfit to mingle with their long-legged ranch breeds. The soldiers ripped the ponies from their loved ones and shot them or drove them into the wilderness, part of which later became the Theodor Roosevelt National Park. It is said, and I believe it to the depths of my very soul, that each horse made a vow in the form of a scream high on the winds of each treacherous winter in the badlands, to one day return to their tiwáhe, families ... and never be parted again." He waited a moment then turned to me. "I will help them keep that promise."

We sat in afflicted silence except for the water trickling. I imagined someone taking Journey, just like that, tossing him out like garbage. Frightening him. Killing him. The thought steamed behind my eyes, and my jaw clenched tight.

Easy Paisley. It's alright. Gram's voice came like a ghostly lullaby. I closed my eyes, thankful for one of her rare gentle moments.

I drew an unsteady breath. Tate looked concerned. He touched my hand.

Go ahead. I gottcha, P, said Gram.

Like a gust of wind, a sudden need to confess overcame me. I clasped his hand in both of mine. "I hear their voices," I said, pleading for him to find the answers for me.

"I know you do. We all do on occasion."

"No. I hear them *all*. *Every* time they're near. *Every* night. In my dreams. They surround me. And words — words I don't understand — rush through me trying to tell me something — something I should do, but I don't know what."

He looked into my eyes. "This is something special, Paisley. The spirits are speaking to you. Keep listening. One day ... you will understand their words."

He leaned on my shoulder. It wasn't what I wanted to hear exactly, but the way he spoke settled me. As we sat in the waning sunlight and the murmurs of our horses — our brother and sister — I yearned for more.

"Why are they called Nokota?" I asked.

He drew an easy breath. "The Kuntz brothers out in Linton created it. They rescued many from sure destruction straight out of the Theodor Roosevelt National Park during the 1980's. Park leaders wanted to change the wild horses' appearance to be more "sellable" at auction and more "attractive" to park guests, so they started eliminating the original stallions. Without Frank and Leo Kuntz, preservation of their bloodlines would have been impossible. The brothers decided the *No* represents *North* while *kota* represents *Dakota*. Spirits of the Northern Plains. Now, our state horse."

"How many do they have?"

"It changes according to their breeding program and what nature decides, but not enough. Smoke-N-Ash is from their best stock. I spent every penny I had on him."

When Tate spoke next, great thought and hesitation laced his voice, like he wasn't sure if he really should say what he was about to say. "Alberta ... everyone ... they are all counting on me." I sat real still. He fixed his almond eyes on the water.

"I will do everything in my power for their well-being, but sometimes ... it is a heavy burden."

My words flowed easily to him, "No one expects you to single-handedly save our world, Tate. Or the Nokota." He looked at me and I nudged him. "I mean, every great super-hero has to have a side-kick, right? Just ask Knut. Heck, you've got seven. *Eight* once Lenny gets here."

He gave a feeble grin.

I went on, doubt never entered my mind. "Forever Fields *will* see better days. But not at the hands of you alone, Mr. Maycomb. Though I suppose you'd like all the glory to yourself."

"I want no such thing," he said with a soft smile. "I just know if my herd keeps producing foals as fine as Ghost Song, these Nokota are destined for greatness. Throngs of people will flock to them bringing business, exposure ... money." His eyes faded. "But the Nokota are not a factory. They are history. And I plan to be a part of securing their future. Only time and patience, as our ancestors tirelessly proved, will carry us along The Quiet Path to rewards. He looked at me with a pained expression. "I worry, sometimes, that The Quiet Path will take too long and we could lose everything."

I had no idea Tate felt such pressure. "Have you told Aunt Bert what you just told me?"

He looked away like he'd surprised himself. "I've never said the words out loud."

I took his hand. Somehow, knowing Tate wasn't infallible gave me even more hope.

Chapter 15

"It's about time you guys got here!" Knut griped standing at the entrance to Sheldon's Thistleweed Arena and Event Hall.

The place stood at the very edge of town. Although calling Sheldon a "town" might be a stretch. Main Street literally consisted of the post office, Sid's Bar, and Saint Mary's Church. Four blocks of neat and tidy houses made up the residential area; the rest of Sheldon's population was rural. True farm country. Not that I came from a big city or anything, but I did kind of miss a fast food joint or discount store now and then.

Thick clouds had moved in, and it was getting dark outside. The wind had picked up too, it batted Knut's hair around like a bunch of tiny wind socks.

"Knut," I said amazed, "you look … *good!*"

He wore a pearl-buttoned turquoise checkered shirt tucked into some *spanking* new Wrangler jeans that actually touched the base of his polished black boots. My mind explained with two words: Aunt Bert. I wondered what kind of fight I missed that got this snazzy ensemble onto his bare bod.

"Yah, yah. Just get inside. Come on," he pestered. "There's a storm coming!"

Prairie and Kola ran to my crazy-haired cousin and doused him in slobber, which he enjoyed. Then the two flopped down onto the sprawling front porch, tongues lolling.

"What are you talking about, Knut?" Tate said. "The forecast said it's just a little welcomed rain coming in."

Knut wrung his hands and moaned, "Just get inside. Everyone's here already. The show's gonna start. I saved your seats!" He hopped up and down like a potty dance.

"We're coming, buddy." I turned to Tate as we dismounted. "So is this show going to be any good?" I expected little more than some small-town hacks on nags plodding to eighties music.

We walked Journey and Little Feather to the old-fashioned hitching posts in a shelter near the entrance and loosened their cinches. I had offered to drive Oscar, but Tate insisted on riding into town and taunted me even for worrying about a little rain. A few other horses stood in the neighboring shed with rears sticking out and bent hind legs.

"Didn't you see the flyer? It's one of the best around. You're in for a treat."

Riiiiight. I mean, let's remember where we were. Sheldon. North. Dakota. Population: Not so much. Although, I *was* surprised to see so many cars and horses parked outside. Quite possibly the neighboring towns, Enderlin, and Alice, had shown up for it too.

I looked back at Journey again. He lifted his head to me, hrred hrred, then hung his head low to nuzzle Kala. Tuckered. They'd be fine till we got back. Prairie came and sat right next to the door, Rope hanging out both sides of her mouth, and looked up at me like she was coming in.

"You stay, girl. Stay with Kola over there." She whined, but I ruffled her ears then patted her butt to send her on her way.

As we walked into the Thistleweed Arena, I heard the faintest rumblings of thunder far off in the distance.

"This way!" Knut yelled as we made our way up the stands in the arena. Then he dragged us both through a crowd of people to get to the seats with the rest of our family.

"Sorry," I said to every person he knocked me into. "Pardon me. Oops. Sorry again."

Tate followed close behind maneuvering *far* more gracefully. Or was it just that people parted the way to let the long and lean, take-your-breath-away Lakota man through?

Strangely, while being jostled like a pinball through clumps of strangers, I actually started to worry about what my wind-blown hair looked like, and I tried to straighten my shirt and brush off my jeans. Chalk it up (if you must) to not wanting to *completely* disregard all the effort Aunt Bert had made to rectify my fashion ... er ... quandary. I imagined by now my hair must have looked about like the Bride of Frankenstein or *worse* ... Knut. And I had dirt smattered all over my gauzy tunic top and jeans.

I could hear it all now. The announcer would say, *"Paisley Noon has arrived folks, and it looks like she's just in time for the mud wrestling tournament!"* (Tate would be *so proud*.) Then the people would all whisper to each other, "What's a girl like *that* doing with dreamy Tate Maycomb?" Then *he* would wonder the same thing.

Tate noticed my fidgeting, grabbed me, and turned me around to face him in the middle of the crowd. Startled at the move, I met his eyes.

He nestled some stray bangs up into the rest of my waves then he cupped my clenched jaw in his warm hands and peered into my eyes with such sincerity, the rest of the world vanished. The two of us stood there among the muted busyness like a stone parts the waters in a stream. Somehow, and I don't know how, I knew he'd heard my thoughts.

His voice came to me and only me. "You. Look. Amazing." Every inch of me tingled as his eyes traveled over me, head to toe, stopping to linger at my chest then again at my hips. Like *that* doesn't make a girl turn seven shades of red.

179

"And I do believe you look…" he paused like he couldn't quite put a finger on the word he wanted, "… eighteen." Then he gave me such a seductive grin, I practically attacked him right there. He just laughed and pulled me in, making me forget my hair and clothes and the people.

"Over here, Paisley! Tate!" Knut hollered.

When I caught sight of his red mop in the crowd, I saw the rest of my family waving. They were all spruced up, even the twins. Heath's locks actually looked like he had swiped a comb through them. I had to shield my eyes from the beacon bouncing off his enormous belt buckle. He could've signaled air traffic with that thing. Henry's buzz-cut glistened. He'd rolled up the sleeves on his black shirt to stretch so tight over his bulging biceps I worried he might cut off circulation by night's end.

River and Bob wore matching black cowboy hats and old-fashioned western shirts with pointy collars and V-piping at the chest. Bert sat between them, white shirt, and white jeans. Her white-blonde head barely reached River's and Bob's shoulders as she flagged me with a rolled-up program. Griff sat on the end with his arms crossed hard over his chest. Surly as ever. He'd tucked in his shirt, though, and *maybe* swiped his hair with some spit, but I couldn't be sure.

Just as I finally planted my butt on the metal seat and began to take a deep breath from climbing the bleachers, a silver-haired announcer sitting straight across the arena floor from us blared, "Ladies and gentlemen, please rise for our National Anthem as Robin Strongwind riding Grand Rock carries our nation's colors."

Holding the American flag in one hand, a long-legged lady decked in red, white, and blue sequins and a white cowboy hat came jog-trotting in on a striking black and white pinto which, if I wasn't mistaking, had all the features of a Nokota horse. The rippling neck muscles and powerful hindquarters slid under a pristine coat. Hooked ears poked out of his dense mane and forelock. Feathered fetlocks wisped freely at his feet as he loped effortlessly around and around the arena. Robin rode him like a rocking chair, her black hair swaying. She looked up into the crowd like a tribal queen before her subjects, her dark, confident eyes peering into us. And though watching her made me feel oddly small, even *I* couldn't deny they were an impressive pair.

We all sang with a barber shop quartet. Small town or not, this was a *real deal* show.

After the song, Tate leaned in as we took our seats. "What about that duo?"

I only returned a quizzical look. An insecure (or I should say *immature*) part of my brain wondered if he'd been more focused on the horse ... or the girl. Instantly, for reasons I could neither understand nor control, I decided I did not, would not, and could not like this Robin Strongwind. And that was that.

"Grand Rock is the newest Nokota stallion in the area," he said. "I'm told his breeding rights are sky high. Straight from Linton." He dreamily watched the horse and rider exit the arena. "His lines would be good for my band."

"Who owns him?" I asked. "Maybe you can cut a deal. You never know, right?"

He met me with a disappointed look. "*Her*," he pointed to Robin nearly out of sight. "And she is a businesswoman, not likely to compromise the integrity of her lines or *cut deals* with *anyone*, much less me."

Now, I *really* didn't like her. "Whatever," I said sounding way more teenagery than I wished. "Anyone can see you know *exactly* what you're doing. She'd be *lucky* to let Grand Rock sire some of your foals. Besides," I nudged him, "you've got us in your corner." I nodded down the row.

He raised his eyebrows and nodded, "You have a point there." Then he laced his fingers in mine and rested our hands on my leg.

181

Warmth flowed through me as my heart fluttered, sitting so close to him, holding hands, in *public*. By most social standards, I do believe such a situation might relay the message that we were indeed ... *an item*. For a brief moment, I asked myself how that had happened, but then I realized I didn't care. But I still had to be careful, of course.

From some visceral place within, a strange and confusing vibe swirled inside me, and I nearly pulled my hand away from his just to make them go away, go back to normal.

Easy, Paisley. Gram's voice floated to me like trying to calm a jittery colt. *Just enjoy.*

"Right," I exhaled in a whisper. Tate rubbed the back of my hand with his thumb as the announcer turned my attention to the entrance on the arena floor.

"Ladies and gentlemen," his voice like golden caramel, "let's give a big Thistleweed welcome to Candice and Evelyn's Little Buddies!"

The crowd cheered as the most adorable mini-donkeys came trotting in with none other than the very same Candice and Evelyn who did our nails at the Ahh Spa that morning. Aunt Bert and I leaned to connect surprised glances.

Leading them out, Candice wore a floral mu-mu and a sun bonnet that flopped down over her eyes. In her arm swung a basket of trailing flowers. She called like Santa to each mini keeping them in line. Evelyn brought up the rear with a candy-striped shepherd's hook and the most ridiculous Bo-Peep get-up. I could barely see her wrinkly tan face buried in all the ruffles.

We all aawwed and ohhed and chuckled at each mini-donkey dressed up with their long, fuzzy ears poking out of straw hats. Some wore flowers around their necks, others pulled little wagons full of flower pots. Their heads pitched down like they were concentrating so hard just to get around the big arena.

Honestly, it was the cutest thing I've seen in ... well ... ever. And get *this*. I stole a glance at the end of our row and caught Griff's mouth twitching up at the corners just as the little act trotted out. Yep. It was *that* darling. Definitely rating high on my cute-o-meter.

The announcer said, "Aren't they delightful, folks? Let's hear it for Candice and Evelyn and their Little Buddies. Thank you, ladies, for bringing your crew from Valley City. Be sure to stop and see them after the show in the stable area. These fine ladies *and* their donkeys would love to visit with you."

Aunt Bert leaned to see me again with an, *I'd say,* look. That made me laugh. Did those women ever know how to "visit." Tate seemed confused, and I have to admit, it was fun having an inside joke with someone. That's the kind of thing you do with people you really know well, right? Like a ... *friend.* Yet another foreign, but I will say welcome, new sensation for me.

The lights dimmed in the arena and a spotlight shone on the entrance. Tate squeezed my hand and whispered, "You're going to like this."

Fluty woodwinds piped through the loud-speakers. Indian music. Like the kind my mother used to play when she thought she was alone with her yoga matt in the spare bedroom. A hazy memory of me in flannel pajamas, hidden in the hallway miming her, faded in and out while the music ricocheted off the arena walls.

The announcer switched into *serious stuff* voice which hung low and rumbled through the stands. "And now folks, the pride of Ransom County. Let's all put our hands together for ..." He inserted a dramatic pause here and shifted into *light 'em up* voice mode. "*Prrrrairie Firrrre!*"

The crowd came unhinged as into the spotlight strode fifteen girls riding bareback. I saw the black and white Nokota stallion saunter out again with Robin Strongwind astride. The immature brat in me decided right then that these ladies *clearly* thought they were hot stuff, better than everyone else. Though I had not a shred of evidence to prove it was true. While my conscience tugged at me over the matter, I forced my thoughts on something else, something undeniably good, no matter what. Drumbeats danced in my mind and unruffled my feathers.

Horses.

The Nokota. These were not quite like Tate's herd. They came in every color, like buttermilk buckskin, dark bay, and dusky dun. Only two had the distinctive sooty blue roan coloring like Tate's Smoke-N-Ash or Mazaska. A couple had a longer-legged, rangier look; otherwise, they all had that square-set, heavily muscled, strong boned look of the Nokota. Their untamed manes and tails showed the prairie winds still lingered in them.

I clapped with everyone else but refused to see what the big deal was about the performance. The young ladies wore basic jeans and faded t-shirts. They all had cocoa skin and long black ponytails stuffed under straw hats or ball caps.

They came in at a walk. Slow and lazy. Slouchy even. Immediately I decided the donkey act had been the highlight. *Cue cheesy 80s music.* I looked at Tate like, *Seriously?*

He smiled and squeezed my hand. His eyes never left them. (Grrrr.) I followed his gaze out to the arena and tried to determine if he was looking at the black and white stallion … or the long-legged Lakota woman on its back. And since my mind was going there, I chewed a fingernail as I tried to figure out if he was checking out *all* of the cute girls sitting so smug on their horses, so sure of themselves. So not like me.

Pull it together, P, Gram said.

Gram was right. I figured, who cares if Tate was looking at them? We're adults.

My stomach twinged.

A sea of pasted grins surrounded me. Knut just about wiggled out of his skin watching the act coming into the arena. Then the lights dimmed, and they began to trot sloppily around in no particular pattern. I decided to be *embarrassed* for them all.

Tate kept his eyes glued. (Double grrr.)

These girls didn't even look like they knew how to ride. They jostled all over the place bouncing helter-skelter around the arena. Half the time they about ran into each other. I couldn't bear to watch. I wanted *so bad* to holler, "Come on! Get your act together! Do those Nokota justice! My *grandmother* could ride better than that!"

Oh Paisley. Her voice sounded eerily disappointed. *You do judge quickly.*

I frowned. Did she have a clear view from the spirit world?

Then I felt a squeeze at my hand as the sloppy t-shirted girls directed their horses into a long line down the center length of the arena. The Indian flute music came to an abrupt halt with a final drumbeat at precisely the same time all the horses fell into position completing the line. The most coordinated part of the show. But they just stood there in silence, heads low, and I *could not* believe that was it. No one clapped even. Tate must have a screw loose or something. I started to roll my eyes, but he saw, I just *know* it, and tugged my hand to get me to keep watching the train wreck.

Suddenly, crashing the awkward silence, a head pounding, earthy drum kicked in, and the girls at either end of the line took off like a shot! Each in turn followed in time to the back-beat of the new music. *That* got my attention. Native voices called behind the drums and the girls threw their hands in the air whooping war cries. Their hats flew off and they yanked out their ponytail bands as their legs gripped their horses' bare sides and tore at blinding speeds around the arena in perfectly choreographed designs.

Criss-crossing within a hair's breadth of each other. Pin-wheeling in perfect succession like an equine kaleidoscope. Silky black hair flying and flapping in the wind they created. Smiles as wide as the prairie itself stretched all the way into the crowd as the girls pumped their free arms to get everyone riled up.

It was all I could do not to cry.

People bobbed their heads to the music and shimmied their shoulders. They hooted and hollered as the ladies swept past each section of bleachers at lightning speed. And then the crowd went *nutzo* when Robin Strongwind and two others stopped in the center, kicked off their boots, and stood on their horses' backs while the rest blazed a circle around them. The music reached a frenzied pace as the girls standing on their horses really worked the crowd and boogied in place while the circling horses nearly dug a trench to China.

Oh my heart. The goose bumps up my arms and all over my scalp betrayed me. Everyone — and I mean EVERYONE — was on their feet cheering and dancing. Even Great Uncle Griff stood up and pumped his fists to the beat. Suddenly, my defenses completely melted. I longed to be with them in their happiness. Not suffer alone inside myself. Forcing myself to see the Prairie Fire girls for who they really were — passionate, talented horsewomen — I realized I was not so different from them after all. The revelation dissolved the heavy weight of bitterness, and I expelled it in the form of a war cry whoop second only to my mother's. The more I released, the more my spirit sprout wings.

Finally, the circling horses moved gracefully into a star pattern surrounding the three in the middle, and then those three girls did flying back-flips off their horses and landed square in the deep sand. In one swift motion, *all* the girls leapt to the ground and stripped off their baggie t-shirts to blind us with sequined flames on red, orange, and yellow show shirts. Each one whipped a sparkler stick out while Robin Strongwind raced down the line lighting them up. They effortlessly mounted their Nokotas and cantered in a circle, sequins dazzling, sparks flying.

"PRAIRIE FIRE, EVERYONE!" screamed the announcer over the bedlam applause.

Tate clapped and looked at me. I felt dumb. Oh the awful things I'd thought about the girls. The embarrassment turned on *me* — and rightly so. I was ashamed. I knew Gram was too. I tried to hide the tears welling in my eyes. I *tell* you, that was a humbling moment.

Leave it to Gram to let me learn the hard way, again. I do judge too quickly.

With the applause still roaring and the girls each taking a bow in turn, I reached an arm all the way around Tate's waist and leaned. He curled me into him and blew a piercing whistle for us both.

"And last but never least, the founder of Nokota Land Ranch and The Prairie Fire Foundation, where all donations and proceeds from shows just like this one, folks, go straight to the preservation of the historic Nokota horse … Robin Strongwind!"

Our applause heightened as she stepped in front of her black and white stallion to take her bow. Out of nowhere came a crack of thunder so jolting I thought the roof might split in two. Everyone in the arena jumped or ducked or grabbed their heart. Then we all fell silent.

* * *

Dang it, you two," River cussed out of character, "get in the Bronco!"

Lightning rippled through the night sky like Mother Nature's very own Fourth of July fireworks show. Cars and trucks scrambled out of the parking area. A few left at a run on horseback, others quickly loaded their trailers.

We didn't have a trailer. We hadn't expected a storm. The forecast had said light rain after midnight. And with the drought, we doubted even that. But the air sank heavy with moisture. A storm brewed.

"Not a chance," I hollered over the gusting wind. "We still have time."

Looking up at the hot, electric sky, Tate said, "She's right, River. We've got time to get the horses home. We can't just leave them here." A low rumble dared us.

My entire family, dogs included, sat smashed in River's wood-grain Bronco. Their opinions split.

"Jeez, you guys," said Henry. "Just turn Journey and Kala loose. They'll find their way home, faster than us even. Come on, we're wasting time!"

Baker Bob agreed, "It's true and you know it, Tate. Little Feather has had to find her way home before. She'll show Journey the way."

Tate looked at me like he knew it was true, but I looked right back at him, determined. "Not. A. Chance. You go. *I'll* bring them home *myself*."

Right then, my mind flashed to the archway joining the living room to the kitchen back in Grover. I was twelve again and shivering in my flannel pajamas while Dad and Gram argued over who would save BG and Journey from the worst Minnesota blizzard in a decade.

Prairie leapt off Knut's lap right out the window. She sat at my side looking straight up.

Knut cried, alone in the way back of the Bronco. "*Someone* has to make sure they're safe!" he wailed, snot dribbling down his lip.

Heath reached an arm back to him and squeezed his shoulder. "It's okay, buddy. Paisley will see to it. Don't you worry."

"She's gonna get herself killed, for chrissake!" Griff growled. He sat smashed between the twins. "Berta, talk some sense into that kid!"

Aunt Bert sat silent in the middle of the front bench seat, her blonde-white hair stark against River's and Bob's dark western shirts. I could see in her eyes she was torn, but I could also see that she knew I was not a *kid* anymore. A flash of lightning lit my face. I did *not* want to fight her on this, but I would if I had too.

"Go," she said with conviction.

I flung around and didn't dare see if Tate followed me. My stomach did whirligigs at the thought of finding my way back to the ranch alone, but I trusted Little Feather to show the way.

The Bronco vrrooomed off.

Then I heard, "Kola. Come."

Chapter 16

I've never, ever in my life been so glad to hear someone's voice.

"Help me with this knot," I said. My hands trembled with each rumble of thunder.

He put his steady hand over my fingers. "Let me do it. You tighten cinches."

I froze for a second to collect my nerve. Focus. Get the horses and dogs home safely. That's it.

"A little help here, Gram?" I whispered.

What? Hold back the skies? Sure. I'll get right on that, P.

Oddly, her sarcasm got me to cool it and take in my situation.

Journey made a quizzical noise and nuzzled me. I placed a shaky hand on his shield star. It glowed in the darkness, superhero bright. Prairie sat at my heels offering Rope like *just in case.* I heard my own voice faintly in the back of my mind. *I guess you never know when a grimy old rope might come in handy. We girls have to be prepared for anything.* I couldn't help smiling at the thought. But the words also took me back to Aurora Way … and Dad … and Gram … and the Blizzard.

Focus.

"Here," Tate said, "put this on." He handed me a wadded-up plastic poncho. "My saddlebags are always packed."

I shook it out. "You wouldn't happen to have a floodlight in there, would you?"

"No," he said. "But these might help." He pulled out two headlamps. He looked pretty impressed with himself.

"Nice," I said with a little more confidence than just a moment before.

* * *

A beam of light lit the path. My butt wiggled back and forth in the saddle as Journey fox-trotted in high gear through the woods, smooth as silk. Tate and Wiyaka Cikala had to canter to keep up, but Tate sat it so easily he might as well have been riding a sofa. Lightning cracked and a hot wind twisted the treetops above us. Still no rain.

We stopped at a clearing looking out onto the stretch of open prairie that reached toward The Lane. Before us sprawled a sight I'd never seen before and doubt I will ever see again. At that moment, I realized just how small and insignificant I really was. It forced me to wonder, "How could I possibly make *any* difference being such a feeble speck?" It made me feel like an idiot for caring about what my hair looked like or for being jealous of some girls. And I couldn't help wonder if Gram felt something similar when she went head to head with the Blizzard so many years ago.

Tate's voice filled with awe. "Would you look at that."

Lightning strips, three, maybe four or five ribbons at a time, popped out of the cloud canopy and crackled down to the earth, splitting the air with deafening crashes, and sending up puffs of smoke and flame.

The *prairie* was on *fire*.

"The Thunder Beings — Wakinyan — are unhappy today," he said as he stared seriously out over the land.

Kola and Prairie sat and stared as well. Both of them held one end of Rope in their mouths. Our horses flinched with each crack, but they did not move. A chill traveled down my neck.

"What?" I asked between strikes. "What do you mean they're *unhappy*? I'd say more like *pissed*. Those fires are going to run rampant out there, Tate! Look at them. And it's so dry ..."

"Sometimes," he tried to explain, "our creator sees an imbalance in our world. He sends Wakinyan to set it right. Though the Thunder Beings can be so terrible ..." Crash! "... the Lakota spirits are also gentle." He twisted in his seat to look back on the woods from which we came. It remained untouched by the lightning. "This is how we learn. Through balance. For every bad, there is good. No wrong deed goes unpunished. And no goodness goes unnoticed."

My breath came in quick gasps. Who made them mad? I think I've mentioned before how I'm not the religious type, but something deep in my bones said it was me. I'd judged the Prairie Fire girls. Gram had said it. I judged good people doing good things. And how much more obvious could the spirits get? The *prairie fire* presented a pretty grave consequence for me here. And not just for me either, but those who stood with me now — the most precious.

But while *I* looked out and saw a landmine of high-voltage death, Tate seemed to gaze upon the face of God.

"Tate, I ... I think this is all my ..." I searched his face desperately, like maybe he could absolve me if I confessed. But I chickened out. "I mean, maybe we should go around." The river bridge wasn't too far north.

"That will take too long. Besides, the riverbanks will be treacherous once the rain hits."

Visions of the flooded river coursing over the road rushed to me from when I first arrived in the spring. That was a force I did not wish to reckon with.

192

"Then do you have any ideas how we might *balance* our way across this stretch?" The words tasted acrid in my throat.

He replied without acknowledging my tone. "I have not tried it on my own before, only heard legends of it in our songs. But I believe ..." He turned to me with a simple look. "I believe I will sing."

Excuse me? Thank the thunder gods I managed to keep it in my head. "Oh. Okay," I said with a *well of course you should sing while we're trapped here between fire and oncoming torrential downpour* kind of tone.

The dogs kept staring like they were watching, waiting for something. Journey and Kala turned their heads to each flash as though calculating the timing of the strikes. Then Tate began speaking words I did not recognize. Lakota words. And I longed desperately to know them. His silhouette blended with the night sky as his words transformed into song. I closed my eyes. I was afraid, but the smells of the smoke and the earth and the drumming sounds of thunder created visions in my mind. A dance.

"Wacipi." Tate kept singing this word in his song. "Wakina," he said too. "Wacipi wakina. Wacipi wakina." Then the notes went up like a desperate cry and down like mournful wail.

I kept my eyes closed tight. The vision faded into view like a mirage.

I am dancing. I can feel my body moving in rhythm, but I cannot feel my legs. I float. Soft as a pulse, I undulate to the sound of the voice. I dance on horseback through tall, emblazoned grasses. *Wacipi wakina.* Billowing smoke. Light shreds the sky. It blazes on either side. Thunder Powers engulf us. We are the smoke. We are the flames. The horses' hooves step in rhythm to it all, slow and sure. To the sound of the voice. I follow but a shadow. It is part of the earth with which we dance. Down a winding, narrow path. Our horses' manes lick up and down.

193

Hind quarters sway elegantly as they place each footfall on safe ground.

Through the billowing smoke, Prairie Fire girls watch me. Their smiles wash over me. Understanding. Forgiving. The Nokota, theirs and ours, swirl like vapors before me, around me, through me. They are me. I am them. The horses are the reason I have come. They are the reason I exist.

Thunder rolls. Poplars hiss. Still the horses dance, carry me along the safe path. Carefully. Slowly. Wacipi Wakina. What does it mean?

The words come.

"Thunder Dance," I said and opened my eyes.

We stood on the gravel road — Little Feather and Journey, Kola and Prairie, Tate and me — safely on the other side. The decaying FFF sign poked out of the bramble. The Lane pointed clear passage home.

"What. Just. Happened?" I asked.

He sat tall on his horse. "The Thunder Dance. It seems as though the spirits found us worthy of safe passage through the flames."

No goodness goes unnoticed... Gram's voice held a rare brightness. I had literally walked through fire and found redemption. Rather, *it* found *me*.

I started to tell Tate, but the hissing sounds from my vision grew loud and *real*. When I looked beyond the smoke and flames, a *wall* with the hiss of a thousand snakes came at us. Prairie, ever the Border collie, yanked Rope away from Kola and started herding Journey and Little Feather. She yapped and spun circles while Kola bounded out ahead of us then turned to wuff. He leveled his wolfish head at the wall. His eyes glowed in the darkness.

Both Tate and I knew better than to ignore our dogs. "M*ove!*" he yelled over the rain that was now extinguishing the prairie like a candle wick.

"Don't have to tell me twice!"

I gave Journey a swift nudge in the ribs, and we were off like a shot down The Lane. Though I thought he'd sprouted wings, Tate whooped and laughed not far behind.

I anchored my fingers into Journey's thick mane. I knew the sharp left turn to the house could sneak up at this speed. I peered down the gravel road and leaned in. The beam from my headlamp flickered across a white speck ahead. Journey's ears perked forward. It stood on the road, small and statue-still. I pulled up in a hard whoa and looked to Tate. He saw it too. His laughter vanished as Little Feather loped to my side. Kola and Prairie ran to investigate, but they stopped halfway.

Sheets of rain pummeled the grass fires and muted the flares of lightning not far behind us. If we wanted to make it home without getting drenched, we couldn't stand around.

"What is it?" I asked trying to hone my light on it.

Tate's eyes narrowed then he opened his mouth just a fraction before speaking. "Oh no." The two words came eerily long and slow.

"What *is* it?"

"Oh. No." Then with mounting tension, "No. No," he said gravely. "Wana Gi. NO. NO! Oka Wana Gi!" He and Kala darted toward the white figure like the devil chased them. When I turned to face the torrents nearly on our tails, I too thought he'd come to claim us.

I slapped Journey's hind end, and we caught up in a flash. My mind raced to decipher the words Tate kept hollering.

"Oka Wana Gi," I muttered, but the thunder and rain drowned out my words. "Oka Wana Gi." What did it mean? The words felt familiar and alien at the same time.

Search, Gram said. *Think, Paisley. Think.*

Then I heard, piercing through the constant roar, a scream. No. A call. Not that even. I listened as the ghostly white figure grew closer blinking in and out of my bobbling headlamp. It was a *song*.

195

Ghost Song.

* * *

The sky opened up and the world became a blur as we moved forward in the beating rain. But she stood still, glowing. Tate's first filly foal out of Smoke-N-Ash. The little beauty with the medicine hat and the song of our ancestors. She must have slipped through a weak spot in the fence. Losing her was NOT an option. She meant too much, if even just in hopes and dreams.

Water streamed into my eyes and pelted my shoulders. I could so easily have whistled for Prairie, turned left down The Drive and been in the horse barn within two minutes, safe and warm. Rain gushed through my flattened hair as rivulets formed in the gravel road. Journey's hooves sucked and splashed in the mire.

A lightning flash gave me a glimpse of Tate's profile. He stared intensely at his prize foal, and his jaw line shifted in the eerie light. I couldn't get a read on his face, but the pitch in his voice told me he was close to losing it. My heart ached.

As soon as we got about fifty feet from Ghost Song she turned on her heels, pierced the thick air with her scream, and ran southward onto a tractor path. Tate and Little Feather never looked back. They took off after her into the darkness. Kola, hot on their heels, howled like wolves in the timber. Prairie started after them, but she stopped when she realized Journey and I hadn't moved. The look on her face cast chagrin. "What are you waiting for?" she cried. "They can't do this alone. Let's go!"

My head told me to turn north toward safety. My gut said otherwise. Ignoring a magnetic draw luring me to the barn, I swiped drenched bangs from my eyes and leaned into Journey asking him to head south. He put his failure-is-not-an-option ears on, and we followed the sound of Kola's already fading howl.

Journey slipped once and I tried to slow him down, but he would have none of it. So instead, I rubbed his neck. "It's just a little rain and mud. You can do this."

His ears twitched back at me, but I knew as soon as the words left my lips, they were for *me*, not my brave knight in shining copper. Journey turned without guidance and barreled through bramble and hock deep mud all on his own. I hung on and listened for Kola's howl. The wind kicked up and rain slanted at us destroying my bearings. I kept listening and clung to my horse.

Soon I heard the unmistakable report of Prairie's alarm bark.

Shining my headlamp down into a waterlogged drainage trench, eight or nine feet deep, I saw them all. Tate, Kola, Little Feather, and Ghost Song stuck and struggling in waist high mud. Prairie yapped, franticly pacing back and forth, searching for footing to take her down to their rescue, but each step she took crumbled beneath her tiny paws making her clamber back up.

They all strained in slow motion to free their bodies from the gripping mud. But the more they moved, the deeper they sank, and the more exhausted they became. Kola had somehow managed to get close enough to the filly. By the way he was able to maneuver himself, it seemed like he could have worked his way to safety with some effort. But he leaned against Oka Wana Gi's flailing body, like he knew the little one could very well panic herself into a frenzy and die of fear, or hurt her legs.

"Tate!" I screamed and scrambled on my belly to look over the edge. "TATE!" Fear gripped my throat as my headlamp shone on his mud-streaked face.

He looked up, startled. "Paisley!" Fear filled his throat too. "Ghost Song! She's so afraid," he yelled above the wind and rain.

"Are *you* okay?" I hollered. He inched toward her, so I prayed that meant he wasn't hurt.

"I'm fine," he said sounding almost bothered. "We're all fine ... for now. Get a rope!" Despair tinted the edge of his words.

I tried to take in the scope of the situation. Little Feather, with the most level head I've ever seen on a horse in such a position, obviously had it in her mind that this would not be the night of her demise, for she lurched toward the other side of the trench — away from Tate's outstretched arms. She dug in on the slant until finally, heaving and snorting like a prize-fighter, rose up on the other side and stood tall, slathered in the mud that had dared defeat her. She screamed "TRIUMPH" into the storm.

And as I cheered for her, I saw Tate's rope firmly attached to her saddle.

"The rope!" Tate hollered.

Prairie looked at me like she wanted — needed — to know the plan. Journey pranced restlessly. He whinnied and snorted demanding a solution.

"What am I supposed to do?" I cried into the rain which streamed down my face hiding my tears. The wind kept gusting and my body felt heavy as though the mud had reached up to drag me down with it. A chill settled inside my bones. I couldn't think straight.

"BARK!"

I looked down. Rope lay on my mud-slogged boots.

"YAP YAP!" *Take it!*

My dog's sharp warning to Get. My. Self. To. *Gether. sn*apped me to my senses.

"Of course!" I shrieked with revelation.

I coiled Rope and tossed it to Tate. Prairie bolted into the darkness. She disappeared, but there's one thing I know about my dog: Prairie always has a plan.

Even when I (or should I say *especially* when I) sooo do *not*.

"Tate! Here!" I yelled. It landed just within his grasp but wasn't long enough for him to work with it. He needed more length.

"Just toss it down," he said.

I let go of my end and helplessly watched him slip it around Ghost Song in a make-shift harness.

"Doesn't Journey have *anything* we can use?" he asked puffing as he wrenched his body.

I ran to Journey and scoured his tack. His body trembled, but he stood steady as I searched. Desperate for anything, I thought about taking off his bridle. The leather reins might be strong enough.

When I ran back to the edge to gauge the distance for length, my headlamp bobbed onto Little Feather still standing on the other side and my dog stood next to her! Through the heavy curtain of rain, I saw her little Border collie legs spring at the rope attached to a front latigo strap. Kala shied away, but Prairie yapped at her and whipped around her legs to keep her still. Then she kept leaping for the coiled rope.

Half in shock, I cheered her on. "That-a-girl, Prairie! That's it. Get the rope!"

Tate caught sight of it. "Good girl, Prairie! Grab it! Rip it off! You can do it."

Finally, with one mighty spring that could have landed her right smack-dab into the saddle, she wrenched her agile body to the side, snapped her teeth at the latigo tie, and hooked one paw in the coil sending her and the rope crashing to the ground. Little Feather stamped nervously aside as Prairie scrambled upright.

"YES!" I screeched and about collapsed from the tension. "Give it to Tate, girl. Send it down now."

She looked at Tate reaching toward her, and she let the rope slide down the bank just within his reach. He grabbed it like it was life itself and instantly had it fastened to the harness he'd made for his inconsolable filly. He tossed the other end up to me and I promptly fixed it to the pommel on my saddle. Journey snorted and pumped his legs. It was his turn.

"Okay buddy," I said trying to steady my voice. We were almost there. But if we pulled too fast and hard, the ropes might snap, or the knots might not hold. "Steady now. Easy boy."

We moved together one inch at a time. Agonizingly slow steps backward. I tried to steady the line with the entire length of my body as I gripped and pulled. Gripped and pulled. Hooves and boots slipping in the muddy grass, somehow finding purchase.

Wind and rain beat down daring us to let go. *Give up,* it hissed.

But we did not give up.

Suddenly, the pull on the other end stopped as though the rope had snapped. I fell on my butt and tried to see through the rain. In the grayness, stood a dark silhouette of a filly foal. The rain revealed ribbons of white as the black mud sloughed to the ground. She let me come to her, and I placed a falsely steady hand on her shoulder.

Words escaped my lips. "Takaku ki," I said, and I knew it meant *little sister.* Ghost Song twitched incessantly and squealed her song as I felt for injury. "Takaku ki." Once I felt confident she had emerged unscathed, I removed Rope and tied her to Journey who nuzzled her close and shielded her from the wind.

When I got back to the edge to help Tate and Kola, Tate's body hung limp over Kola's back. The faithful dog was trying to carry Tate up the trench, but it looked as though exhaustion had devoured them both. Barely thinking, I grabbed Rope and leaned dangerously over the ledge.

Sliding and sinking, I called. "Tate! Grab Rope. Kola, take it boy. Take the rope!" Neither responded.

Prairie did not like my plan of action. She yapped at me from the other side, but I had no other ideas. Then she grumbled and started herding Little Feather along the length of the trench, away into the darkness.

Tate lifted his head just feet out of my reach. "Paisley." His voice was weak and distant.

"Tate! Grab the rope! Grab it!" I commanded.

Kola whined and licked Tate's face. I held my breath as Tate weakly took hold of Rope and tied it around his waist. I tried to pull, but I just wasn't strong enough. Instead, with each effort, my body slid further down the bank, the ground crumbling away with every movement.

The wind whipped over me and the shelter belt trees thrashed and writhed into a twist above us. No more than thirty yards away, a cottonwood groaned as its roots ripped from the earth and crashed down spanning the trench. A roar vibrated the earth. I gave one last yank on Rope and plummeted through the mud to Tate's side.

Kola barked feebly. Tate turned to me. His beautiful face just inches from mine. We lay in the mud together, limp. Unable to move one more muscle. My mind swirled inside my skull.

I heard a thundering crash, and then darkness inked its way over my eyes.

Chapter 17

I woke to silent darkness.

Chilling memories of rain and wind and mud scoured through me, but it was quiet now. I didn't know how long I'd been out, but every muscle ached with cold and wet as I rolled over to check on Tate. I touched his face carefully with my trembling fingers and pulled aside a matted strand of hair. He opened his eyes and looked into mine. Dark and rich even in the moonlight.

Moonlight. The storm had come and gone.

We looked up to twinkling stars. The night sky canvas beamed pinpricks of light through the crystal-clear air, and the moon rode high. It lit our surroundings like daylight. Kola lay next to Tate, exhausted but alert, and I wondered how long he could keep up this vigil. Thick-trunked trees sprawled across the trench just feet away.

Summoning strength, I worked my way up the slope.

Tate's voice came to me weakly. "Paisley, be careful." He struggled to follow my lead but fell back with an agonizing scream. "My leg!"

I slid back to his side. "Don't move. You hear me? Do not move!" Fear zapped my chest. A splinter of fence post stuck straight through the fleshy part of his calf. "Holy Saint Francis ..." I clapped a hand over my mouth trying, for Tate's sake, not to freak out. But this was *bad*. Dark blood soaked his mud-caked jeans. No way could I pull that thing out.

He took it all in too. "Ohh." Huff, pant. "This is not good." Grimace, huff.

Kola whined and tried licking Tate's leg. Tate pulled him off and buried his face in his dog's thick fur — a place I dared guess he'd gone before in search of strength.

"He stayed by your side the whole time," I said trying to sound strong.

"I know." He stroked Kola's muddy fur. "A true friend."

Glad his thinking was lucid, I started to get up again. I had to get him out of there. Then he reached for my hand and held it so tightly I could feel his heart beating through our touch.

"You stayed too. When you did not have to ..."

"Yes. I did." I held his hand over my heart. "A true friend." We smiled. "Now don't move. I'm going to shinny up this ditch and get us out of here."

At the top of the slope, Journey's white shield star shone in the moonlight. He whinnied when he saw my head pop up. For a second, I thought he was alone. Then, as my eyes focused in the starlit night, I saw four spindly legs crisscrossing behind his.

"Ghost Song!" I hollered down to Tate. "She's alright! Journey's got her. She looks fine, Tate." I saw his entire body slump in relief. Kola looked up and pant-smiled.

"Thank the Great Spirit," I heard Tate murmur.

I called for my dog. "Praaairie!" The last I'd seen her, she was on the other side of the trench herding Little Feather away. Neither were anywhere to be seen now. And though part of my heart lurched with worry, a greater part knew she'd somehow gotten herself and Tate's frightened horse to safety.

Off in the distance, I thought I heard something. Something ... moving. A mere scratching sound at first, then it grew louder as it approached. The batteries in my headlamp had died, but I caught a quick glimpse of something reflecting in the moonlight. A flash. Then a flicker. It grew brighter as the sounds came closer.

Journey nickered and blew out his nose. I laid a hand on his neck. He held his head high and flung it up and down like nodding approval.

"Bark bark!" Prairie came shooting out of the darkness. "Yip yap!"

"Prairie!" I dropped to my knees and held my arms out wide. She leaped onto me and snuffled me all over so furiously, I thought she might hyperventilate. I was so happy to see her, my throat got all tight and I felt myself pushing back more tears. "Oh my baby girl is okay." I looked at her smiling face. "There's my girl."

She whined and made her little worry-wart monkey noises. Journey dipped his head down to nuzzle her fur too. Prairie licked his nose. Then Ghost Song gave such a pretty little whinny, I had to laugh out loud. But the filly wasn't singing to us. She was focused on more movement still coming.

With Prairie in my arms and Journey standing over us, I watched a sparkling light bob in the darkness until I finally made out a silhouette. Several silhouettes. One of a horse. I could hear its tack squeaking and jingling now. Another of a man. Two, three men. The glimmering light came from the waist of one of them. That's when I realized who it was.

"Heath!" I cried and ran flailing my arms. His gigantic belt buckle reflected the moon like a homing beacon.

His clear baritone voice called back as he broke from the others, "Paisley, is that you?"

I flung myself at him and he lifted me off the ground in a bear-hug. "Oh my land sakes. You're okay?" He held my face in his hands and swiped some mud off my forehead. "You look horrible."

I let out a whimpered cry and feebly smacked him on the shoulder.

"She's okay," he hollered to the others. "I got her!"

I began to shake. Maybe from relief, maybe from delayed shock, but my muscles trembled in the safety of my cousin's arms, and Heath helped me to the ground as the others rushed up to us.

"Tate," I said trying to focus. "He's hurt!"

River stayed by my side while Heath and Henry sprang into action.

"How did you find us?" I asked as I reached for River now stooping above me.

He held Little Feather's lead but supported me slumped on the ground. "When you and Tate didn't show up at the house by the time we'd sent all the horses out to The Swale to weather the storm, we started out on foot looking for you. The power got knocked out early on. It was so dark. I'm not exactly sure what kind of damage we'll be going home to. By the size of some of the trees we've seen downed, I ..." He paused to rub his stubble. "... I just hope everyone got into the storm shelter." We sat in worried silence for a moment then he took a deep breath. "Anyhow, we just took off looking for you on foot without thinking a whole lot. Don't even have a flashlight." He chuckled and shook his head. "We were going in the wrong direction until *this* little girl showed up, leading Kala by one rein." He flapped Prairie's ears. She looked thoroughly proud of herself sitting inside our huddle.

I squeezed her to me again and whispered, "I knew you would find me."

She dabbed her tongue on my nose and gave me the most sincere look. "Always," she said to only me, and then she nudged me to say, "There's still work to be done here," and scampered to the twins at the trench ledge.

Soon, a nearly unrecognizable Kola emerged, his brindle wolf fur slathered in congealing mud. Next came Tate, wrapped in a t-shirt sling, sliding inch by inch in the twins' arms carefully over the edge. His leg looked worse than before, and his responses made me nervous.

"Wiyaka Cikala?" he moaned, his eyes barely open.

River's soothing voice replied, "Little Feather's right here, Tate. Sturdy girl's just fine. We got her."

"Gh...ghost Sssong?" It was nothing more than a whisper.

"She's here too, Tate. All doing just fine. You stay quiet now. We're gonna get you home quick as a wink, hear?"

Something was not right. "I told him the filly was fine just moments before you got here. He thanked the Creator and everything," I tried to explain.

Tate moaned and tried to sit up. "Pais...ley..."

And just as I rushed to him, his eyes rolled back in his head, and he was out cold.

* * *

A hint of dawn rolled over the horizon as we walked home on the tractor path. Heath and Henry had Tate situated carefully across Little Feather's back. They had secured him with mud-caked Rope, but they also held onto him on either side, careful to support his leg with the post splinter still jabbed through it. Tate's head hung low, and frighteningly weak sounds escaped him now and then. He had to get to the Valley City hospital fast before his leg turned septic.

With Ghost Song ponying at our side and Prairie trotting close behind her, Journey gingerly placed each step. I worried he might be sore and already started thinking about how to best recoup him. That made me think of BG and all the other horses on the ranch, especially the fragile seniors. Where did they go to find safety from storms? River had said something about The Swale, but I tried to mentally prepare for the possibility that some of our old friends may not have made it through the night. The thoughts twisted in my stomach, pain spiraled through my shoulders into the base of my skull.

Nothing, however, could have prepared me for what came into view as we approached the ranch. Air caught in my throat as I clenched Journey's mane in my fists.

River was the only one to find words. "Holy Saint Francis..." was all he could manage, but this was far and away beyond anything having to do with Saint Francis. "... they better have made it into that storm shelter."

Henry stopped in his tracks and words clipped from his mouth, "They'll be fine. They'll be fine." But the words alone could not hold him back. He tore up The Lane leaving Heath to support Tate on his own, but River stepped in to help.

It's difficult explaining the image still seared in my memory. How does one explain when the world she's fallen in love with has met the devil? A winding, twisting, picking and choosing demon. And though my spirituality was in its infant stages, even *I* knew that only an unearthly evil could destroy so much goodness.

My bunkhouse roof lay in splinters strewn everywhere like a game of Pick-Up-Sticks. The door sprawled flat on the porch. A two-by-four stuck out of Oscar's passenger window. The paddock fence in the back was flattened. Prairie and Kola ran to investigate.

"BG!" The sound of the letters sucked inward even though I'd meant to scream them.

River touched my leg quickly. "We turned all the horses out to the east, Paisley. We always do when a storm hits. Trust me. Boss Girl found The Swale along with all the others. It's the safest place for them, especially when there's a tornado on the loose. They know it."

Heath added, "Seriously, Paisley. They really do. We'll find them all cozied up down there chowing on sweet grass. You'll see."

River said, "I'll check on them ..." His eyes flickered seriously to Tate swaying precariously atop Kala then to Henry running full speed up The Drive. "... well, as soon as I can."

I believed them, but I couldn't douse the fear. Boss Girl remained my connection to my mom. I had never entertained the idea of her just ... not being there some day. And let me tell you, reality bites hard when it sinks its teeth in for the first time.

I tried to focus my attention elsewhere, on matters right in front of me rather than those clearly out of my reach at the moment. The guys' bunkhouses still stood, but both had a chunk missing. A wall here. A roof there. A porch rail here. Another wall there.

Doubt. Again. Crept in. Was it a sign? Was it *all* a sign telling me to get the hell out of here?

Gram's voice came to me sure and swift. *Are you kidding me, Paisley? That's what you get out of this? Unbelievable. Look,* she said. *Really look.*

I closed my eyes, let Journey's slow rhythm pulse through me clearing the disaster before me, and then opened them again. It looked different this time.

Chickens wandered across The Drive. The Quonset remained untouched. The machine shed hung together by a thread, its roof rolled off the top like a sardine can, but the mountain of Heath and Henry's tarp-covered secret project still loomed in the shadows. I saw Knut's little barn blown to smithereens, but counted every kitten, chicken and duck wandering waywardly out of the rubble. Prairie attempted to round them up but only scattered them more. Even Flash Goaton and Phyllis, the ornery Shetland pony that bites, found a spot in the yard to graze. Shredded hay bales were scattered everywhere like tumbleweeds in a ghost town — the hay shed a skeleton but still upright. The newly renovated horse barn stood untouched.

Last, I saw a farmhouse at the end of The Lane — half the porch sunken in, gaping holes in the roof, broken glass in every window pane — standing tall. Henry skidded to a stop at the storm shelter attached to the east side of the house. He pulled up the slanted doors. I felt River squeeze my knee again. When we saw Henry help three, four and five figures emerge safe and sound, I grabbed his hand, and he reached his other arm across Tate's back to meet Heath's grip.

Aunt Bert, Knut, Baker Bob, Henry, and Great Uncle Griff stood there rocking in a hug huddle as the morning sun streaked into the yard and Knut's rooster crowed good morning from the top of a busted feed bin. I swear I heard that old house say, "Not to worry, young one. I've been around far too long to let a little wind take me down."

The winged horse that topped the turn-about fountain spewed crystal clear water into the sunlight. Rainbows in misty diamonds showered into the pool.

See? Gram whispered. *Now is the time you belong here the most.*

* * *

In a flurry of movement the scene changed quickly, like someone switched the channel and hit the fast forward button. Before I even grasped what was going on, Tate lay sweating in the back seat of the Bronco with his head on Aunt Bert's lap, Henry in the passenger's seat, and Knut in the way back donning his superman cape. Kola panted next to him. Baker Bob looked from the driver's seat with a grave expression.

I opened the back door to hop in. "I'm coming with you." Prairie pranced at my heels.

Tate raised a hand and moaned, "No Paisley."

Aunt Bert shushed him. "Don't talk. Paisley, scoot in under his legs here."

"No," he said, this time trying to sit up.

My heart sank right down into my boots. After all we'd just been through, now he didn't want me near him? Even Aunt Bert looked taken aback. I tried to save face, "Oh ... yah ... I mean of course. No ... you guys go." Whimper.

"Iyá yo," he said weakly. "Go to them. The Nokota wait for you."

He sounded delirious, but somewhere deep down I got it. Of course the guys were perfectly capable of seeing to the herd; they knew them better than me. But Tate spoke as though it was my duty.

"He's gonna be just fine, Paisley," said Aunt Bert with understanding. She glanced at Bob then back to me. "You go. By the time you meet us at the hospital, he'll be all patched up."

I hesitated. "See you soon."

The door shut and the Bronco vroomed down The Drive.

As soon as Journey, Wiyaka Cikala and Oka Wana Gi were safely tucked into the horse barn with clean hay and fresh water, we piled into the ATV. River checked his vet kit, but Griff held in his lap a pistol.

When he saw horror in my face, he said, "This gun has the same bullet in it that sat in the chamber on the last day of Bob's service with the Marines. I don't aim to use it up lightly."

I squeezed Prairie closer to me and we drove off to the east in silence.

* * *

Out on the east prairie, you couldn't tell much more than a summer sprinkle had dampened the grass. Lightning hadn't touched this wide open section. Heath drove the ATV over the grassy road trying (occasionally) to avoid gopher mounds. I hung on to Prairie squished on the seat next to me. She sensed my nerves because I felt her lean into me. I didn't know if I had what it would take to handle whatever we happened upon in The Swale. I didn't understand how a place could be safe from a storm like that. Racing the herd along the ridge and into the valley just hours ago felt like a distant memory.

When we reached the crest, Heath slowed to a stop, and we got out finding the most perfect scene like something straight out of a painting. Something about the lay of this land — yawning slopes, gentle curves, trees and water — did not invite the Thunder Gods. The herd roamed and grazed like no big deal.

I took mental inventory. The Old Ones mingled in with the Nokota. Smoke-N-Ash and Mazaska stood watch over opposite ends, their nickel plated bodies glistening in the sun. The Not-Yets and young ones frolicked in the morning light reaching down the slope. My heart sang when I saw a flea-bitten, slightly sway-backed Arabian — my beautiful Boss Girl — swinging her head and prancing along with the Little Ones, showing them some moves, no doubt. It was such a sight for my aching eyes, I cannot tell you how hard it was holding back the waterworks.

"See, Paisley. What did I tell ya?" Heath's words sounded like an angel choir. All I could do was chortle and cover my mouth in amazement.

The guys grabbed their clipboard, and I sunk to my knees. A warm breeze swirled over me, and I took in a deep, cleansing breath. But when I heard rustling papers and counting again and again, I noticed the guys rubbing their chins.

"What's the matter?" I asked.

Griff grunted, "Not adding up."

Of course it looked like a full herd to me, but I didn't even begin to think I knew each one like they did … by name even. I knew there should be about 55 horses down there, but I attempted to take mental stock of each.

I saw BG playing with the Little Ones. I found Jesse, River's paint horse, easily enough next to Edison and Einstein, the twins' matching bays, grazing quietly with Bullet, Uncle Griff's red roan Nokota. I could pick out Jimmy, the dressage saddlebred, because he stood at least a couple hands taller. Of course I recognized Tate's two Nokota stallions on either side of the valley, and I was pretty sure I recognized Sica Hota — Gray Squirrel — Ghost Song's mother. But I fell short when trying to account for the rest of the herd. I cursed my poor memory and started counting and counting again.

"Twenty-five Nokota, right?" I asked squinting into the sun rising higher.

"Yep. Oka makes Tate's twenty-sixth," River said. "All Nokota are here. It's ..." he hesitated, "it's one of the seniors we can't seem to find."

My eyes raced over the area where the Old One's seemed to congregate most and started counting. Twenty-nine every time. When there should have been thirty. We scanned the far reaches of the valley then the papers then the landscape again.

Finally, the words we all dreaded came long and slow from River's lips. "Oh no."

We honed in on the spot he sighted. Heath's shoulders just sank, and he dragged his feet back to the ATV.

Griff squinted and grimaced, "Aw ... damnit anyway," and he swiped his cap off and pinched the bridge of his nose. "Like she doesn't already have enough heartache."

"Who is it?" I asked and got up. "Who are we missing? I don't see anyth..."

River took my shoulders gently and turned me so I could see in his line of vision. Northward, farther down the valley, away from the safety of the herd, laid a soft mound my fool eyes had taken for a freshly dug pocket gopher den. But it was not. Only one horse at Forever Fields had a coat that color, a coat of chocolate and a flaxen mane. Methuselah, Aunt Bert's Rocky Mountain, at age thirty-five had decided this would be his day to return to the prairie earth and run again with his ancestors in the forever fields.

With somber hearts, we rode carefully down to the herd. River and Griff set to work going over the Old Ones with a careful eye, only needing to treat a few scrapes here and there. Heath checked on the Not Yets and Tate's Little Ones. I fussed over every square inch of BG. She stood stock still crunching slowly on the mint I'd slipped her. Her eyes told me, "I'm not going anywhere for some time." I hugged her neck and buried my face in her silver mane. She tipped her head over my shoulder, hugged me back, and said. "Go to them."

I went to the Nokota.

Warmth poured through me as I wandered among Tate's horses. Birds flitted from rump to rump. Grass rippled in the warm morning breeze, and I felt my body lift. My shoulders relaxed. The crevice in my brow melted as the stallions watched me approach from their opposite vantage points then continued grazing as though I was a common part of the scenery.

Then, so slowly at first, the bodies began to flow like a current in one direction. Around me. I turned with them. Their pace quickened. My heart beat steadily. This was the scene that played in my dreams.

I stood still, closed my eyes, and drew in a deep breath. The voices came. They whispered *Paaiisley* across the tips of the tall grass and into the air until the sounds swirled above my head lifting my arms. When I opened my eyes, blurry dark faces circled with the horses in grey smoke. *Hunka* they called. Though I did not know who they were, I knew this word meant I belonged. *Go to them, hunka.*

213

The river of horses came to a gradual stop. They looked at me with curious, gentle eyes. I wound around them just like my fingers had worked through the gnarled crabapple tree in the front yard. Patient. Getting to know them one by one. My fingers slid down their necks and over their backs. Never once did they flinch at my touch. I picked feet and searched for stone bruises, checked legs for heat or swelling, and wiped faces free of flies and tears.

Not until I stooped over to pick a stone out of the last one's back hoof did I realize that I had a shadow. Right next to me stood Mashte (MAH-shday). I remembered his name because he was a one-of-a-kind, a Nokota pony cross named for the sunshine in his bronze coat. The little guy's thick flaxen forelock always hid one eye making him look bashful. And the fact that he stood maybe 13.3 hands, tops, made you just want to stuff him in your back pocket and take him home with you, which I'm pretty sure he would have loved. He rubbed his lip like a back scratch over my hunched shoulders. When I stood up, he nuzzled into my belly, and I hugged him.

"Was that a scary storm last night, Sunny?" His head lay heavy in my arms. "Ohhh now, now. Everything's gonna be okay." I looked off to the north where Methuselah lay, soft and silent, and wished someone could have been here for him in his final moments to tell him he would be okay … that his forever fields awaited him, and he had nothing to fear.

Even though the rest of the horses were safe and sound, I could sense the sorrow in the air, for our brother — our tiblo, our ciyé — had left us, and we would miss him.

Griff promised to go out to The Swale with the tractor as soon as we returned from the hospital. Thusie would be laid to rest in a proper burial place like he deserved for his years of dedicated companionship and hard work.

Trying to ease our heavy hearts, I'm sure, River said, "I've never seen anyone work with the Nokota like you did out there, Paisley. Save Tate, of course."

This took me by surprise. "Really?"

Heath said, "Yah, P. They hardly budged while you fussed all over them. Usually it takes a few of us to catch and hold 'em. Sometimes they can get a little wound up, especially if Tate's not around. And after a storm like last night ... well, that was pretty impressive."

"Really?" was all I could say again. Then I realized that somehow, I knew it would be that way. I had always known it. From my dreams.

Even Griff offered, "Damn nice work, yah," as he stared, hard and squinty, over the open prairie.

A smug grin twitched the corners of my mouth, but I brimmed with genuine gratitude before replying, "Thanks guys. It felt ... natural. I guess they just kind of thought the same."

River smiled. "I guess so."

Chapter 18

Outside Tate's hospital room, I took inventory of my appearance — my *new* clothes had finally dried so that my gauzy tunic top — now a stained, muddy train wreck — hung like cardboard. I attempted to run my fingers through my gnarled hair. So much for my new look. But after everything that had just happened in the last twelve hours, I didn't give a rat's butt.

Tate lay on his hospital bed with his leg wrapped and hoisted up like a mummy. Everyone looked expectantly as the doctor came in with his report.

"Well, son, whatever this old drill sergeant is feeding you out there on the open prairie, just tell him to keep it coming. You've got a leg of steel, young man, like Clark Kent himself," Dr. Bjorn said. "Be sure to tell Knut I said so too."

Tate smiled, relieved. "Sure thing, doc." Then he rested his head back on his pillow and reached for my hand.

Not Aunt Bert's hand. Not any of the other five people jammed in his room either. Mine. So I took it and leaned against his bedside. I wondered if anyone could hear me purring.

"The herd is fine," I told him. "Hardly a scratch on them."

Trust poured from his eyes as he softly squeezed.

River interjected, "She's got a real gift with them, this one."

"I know," he said and held my gaze giving me butterflies.

But before any of us got too comfortable, there came a voice from the hallway that sent shivers down my spine.

"Don't you worry your pretty red head about it. I'll find my way."

Remmy Stone prowled down the hall.

Tate's grip tightened like a vice, and I nearly cried out in pain but for the panic locking my throat. Heath and Henry stationed themselves at the door, and by the looks on their faces, this guy wouldn't be getting close to our family today.

Between the twins' shoulders appeared a slick, black haired, cocky face, and it pained me to see, now that I knew the story, the resemblance. Remmy and Tate shared the same almond eyes, high cheekbones, and powerful jaw line. By portrait alone, anyone could see they were brothers. My heart grew heavy for Tate who was unable to escape.

Dr. Bjorn tried to help. "Mr. Stone, this is *family only* visitor time. I'm going to have to ask you to leave."

"Oh, but my dear, dear Dr. Bjorn ..." Remmy sneered, "don't you see? I *am* family." He spread his arms in *too* grand a gesture but was met with stony silence from every face in the room. Tate looked away, disgusted.

"No? Well then. I guess I'll have to switch this to a business visit." His mock friendliness disintegrated into a dark and eerie glower. Chills prickled the back of my neck as Heath and Henry turned back to us showing a flicker of concern.

Aunt Bert stepped forward, all four-feet-eight inches of her, and took charge. "What's your business here, Remington?"

Sharp as a knife he said, "I just happened to swing by your place this morning and thought it only fair to tell you upfront ..."

Uncle Griff growled as he stepped next to Aunt Bert, "Tell us what? We know well and good our place got hit." He put his hand on Bert's shoulder, while Baker Bob and River stood firm behind them. The air was rank with worry, but no one showed it.

"Well ..." He drawled it out as though he didn't want to have to tell us whatever he was about to say, but we knew better. "I'm afraid perhaps you don't quite understand just exactly how the whole insurance world works. You see, it's just been out of the goodness of my heart that I've been letting you slide on your payments for the last year. But the one thing I have no control over is the fact that without making said payments, you in turn have no home owners insurance. My company has no choice but to deny any claims you send in. You see, it's nothing personal, just business." His bleached smile went *ting*.

Low and throaty, Henry snarled, "Why you..." and in a flash he was on top of the man, barreling him onto the cold tile in the hallway and pummeling him with rock-hard fist after fist.

Heath raced to pull his brother off Remmy, but not before he got a few punches of his own in, which made Bob and River step up with a strong hand to yank them all to their feet, chests puffing and faces sweating. Dr. Bjorn grabbed the phone. I stood protectively in front of Tate. Aunt Bert stomped right to the doorway as Bob wrapped Remmy's arms backward.

For a second, I swore Bert was going to land her fist smack in the center of his gut, but she just stood there looking straight up at his bleeding lip.

Her voice rumbled so low in her throat, I had to lean in to hear the word, "Iktomi."

Remmy's arrogance flickered but an instant then he tried ripping his arms free, but his weaselly frame was no match for Baker Bob's one-handed Marine Corps grip.

"I think you've over-stayed your welcome," River said steadily.

"Fine," Remmy said. "Let me go, and I'll throw you poor dogs a bone."

Aunt Bert stared him down with pitbull intensity then gave a nod for his release.

He straightened his suit and hair as he sauntered away down the hall saying, "I'll make you a deal ... since you're *family* ..." He gave a sarcastic bow. Heath had to stop Henry from lunging again. "You can either come up with the missing payments *plus fees and interest* ... or ... you could forfeit the whole junk pile of a ranch to me. Either way," he straightened his tie, "if I don't get what's coming to me by summer's end, your little operation is closing down just like it should have over a year ago. Forever Fields is out of time."

Just as hospital security rounded the corner, Remmy Stone slicked back his black hair and strode the other way out the double doors.

* * *

In just two days time, Tate came home. And by "home" I mean we moved him temporarily to the ranch. He and Griff bunked together in what we eventually coined The Recovery Cabin, and we devised a schedule for all of us to take shifts looking after his place.

I spent the better part of a day trying to find my few things strewn all over kingdom come. Honestly, all I really cared about was my old paisley pants, which had somehow gotten stuffed under Oscar's hood (no lie), and Gram's picture, which I found over by the Quonset. Finding her sitting upright, hands in her lap, loose, gray bun framing her resolute face ... well ... it gave me strength.

A little old storm can't take me out.

I laughed out loud at the irony and held her picture close.

Pages from my journal turned up in the oddest places. Everyone collected them whenever they found one or two. I kind of panicked about other people reading my private thoughts. Thankfully, it seemed they were respecting my privacy as they handed them over throughout the days that followed.

Even Heath said when he found several sheets stuck in the roof of the machine shed and I snatched them defensively out of his hands, "Don't worry. We don't *want* to know any of the drama going on up there." He knuckle tapped my head. Still, I hugged the pages close and stomped away.

I had to sleep on the sofa in the big house living room for a few nights, which was fine, but I did feel out of place and my back started kinking up. Aunt Bert had made Knut offer me his room upstairs until my bunkhouse could be fixed, but who knew how long that would be? It's not like we could afford to rebuild anytime soon (or ever). Remmy Stone's doom hung over us like a dark cloud. So when I told Knut no, I was given two options: sleep in the basement spare bedroom across the hall from Baker Bob (who, by the way, confessed openly to snoring like a freight train and sleepwalking in his underwear to the kitchen) *or* convert the old tack room into living quarters.

"Barn it is," I said.

Everyone concurred. Definitely the wiser choice.

"And Paisley," Aunt Bert said, "we should really give your dad a call and let him know what's going on. I'm sure Peter would want to know you're safe."

Panic seared my shoulders instantly. "No!" I cried and I felt the crease in my brow dig deep. "He doesn't need to know anything."

Aunt Bert said steadily, "But he is family. And family has a right to…"

"I'm eighteen. I'll decide what he has a right to know." My teeth ground as I worked my clenched jaw.

"Well, I'm just saying, is all," Bert finished the conversation with a wave of her fork.

Tate looked down at his plate. I felt childish. It's not like Dad would make me go back to Grover with him and Cindy. But I couldn't risk it.

Baker Bob set a freshly opened jar of chokecherry jelly on the table and changed the subject. "So did anyone hear what kind of shape old Crazy Ned's land is in now?"

"Crazy Ned?" I asked thankful for a shift in conversation.

Tate took a spoonful of jelly for his toast and passed the jar. "You could say he's our next-door neighbor. He owns the piece of prairie across from The Lane. The land we danced through."

"You did the Thunder Dance?" asked River.

Aunt Bert said, "That's burned cinder crisp."

Tate chewed and nodded. "Mmhm." He looked proud. So did everyone around the table.

"It's horrible, what the fires did to that land," I said picking at my omelet. "So sad."

Seven full mouths replied *no*. River explained, "Quite the contrary, Paisley. Fires on the prairie are good things. I'd say that land was due for a grass fire, all choked out with weeds. A burn like that will revive it like no fertilizer ever could. It will come back, don't you worry."

"Something good from something bad," Knut sing-songed and stuffed his mouth full of jelly toast.

"That's right, Knut," Aunt Bert praised and patted his hand. "That's what we try to teach. There's always some good that can come from something bad." Through her cheery façade, my aunt looked tired, and I wondered if she truly believed the words herself at the moment.

I spread chokecherry jelly on my toast, and we all sat quiet for a moment listening to each other chew. No one had said a thing about how we were going to fix the damage from the storm, but it hung like skunk in the air. I wanted so bad to ask how we were going

221

to pull something good out of this one, but Griff beat me to it.

"How the hell are we gonna repair this place?" he barked.

Everyone sat rigid, not knowing what to say, but I'm guessing also glad he had the balls to ask it out loud. Forks clinked on plates. River and Tate exchanged glances, but I tried not to make eye contact with anyone and stared at the jar of jelly in front of me. The morning light shone through the rippled glass making the red sweetness shine like jewels.

River studied me from across the table. "Something on your mind, Paisley?"

Dang it if all eyes weren't smack dab on me again.

"Actually," I started with hesitation, "I kind of do."

"Well, what is it?" Griff demanded.

I knew it was a hair-brained, little kid idea, but it wasn't really my idea at all. Aunt Bert brought it up all the time and everyone always laughed it off. But the silly idea visited me at every meal when I saw those jars glistening like rubies lined up on the baker's rack in the window. And every time I rode past the heavy-leaden chokecherry bushes all the way down The Lane, or hanging over the water at The Spring, or reaching over the iron fence on the west side of the front garden.

I stared at the jelly jar, bit my lip, and went for it. "We should sell Baker Bob's award-winning chokecherry jelly?" I didn't mean it as a question.

No one said a word. They all sat there like I'd spoken Klingon.

Deep breath. "I mean, really, you've all said it before. It's the best jelly in the tri-state area. People would flock to stores to get it once they tried it even once. I know it's not like it would pay for everything, but maybe it could be a start. I'm sure we can think of other things too." *And hold.*

222

Knut, always a young man of reason, agreed as he swiped a glob of this very jelly off his chin. "Mmhmm. It's the best," he said. A high-class marketer couldn't have directed him better.

"There's our slogan." *End pitch. Wait.*

Slowly, forks clinked onto plates. River dabbed his mouth with a napkin. Bob grinned politely and looked at a jelly jar. Why wasn't anyone saying anything?

Aunt Bert smiled gently. "What do you say, Robert? You ready to go commercial like I keep harassing you to do?"

Baker Bob's smiled gently too. "It's a lovely idea. I'll check with Billy at the diner for price on pectin and sugar."

Henry added, "Shirley and Lars Anderson will sell it at Norse Drive Market, I'm sure. Filip is home from college this weekend. I'll catch up with him. See what he thinks."

Tate offered, "We could set up a booth at the local horse shows and auctions. I can talk to Robin Strongwind and see if she'd be willing to do a little promoting for us on her tours with Prairie Fire."

"And we should make flyers to hang in storefronts, like that Ahhh Spa you and I went to," said Aunt Bert. "If we put a bug in Candice and Evelyn's ear, those two gossips will make sure everyone from here to the Black Hills knows about it."

Everyone's eyes sparkled a little brighter than just a few minutes ago. That alone was worth speaking up. But I couldn't help feeling it all seemed a bit gratuitous.

Enter Wet-Blanket Uncle Griff.

"Hold on just one goll dang minute!"

I cringed. The rest of my family froze.

"Have you all gone off your nut? Have you forgotten the cost of running this place?" We fell silent. "Feed. Medication. Machinery. The electric bill alone nearly puts us under every month. Why don't you set up a lemonade stand while you're at it."

Wow, did I feel stupid.

Aunt Bert stared at him. Her jaw set and her eyes frustrated. "Griffin Cy Tuson…" She let out a deep breath. "There's no harm in a little hope. Small dreams breed big dreams."

Griff harrumphed.

Heath eyed Henry, and their devilish smirks showed they were up to something. "Actually, Bert's right on track."

Henry said, "We've got something you all should see."

* * *

"Ladies and gentlemen, what you are about to see will astonish and amaze."

We stood inside the machine shed in front of the ring master twins' tarp-covered monstrosity about to make its debut.

Griff grunted.

"What is it! What is it!" I thought Knut's red head might explode if they didn't pull that tarp off quick.

Heath said, "Brother, are we sure they're ready?" His theatrics left something to be desired.

"Indeed, Brother. I believe the time has come." Henry shouldn't quit his day job either.

They walked to opposite sides of the shed and grabbed hold of identical, red levers on the wall. They looked at each other, nodded one – two – three, and threw the levers down setting off a pulley system which raised the tarp slowly all the way to the ceiling. Heath and Henry looked at us with wide eyes, and though I could tell they thought we should have been leaping for joy and applauding, maybe even swiping a tear, I'm pretty sure we all just saw a pile of metal sitting on several flatbed trailers.

"What is it?"

Thank you, Kah-noot.

"Isn't it obvious?" Griff's sarcasm cut like a knife. "It's a bunch a scrap metal we'll get about a dollar for at the recycle yard."

The twins grinned completely unshaken and continued their presentation. Heath disappeared as Henry continued.

"Ah, the unaided eye might see just such a thing. But if you take a closer look, you will see ... the future." They'd obviously put a lot of time into this little demo. It was kind of adorable.

Heath drove a four-wheeler out from the back of the shed, hooked it up to a flatbed, and pulled it into the sunlight. It wasn't pretty. Odd shaped metal sections bolted together to create gigantic half-pipe – ten, maybe fifteen, feet high each – nested on the trailer. Henry came out on the tractor pulling another flatbed with long, wedge-shaped sections that, as best as I could decipher, when put together might make propellers. It wasn't until Heath came back out with another trailer carrying an enormous egg-shaped cylinder — what I can only guess contained a motor of sorts — when I actually started to get the picture. Tate and River and Bert and Bob and Griff must have too, because you should have seen the look on their faces melt from skeptical grimaces to sheer disbelief.

"It's an airplane!" Knut screeched.

Awestruck, Aunt Bert shook her head and said, "Oh my holy Saint Francis, boys. Is this what I think it is?"

Those two hounds just crossed their arms and nodded proudly.

Knut reiterated, "It's an airplane!"

Struggling for words, River asked, "And it ... works?"

The boys gave him such a look. But when no one knew what else to say, Henry explained, "It's not an airplane, Knut buddy. It's something even better. This little wind turbine will power our entire ranch, and Tate's place too, just like the big wind farms."

Baker Bob said, "Oh my Lord, boys. I knew you were crafty, but this ... this is a bit more complicated than converting an old washing machine into a lawnmower like you did last summer."

Cocksure, Henry came back, "It'll work. Just wait and see."

At this point, we believed. We had to. Even Griff took off his hat to scratch his head.

Henry went on, "And in time, if we want, we can extend it to neighbors. I imagine Crazy Ned will be *quite* happy to get his juice from us."

"All contingent, of course, on Tate's namesake, that is."

Tate straightened and spoke with great pride, "Taku skan skan — the power of the sacred prairie tate will endure just as they have for ages past." No sooner than those words left his lips did a stiff gust come along and nearly knock us off kilter.

Griff, still scratching his head, started mumbling to the ground as he walked away, "...with the saddlebred and a few others ... auction this weekend ... just gotta finish that three-year-old ... just might ... maybe a clinic ..."

"What's that you say, Griffin?" asked Aunt Bert, and he startled. "You wouldn't happen to have an idea brewing under that gray ponytail of yours now, would you?"

Everyone stopped and gaped.

"No. Of course not," he snapped, but then he stopped in his tracks, looked back at us, then down to the ground again. He calculated something in the dirt with his toe. "I don't know." Snort. "Well ... maybe." Grumble.

Now, a Griff Tuson rookie would have guessed that wrinkled old Cayuse was right ticked off at the mere thought, but if I'm not mistaken, I dare believe I heard the slightest, ever-so-tiniest hint of a smile in his voice. But I also got the distinct impression that we were all to leave it at that — not say a word more for fear of destroying the possibility of the great Griff Tuson working his magic with the horses of Forever Fields once again.

Instinctually, taking the attention off Griff, River changed the subject quickly. "I believe we better get started assembling this monster as soon as we get back."

"Back from what?" I asked.

A second silence took over the energy in the air as our attention turned from Great Uncle Griff to Aunt Bert looking off into the sunrise. "Companion Fields. I have a friend to say goodbye to."

* * *

It's a sacred place, Companion Fields, filled with memories whispering over gentle, open slopes and through cottonwood trees — a place where a person could perhaps catch a glimpse of the Forever Fields in the beyond. A place to remind us that Forever Fields Farm is only a temporary rest home for the Old Ones. And they cannot live forever.

Oval patches scattered the hills and valleys, each a special site much like a church yard. Some had monuments of piled rocks, others simply covered with a blanket of wild roses. Aunt Bert stood far away by a soft, fresh mound. Her stance was strong, her hands on her hips, but her blonde head was bowed low.

"What's she doing?" I asked Tate.

"She is having a conversation with her tiblo. This is not the last she will have with Methuselah, but I believe, for her, it will be the most important." He shifted on his cane to look at me. "So often we do not get to say goodbye to them before they go. No one can predict when the spirit world will come for the Old Ones. This horse was special to your aunt, and she

227

needs her time with him before he fades into the sea of spirits roaming the Forever Fields of beyond."

I digested that. It felt good to think our horses didn't fade away into nothingness. It comforted me to know they were still there. More importantly, it reassured me that the horses in my dreams were indeed real. I knew it now. They were the horses of our past. They run with my ancestors. That is why I heard the voices in the winds as they circle me. Though I still didn't recognize the human faces that accompany them.

The horses. The spirits. The voices. The faces. They are of me and I am of them.

I looked at the people by my side, holding their hats in one hand and their horse in the other. They looked down at the ground or off into the hills. Journey stood behind me with his head lightly touching my shoulder. I could feel his breath flutter down my arm. Prairie and Kola sat side by side.

I took in the diversity. Tate's black silk tresses blew in the breeze blending with Little Feather's mane. Heath's blonde curls and Henry's blonde-white buzz cut made a sharp contrast against Edison and Jefferson's dark bay coats. Knut's red crazy curls flopped in the wind like Phyllis's bushy forelock. I had to laugh at how ridiculous he looked riding that little pony with his feet practically dragging. She never seemed happier, though.

River's trimmed black hair lay in sleek waves like the curved black-against-white lines of his paint, Jesse, standing regally with his nose to the wind. Baker Bob's silver Marine Corp cut glinted in the sunshine next to his silver Nokota named Sheriff. And then the two dark-skinned, wrinkled men standing side by side with their thin, gray-streaked ponytails trailing down their backs next to their matching red roan Nokotas, Bullet and …

Two dark-skinned, wrinkled men? Two red roans?

228

Gram's voice came echoing in from a distance. *You know who it is.*

And she was right. I knew exactly who had joined us. I touched Tate's arm gently and nodded down the line. He remained calm but as he returned my glance, I could see excitement in his eyes.

The newcomer asked, "Methuselah?"

I could literally feel Great Uncle Griff's muscles tighten, but he didn't budge. He knew exactly who stood next to him too.

Griff's brother had joined us on the hill, unannounced. Lenny Tuson's part in our story was about to play.

Chapter 19

On the awkward ride back to the house, Griff's face and neck seethed red. Anyone could see he harbored serious resentment for his brother abandoning him and the ranch back in the day. I tried to imagine a time when the famous Tuson brothers performed horse training miracles, but the images just wouldn't come. I couldn't see beyond Great Uncle Griff's crusty shell, and I doubted if he ever had any real talent with horses. Lenny probably did it all. Now Lenny, *he* I pictured calming a wild one in his day. His easy way and gentle eyes ... *he* had the magic. Regardless, the two brothers' paths had joined again, and who knew what might result. I only hoped, as he stomped off to his bunkhouse, Griff would get over himself soon.

The rest of us ... oh my, were we happy to see Lenny. We each had our own reasons. I can only say mine for sure, but just his presence injected something different here at the ranch. He hadn't been through the storm. He hadn't been dealing with Remmy Stone. He came to us fresh, and I believe hope rode with him.

Heath and Henry watered and turned out our horses first before taking Lenny's little red roan Nokota named Slingshot to the guest stall to bunk next to Journey and Boss Girl. They would make sure he felt welcome.

"Lenard, where's your rig?" asked Aunt Bert, her face all lit up. "You didn't ride all the way from Grover!"

"By golly no!" said Lenny. "Hitched a ride with …" His eyes shifted slightly. "… a guy."

A *guy*? Kind of vague.

River voiced my thought. "What guy?"

Lenny winked and shook River's hand. "Said he'd heard you got hit hard by the storm." I swear Uncle Lenny kept shifting glances at me. "… I don't think you'd know him."

"Oh my good Lord in heaven, he saw the place like *this*?" Bert swept a hand to her head and looked at the boarded-up buildings, the tar papered roofs, and the patched corrals and fences. Though we had started putting it back together, the whole place still lay in ruins.

Lenny waved his hands. "Not to worry, Bertie." Here, he searched hard for his words. "He told me … uh … he'd send some business your way."

He was so hiding something.

I thought Aunt Bert might've bust out crying though. "Oh Lenard. I don't know exactly what kind of business we could offer *anyone* at the moment, but bless his heart for saying so. Who was it?" She looked to River. "Maybe we'll recognize his name from the auctions."

"Oh. Yah. His name. Now what was the name? Rusty was it?" He rubbed his stubble beard a little too emphatically and looked around the place pausing at a broken fence board with nails sticking out. "Yah. Rusty Nailer. You know him?"

Cockamamie. But why would Great Uncle Lenny make it up?

Both River and Bert squinted real hard. "No." Bert looked at River. "You, River?"

River only eyed Lenny and slowly shook his head. They knew something was up too.

Lenny threw his hands in the air. "Look at us. I been standing half a hop from you for how many minutes now and I haven't gotten so much as a peck on the cheek from my little niece-in-law. How's my Alberta Lynn?" He drew her in and I thought he whispered something in her ear. When they held each other at arm's length, Aunt Bert had an everything-makes-sense-now expression. She nodded and winked at River confirming my suspicions. But I worked really hard to shove them aside because it was ruining Lenny's homecoming.

We stood around Great Uncle Lenny at the fountain asking questions and telling him the latest. Knut even ran inside for his comic book collection.

Everyone had some kind of connection to the man. I remembered like it was yesterday buying Oscar out of the church parking lot and sharing a Baby Ruth with him three years ago. His eyes twinkled knowingly when I shook his hand.

"How's that old tin can doing, girly?" He tipped up his cap and looked at good old Oscar parked in the tall grass by the machine shed.

I gave a sheepish grin. "Oscar? Well, he doesn't get much use these days. I mostly get around on horseback here."

"Aw, that won't do," he said. "The more you use that tough old so-n-so, the longer he'll last. That's the truth for most things getting up in the years." He winked and elbow nudged me. "Humans too, ya know what I mean."

Everyone laughed. I wondered if that was the reason he'd come. Then I thought about Griff harrumphing inside his stuffy old cabin.

Once we had all said our hellos and caught up a smidge, it was time to get back to business. I don't know what our deal was, but Lenny's arrival kind of threw us all for a loop. In a good way. (Except Crabpot, of course). It kicked us into high gear, thinking and making plans. Our world started turning a little faster. And though he and Griff could darn near have been twins not only in looks but voice and mannerisms, the younger brother popped around spry enough to transfer his energy onto us.

And things got done.

The twins set straight to work on the wind turbine. River went to repair paddocks and shelters. Knut got to work fixing up his little barn. Baker Bob took off for Billy's to get a Bronco full of sugar and pectin. The twins started slapping temporary plywood walls onto bunkhouses.

I set Saint Francis of Assisi upright next to the swing in the front yard. I knew I needed to start clearing out my quarters, but the jumping beans popping in me wanted so bad to stay and talk to Great Uncle Lenny. Instead, however, of ruining Aunt Bert's time alone with him — I am proud to say I didn't even need a reminder from Gram this time — I settled with listening through the fence.

"It's so good to see you again," Aunt Bert said again once they were alone, and she nearly squeezed the daylights out of him. "Just so good."

Lenny gave it right back. "Yah," he said with his thick Scandinavian accent. "But what the hell d'ya do to the place, Berty?"

She let out a burst of sunshine laughter I hadn't heard in days, and I knew right then, these two had history. Good history. "Question is, what are we *going* to do with it?"

Lenny just shook his head and slapped his hands on his bony hips. His crinkled eyes squinted even more in the sun and the two of them stood there by the trickling fountain looking out over the yards … and then at Griff and Tate's bunkhouse. "Well, I'm not sure how much help I'm going to be if big brother doesn't warm up to the idea of me being here. You know I'll do what I can, but I don't want to cause problems."

"You just let me handle Griffin. He can't lock himself up in that hut forever. A *conversation* will set him right."

* * *

"No. Not that one."

By early afternoon, Tate (thank God) saved me from neck deep garbage in the horse barn's old tack room. Let's just say it would be a while before I could call it my own. He picked me up in the UTV since his leg was still mending and asked me to help him with the herd.

On the advice of his uncle, Tate had been told to always have a few Nokota horses available to sell in case of emergency. River had explained to him several years ago, "Gentled and trained, they'll bring a good price."

Tate had been quick to reply, "It's not about money. It's never been about money."

River had explained, "Oh I understand that. Believe me, I do. But sometimes you have to do things you maybe don't want to ... and you can't keep things clutched tight all the time. So you settle in with a deal you can handle without losing too big a piece of yourself."

This hard lesson brought both Tate and me to the south pasture where the full herd gathered every day at the windmill watering hole. Sitting in the tall grass, we watched the Nokota babies nurse and the geldings play "bite, bite, rear, kick." A few stretched their thick necks and lifted their lip way up like having a good laugh at our expense, but I knew this was their way of catching our scent. Then Prairie and Kola got a wild hare and stirred them all up, so Smoke-N-Ash got the herd on the move. Their hooves sounded like rippling thunder breaking over the gentle swell of the land. We got a good look at them as they swept past, circled and came to rest on another nearby slope.

"Okay." I tried to keep my patience in check. "How about *that* one?" A black speckled stud with a solid black face kept his eye on us and snorted.

"No, no, no. I can't sell him. He's got the best sense of humor."

I could not hold back a *look* for that, but I pointed to a little strawberry roan.

He said, "No! No one gets him. He's the fastest in the field."

By the end of a half hour of this, we had identified the shyest, the bravest, the calmest, the meanest, the craftiest, and the laziest. We also found the ones with the most balance, the most wisdom, the most people sense, and the most level-headedness. When we'd gone through the full herd, only five horses remained. Son-of-a-Smoke, a two-year-old blue roan stud always looking for trouble. Appledance, an energetic strawberry roan filly no bigger than a pony. Tumbleweed, a leggy three-year-old bay roan gelding. Switchgrass, a four-year-old buff gelding with a black mane and tail. And finally, three-year-old Cloud, a mild-mannered black and white painted mare with a homely face. The pain washed vividly across Tate's expression as he struggled to come up with a reason not to offer these five up for sale.

"They're good horses too, Tate," I said. "It's not like just because you're willing to sell them that you don't think they're good enough to keep."

I was trying to comfort him, but at the same time I knew how bad he wanted — no ... needed — to contribute somehow.

"Anyone who gets these horses," I continued, "is inheriting an excellent representation of the Nokota breed. You *want* that. You want their new owners to be happy and be able to say '*I* have a Maycomb Nokota horse,' and that's got to really mean something."

He drew in a deep breath and stared out at the herd. I wasn't sure he was convinced.

"Tell me again, Tate, what's so great about your horses?" When he looked at me, I gave him a cheeky grin. "What's different about your horses compared to those wimpy-ass Prairie Fire brands?" I was egging him on, of course. He'd preached this lesson to me a hundred times, but I think he needed to hear the words come from his own mouth right then.

"They are a true line," he said. "They possess the most historic Lakota influence anyone will find short of those bred by the Kuntz's in the Missouri River Valley."

I smiled proudly. "Sitting Bull would have wanted these horses to live with the people. You told me once, 'They are searching for their families.' Remember?" He looked at me and waited for my words. I waited for them too. Something swallowed them into the back of my throat.

Get it out. It's time to get it out, Gram said.

"I know ..." I looked at my feet. "... how it feels to wonder where your family is. And I also know how good it feels when ... when you find them," I whispered. Tate took my hand. "Let them find their tiwáhe, Tate, one horse, one person at a time."

Gram's voice sighed on the wind, *Well done.*

Tate didn't speak, but I could tell he was thinking — thinking about the history of these horses he called our brothers and our sisters. About tiwáhe, family. Meadowlarks called while the prairie winds swept over our silence.

"They will make good companions," he said at last. "And will only go to the best families."

Like he had to tell me that.

"Well duh," I rolled my eyes and nudged him out of his seriousness. It took him a second, but eventually he smiled and pulled me in for a long, soft hug. The kind I thought I'd never feel again. The kind I'd decided to never give or receive because I was so sure there would be no one on this planet honest enough to share it with.

236

I sank into it, warm and easy, and hugged him back.

* * *

With the help of the ever-capable Prairie and her apprentice Kola, Tate and I cut out the five horses with the UTV and herded them back to the farmyard.

"Those there are some nice animals," Lenny's voice came to us as he too leaned his tiny frame against the round pen rails. "Whatcha plannin' on doing with 'em?"

Tate straightened and took a breath. I could tell Lenny's legendary reputation as a horse trainer and breeder made him nervous. "I aim to gentle and train them," he said never looking away from the five Nokota. "Then sell them for a good price to good homes." Only then did he look to Lenny, and though I know he was trying to exude confidence, I could hear question in his voice. Oh, how many times had the very same self-doubt plagued me. But I *knew* this was right.

Lenny simply nodded, looked down at Tate's bum leg, and looked back out to the horses. He was smiling. "'Course you are. That one there." He pointed to Son-of-a-Smoke. "That's a nice animal. Look at his gait. A runnin' walk, sure as shoot. See how he's always got one foot on the ground goin' this-a-way and that? That's a smooth ride."

Tate perked at the observation. "Many Nokota are naturally gaited horses. It helps them travel long distances with an efficient pace."

"Is that so?" Lenny asked, but I suspected he already knew it.

Tate asked, "Do you know much about the Nokota?"

"Ohhhh," Lenny dragged it out and kind of shook his head as he inspected the top of his boot. "I guess I know a thing or two."

I knew full well that this was mostly Tate's deal, but I couldn't hold myself back. "Lenny." Tate gave me a quick glance. "I know you just got here and all, and I'm not sure what it is you plan to do to help out, but we all know you were a legend when you and Griff used to train and breed here back in the day. When this ranch was really rockin'. I don't suppose you could help work with these horses?"

Oh mah gah. Did I really just do that?

Tate's eyes grew the size of saucers. He whipped his head to hear Lenny's reply.

Lenny squinted and smiled at the five Nokota in the round pen. Then he looked across the yards to Uncle Griff's closed-up bunkhouse.

He bobbed his gray pony-tailed head and tipped his straw hat up. "I believe I told you what I think about that, girly." He leaned so he could look both Tate and me in the eye. "The more we tough old so-and-sos get used, the longer we last." Wink. "Get me a rope."

Prairie's ears shot up like darts at the word. She bolted to the horse barn and came back with Rope. I thought she'd retired the disgusting thing after its traumatic experience in the storm.

"Bark!" she yipped as I ignored her and handed Lenny a lunge line. "Bark, BARK," she demanded.

Lenny raised an eyebrow. "That one, huh?" he said to little miss bossy pants.

"No, Lenny," I said, "here. Use this one."

"*Growl.*"

I rolled my eyes. "Seriously?"

Lenny ambled over to Prairie. "Say, say now. Let me see here. What do you have?"

Her whole rear end wrenched back and forth.

Lenny, being too kind, examined Rope. He twisted the frayed ends in his fingers, snapped it several times in several places, twirled it and coiled it. Prairie sat with perfect posture observing, her head tipped and ears cocked like awaiting a doctor's report.

"Hmm," he said. "It seems we have here a perfectly good rope looking for a job. I like the tough old ones ya know. They don't make 'em like they used to."

Prairie's mouth opened wide and pant smiled.

"Let's have a look, shall we?" he said as his crouched little body clambered up to the top rail. Tate and I joined him. He slapped Rope on his leg and clicked. "Get along," he said as he flung it out to get the five Nokota moving around. His crinkled eyes studied them while he coiled Rope. "Watch 'em now."

He chuckled and pointed to leggy Tumbleweed and the buff-bay Switchgrass pecking at each other and romping every which way. "They gotta get the nonsense out first."

Cloud and Appledance, the mare and filly, set their heads low and trotted around steadily. "The mares," he said without taking his eyes off them, "always so serious, get down to business. Just like a woman."

"I heard that!" hollered Aunt Bert coming down The Drive to join us. "Smart-aleck."

Lenny ducked and winked at me.

Son-of-a-Smoke stood in the center, his black head held high, staring at us. Lenny squinted hard at him for a second, sucked something out of his teeth, and leapt down into the pen. He stood up slowly from the jump down, pulled up his saggy pants and cracked his back.

"Tell me about this guy," he said.

I looked to Tate, and I have to be honest, I was a little concerned for Lenny's safety. He just seemed so … I don't want to say *old*, but … maybe just not-so-sturdy.

Tate explained, "Son-of-a-Smoke is one of Smoke-N-Ash's, a stallion I got from the Kuntz brothers in Linton."

"Mmhm. Fine animal."

Son-of-a-Smoke snorted and shook his head sending his black mane flying in the breeze.

"He's not too sure about all this fuss," Lenny said and he flapped Rope up high then, with amazing accuracy, it lightly tapped the two-year-old's rump. Son-of-a-Smoke moved on into the flow of the other four horses. Lenny pulled a ratty hankie out of his back pocket and swiped his bulbous nose a few times as he kept studying.

Aunt Bert joined us on the top rail. I whispered to her, "Is he okay in there by himself?"

She looked back at me like I'd just called Saint Francis a nincompoop. "Paisley *Alberta*." Her mouth gaped at first then settled into a sly grin. "I don't know. Tate, what do you think? Does *old* Lenard here need help with this wild mob?"

I could've lived without the sarcasm.

Tate smiled gently, nudged my shoulder. "Watch."

Great Uncle Lenny moved toward the center of the pen, and as he walked … he changed. With each step his shoulders lifted and his footfalls lightened. Lithe and springy, he moved among them. Their heavy feet sent gravel flying. Their thousand-pound bodies shuffled this way and that, often bumping at the barrel or hind quarters warranting a swift blow from behind, or jab from the front, or a nip at the neck.

Relaxed, Lenny held his head high and kept walking right through the five scrambling horses as though taking a stroll down The Lane for the mail. His eyes flitted from one to the next. They watched him too. Especially Son-of-a-Smoke. Lenny meandered among them as though protected by a magical force-field.

Once he reached the center of the round pen, he stood. And without doing a single thing, save raise his hands slightly, the jumbled horses slowly began to sort themselves out until they created a single line. Bay, blue and strawberry roan, buff, and black and white all melded into one sea of movement. No horse

240

led. No horse followed. Their hooves shuffled rhythmically through the soft footing — breaths puffing in and out in time, mouths licking and chewing, eyes waiting. They created a circle, and Lenny was their center.

"Wow," I said feeling chills.

"Mmhm," said Aunt Bert. She smiled wide and put her hand on my shoulder. "It's quite a thing," she said and leaned her head against mine.

Tate whispered, "He's not done. Keep watching."

After several minutes, Lenny steadily lowered his hands and the horses slowed their pace. Gradually, they all came to a stop then, one by one — Cloud first, Son-of-a-Smoke last — sauntered to the center where Lenny rubbed their heads and talked to them softly.

He looked up at me and grinned. "Your turn."

* * *

Throughout the afternoon, Lenny taught me how to gentle the horses. I started with Cloud, and he started with Switchgrass. The others waited in an adjacent pen. Prairie and Kola sat next to each other staring in, ready to spring into action should duty call.

Patiently coaching me through every step, Lenny and I lassoed our charges and taught them how to give to pressure so we would be able to lead them. I put even pressure on Cloud's neck just until she gave then I released immediately.

"Reward with release. Always reward with release," Lenny said over and over.

"Reward with release," I said to myself as I tried to get the timing just right. Each time my little three-year-old Painted Cloud gave me a little bit more and a little bit more until she let me lead her all the way around the pen.

Then Lenny showed me how to use a stick-n-string to get her used to being touched all over. I gently slung the string around her hind end and her legs and her neck and even her belly. Once I got her to the point where she didn't flinch a hair while I did this, we moved on.

Next, we played "Accept the Human" with me jumping up and down, rubbing and bumping, and hopping halfway onto her bare back then sliding off. This took some time. She kept stepping to the side while I rubbed or bounced.

Lenny told me, "You keep at it until she stands still. I don't care if you have to bounce like a baboon from here to China 'til she stops. But soon as she does, you stop and pet her like it's her birthday."

By mid-afternoon Lenny and I got four of the horses to the point where anybody could rub them and put a rope halter on and off without much fuss. Tate and Aunt Bert worked with us a little, and at one point, Heath and Henry joined in with Appledance and Tumbleweed for a few minutes before they had to get back to assembling their nearly operational wind turbine. Even Knut popped over from his barn for a quick lesson from Great-Uncle Lenny.

All the horses came along beautifully. Except Son-of-a-Smoke. That two-year-old stud colt flicked his tail like a black barbed whip every time anyone tried to pet him.

"I don't get it. What's his deal?" I asked no one in particular.

"Don't worry about him," River said as he passed by carrying a hay bale. "Lenny will show him the way."

Lenny tipped his cap high on his forehead and flagged River over. "Come take a look at this one's feet. Tell me what you think."

As Tate joined them and they all gathered around homely bald-faced Cloud standing patiently, I saw Aunt Bert coming out of Tate's and Griff's cabin. I realized I'd been so busy, I hadn't noticed her leave. But there she went tromping off the little porch and away into the big house. The curtains on the Recovery Cabin were opened.

After inspecting Cloud's white hind foot, River brushed his hands on her rump and said, "She hasn't been self-trimming quite like the rest of them usually do. Sometimes the white hooves need a little more attention."

"That's what I figured," said Lenny.

Tate said, "Cloud is such a gentle spirit. I had hoped she would be able to pass that on to her foals, but I wonder…"

Lenny stopped him. "This girl will make a good brood mare *and* trail horse for someone. Not to worry. Nokota feet are made of stone. She's no exception. Nothing some light farrier work can't mend."

River nodded. "I'll get her trimmed soon as you think she's ready."

As they continued talking about genetics and bloodlines (something I was not quite up to speed on yet), I watched the other horses. Appledance pranced around like a strawberry princess while Tumbleweed, still adjusting to his three-year-old legs, tried to catch her. Switchgrass knelt on his front knees and reached his head under the round pen to try for a couple of weeds calling his name on the other side. But Son-of-a-Smoke, he just stood at the far end with his nose pointed into the hot wind. I could feel his heart aching for the prairie. He flicked his tail, snorted at the ground, and stared far away again.

A slamming screen door startled me, especially when I realized it had come from the Recovery Cabin. *And even more* when I saw Griff sitting in his rocking chair. His owly, wrinkled mug peered at us from the shadows of his weather-worn cowboy hat. His leathery hands cast a spray of wood chips as he whittled away at some poor unsuspecting piece of poplar. I so wanted to know what Aunt Bert said to him when she had her "conversation" with him earlier — oh to have been a fly on the wall. But whatever

243

they talked about, I believe I witnessed the effects. True, I didn't expect a family reunion with sappy music and slow-motion running, but getting Griff's rear out of the cabin was definitely a start.

Son-of-a-Smoke turned to face the bunkhouse, his head level, his eyes intent. A dry wind swept in at his back sweeping his gnarled mane and tail forward. I swear the prairie floated a *part* of that horse on the back of a dragonfly and landed it on Griff's railing. As the wind bucked in my ears, I closed my eyes, took a deep breath, and listened for the voices.

A single voice drifted in calling long and low. *Griffin.*

* * *

The next morning Prairie and Ernie got me up before Knut's rooster. I'd spent all evening clearing out my new space in the horse barn's old tack room, and though it wasn't exactly the Ritz Hotel, I found it cozy enough. I liked hearing my horses steady breathing coming from across the aisle, and I have to admit I did a pretty good job making it my own. Once I'd gotten all the junk "relocated" to the Quonset, it turned out to be a pretty decent-sized space with a south window. Tattered photos of years past decorated the walls, and to my amazement, I recognized almost everyone in them. My family. I pinned Mom's picture up with them.

I situated a wobbly desk and chair beneath the window. Gram's and Mom's framed photographs took a seat under a metal lamp. Aunt Bert found a cot and mattress, and River fixed up a dresser that had two-broken legs and three drawers that stuck when you pulled them out. The utility sink made my room fully functional, sorta. Deep down, though, I longed for my bunkhouse. (There's a sentence I don't say every day.)

I couldn't sleep. Today was chokecherry picking. Baker Bob rigged up the kitchen into a full assembly line of sugar canisters, yellow Sure-Jell boxes, giant stainless steel pots, cone-shaped strainers with round wedge mallets, and piles and piles of gauzy cheesecloth. It spilled way out into the back yard onto folding tables underneath the clothes line.

He'd announced at our late night, Griffinless supper, "I know you've all been working your tail feathers off, but tomorrow, I need chokecherries."

Knut asked, "*Then* what do we do with them?"

"Leave that to me. Just get them here. Slugs of them. I want to swim in red, juicy berries by day's end."

I itched to get started, so I slipped on my whipped and ripped paisley jeans and a white tank top, wrapped my hair into a braid that hung over my shoulder, then snuck out into the aisle. Journey and BG lay curled up in fresh straw sleeping peacefully.

Misty fog sank heavy in the yards and down The Drive. I stretched the sleep out. These cool mornings at Forever Fields had a way of breathing new life into me. Out here on the prairie, the winds sleep with the sun and rise with it too, so I treasured the moments when everything laid quiet and still.

But this morning, everything did not lay still.

A slow creaking screen door opened and closed, and then the sound of heavy-booted footfalls on the gravel walked down The Drive. And though my Spidey senses still had a few crusties this early, Prairie's were on point. She leveled her head and slowly crept in the direction of the footsteps. Their pace was slow but even — purposeful. I knew it couldn't have been Tate since he still had a heavy limp. River stepped too lightly for it to be him. And I couldn't even keep a straight face picturing one of the twins up this early.

It had to be Griff. But where was he going? Curiosity poked me in the butt and I followed Prairie through the haze. We passed Knut's barn, then the machine shed and the massive base of the wind turbine which disappeared into the low hanging clouds. Then, instead of turning onto The Lane, we kept going straight down the tractor path that followed the shelter belt, the one Tate and I chased Ghost Song onto during the storm. Griff was on his way to the south pasture. I didn't remember seeing any chokecherry trees down there.

By the time we got to a clearing, the fog had started to lift. I still couldn't see real well, but I definitely saw Griff. Prairie and I hung back and kept low. Yet another covert operation.

He carried nothing with him. Not even so much as a hankie. He stood in a hollow where the morning fog sank heavily. His arms hung straight at his sides as he looked around as though searching for something.

Crunched in the tall grass among several tufts of black-eyed Susans, I watched him. In the cloud. He stood and searched. And for a moment I wondered what he expected to find. But deep down I knew.

Answers.

After some time, I saw his shoulders slump. He sank to his knees and buried his face in his hands. The fog consumed him. A strange part of me wanted to go to him. I wanted to kneel next to him and let him know he wasn't alone. I wanted to put my hand on his shoulder and let him know that things could be okay again — that he had so much to give still. He had to. Because he, in more ways than I care to count, was so much like me and I so much like him. And though I tried to act all confused when he behaved the ways he did, I always knew how he was thinking because *I* think just like him most days. I thought of the grudge I held against my dad. And Cindy. And snapshot boyfriends. And backstabbing girl friends. Griff *had* to be able to rise above himself … so that I could too.

Palpable, as though I could project it with nothing but will, my spirit reached out to him. Prairie pricked her ears and looked at me then her gaze drifted toward Griff. A faint breeze rustled the grass over our heads and I heard soft, plodding sounds coming through the lifting fog. A rhythm thrummed. One by one, slowly emerging from the haze, came the horses. The Nokota.

First, a grey head appeared like out of a dream. Then a brown face and silver neck. Then a black one, nothing more than a shadow. As more and more arrived, I recognized Mazaska, the silver stallion and Mashte, the sunshine pony. Ghost Song's small, white body with black ears showed a stark contrast walking quietly next to Zica Hota's charcoal coat. Once Oka Wana Gi tried to let out a snip of a song, but Grey Squirrel murmured to her for silence. Now was a time for quiet.

And though I heard their voices ... they did not come to me.

Sunkaku, they called.Little brother.

They went to Griff. Unhurried at first, they circled him. Then they gradually built momentum. And like a carrousel, they cantered around and around until their own wind lifted the fog up and away drawing my great uncle to his feet inside a swirl of mist. I saw his face. His eyes followed the Nokota. He turned and turned until his arms lifted and he began to sing.

He sang low notes at first, then high and wailing sounds, then soft and low again. Between verses he turned to face a different direction. On the last, he looked to the earth and moved his feet in rhythm. His voice pulsated tones in a language I now recognized as Lakota but still could not understand. His raspy voice carried on their wind as they all spoke to one another. The earth lay quiet but for the familiar pounding hoof beats from my dreams, swishing prairie grasses ... and the repeating words of the song.

Cekiya yo, cekiya yo!
Ahitunwan yankelo!

Chapter 20

"All right you guys, the day's a wastin'!" said Aunt Bert donning a red kerchief on her head, a checked sleeveless shirt that tied in front, and cut-off jeans. "It's nearly nine. Listen up good. Baker Bob has gone and set us up with a sweet deal if we can make it happen. Turns out Norse Drive Market in Valley City is willing to be part of Sheldon's Crazy Daze Extravaganza next week on account of feeling like they might be wanting to branch out a bit since Remmy's got them in his sights these days. Looking for some fresh space and new customers. Anyhow, Lars and Shirley Anderson have agreed to showcase our jelly. They say if it takes off, they'll stock it in their store. Isn't that right, Robert?"

"It truly is," he said looking like he might bust right open.

Aunt Bert went on like a coach, "So I don't have to yammer on about the importance of every person here today. This could not, would not, will not, get done without each and every one of you. You hear?"

We nodded and murmured agreement. The sun crept into the sky behind the giant propellers on the twins' working wind turbine casting shadow flutters over us.

"Let's get pickin'!" she said and hopped behind the big truck's wheel while Knut bounced on the bench seat. She could barely see over the dashboard and had to reach tippy toed to the gas pedal, but she revved the engine as Baker Bob flung one last five-gallon pail full of empty ice cream buckets into the back and got in.

I turned the key and Oscar roared to life like a crazed lion, but I revved his engine and he settled into a nice little purr. He knew Lenny was watching. The horses would get a well-deserved break for this hot July day. Lenny sat shotgun and hung his arm out the window while Prairie sat in the middle pant-smiling. We had already loaded as many ladders, tarps, and clippers as Oscar's truck bed could pack. Tate sat perched on the ATV out my window, and Kola waited patiently ready to lope along. River, Heath, and Henry piled into the Bronco, but they had one extra spot ... and it made me sad.

This day, to me, wasn't just about picking a bunch of chokecherries so we could sell a few jars of jelly. It was about all of us being together fighting against the destruction the storm left behind and the dark cloud of debt Remmy Stone held over us. Like a super-hero team against the forces of evil! Our family *needed* this day together. It wouldn't be complete without *everyone*. Great Uncle Griffin never knew I had watched him with the Nokota in the field, nor did he know I'd followed him home and saw him slip back into his cabin before anyone else got up.

Bert said, "Let's start on The Lane and save The Spring for later today when the sun starts to get to us."

"Fair enough," said River. "Let's move out."

I had to stall for just one more minute. "Wait! I have to pee!"

"Again?" asked Lenny.

"Peanut bladder. Be right back." I mumbled to Tate, "You *sure* he's not coming?"

He gave me a doubtful head shake. "He just sat in his chair and stared out the window when I tried to talk him into it."

I eyed their bunkhouse. All but one of the shades had been pulled down again.

Screw it, Paisley. Just go get him, said Gram.

She was right. Enough with the games. Great Uncle Griffin belonged out here with us, no matter what issues he still had to work out in that wrinkled brain of his. Forever Fields Farm needed him. I hiked up my paisley jeans, straightened my straw hat, and marched myself right up to his door. I glanced back at everyone in The Drive gaping at me but shrugged them off and raised my fist to pound his door. As soon as my hand about connected with the chipped paint, the door swung open and I darned near clocked Griff on the forehead.

"What are you doing, Girly, lazying around on the front porch?" He growled at my fist suspended in the air. "We got to get a move on. Chokecherries won't pick themselves!" Then *he* hiked *his* britches up, straightened *his* cowboy hat over top of his gray braid, and marched *himself* right down the porch steps to the vacant seat in River's Bronco.

I strolled back to Oscar like that went exactly how I'd planned it. When I crawled into the driver's seat, Prairie shoved her head under my arm.

"Gotta pee, do ya now, Peanut Bladder?" Lenny had such a look on his face.

* * *

After the first hour of reaching overhead, or way out to loaded branches, my arms screamed for relief. I gritted my teeth as nearby Russian olive trees gashed my skin. But as I became immune to the bug bites and scorching sun, I really started to appreciate the job.

There's something pretty awesome about the way everyone's hands reached and their eyes looked up into the trees together. We swung pail after pail and bucket after bucket — full up with blood-red cherries — from one hand to the next and lined the truck beds corner to corner. The prairie wind aired my damp shirt and cooled my sweaty neck. Katydids and grasshoppers scratch a tune above the wind, the wind, always the wind. My three-legged, one-eyed, crimp-eared orange tabby cat led Knut's kittens through the ditches, showing them the ropes of pounce-and-catch — although there was a lot more pouncing than catching going on if you ask me. Prairie and Kola patrolled The Lane like supervisors. Then there's nothing like sitting on Oscar's tailgate surrounded by family – tiwáhe – sipping a perspiring cup of lemonade and enjoying one of Baker Bob's turkey and strawberry sandwiches on his homemade whole grain bread smeared with honey-almond butter.

Everyone's smiling and squinting in the sun — trying not to get caught watching my two great uncles inch toward each other with arms folded at first then loosening up while they worked their hands as they talked about horses, *carefully* reminiscing. All the while, the Nokota grazed not too far away, keeping an ever-watchful eye, tails swishing at flies.

Down by The Spring we splashed around, tossing berries to the fish. The shade felt good. Griff meandered into the woods and emerged carrying a dozen or so diamond willow branches.

Knut said, "Nice ones, Uncle Griff!"

"That they are, Knut-head. Dandy I'd say."

Lenny, picking a few feet from me, murmured to Bert at his side, "Still working his magic with the diamond willow, I see."

"Yes indeed, he is," she said. "Does his best work when he's cheesed about something. Filled up a whole shed of walking sticks and candleholders since the day he found out *you* were coming." Her sunshine laughter filled the trees and rivaled the birds.

* * *

Back at the house, we unloaded all the buckets, our hands stained red like kindergarteners that raided

251

the finger paint. But since so much work still had to get done around the farm, only a few of us set to work on making the jelly. Lenny and Tate planned to continue working with the five Nokota, River and Griff would start putting the finishing touches on one of the Not-Yets, and Heath and Henry were in charge of evening chores and more repairs. Bob, Aunt Bert, Knut and I rolled up our sleeves and prepared to turn cherries into jewels.

First, we poured them into bleached clean troughs and stirred them around until all the leaves or bugs and what-nots had sunk to the bottom. Then we strained them out and put them into stainless steel stock pots where they boiled into mush.

Next, we rolled a pointed wooden mallet over the berries in the cone-shaped colanders situated over more pots. Juice and pulp oozed out, and we dumped it into cheesecloth sacks to hang from the clothesline over screen-covered kettles sitting on folding tables underneath. We gently twisted and tied the sacks and let the juices drip clear. In the meantime, Aunt Bert melted blocks of paraffin.

As soon as the pots filled with clear red juice, they went straight back to the kitchen where Baker Bob added Sure-Jell pectin and brought it to a rolling boil. He'd already prepared bowls of sugar, and when the boiling juice didn't quit boiling even when he stirred it, we knew it was time to dump in the sugar. Then he'd make us all skedaddle while he put in the final, secret ingredient.

"Really, Bob?" said Aunt Bert. "Even me?"

"Out," he said and tapped his foot.

Immediately after adding his secret ingredient, Baker Bob carefully skimmed off any foam, then ladled the hot jelly into sterilized glass jars waiting on the sup deck's dining table. Knut and I wiped the rims, and Aunt Bert poured melted paraffin over the tops to seal them up tight. Then we went back to the beginning.

At dusk, the guys came to pitch in all night long. Tate stationed himself next to me the whole time. His smile lit up the room when I harassed him about needing a hairnet, so he wound his hair into a bun that shot out spikes.

"Is that better?" he asked.

I circled him. "Hmm. I guess it'll do. You look like a ticked off grackle though."

He lunged for me, but I ducked and scooted underneath River carrying a pot outside to the lamp lit backyard. I could hear him chasing me then I remembered his leg. I stopped in my tracks only to turn around and find myself captured in his arms.

"Gotcha," he said. My insides melted and we laughed until we collapsed into the grass. "You've got a little ..." he said as he brought his thumb to my lips, "cherry juice." He wiped it gently away. My heart flip-flopped. Then he said, "Oops. I think I made it worse."

"Is that so?"

"Yah. You look like Knut put lipstick on you."

Laughter rippled through me as warmth radiated into my cheeks. Tate rose and offered a hand at brushing the grass off my butt. How *convenient*. I didn't shove him away though.

Heath yelled from the wash troughs, "Get a room!"

Then Henry squirted a stream of water out of his hands at us. "Somebody get the hose!"

"Why I oughta..." I growled as I lunged for them. Knut flew off the porch to join in, so we all splashed each other like kids in a kiddy pool.

"So help me," said Aunt Bert, "I will hang you all up by your ears if you don't get back to work. I need someone to measure out sugar here!"

Busted, we sing-songed, "Okay," and flicked a last sprinkle at whoever stood closest.

Back in the house as Tate and I measured sugar and opened pectin boxes, I watched Griff and Lenny mill about at different tasks. I noticed how they didn't necessarily chum around or even speak much for that matter, but worked with purpose. Somehow, Griff's "conversation" — be it with Aunt Bert, or the Nokota, or both — had given him a new attitude. Still no warm fuzzies, but no waves either.

We told jokes and stories, laughed and high-fived at the littlest things. At one point, Knut even got us all to sing the theme song to Indiana Jones. By our last batch of the day, however, cricket and frog choruses took over, our feet dragged, and our hands slowed.

Aunt Bert said as she wiped a dish with a tea towel, "River, why don't you tell one of your old Lakota children's stories?"

He looked to her and she eyed him back.

"Tell about Iktomi," she said. "I think I'm in the mood to hear it now."

River raised an eyebrow. I'd heard that name before. Iktomi. It's what Aunt Bert had spat in Remmy Stone's face the last time we saw him at Tate's hospital room. I'd just assumed Iktomi was some Lakota swear word.

River rolled a mallet in a cone-shaped sieve as he began. "In the days of our ancestors, a man who looked much like a spider, came to walk about the earth." His low, soothing voice lulled us as we finished our jobs and started to clean up. "His name was Iktomi. In the ancient days, he was known as Ksa, wisdom. But because he looked so odd, people made fun of him, so he used his mysterious powers to play malicious tricks. For this, he was stripped of his title, but he became even more sly and cunning. It is said he mixed potions and pulled his spider web strings to control humans like puppets."

The kitchen lay silent but for a clang of a pot and the frogs and crickets outside. I knew we all pictured Remmy. Tate sat at the table and stared at the floor.

River continued, "In the end, Iktomi's schemes backfire, and he falls to ruin. But we must remember that, to the Lakota, Iktomi is not evil. He is a teacher.

254

For through Iktomi and his wily ways, we learn that everything has its purpose. Even the Bad Ones. For *they* are who teach us how *not* to live."

* * *

By the time we transported the jelly-filled jars to the Quonset, the clock read 2:00 AM, my butt was dragging, and I'm pretty sure I looked like a character out of a slasher movie.

"I'm calling it," Baker Bob said finally. "Got another truck load to go tomorrow, so let's get some rest."

Knut protested, "I'm not tired!" Then he gaped his mouth into the yawn of the century. He might've sucked in a bug.

Aunt Bert said, "Robert's right." She took Knut gently by the shoulders. Cherry-red highlights streaked her white-blonde hair. "Got lots of fun waiting for us tomorrow."

Tate walked me to the horse barn. I don't think he really needed his diamond willow walking stick anymore, but something told me he liked having it.

When we got to my door, I said, "Your leg's healing up real well, yah?"

His eyes looked heavy as he leaned against the door frame. "My leg is healing well." He seemed so quiet. Sure, it was 2:00 AM, and we had worked ourselves silly, but he was quiet in a different way.

"Paisley?" The faint light in the aisle made his skin glow.

"Yah?"

"I ..."

I looked into his eyes, worried. "What is it? What's the mat..."

Before I could finish my word, he swooped down and kissed me. Just a quick, feather-soft peck, but I felt the heat of his body and heard his uncertain breaths. He waited, searching my eyes. I answered by reaching up the long lines of his neck and carefully undoing his hair tie. I let the long strands wash down the sides of his face.

In that moment, I hesitated. A kiss, even if it led to nowhere, meant something would have to change. Did I want that? Part of me wanted life at Forever Fields to stay just the way it was. Full. Full of family, full of hope, full of something I'd not felt since before Mom left and before Gram died. I just couldn't do anything to mess all that up now.

But I knew right then, standing in the shadows with Tate, that my empty, pitted pail had been filling up drop by drop since the moment I set boot onto this soil. Forever Fields overflowed within me.

Journey softly nickered and BG sighed, somehow moving me closer to Tate. The search for the other half of my whole ended here. I pulled him in and kissed him back.

Chapter 21

The next morning at breakfast, we sat among another day's worth of jelly-making paraphernalia. Baker Bob estimated another day would get us down to the last of the cherries.

"But that's only if I've got all hands on deck," he said as he replaced a stainless steel pot with a mountain of buckwheat pancakes."

I reminded him as I filled my plate, "I still have to pick the ones just on the other side of the front yar..."

"I'll help you," Tate said before I even finished.

Everyone froze. I felt the eyes around the table gawking, so I shoved a forkful of pancakes in my mouth. They knew. They all knew. I could see it in their faces. Heath and Henry sat right on the edge of some smart remark. And the rest of them — except Knut who was too busy pouring a quart of syrup on his plate — tried to casually look away, but I saw the curls at the tips of their mouths. I think I even noticed *Lenny and Griff* eye each other with a wink. I cringed inside. Exactly what I was afraid would happen. Just when I was getting comfortable with the way people saw me around here, and the way I felt around them. Now ... if Tate and I ... if we ... well, it would all change.

Tate's calloused fingers softly touched my hand. I looked up into his coffee brown eyes filled with certainty. Then forks clanking and conversations resumed just as quickly as they had stopped. I felt a gentle squeeze and dared to think that perhaps I was wrong. Again. I looked around the table and realized that actually … *nothing* had changed. We just … moved on.

Baker Bob said, "I nearly forgot about those trees out there. Get 'em first thing today?"

"First thing," I said and gripped Tate's hand right back.

* * *

We finished our picking in about an hour, but the way Tate and I saw it, no one had to know we had finished so quickly. We rested against a cottonwood with our few stolen moments. That's all. And it felt nice. Natural even.

With our dogs sprawled out in the grass next to us and our legs outstretched, we listened to the wind in the trees and watched through the paddock fences the goings on of the farm. The sky seemed bluer, the air cool and dry. Lounge cat Ernie demonstrated the art of cleaning and sunning in the middle of The Drive. Sadly, the kittens learned quickly, and I worried nary a mouse would ever be caught on the property again. Just past them, Journey and BG rolled in the paddock outside the horse barn. The dust kicked up as their legs flailed and they ground their backs into the dirt. When they finished, they just laid there in the sun snoozing.

Aunt Bert and Baker Bob chattered over the water trough cleaning chokecherries. Knut had his little pony Phyllis taking a bit and saddle real nice. I wondered if he'd ever get her to quit biting strangers long enough to find her a good home. So far, three different people had come to check her out, but they all left holding their fingers or cussing about a ripped shirt.

River, Heath and Henry came riding down The Drive with a few horses — Not-Yets as far as I could tell because I recognized Jimmy, the tall saddlebred. Lenny moved slow and calm in a round pen with Son-of-a-Smoke putting up a stink. Flapping and unfurling

Rope toward the blue roan's rump, Lenny sent the young stallion around and around and around, but I could tell that horse was not buying what Lenny was selling.

Just as I drew in a deep, content breath, ready to get back to the house, the screen door on Tate's and Griff's cabin slammed and I saw my great-uncle's gray braid and bowed legs stride across The Drive toward the round pens. He stuffed a hankie in his back pocket and tucked his plaid cotton shirt into his jeans as his heavy boots scuffed the gravel.

I tapped Tate's arm, excited. "Look."

"I see them," he said. We both sat up squinting.

Griff leaned up against the pen. Lenny joined him. Lenny shoved his straw hat way up and rubbed his forehead. Fragments of their voices drifted on the wind.

"Will you look at that," I said.

"I don't claim to understand the workings of another's heart, but I do believe Griffin may have had a *conversation* recently." He squinted harder at the two men now using their hands as they talked.

I looked at Tate and asked, "What do you mean?" even though I already knew. My own heart told me, but I wanted to hear what he had to say.

"We all from time to time lose our balance. We go searching for our center, wherever it calls. If we ask in a proper way, our ancestors and the spirits come to set us right again."

My heart skipped and I looked at him hard. His words sounded dangerously close to ones I'd heard so many years ago. Words uttered just before my arms flung wide at the sound of my mother's war whoops and Boss Girl's hooves pounding across the meadow. This time, though, thoughts of her did not stir mystery or loss, for part of her, I knew, would always be here.

I asked him, "Have you … had these *conversations*?"

He reached over to kiss my forehead. "Many times." He smiled, and I blushed getting the distinct impression that at least one of those conversations had involved me somehow.

Prairie stretched and plopped her head on my lap. I stroked her silky fur absentmindedly. I leaned against Tate and continued watching Lenny and Griff talk. I knew I had witnessed Griff's conversation as I had crouched in the grass while he sang to the Nokota, and now I felt kind of guilty for sticking my sneaky nose in his business that morning. Then I realized I had had conversations too. I've been having them ever since my first dream of horses circling me in the head-high grasses, whispering to me, and the dark faces fading in and out of the smoky wind, and the voices speaking to me with words I didn't know.

"Tate," I asked, "what does Cekiya yo and Ahitunwan yankelo mean?"

I probably massacred the pronunciation, but he looked at me surprised … and I think a tad impressed. "Those are words from the Four Directions song."

I remembered how Griff had turned each time he started a new verse, looked up for another, and looked down for the last.

Tate picked at the grass. "It is a song one might sing to call upon our ancestors, the Great Spirit, and Grandmother Earth to hear our prayers. It says *Pray to him. He is sitting there looking this way.* It is a song to remind us that our people still live on, and it is right to look to their ways for answers." He paused studying the grass with such a pensive look that I could tell he had memories of this song, perhaps memories of how he'd sung it in search for answers about his own brother, but I didn't pry.

We sat in quiet, watching the brothers move from the rail. Lenny handed Rope to Griff and climbed to the top rung. Griff stood in the center of the ring — relaxed with one hand on his hip — and slapped his leg with Rope just once. Son-of-a-Smoke jolted here

260

and there, and Griff allowed it for a long time, then Griff tried to get him to switch directions or make him run harder. That blue roan wanted nothing of it. Dirt flew from his hooves. He reared and shook his head wildly.

Instinct told me to run and help, but Lenny just sat on that top rail looking on. Tate watched calmly as he stroked Kola's fur.

"Don't you think it's a little dangerous for Griff to be in there alone?"

Tate's eye never left the scene. "I forget Griff had his heart attack your first day here. You have never seen your great-uncle work his magic, have you?" A smile crept across his face. "He's got this."

Son-of-a-Smoke blasted a whinny so loud it carried on the wind lifting me to my feet. The young stallion stomped hard at my tiny, wrinkled great-uncle. I just knew he'd send us all on yet another trip to the hospital. But at the very last second, Griff threw his hands in the air and made such a racket like a madman that Son-of-a-Smoke jumped back, stunned. Griff stood casually again in the dust and calmly coiled Rope. Son-of-a-Smoke snorted and dipped his head to the ground then swung it back up, snorted again and lashed his black tail.

Griff turned his back. Kept coiling Rope. And then, as Saint Francis is my witness, something magical truly did happen. Son-of-a-Smoke lowered his head, started licking and chewing, walked to my great-uncle, and swished his big lip against Griff's plaid shirt. At first Griff didn't do a thing, but after a moment he took a few steps *away* and kept working Rope.

Son-of-a-Smoke followed, slow and calm, head low.

At that moment Griff turned around easily and rubbed the stallion's face. In a few moments, he slid a Rope halter right over Son-of-a-Smoke's head. Griff led that horse around like a puppy dog until the dinner bell clanged declaring this round officially ... over.

261

* * *

The next day liquid rubies filled the basement, the sup deck, and the Quonset. And the heavens sent a light rain to settle the dust.

After breakfast no one was in too big a hurry to work in the rain, so we lined up chairs along the front porch and listened to the sprinkles tap the roof. I absorbed the stillness all around, and comfort soaked into my bones. A misty drizzle airbrushed the farm. Hazy figures stood with heads low in the paddocks. Solid gray skies stretched a dingy canvas far and wide.

Griff whittled some diamond willow while River read the paper. Heath and Henry tinkered with something that looked like a motor, and Knut sprawled out with a comic book next to the dogs.

Twirling my ponytail, I thought about how hard we all worked every day to keep this place running — the new seniors we'd gotten several days ago, the training with the Not-Yets and Tate's five Nokota, the wind turbine the guys made from scratch running the place. I stared at a couple jars of jelly on the porch railing.

"We need a name," I said. "Our jelly needs a brand name. We can't go selling it all naked like that."

"The girl has a point," Baker Bob rubbed his three-day whiskers as he tipped back and forth in his rocking chair. "How about ... Greene Jelly?"

"Yah, Green Lantern Jelly," Knut snorted.

"Very funny," Aunt Bert said. "How about Baker's Jelly?"

"Anyone up for Noon Jelly?" I only got a couple *fat chance* looks, but Tate gave my arm an obligatory squeeze.

"Here's an idea." Lenny strolled out carrying a box. Everyone looked up.

"What have you there?" asked Aunt Bert.

"Ohhh," he said, "just a little something from someone who wanted to help." He looked at me and pushed his straw hat way up on his head.

Baker Bob went to him. "A little something, eh?"

I don't know exactly why, but the look Lenny gave me creased my brow. "What do you mean?" I tried to hide the suspicion in my voice, but he kept looking at me like he was about to spring some sensitive news which sent a twinge into my jaw.

He took off the box lid. "Come see for yourself."

Inside laid several neat stacks of blank three by six-inch papers. We just stared at him.

Lenny chuckled. "The *other* side."

Aunt Bert turned one over and gasped.

Baker Bob grinned and nodded. "Well would you look at that."

The background showed a faded prairie scene with a single, windswept horse standing in the tall grass. Across the top it read in letters designed to look like wildflowers: *PRAIRIE JEWEL JELLY.* At the bottom in deep red, scroll-type font it said *Chokecherry.*

"Where did you get these? They're perfect," I said. "Must have cost a fortune."

"Well," he started, "funny thing is…"

I kept looking at the details, admiring the colors and artistry. Whoever made these jar labels captured Forever Fields like nothing I'd imagined possible on such a tiny piece of paper. The prairie. The sweeping sky. The Nokota horse. The flowers. The wind. Everything.

"… the guy I hitched a ride with wanted you all to have them. The boxes just arrived by FedEx yesterday. I don't know about you, but it just doesn't feel right to turn down such a generous offer. Ya know what I mean?"

Aunt Bert and Baker Bob both looked at him then quick at me.

"What?" I asked.

Baker Bob looked back down at the paper. Lenny shifted and slowly put the lid back on the box. Aunt Bert pointed to the bottom left of my label and put her hand on my shoulder.

Five teeny tiny, handwritten words froze my insides as my fingers gripped the edges.

Floral Daze by Cindy Petals

"*Excuse* me?" I said sounding way more like the Paisley Alberta Noon of two months ago than I'd wanted. Aunt Bert held both my shoulders, and it took everything I had not to shrug her away, rip up the label, kick the box sky high out of Lenny's hands and go stomping off.

Cool it, said Gram. *Get a grip.* Her voice sent relief through my veins.

"I *mean*, I don't understand." Somehow, I maintained fractional composure.

Lenny tried to explain. "Your dad, you see … Paisley … he and I kind of um …" His eyes pleaded with me then to Bert.

"I *think* what Lenny's trying to say," she said as she turned me to look her straight in the eye, "is your dad brought him and Slingshot here." She cut me off before I could squeeze one word in. "*And* for some time now, he and Peter have been …" Here she looked to Lenny like she was searching for the right words. "… wanting the very best for you."

"But…"

"*And* your stepmom too." Her eyes stuck to mine.

I could not contain my eye roll.

Lenny tried again. "She wanted this to be the start of something like an olive branch. You know? For the family."

Huff.

Enough already, P. Get your big girl panties on.

My eyes flitted from one person to the next. I heard the kindness in Great Uncle Lenny's voice. I saw the sincerity in Baker Bob's eyes. I felt the steadiness of Aunt Bert's hands on my shoulders. I thought about everyone — the big brothers I'd found in Heath and Henry, calm and wise River, crazy Knut keeping it real, the promise I felt in Great Uncle Griffin, and my beautiful Tate — all holding me up in their own way.

I took a deep breath and calmly flattened the crinkled jar label.

"That was..." I sucked in my lips and created a smile. "... very nice of her ... them."

"Yes, it was," said Aunt Bert.

"And... it's a good name too. Yah?" asked Lenny. I think it might have been his idea.

I swallowed my pride and forced the words passed my lips. "Yah. It's good." Tate's thumb rubbed my arm, and I looked back down at the paper. Cindy had made a really nice gesture here, and a teensy weensy part of me treasured the fact that they were thinking of me ... of all of us. And even though everyone was looking at me, the words came easily. "It's really good."

Chapter 22

By late afternoon, the rain let up enough for us to get some outside chores done. Tate and I, however, found ourselves on our swing in the fenced in front yard with Ernie sprawling across both our laps. Sadly, Tate had decided his leg felt good enough to move back into his place.

"I feel like a piece inside me is withering. I haven't touched Oka Wana Gi for days. Or Mazaska. I haven't been there to scratch him in that spot under his chin like he loves so much." He sighed. "I just need to be near them."

"I get it. You go." Heartache. "I'll probably get more done without you hanging on me all the time anyway." I smiled.

He kissed me. "I'll be back for supper."

"Perfect. Now git." I slapped his tight butt and watched my dog herd him and Kola away. It surprised me how much I'd sounded like Gram just then. Or maybe Aunt Bert.

Tate met Bob coming home in the Bronco way down at the corner leading onto The Lane. They stopped to talk for some time. I thought nothing of it and went back to the front yard garden to give it some finishing touches. Since the storm, I'd gotten it back into Gram-worthy condition. Only Saint Francis of Assisi, with his newly broken nose, bore record of any natural disaster taking place here. Prairie and I stood back to admire the space. The crabapple tree stood laden with tiny green fruit. Daylily trumpets arched along the far wall. The flagstone path meandered throughout taking visitors on a little prairie flower tour past tufts of bright yellow black-eyed Susans, cheery daisies, delicate bergamot, and tall stalks of purple coneflowers. I had nurtured mounds of yellow lady slippers, bellflower, and primrose creating softness against the jagged stones. Every corner held a little surprise of color, tokens from the prairie.

The Bronco's tires crunched up The Drive. Though my view was blocked by two monstrous lilac bushes on either side of the swirly iron gate, I could hear Aunt Bert come down the porch asking how things went. I saw through the dense foliage that Bob was silently waving her to him and putting a *shush* finger to his lips.

I looked at Prairie. She looked back at me with ears out to the side. And once again, we went into Covert Operation Mode. (I'll just never grow up, I guess.)

She snuck behind one bush, pant-smiling at me from across the flagstones, while I crouched behind the other giving her the stay signal. Together, we listened in.

Bob shushed Bert and said, "Is anyone else around?"

Bert gave a quirky look. "Not as far as I know. Everyone's out doing chores. Why?"

"I mean especially Griff and Lenny?"

"Yah, they're working with River in the horse barn getting those Nokotas and a few of the Not-Yets all prettied up, cleaning sheaths, trimming feet, updating shots and such. Lenny says they're all coming along so nicely, they might be ready to sell soon. Thought maybe this weekend with Sheldon's Crazy Daze and all. What's going on?"

"Oh my blessed spirits, this could not be more perfect!" Bob sounded like a helium balloon about to bust. Prairie's eyes widened and she pricked her ears at him when he started doing a jig and flapping his tattooed arms.

"What couldn't be more perfect?" Through the leaves, Bert looked thoroughly amused with Bob's antics.

"Well," he settled down and they sat on the fountain's cement bench. I had to lean into the lilac branches to see them. "When I went into Valley City just now, I made a few stops. Lars and Shirley Anderson first — they loved the jar labels by the way — and then the Ah Spa to talk to Candice and Evelyn, the donkey ladies. They are just lovely, lovely women and such a stitch!"

"Yes, I remember them," said Aunt Bert clearly wishing he'd get to the point.

"Wouldn't you know they've spent the better part of the summer organizing a Sheldon Summer Shindig Reprise and it's going on *this* weekend." He pulled a flyer out of his back pocket. "Look here. They're putting on a whole new horse show, adding a flea market, an auction, a dance, horseshoe tournaments, and fireworks. Prairie Fire will be there too. Those ladies are pulling out all the stops. They say it's just something they love to do."

I gave Prairie my excited face, which she gave right back.

Aunt Bert examined the flyer. "That's great, Bob! But what's the big secret?"

"Don't you see, Bertie? This is our chance, and I don't mean just to sell jelly."

"Then what *do* you mean, Robert?"

"I mean … it's time for the legendary Tuson brothers to make a comeback."

My eyes about bulged out of their sockets, and I clapped a hand over my gaping mouth. Prairie wagged just the tip of her tail as I soundlessly sank into a cross-legged position.

Aunt Bert sat still as stone looking straight at Baker Bob then slowly shifted to look back down at the flyer as she whispered, "Oh Robert, do you really think? It's so soon. They've just started talking again."

"For the greater good of the farm? For the *family*? I *have* to believe they'll do it." Bob's voice held such hope it nearly made me cry.

"I don't know. How would we even begin to think of approaching them with the idea?" asked Aunt Bert.

Baker Bob got up and went to the Bronco. I squirmed to see him reach in and bring out a couple of his cloth grocery sacks.

"Not to worry, Bertie," he said hoisting the heavy bags effortlessly into the air. "I'll fill their stomachs while you work your magic."

* * *

That night we ate filet mignon done to perfection, the sweetest corn-on-the cob I ever did typewriter my way across, cheesy skin-on mashed potatoes drenched in butter, and the richest French silk pie, which lingers *to this day* on my thighs. Heath and Henry about looked like they'd died and gone to heaven, and I caught Tate closing his eyes with each bite too. Needless to say, everyone (and I do mean *everyone*) was fat and happy by the time Baker Bob started clearing the table and gave Aunt Bert an elbow nudge bumping her last bite of pie right off her fork. He kept moving into the kitchen, but I saw him give Bert the get-the-goods eye.

Bert cleared her throat and dabbed her mouth with her napkin. "Eh hem. So River? Let's have a report on the Not-Yets. Any promising news?"

River nodded. "Jimmy is coming along beautifully. Anyone with a lick of sense will see that horse has serious dressage or jumper potential again. Attitude's improved too."

I pictured the blood bay American saddlebred gliding along in a show arena — his airy tail sweeping behind him, his impossibly long legs dancing, his black feet hardly bothering to touch the ground. With the right rider, he'd be unstoppable.

"The new one we just took on last week is a really nice boy," River continued. Several of us hadn't had time to meet the newcomer yet. "His racing name was Pocket Full of Change, but I've just been calling him Pocket. Turns out he's only ten years old, gelded. Took him for the nicest trail ride a few days ago. He was calm and steady as a rock. Kind of rare for those retired racehorses. Usually, they're full of spring and jitters. But he's got a low head and a kind eye. I don't see why he couldn't go to someone looking for a good trail buddy."

"Good," said Aunt Bert. "I'm glad we talked his owner into selling him to us rather than boarding him here as an Old One."

"Mmhm. It's not his time. That horse has some of his best miles ahead of him. Other than those two, I don't think anyone else is quite ready for adoption just yet."

Aunt Bert paused. (More like *stalled* — and who could blame her?) A cough that sounded suspiciously like *ask 'em* came from the kitchen. She turned to Knut. "Would you care to share how Phyllis is doing?"

Knut scrunched up his nose and pushed his thick glasses up. "Um. Well … er…" He made some guttural noises as he twisted his red curls. He shifted in his seat like his thoughts poked needles in him. Whatever he had to say obviously didn't want to come out. Finally he blurted, "Oh all right!" Everyone just sat and waited patiently for the rest. Bert rested a hand on his shoulder, but he shrugged it off.

"What's got you upset, Knut honey?" she asked steadily, not coddling.

After a little whiny moaning, he slumped and stared at the table. "She's perfect. Phyllis is ready to go." No tears. But his sadness engulfed the room.

It occurred to me then how difficult this must be for him. He has such a hard time showing emotion, but somehow the animals draw it from him as naturally as a bee makes honey. Here he was being

270

asked to turn this Shetland pony into a gentle, people-loving, well-mannered … adoptable … little pal, and then give her up and send her away just like that. When I thought more of it, I realized how strong Knut had to be to know this and still manage through it.

River's buttery voice floated like a leaf on the water. "You've worked magic with her, Knut. She's lucky you saved her from the slaughterhouse. She will only go to the finest of homes. You have my word."

Knut shoved his glasses again and looked at the ceiling. Everyone around the table reiterated River's words to Knut. I even patted him on the back, which he didn't particularly like, but he did stretch a smile up one side of his mouth. I wanted him to know how my heart went out to him, but I didn't know what words to use.

I said what I thought might help. "Wonder Twins or Batman and Robin?"

His eyes lit up with a combination of surprise and relief. "Wonder Twins."

I smiled at him, and I cannot be sure, but I believe it felt like the kind of smile a big sister might give her little brother to let him know everything was going to be okay. "That's what I thought."

Henry said from across the table. "The Dynamic Duo all the way. *Gadgets*, buddy. It's all about the gadgets!" That lightened the mood immensely.

Then Griff offered, "Captain America or GI Joe," and gave us all a *top that* look, which made us laugh because he didn't usually join in on this weird little game. But from there, everyone took their turn playing a few rounds of superhero until Knut seemed thoroughly distracted from his sad thoughts.

Unable to stall any longer, Aunt Bert finally took a deep breath and folded her napkin. "Say, Lenny. Griff."

They both looked at her and waited. I read the *no turning back now* expression across her face. Then, like ripping a Band-Aid, she let it fly. "How would you

271

feel about doing a demo at the horse show in Sheldon this weekend?" Before anyone could blink, Baker Bob appeared at her side with the flyer. "They're putting on another Sheldon Summer Shindig during Crazy Daze. And see here? They're having a flea market and horseshoe tournaments and a dance and fireworks."

Tate kicked my foot under the table and gave me such a look. I'd never seen his eyes so wide. I kicked his foot back and tried to suppress my smile. Heath and Henry both whipped their heads toward our great-uncles. I felt the wind from Heath's hair. River slowly leaned back. Aunt Bert kept pretending to study the flyer while Bob nervously wiped a dish.

Griff and Lenny said nothing.

Knut, thank the good lord, broke the silence. "Yes, yes, yes!" The shift in his spirit just as fluid as River's voice. "You can show them how to gentle, and how to lasso and train." His hands flitted around his head the more excited he got.

Griff and Lenny did not move.

I tried. "Maybe I could set up a stand next to Norse Drive Market's and see if I could sell some of those diamond willow walking sticks you've made, Uncle Griff. And candle holders too. People will love those. You do such fine work."

Still nothing.

I kept on toward Bert now. "I've got some perennials I can split too."

She nodded with encouraging eyes and a smile.

Nada.

Aunt Bert set her jaw, placed her napkin down too tenderly. "Everyone, can I have a moment alone with Griff and Lenny?"

No one had to ask us twice. We scooted our behinds out to the front porch just as fast as you can say skedaddle. While the minutes ticked by, and the muffled voices rose and lowered, I tried to contain my excitement at the possibility of the legendary Tuson brothers making a comeback. By the looks on everyone else's faces, they thought the same.

When we heard footsteps coming down the hall toward the door, everyone tried to look casual. Griff tromped out first followed by Lenny. They both hiked right on past us, down the steps, and out to the horse barn. I only caught snip-its of their conversation. Something about Cloud and how "they'll get a kick out of that" then how Son-of-a-Smoke "might be a challenge" but their voices drifted off with them.

Aunt Bert stepped onto the porch and let the screen door slam behind her. She stood on the welcome mat with her arms crossed looking pretty darned smug, I must say. We waited to hear the verdict. I thought Baker Bob might twist his hands into a pretzel if she didn't spill it.

She swiped her hands together and let out a deep, satisfied sigh. "They're in."

Chapter 23

Dawn lit a banner that read *Welcome to Sheldon* as the Forever Fields caravan drove under it. The tiny town buzzed with activity, and we hadn't even reached the Thistleweed Arena and Event Hall where the shows and demonstrations would take place. Oscar idled down Main Street until we found our stand set up right between the one-room Community Center and Norse Drive's booth already glistening with red Prairie Jewel pyramids of jelly jars. Lars and Shirley Anderson in their matching Norwegian t-shirts and yellow-blonde hair waved to Bob, so he and Aunt Bert rolled the Bronco to the side of the road and started unloading our wares. We had more jelly, Griff's diamond willow, my pots of baby daylilies and daisies and primrose, plus a generous selection of collector's comic books Knut insisted on selling regardless of Aunt Bert's emphatic, "No way, José." She hid them under the counter all day.

Behind us River, Heath, Henry and Knut were all crammed into the king cab truck hauling the three Not-Yets. Griff and Lenny brought up the rear pulling the stock trailer full of our Nokota hopefuls. Tate and I, even though clear skies stretched out to the horizon and the forecast called for *zero* percent chance of rain, decided to drive our horses in this time.

I glanced in my side view mirror at the dogs in the truck bed propped up over hay bales, tongues lolling out of their happy faces. I heard Journey and Little Feather's soft nickers as we rolled along too. It had been a while since I'd taken my boy anywhere, so I knew Journey would have some fun getting out. He and I were going to be one of Griff's and Lenny's helpers. The plan was, while either Griff or Lenny worked with one of the young Nokota on a specific skill inside a round pen, they would explain their process to the audience, and then Tate and I would demonstrate it for the crowd. I got butterflies every time I thought about it, so I was glad to have plenty to do to distract me before we got to that point in the afternoon.

We pulled around to the back side of the event center. A long row of twenty, maybe thirty temporary stalls stretched out before us. Several at the far end already had rumps sticking out, and a few had a bunch of mini donkeys tethered inside. Then a lady in a white cowboy hat came walking toward us. Robin Strongwind. with her perfect flowing black hair and her perfectly proportioned skinny body in that perfect Prairie Fire sequined outfit, waved, jogged up to Tate's side, and crossed her arms on his window ledge. A small, *extremely* immature part of me willed Oscar to leave a rust scuff across her chest and maybe pick off some sequins for good measure.

"Good morning, Robin," Tate said.

"Good morning, yourself." She flashed a toothy smile. Then she looked at me. "I don't believe we've met."

I don't believe we've met I heard the six-year-old inside my head mimic.

"I'm sorry," Tate said. "Robin Strongwind, this is Paisley. Paisley Noon, Robin Strongwind."

I forced myself to grow up. "I'm excited to see your crew perform again. You guys put on a great show."

"Thanks," she replied then looked at Tate. "I'm excited to see some Maycomb Nokota."

Before he could respond, she swung around and pointed toward the stables. "These first eight spots

275

are for you. Water's over there. Manure pile's over there. Warm-ups start at eleven."

She smacked Oscar's hood twice and sauntered off in her white jeans. My conscience cringed at the sight of Oscar's parting gift, a brown-orange smear across her hip.

* * *

By 8:00 AM the town teamed with people. The locals roamed around in their bib overalls and tractor hats or broken-in jeans and scuffed boots. The *non-locals* wandered about in never-been-worn western shirts and expensive boots that looked like they made their feet hurt. In the parking areas, fancy cars sat next to rust-buckets. When I saw a creamy white Lexus with gold trim and out-of-state license plates parked next to someone's age-old Farmall tractor with a cat sitting on the seat, I knew this event was something special. Somehow, Candice and Evelyn, had managed to reach a wide swath of population and get them hyped up about the simple ways of little Sheldon's Shindig. I couldn't help wonder if people these days felt starved for something like this. Like they've been looking for a long time, they just needed someone to point the way. Note to self: Never, and I mean *never*, underestimate the power of a good pedicure and gossip.

And were people *buying*! Antiques, art, crafts, furniture, jewelry, you name it. Booths lined the streets. Face painted kids carried balloon animals or drippy ice-cream cones. Someone was grilling burgers, and I dare say my nose detected a mini-donut and possibly a deep-fried cheese curd. A constant *clink clunk clank* rang in the background as the horseshoe tournament got underway, and a bunch of people were already setting up a big tent for the dance plus a seating area for fireworks. When I

276

got to our stand, Aunt Bert and Baker Bob had a line ten people deep, so I jumped right in to help.

Aunt Bert was in the middle of a sale, and though I saw pure delight in her eyes as she bustled around nodding and smiling to folks, she looked grateful to see me. "Hey sweetheart, did everything go okay? D'ya get the horses settled? Bob, you got change for a twenty?"

"Wow," I said grabbing a plastic sack for one of Griff's diamond willow candleholders. "You guys are doing well!"

"Oh yes indeedy we are. Where are the guys?"

She wiped her brow and counted out some cash for a lady wearing a fifties-style red and white polka dot dress. The lady elbowed a man with an opened wallet.

"See look, dear," she said to him as she held a Prairie Jewel jar up to the light. "It's like liquid rubies, isn't it?"

He didn't look but took his change from Aunt Bert. "Mmhm, hun. I see. Very nice."

"They all stayed to set up in the arena," I said. "I think everything's about ready."

Baker Bob, as he scooted by to grab several walking sticks for a customer to choose from, said with a nod, "As soon as Shirley over there cracked open a box of butter crisps and started handing out samples of our jelly, sales have gone berserk. I might have to make a trip home to get more! In fact, be a dear Paisley, will you, and run to the Bronco for more of Griff's diamond willow." Bob was giddy with excitement.

Aunt Bert added as I started away, "And more of your plants, darling! The last of those went an hour ago."

A sugary blend of pride, joy and relief chased goosebumps right up my arms and tingled the back of my eyes. This was not the time for waterworks. But I have to admit, though it had been many, many days since my last tears, I realized I wasn't afraid anymore to let them come.

* * *

Deja vu moment.

A vaguely familiar voice came over the loudspeaker and I recalled the silver-haired announcer from an earlier version of today's event. "Ladies and Gentlemen, please rise for our National Anthem as Robin Strongwind riding Grand Rock carries our nation's colors."

This time, I sat astride Journey as we waited in the warm-up area with Tate on Little Feather. Griff, Lenny, River, Heath and Henry all took off their hats as they stood holding a Nokota. Robin, sitting tall and sparkly with the flag, walked Grand Rock by nice and slow.

When the music started, my heart beat a little faster. Not really because I was nervous, but because I wanted everything to go well. I wanted everyone in the crowd to be thoroughly impressed with my great-uncles, and not just because I knew it could mean a lot for the future of Forever Fields. Griff shifted his weight on his bowed legs, and Lenny squinted his crinkled eyes, snuffling his nose with a hankie. They both fidgeted with the headsets they'd been given, trying to make the microphone bend just right. I wanted them to do well ... for *them*. So that they could be reminded of how good they were, how much they had to offer ... yes, even at *their age*. I wanted them to show the world that just like Pocket the ex-racehorse, they still had some of their best miles ahead of them. My heart swelled at the honor of being a part of those miles.

The music ended and Robin rode out past us again. This time we all smiled and called out "Nice ride" and "That was great."

Our turn!

The announcer began. "And now folks, Sheldon's Second Summer Shindig and Crazy Daze Combo has a real treat for you. Starting things off for us today is a legendary duo that goes way back." Some mysterious kind of woodwind music started to play. "These men and their history with training and breeding is unprecedented. Matched by none. They can soften the wildest of horses, teach them how to trust again and be partners with the two-leggeds in our human herd." Laughter rippled softly. "And though time led these brothers' paths in different directions, they come together today, not for fame, not for fortune, but *for the horse*, sunka wakan, our beloved *state* horse. The Nokota. Ladies and gentlemen, please give a hearty welcome back to Mr. Griffon and Lenard Tuson!"

Griff grumbled out the side of his mouth, "Who the hell wrote this guy's script?"

Lenny smiled. "Ya, I'd like to shake his hand."

River offered his hand and gave a modest smile. Lenny winked and grasped it firmly. Griff growled, but I saw the edges of his hard face soften.

Tate interrupted them. "Guys. That's your cue. It's time to go."

My stomach twisted into knots, but not in the jaw-clenching, shoulder pinching way like usual. Just excited and wanting to do my best. I gripped Journey's reins and nudged him forward, but he would not move for me. Just twitched his ears back and forth nervously. I forced myself to take a deep breath, unclenched my butt cheeks, and relaxed into my seat. Only then did he walk on.

Griff leading Son-of-a-Smoke, and Lenny leading Switchgrass, strode into that huge, cheering arena like walking to do barn chores. When I focused on them, natural and relaxed as can be, my insides settled. Tate smiled and nodded as we stood quietly. River, Heath and Henry took Appledance, Tumbleweed, and Cloud into a holding area off to the

279

side then grabbed some gear and brought it to the two main round pens in the center for Griff and Lenny.

I saw a flash of red in the audience bobbing up and down with flailing arms trying to get my attention. I lifted my hand halfway to wave back at Knut. Aunt Bert's blonde-white hair and smile like the sun shone down on me. I breathed a little easier, thankful the rest of the eyes in the stands were *not* on me.

The hour flew by. One minute, Griff was showing Son-of-a-Smoke how to accept the saddle for the first time ever, the next minute, he was trotting around the pen on the young stallion. Tate and I demonstrated left and right lead changes on the outer rim while Lenny explained where to put your feet and how to shift your weight in order to communicate with your horse. Then in a wink, he was getting Switchgrass to accept a snaffle bit.

Lenny did most of the talking. Surprise. And he was so good at it. Educated, funny, even charming. He explained how these Nokota had been caught and gentled just a few days ago, so the audience understood these were not *wild* horses necessarily, but he also expressed the Nokota horses' unique ability to adapt and learn quickly regardless of circumstance. And though I concentrated hard on my part most of the time, I did listen when he told the audience a brief history of the Nokota breed. I never grow tired hearing how they have escaped extinction twice in their desperate quest to find their families.

Before I knew it, the crowd was cheering. Somehow, within the time given, the Tuson brothers had all five horses saddled, bridled, and riding. Griff tipped his hat as he cantered Son-of-a-Smoke in one round pen, while Lenny trotted Switchgrass in the other. River rode sweet little Cloud at a soft jog next to me and Journey. Then, to show off just a tad, Heath and Henry took Appledance and Tumbleweed around the arena at a brisk pace with Tate and Little Feather.

Finally, the announcer said, "Aren't these Nokota some of the loveliest creatures you ever did lay eyes on, folks? And as if just having a chance to watch them in action wasn't enough, wouldn't you know, each one of these fine animals is for sale. Imagine having a piece of living history in your herd. Be sure to stop by the stables after the show to see them up close and personal and learn more about this amazing breed. Let's give the Tuson brothers and these hard workers another round of applause!"

Journey whinnied like a trumpet and threw his head up and down as we all soaked in the praise. I looked around in awe at the packed seats and the energy in the air. The smiles. The hoots and hollers. Squinting into the sea of faces, I found Aunt Bert in time to watch her wipe her cheek with a tissue while Knut practically leapt out of his Hulk shirt. Lenny lifted both his hands and waved at the crowd, thanking them, cuing the rest of us to do the same.

Griff, however, did not. My heart twinged for a second as I watched him, head down, shoulders slumped, the top of his cowboy hat concealing him. His hand moved quickly to his face then back to his reins again. At last, when Griff raised his head revealing red, watery eyes and a sideways grin, he straightened in his saddle and saluted every corner of the arena. Then his eyes came back down ... on his brother. Lenny kept waving but turned to Griff and smiled.

Chapter 24

Nickers and snorts woke me from the deepest sleep the next morning. But before I opened my eyes, I watched the fireworks in my mind one last time and felt Tate's arms wrapped around my exhausted body on the dance floor. I remembered his calloused fingertips softly trailing down the long line of my neck to the small of my back. A shiver rippled through me and I snuggled deep into my covers treasuring it all for myself.

Still refusing to leave the comfort of my dreams, I saw the faces of *all* those I love, young and old, two-leggeds and four-leggeds. I let the feelings linger until they seeped into the farthest corners of my mind so that no matter what happened from here on, I would know fragments of the day, start to finish, were carefully tucked inside me. Mine forever.

A wet tongue and serious dog breath forced my eyes open. Prairie had had enough sleep. Ernie, crouched motionless on my chest, stared at me all creepy like. Dream time over.

While I dressed, I heard voices outside the barn. Though muffled, I knew I didn't recognize all of the speakers. Visitors? So early? I yanked on my paisley jeans, Supergirl t-shirt, and boots. As I ran my fingers through my hair, my reflection in the cracked full-length mirror caught me off guard.

My short frame stood before me, and I couldn't use words like slender or skinny to describe it, more like ... fit and ... healthy. I felt my ever-present pooch belly, and though Baker Bob's cooking was as hearty as it comes, I could tell my waist lay flatter than it ever had before. All those two and a half mile jogs with Prairie down The Lane to the mailbox and garden work and chores and the constant motion of our day kept me trim. In the dim light of my little tack room, my skin glowed like honey. My hair waterfalled in long, blonde streaks down the sides of my face and over my shoulders. When I tucked one side behind my ear, it felt smooth and strong.

I was no longer the same person who had left Aurora Way in Grover, Minnesota with questions swimming in her head and a sneer on her heart. I was better. This place made me better. My *family* made me better.

Car tires crunching on the gravel joined the voices outside and then more new voices after car door thuds, so I decided I better at least brush my teeth for company, whoever it was. As I held my hair to the side and let the water run, I thought about our situation. True, we hadn't gotten any solid offers on any horses at the Shindig, just a lot of "They're amazing" and "I'll give you a call" or "I'll have to stop out there sometime." And even though Tate felt miserable about not making a sale, we didn't let it take up space in our thoughts. We rejoiced in the fact that we sold out our entire booth — jelly, diamond willow, and plants — and could have sold more. Even Lars and Shirley Anderson sold every last jar of Prairie Jewel Chokecherry Jelly, and they told Baker Bob they looked forward to putting it on their shelves.

I felt proud to be a part of it all. Still, something deep inside told me I had to do more.

I heard the phone ringing all the way from inside the house. Then shrieks of laughter. Then hooves clopping, screen doors banging, and little happy yips I recognized as my own dog's. At some point, Prairie and Ernie had started their day without me. The clock by the bed showed 9:45, so I gave Gram's and Mom's pictures a tap goodbye for the day and ran out.

Someone had already turned Journey and Boss Girl out, so I went straight for the barn door. When I shoved it wide open, nothing could have prepared me for the scene outside. Cars and cars lined The Drive and people upon people milled about the yards. Prairie gave a happy yip and jetted to me. I had to get in on all the fun.

Tate, Griff, and Lenny leaned against a round pen with the five Nokota and visited with several people. River had a group of teenaged-looking girls and their parents watching him take Jimmy through some fancy dressage moves. While the girls' eyes were glued to the long-legged, dark bay saddlebred, I do believe the moms' eyes were glued to the long-legged Lakota man in the saddle. Pocket-Full-of-Change stood tied to a post and munched at a hay bag while a couple older guys and a lady patted him and looked him over.

Way down at the end of The Drive underneath the wind turbine, Heath stood talking to several strangers who stood with crossed arms and nodded their heads a lot. I even saw people coming and going from the Quonset with arms full of junk asking Henry "How much?" as they held up an old rocking chair or a rusty gas can. Someone even sat on the swing in my fenced yard, while another person scrutinized the crabapples.

But perhaps the biggest commotion came from Knut, wearing his Superman cape, leading a bunch of kids around on Phyllis. Toddlers and their moms came and went from Knut's barn, ducks and goats trailing behind. Kittens scampered every which way in all the fun. Ernie hung like a sack of potatoes over some little kid's arm, and I couldn't tell if his one-eyed, crimp-eared face showed misery or heaven.

Somehow, while I had slept in, this place had turned into a theme park.

"Whuff," Prairie's eyes pleaded to be excused.

"Go on," I said. "Keep everyone in line."

"Whiff woof." Translation: Yes ma'am. She scampered off.

I caught up quick with Baker Bob as he scurried to the house with an empty platter.

"What's going on?" I asked getting the door for him.

He kept moving and said, "A miracle of miracles, by good Saint Francis, is what's going on. Help me with more refreshments."

Aunt Bert came behind us humming. "Good morning, Sunshine! Did you enjoy your sleep-in time?" She side-hugged me (something I'd grown to look forward to every morning) and combed her fingers through my un-ponytailed hair. "By the looks of it, I'd say you did indeed sleep well. You look lovely, Paisley."

When I thought about it, no one here had ever seen me with my hair down. The thought suddenly made me self-conscious, but instead of making a big deal about it, I tucked my bangs and said, "Thanks." Truth is … I *felt* lovely. So sue me for enjoying the compliment.

She gave me a knowing smile. "Here, help me with this orange juice."

Baker Bob flung around the kitchen like a tattooed pinball. "Incoming sticky buns! Hot, hot, hot!"

We jumped out of the way. "Plates," Aunt Bert pointed with a knife to the ones drying in the dish rack and started cutting the fresh rolls apart.

While I dried and stacked, I asked again, "Is somebody ever going to tell me what is going on?"

"Business, Paisley." Her voice squeaked as she said the word again. "Business!"

"Seriously?"

"Seriously. These people were all at the Shindig yesterday and wanted to come see the place where the *legendary* Tuson brothers worked their magic on our 'Pieces of History.' Once people started arriving, and took a half a second to look around, they started

285

yanking out their cell phones, holding them high in the air and wandering around the yard, looking for a signal. Eventually, I heard them telling their friends to come take a look." She looked giddy with her sticky fingers in the air. "Tate's already got a crowd interested. And as far as I can tell, River's got himself a real bidding war going on over Jimmy."

Stunned, I carried the tray of orange juice while she brought the rolls. Could this be real? Or was I still dreaming? I stood on the front porch trying to take it all in when I felt the boards beneath my feet vibrate. Off to the east, I just barely caught a glimpse of Mazaska's silver coat reflecting in the morning sun as he moved the herd, which added to the full-on circus. Tate waved me over. I looked at the tray in my hands then at Aunt Bert.

"Go ahead. Just leave the drinks on the fountain bench where folks can help themselves."

"I'll be back," I said.

"Don't hurry. Robert and I have this under control."

When I met up with Tate, I whispered through the rails so not to interrupt Lenny's discussion with a crowd of people. "Can you believe all this? What can I do?"

Tate politely excused himself from the conversation and slipped out of the pen, Kola jogging in his shadow. Our eyes zeroed in, and he bent his knees to fully wrap his arms around me. I felt his whole body breathe deeply, in and out, his head snugged over the nape of my neck. And even though people probably noticed us from any corner of the farm yard, I allowed myself to melt with him in his joy.

After a moment, he studied me and laced his fingers through the long tendrils of my hair. Pure contentment filled his voice. "I just want you with me."

A puff of air caught in my throat, but I replied, "Well here I am."

He lit his knee-weakening smile. "Here you are."

286

Griff's gravel voice cut short our intimate moment. "Hey, *lovebirds*. You wanna have a say in this deal or what?"

Tate grabbed my hand and whispered as he pulled me with him, "Tell me if you think these people are right for the horses they say they want."

"How am I supposed to do that?" I whispered back. "I don't know any of these people."

"Just watch them and listen. Listen for the voices, the ones I know you hear so clearly drifting on the wind. Tell me what they say."

"Tate, I can't just hear them whenever I want. It doesn't work like that."

His eyes pierced mine and then he touched my cheek. "I have a feeling, if you try, you might find differently."

Something about the way he looked, and the way he spoke, told me he was dead-on right.

"I'll try."

The first man wanted to buy Cloud. He was in his thirties, tall, lean, and talked real fast. He smiled a lot too. Like he had something to hide. Or maybe he was just excited. I don't know. I listened to him talk about the team penning events he'd been in and all the trophies he'd won. I listened for the voices. But none came. Certain parts of this guy and our gentle Cloud did not fit together.

I tugged on Tate's little finger and shook my head so imperceptibly, I worried he might not see. But he did.

"Mr. Ring," Tate said.

"Gary. Please call me Gary."

"Gary, I know you said you particularly liked this little paint mare here, but I wonder if you might be interested in meeting the others before you decide for certain."

Smooth.

Griff and Lenny, as though they read our minds, picked up on our strategy immediately and backed off their sales pitch for Cloud.

Lenny suggested, "There's an old way we used to go about finding a horse suited for us, ya know." He grinned and tipped his straw hat up high on his head and stood real square on his bowed legs. Lenny had a real knack for drawing people in and getting them to listen. "Cross through the herd." He tapped the young guy on the chest. "Let the *horse* pick *you*."

"Cross through the herd?"

"That's right. See how they're all clumped up there in the middle of this pen here? You go walk straight through 'em now. Then come back the same way. See what happens."

Gary looked at Tate and me. We gave him a thumbs-up. Then he looked at Griff who just coiled Rope.

"All right. I'll give it a try." The man strode out to the five horses coolly. A bigger crowd developed to look on.

While I watched him, I expected him to be all cocky with stiff, jerky movements. He just *seemed* like a cocky kind of guy. But to my surprise, the closer he came to the horses, the softer he got. He walked real slow but sure and offered a sniff of his hand whenever a horse seemed interested. They milled around with him a little, except Son-of-a-Smoke, who turned away.

When Gary got clear through to the other side, Lenny instructed, "Now come on back. And don't be in a rush about it either. Take your time."

He nodded and started walking again. This time, I saw his eyes work up and down each horse, not intense but definitely busy, drawn especially to Cloud several times. Cloud, however, didn't seek out his attention. Neither did Tumbleweed, which was odd because I thought the playful, leggy bay roan might be a good fit for Gary. When Switchgrass turned away too, I was baffled. The young buff gelding would make a good competition horse, tough and adventurous.

But silly little Appledance couldn't quit nosing Gary as he passed through. He smiled, trying to ignore her lipping at his shirt sleeve. She was so endearing. He stopped to let her nuzzle him.

I watched intently and listened. No voices.

But when the young man laid a gentle hand on her forehead and rubbed in smooth circles — the moment they *connected* — soft whispers floated on the wind singing to me. I still didn't know what the words said, but I felt their warmth flow through me as I watched the young man and the filly. I listened until two of the words swam in my veins all the way to my lips. My skin tingled as I formed the sounds. "Chee-yay. Choo-way."

"Ciye. Cuwe." Tate's earthy voice said with tenderness and pride. "Brother. Sister."

Gary Ring and Appledance stood together. Connected. *Tiwáhe.* Family.

Lenny said to him, "I think that strawberry roan's pretty much made up your mind, ya?"

Gary laughed and patted her solidly on the shoulder. He seemed surprised at first, but when he turned to us, his eyes danced. "I guess I'd say so."

While the two got to know each other, the four of us huddled casually outside the round pen away from the other people.

Griff popped an eyebrow at Lenny. "I don't recall any '*old* way' for pickin' out a horse."

Lenny grinned slyly and gave me a wink. "*Old* way, *new* way. What's the difference?"

Tate put his arm around me. "How about *our* way," he said.

"Call it cockamamie for all I care." Griff shared a rare chortle. "It works!"

Chapter 25

And so I played equine-human matchmaker.

Tumbleweed ended up going to a tall and skinny-as-a-post, middle-aged woman whose legs rivaled his own. Turns out, she was a middle school teacher too, so we knew she'd be able to deal with this three-year-old gelding's attitude. But she also had this great way of shrugging off his nonsense, and I think she actually kind of liked it.

Switchgrass, probably one of the most striking horses in the entire herd with his rare buff coloring, selected a young single lady from nearby Lisbon looking for her first horse. She said she hoped to try a few horse shows and do a little gaming maybe, but mostly she wanted a friend. This match was easy. Call it love at first sight or whatever, but I think we *all* heard voices ... and maybe bells ... and slow-motion-running-on-the-beach music when these two laid eyes on each other. End of story there.

Cloud. Humble, unassuming Painted Cloud went to someone *really* special. We all knew she had to, so when she found a mid-fifties man who'd been looking for a companion ever since he lost his wife to cancer, we couldn't have imagined a better place for her to work her simple charms. And though he seemed very friendly and knowledgeable, sadness clung deep and dim behind his eyes. The man looked as though he carried a heavy burden, one she could lighten for him. Cloud would show him how to enjoy life again.

Son-of-a-Smoke never so much as turned his head to a single soul. He stood alone at the far end of the round pen. Griff even led him up to one person at a time. That's when I heard the voices, faint and distant, but definitely present. They floated here and there, changing course, striving for a target they couldn't quite reach. It made me think. Then … it made me smile.

"Hey Uncle Griff," I called. "Can you just stand there with him a minute?"

He gave me a hard stare, and I believe I caught a hesitant glimpse that said, "I know."

And sure enough, when he looked the young stallion square in the eye, the match was made. Griff slid his calloused fingers to Smoke's head, and I knew he heard the voices too.

Tate said, "Smoke stays." His voice carried equal parts sadness and relief.

Griff rubbed Smoke's neck. "I guess old Bullet could carry Bert around for awhile."

Son-of-a-Smoke would have brought a hefty price, but no one said a word of it. There could be no argument. Smoke would stay with his family.

* * *

As far as the Not-Yets were concerned, ex-racehorse Pocket-Full-of-Change became a college vet student's trail buddy. They roamed around the farm yard and took off out into the south pasture for a while like they'd been trail riding for years together.

We managed to send Jimmy home with a down-to-earth family just getting into show horses. Jimmy behaved like a perfect gentleman. Their polite teenager took the reins timidly and grinned ear to ear as they jogged around the pen. I watched carefully as she *asked* him for every move they tried, didn't push. I pictured them as partners in their rides to come. I just hoped the competitive world of show jumping and dressage wouldn't affect the joy I saw on her face.

291

By late afternoon a few folks lingered, but most of the cars cleared out. Only Phyllis remained, and it bugged Knut. You'd think he'd been sabotaging any potential matches, but not so. He'd taught her how to be a nice little pony, but she refused to cooperate. I thought maybe she was Knut's match, but the voices didn't come to me. Regardless, by the way she kept biting people the second Knut turned his head, I ventured a wild guess that she'd be sticking around for some time.

But I was wrong.

A van drove in with the words *Up, Up and Away* painted on the side with paper doll silhouettes framing it. Five kids got out. One had arm crutches and glasses that hung down at the tip of his nose. A couple others were pudgy little cuties wearing awe and wonder all over their baby faces. The wheelchair lift on the side of the van lowered another boy to the ground. A heavier-set woman with quick reflexes and gentle words reached a hand over two kids' heads to River who was finally free from the gaggle of horse show moms.

He gave her a warm greeting with those comfortable, buttery tones that belonged solely to River. "Welcome to Forever Fields."

The teacher looked grateful for the welcome. "I hope it's okay we got here so late. It always seems to take us a while to get moving." She scrunched up a little girl's hair then gave her a side-squeeze.

"It's good to have you, Miss …"

"Newton. Vivian Newton. Thank you so much. I try to get the kids out as much as I can, and the news about this place sounded so great. We've been thinking of getting a few new pets out at our little five-acre facility. Animals are so good for the kids, you know."

Aunt Bert came to greet them. "Alberta Greene. Good you could come."

"Oh, you're the one I spoke to on the phone?" They shook hands. "Thank you for having us. You should hear the whole town buzzing about what a wonderful set-up you have out here."

Aunt Bert said, "Well, we have *sure* enjoyed showing folks a little of what Forever Fields is all about. And we're thankful for the business." She turned to me. "Paisley, why don't you show 'em around Knut's barn. I'll get Knut. He's just having a snack inside."

I hopped to. "Sure thing."

Tate rubbed my back quick. "I'm going to help Griff and Lenny with those few folks. They've been asking about foals for next spring."

I gave him a peck on the cheek. "Come join us when you get a chance."

"I will," he said.

After having him by my side all day, I hated separating, though I didn't mind the view of his long, black hair flowing over his broad shoulders as his faded-jeans butt walked away.

Vivian counted her little flock. "Rufus." She looked back at the van. I saw a tuft of hair sticking up in the back window. *"Rufus,"* she said and the tuft of hair slowly emerged.

Inch by inch, Rufus painstakingly made his way to the front of the van. By the time he reached the door, Heath and Henry had come over to greet the new guests. Rufus didn't say anything, but as he hung like an orangutan in the van's open door, he had a this-is-as-far-as-you'll-ever-get-me-*alive* look on his face.

Henry tried to help. "Hey Rufus, my man. Come check out all this cool stuff."

Heath chimed in. "Yah, bud. What say I show you how to rope a pony."

Their charms, however, did not budge Rufus.

"I'm sorry," Vivian said. "He's a little reluctant to try new things. You go on ahead."

River stayed with her while Heath, Henry, and I took the kids over to Knut's barn. Prairie herded from behind keeping all seven of us in a neat and tidy huddle. We got them playing with the kittens and splashing a little in the ducky pool.

Knut, still wearing his cape, came flying from the house and bee-lined it to the barn. I loved how much fun he had showing off. The kids clung to him too making him show them tricks and asking to try on his cape.

Vivian and River had managed to get Rufus out of the van. They moved at a snail's pace three steps forward, then two steps back, but eventually, he could watch from a safe distance.

When Knut brought Phyllis out, everything changed. She sniffed around at all the kids, those bushy bangs flopping here and there as she decided which one looked tasty.

Knut kept her in check. "Come on now, Phyllis. Just say hi to the nice kiddies." He behaved so grown up around his animals. "Let's go see this nice, young man."

He tugged on her lead, and she took a few steps with him, but as soon as she got Rufus in her sights, she stopped short. Rufus kept a wary eye on her.

Knut said, "Phyllis. Come along."

She stood rigid, head high, nostrils blowing.

"I don't know what's wrong with her." Knut scratched a bug bite on his arm and shoved his glasses up.

"Maybe, Rufus," I suggested, "you could meet her half way."

Aunt Bert said, "Yes, see how she's looking at you? She's thinks you're really something special, I tell you."

"Yah. Come over," Knut said. "Give her a pat. I got my superhero cape on. I'll protect you. She won't bite."

Promises, promises.

Suddenly, something inside Rufus' head seemed to just click like a light switch, and he marched himself right over like he owned the place. Phyllis stepped right up to meet him. The boy and pony stood inches apart, both studying each other. Then Phyllis dropped her head allowing Rufus to touch her shaggy forelock. The two stayed like that for a moment, and I watched the expression on Knut's face turn. This pony belonged to this boy.

She lipped his jeans, but never once even tried to bite. In fact, she licked his hand like a dog after he gave her a treat. A little smile carved across Rufus' face.

Knut, however, before he'd consider letting Phyllis go, had one important test to perform. He said to Rufus scratching the pony's ears, "Hey. Incredible Hulk or Captain America?"

Oh my. This meant trouble. Knut loved both of those characters. Rufus would have to come up with a pretty impressive explanation for whichever one he picked.

Rufus didn't make eye contact with Knut, just kept rubbing Phyllis till her lip quivered and she leaned into him to make him scratch harder. He stared at a spot on her shoulder and pursed his lips. Knut waited.

Finally, a tiny voice answered, "Captain America."

Knut showed no emotion. "Why?"

Everyone leaned in. Vivian and Aunt Bert looked at each other. I don't think Rufus talked a lot.

The boy's words came out small but sure. "Because good goes all the way through him. He doesn't know how to be mean."

Knut stood there with both a surprised and pleased expression. Then he gave a little grunt, shoved his glasses up, and handed over Phyllis' lead rope. "Here. You can have her."

River went to Knut, and I could tell he was proud of him and maybe wanted to give him a pat or side squeeze, but we all know how Knut doesn't really like that sort of thing. I laughed at myself for having that same attitude not long ago.

River said, "You made a good decision, little man," and ventured a gentle hand on his shoulder.

As Rufus led Phyllis away, Knut leaned into River and hugged him. With two arms.

* * *

As the last car drove away, and the sun cast shadows, a white truck rolled up The Drive. Tate sobered a little and looked kind of confused as he squinted to get a good look. When I saw the sparkly flames painted on the side, and a white hat sitting behind the wheel, I knew Robin Strongwind had arrived.

"What's she doing here?" Tate's voice spoke *my* words.

We walked slowly to her as she parked and got out of her truck.

She approached us in her too-tight jeans. "Word's out you can't sell that young stud, Maycomb." I watched her eyes take in my paisley jeans and Supergirl t-shirt.

Calm yourself, Paisley, said Gram.

Tate said coolly, "He's not for sale anymore."

She eyed him hard then acted like it was no big deal. "Huh. That's too bad." She planted her hands on her non-existent hips and looked around the place. "Because I was willing to pay top dollar for him." Her eyes settled straight back on Tate.

I hitched up my pants and straightened my shirt. "Perhaps you'd be interested in breeding one of your mares to Son-of-a-Smoke instead?"

Well played, Gram said.

Tate looked at me like I was a genius, and I felt a little insulted at his shock, but I saw Robin trying not to let on that this idea hadn't already crossed her mind. She made an oh-I-don't-know *icky* face as she inspected her fingernails.

Tate seized the opportunity. "If that sounds like something you're interested in, I'd be willing to negotiate a reasonable arrangement for multiple standings. Son-of-a-Smoke has excellent bloodlines."

A fraction of surprise flit across her face then disappeared. "I *might* be interested. Depends on how 'reasonable' your idea of a deal is. Let's walk and talk a bit. Shall we?"

As if someone had radioed in, "Cue the Nokota," Mazaska trumpeted and he thundered his band into the western tree line where we all had a front row view just like the one I got that first day Prairie and I flew with them down The Lane till my legs gave out. And though I'd seen them sweep across the grassy lands and through the cottonwoods many times since, their beauty and mystery took my breath away *every* time. In fact, in some ways, now that I had just begun to understand the Nokota, everything about them had magnified. Deep down, I knew this feeling would keep growing with time.

Answering my thoughts, I heard the sweetest little song high above the pounding hoof beats. When I peered through the trees, the sunlight beamed off Ghost Song's bright white body. Then for one brief moment, she stopped. The rest blurred behind her. She twitched her black ears, tossed her head so hard it raised her front feet off the ground, and sang a song of our ancestors to us.

Not too many days ago, I didn't really believe the superstition that the medicine hat brought good luck. But now. Well. I believed.

Robin Strongwind stopped in her tracks as Oka Wana Gi and the herd worked their magic on her. She would not resist the opportunity to have this steely river of Sitting Bull's war ponies run in her own herd's lines. The woman's cut-throat reputation was powerless here. Against the medicine hat.

As I reached down to pet Prairie, I realized I didn't feel the least bit threatened by Robin anymore, even as she and Tate meandered away together. She needed us, I could tell. And the truth of the matter was … we needed her. So I did the only thing I could. I walked away.

When I turned toward the house, I saw the rest of my family sitting on the front porch. They all looked as exhausted as I felt, so I joined them. Soon enough, Robin's truck vroomed off and Tate returned with the good news of a lucrative deal he'd made with Robin, like we all knew he would. The sounds of creaking rocking chairs, frogs and crickets serenaded the sun down into the cool, long shadows of evening. We sat in quiet closeness knowing Forever Fields — and all the good things that we did here — would survive just like the Nokota.

* * *

Heath's stomach growled.

Baker Bob asked, "How about some comfort food? I'm thinking grilled cheese and tomato soup."

Heath held his stomach and groaned, "BB, add bacon and tomato, and you'll be my one true love."

Bob scuffed the back of Heath's head and took off for the kitchen.

"I'll give you a hand," said River. Aunt Bert followed.

I looked toward my fenced-in front yard. Echoing voices whispered to me. "I'll be there in a minute," I said. "I just gotta … check on something."

Tate said, "I'll come with you."

"No, no. You don't have to. I'll just be a minute." The look in his eyes told me he understood, and I was grateful. I just needed a moment alone. Prairie padded softly by my feet. I welcomed her.

We walked past the trickling fountain and swung the swirly iron gate open to find my swing and Saint

Francis waiting in the twilight. I sat down, sighed contently, and felt the rhythm moving back and forth. Prairie sat close with a paw on my leg. We listened to the frogs and crickets tuning up and the prairie wind gentling for the night.

The voices drifted in on the evening breeze. "Tanksi, hecheto welo." I stopped swinging and held my breath. The words came to me. "It is good, sister. Well done." A wonderful chill sifted over my skin and coursed through my veins swelling my chest with all things good. And I cried.

The phone rang inside and I heard Aunt Bert's brisk footsteps. Her muffled voice sounded surprised at first then settled. Prairie nosed my tears then gave such an earnest look. She half-barked, "Uf."

The screen door squeaked open. "Paisley. It's for you."

For me?

Aunt Bert paused. Her next words flooded through me. "It's your dad."

Tears flowed until they soaked my t-shirt. I didn't reply.

Gram's voice came from a great distance. *Go. Your family's calling.*

My heart quivered. I took a deep breath and touched Saint Francis' outstretched arms.

I called toward the house, "I'll be right in."

The End

If you enjoyed this book, please leave the author a review.

BWL Author
Julie Christen

Julie Christen lives on a small farm in central Minnesota. Her superhuman husband, dogs, thirty (named) chickens, barn cat, fat donkey and horses keep her thriving and provide endless material for writing poetry, short stories, kids' books and novels. She's a daydreamer and a cloud watcher. She's a hiker and a Harley rider. She's taught middle school English and health for nearly thirty years and is still going strong in the classroom. Lately, she has accused herself of having "just too many hobbies," from gardening to training her young Nokota® RainyDay. She spends her never-enough-minutes-in-the-day doing these things, not because they are things she just enjoys, but because they are things that *bring* her joy. And that, she believes, is what life is about.

BWL Publishing

BWL

bwlpublishing.ca

Made in the USA
Monee, IL
23 June 2023

36006596R00167